About the Author

Catherine Doyle was born in rural Ireland, where local Gaelic legends gave her an appetite for the world of fiction. Emotions the imagination can stir inspired her to create a new spin on the world of supernatural fiction.

Dedication

For Gemma.

In memory of

Elizabeth Leslie
&
Mary Doyle

Catherine Doyle

SUBLIMINA

AUSTIN MACAULEY
PUBLISHERS LTD.

A CIP catalogue record for this title is available from the British Library.

ISBN 9781784556181 (Paperback)
ISBN 9781784556204 (Hardback)

www.austinmacauley.com

First Published (2015)
Austin Macauley Publishers Ltd.
25 Canada Square
Canary Wharf
London
E14 5LQ

Printed and bound in Great Britain

Chapter 1

Karen's eyelids danced as she slept.

Rapid eye notions, Rick called it, and no one was awake to correct him. He wondered what dreams lay behind her pretty brown eyes; he wondered until he began to feel uncomfortable.

He peeled himself from the doorway that supported him and decided he shouldn't be in her bedroom. His nicotine addiction disagreed. *It's poker night*, it argued; *no one takes you seriously when you tell them you're quitting.* His argument solidified at the sight of his pack of cigarettes. It drew him closer with the promise of comforting breaths of smoky satisfaction. But it lied; there was nothing inside but the silver foil, which seemed to mock him with indifference.

She'd cut them up, he realized in horror.

"You're wasting your time."

Rick jumped at the voice from beneath the sheets.

"I beheaded them." it said.

Rick turned to face his friend. "I just lost two hundred to your brother," he whispered. "This family owes me."

Karen ignored him.

But a clumsy plop on the side of her bed told her he wasn't going away.

Rick wasn't someone who knew when to leave. Rick was a talker.

But Karen thought much of Rick's talk was tiresome, filled with useless and incorrect information. She recognized it as a cover to hide his insecurities. He reminded her of a lost schoolboy, one who had never found the classroom. It was for this reason there would never be anything between them. Not because he was insecure, but because she was. Opposites attract, her mother always said, and she and Rick were just too alike in the desert of the lost schoolboy.

"I'm glad you woke me," Karen confessed. "I was having a bad dream."

"Someone kill your cigarettes?" When Karen didn't respond with her usual cackle, Rick saw sadness in her eyes and he quickly backtracked. "Tell me." he pressed.

Karen felt her face redden in the darkness. She didn't feel it was the kind of nightmare that could compare to the sort of horror scenes Rick was used to. In fact, it would probably be categorized as comedy in his movie collection.

Rick sensed her hesitation and gently nudged her over until he'd created ample room for his long and clumsy legs. He lay beside her with one arm positioned firmly around her shoulders, forming the protective embrace she'd become accustomed to.

"You know," he began, "the longer you put it off, the more likely your brother will find me in your bed. And you know he'll break my legs!"

"You won't laugh?"

"Promise!"

"Okay. I must be young in the dream because Connor and I have our fishing nets ready to catch tadpoles down at the stream. You can get to it through the ditch in my grandmother's back garden. We're climbing the fence when I hear it."

"Hear what?"

"A dreadful screaming sound," Karen whispered. "It goes through me like a current, so intense I wish it would kill me. My knees buckle and my chest implodes; the skin on my face starts to crawl like its melting off the bone."

Rick was intrigued.

"What then?"

"That's it." Karen sighed. "It's just a scream. Then I wake up."

After ten minutes of trying to explain how REN sleep works, Rick scurried down the stairs with his tail between his legs.

Some dreams just couldn't be analysed, he concluded.

Chapter 2

Connor and Karen O'Driscoll were twins. They didn't look alike.

Connor was stocky and well built with black hair.

Karen was petite, with a head of chocolate-brown curls like her mother. Her cheeks were speckled with freckles that spread like a sandy bridge across her nose.

The siblings shared a home in the city, about a quarter the size of the one they came from in Griffin. Griffin Town was full of large old farmhouses. It was a small rural community where Sunday conversations still revolved around the Mass, and people liked to disagree a lot with That Sort of Thing.

Catherine O'Driscoll was the town GP. Her husband, Daniel, had been a simple farmer, or so everyone had believed. Daniel died in what the authorities described as unusual circumstances. Karen and Connor were only six when their mother undertook the difficult task of explaining the circumstances surrounding his death.

Daniel's body had been found in a rented duplex in Spain after suffering what appeared to be a massive stroke. He was discovered with a fake passport and other forged documentation. Some people thought he'd simply left his wife and family to start a new life. But those people hadn't known him very well.

Daniel O'Driscoll was solid: a quiet man, perhaps, a simple man of simple pleasures. He'd never lived anywhere but Griffin. He'd never even been out of Ireland, blaming his work commitments rather than admitting to an overwhelming fear of flying. He liked to keep his feet on the ground, both metaphorically and physically.

Karen didn't remember much about him, except for a fragrance.

The smell of rum and maple, which Catherine attributed to the pipe he nursed by the range in the evenings. "It was a rum and maple blend." she'd told her daughter in a distant tone that made Karen regret asking.

Catherine said Karen took after her father. It must be where she got her love of animals. People often said that Catherine O'Driscoll's consultancy was more like a veterinary clinic than a surgery. Karen had brought home strays of every variety, from injured birds to abandoned dogs, kittens to snails with broken shells.

Growing up without a father hadn't left the twins feeling deprived. Daniel's brother, Andrew, stepped up to provide anything he could for his niece and nephew.

Andrew worked on the family's farm with his mother, Esther.

Karen's earliest memories of childhood took place there.

Daniel had built his family's home next door to his mother's, separated only by a sorry little fence the twins would jump in search of sticky chocolate mice and butterscotch.

On cold winter evenings, it wasn't their mother's call that summoned them for supper, but the smell of Esther's famous scones that brought them indoors like sniffer dogs.

Getting the children to bed had never been a strong point of Catherine's, who relied heavily on her mother-in-law's gift for storytelling. Esther was the town's seanachaí.

Karen thought of those evenings now.

Reliving happy memories could induce sleep, she'd read somewhere; and none were happier than moments spent listening to Esther's tales.

Chapter 3

Karen woke early to the sound of raindrops heavily hitting her window. The sound jolted her into consciousness. Daylight fought to make its way through a parting in the curtains but a moody mass of clouds made it feel silly for even trying.

It was a grey and grumpy day.

Karen stared out the window at it now in her dressing gown. The little park across the street had had no one to entertain for days now, and she was beginning to feel sorry for it. She ought to have been getting ready for work, she knew, but still she stood there, staring out at the soaking swings as they swayed silently in the wind.

Her listless trance was interrupted by the sound of her alarm shouting at her from the bedside table. Eight thirty, it complained; she was late. She would have to grab breakfast on the go.

Karen watched her reflection hurriedly brush her teeth. She muffled a groan as she noticed the black bags under her eyes that informed the world she hadn't been sleeping. Shortly after leaving the house, Karen regretted her attire. *Why didn't I wear the three quarter lengths?* Sitting in wet trousers for the day was not a good way to start the week. After a silent prayer for the flu, to get a few days off work, she made her way to the station.

Karen had been working at Penbrook Insurance for the past three years. It was a far cry from the hopes and dreams she'd had as a girl, but there were worse places. Penbrook shared its offices with countless other firms and Karen felt blessed she hadn't ended up in Cannacord Advertising, where each girl appeared more orange than the next.

Yet another Dart delay meant she was an hour late for work.

Penbrook's offices were anything but private and late starts never went unnoticed, especially if you worked for Brenda Butcher. Desk dividers stood just four inches tall, making for a very intimate work experience.

"Thompson Motors called twice already about their policy," Zara told her. "They want a call back by ten or they're transferring." Zara Mercer was twenty-seven. She'd been twenty-seven for four years now, and her work ethic was as convincing as her age.

****

Sam came over for a routine tea break at midday, but Karen was more excited about the cup of steaming coffee she'd brought. It didn't even matter that Sam repeatedly forgot she took sugar. Sam had been at Penbrook two years now, a lifetime in her book. She favoured travel over stability. Generally she only worked a twelve-month cycle at a time, just to finance her next trip.

Karen had no interest in travelling. She must take after her father, she thought, because she hated flying. She didn't, however, hate hearing Sam's travel tales.

Sam's most recent trip to Egypt taught her about Gorgon mythology. The story of the Gorgon Medusa was well known, but what most people didn't realize was that Medusa was born the only mortal sister of three, Sam told her.

Karen promised that one day she would take a trip with Sam, but it had to be somewhere tropical. For today, though, lunch at Super Mario Brothers with Will Fitzgerald was as tropical as it would get.

Super Mario's was an eccentric little diner. The walls were covered with caricatures from the classic video game. They took their favourite booth in the corner because Sam liked to sit under the image of Princess Peach.

After Will pointlessly scanned the menu – everyone knew he'd just order a Bowser Beef – they began to make plans for the weekend. According to Will the most important event of the weekend was the Lions rugby tour in which England would take on Wales.

Unlike most of the girls at the office, Karen and Sam loved to watch the rugby matches at Broderick's Sports Bar. They served a brand of lager called Toohey's, the most popular lager in Australia, according to Sam. Of course the game itself was complete gibberish. For an avid sports follower, Will played little sport himself, though he'd argue that he was a keen snooker player. Karen suspected this was because it involved the least amount of physical exertion. Will's skills lay more in his mental faculties, which were famous at Penbrook. He could spend days creating computer formulae to build the most sophisticated reports. He'd then sit back and let others take the credit. His original position had been as an in-house auditor but he was always willing to use his technical expertise. Karen got the feeling Will just liked to feel needed.

Her thoughts were interrupted by a rumbling in her belly, which still hadn't forgiven her for withholding breakfast.

"Tagliatelle Luigi," she told the waiter.

Sam had a Yoshi Burger and Will asked for the spiciest Bowser Beef pizza on the menu.

"How's Connor's new job?" Will asked, between mouthfuls of mozzarella and meatballs.

"He's not permanent yet." Karen sighed.

Connor had only been at Galford Construction for six months. It wasn't easy to find employment with a criminal record, either, Karen surmised, but she kept that thought to herself.

"He's too handsome to work anyways," Sam sighed. "He should put those biceps to proper use and carry me across the world."

Karen squirmed uncomfortably. Connor's track record with women was murky at best. While Rick would be proclaiming love after two days and racing to the nearest jewellers, Connor could build the emotional equivalent of the Great Wall of China.

****

The afternoon went by painfully slowly and Zara took it as an invitation to discuss her favourite topic: Zara. She was one of the most delusional people Karen had ever met. During a rebellious period she had spent time as a stripper in downtown New York, but she preferred to tell people that she had been following a lucrative ballet career. Apparently Zara's boyfriend Jake had taken up gymnastics. "Well, he *is* a fitness instructor." she barked at Will, who couldn't help sniggering under his breath. "He has to branch out and practice more difficult exercises. How else could he empathize with clients?"

Jake was, of course also a gifted musician. His band Suns of the Underworld was competing at the Battle of the Bands next Saturday night and the entire department was invited. Even Olivia Newton, a forty-four-year-old mum of two couldn't resist the chance to check out the talent.

By the time Karen got home that evening she was feeling perkier. Her nostrils flared when she opened the front door to the smell of homemade stew. Connor was a deceptively impressive cook. The kitchen was a mess but two happy-looking Yorkshire puddings told her it was worth it. "I'm going over to Raptures later with Rick if you want to come?"

Raptures was the skateboard park on the other side of the city. It was adjacent to, and managed by, Raptures pub, a popular venue for music events. In fact, it was the venue for next week's Battle of the Bands. Karen declined in favour of a soak in the tub. Connor followed her gaze to the camcorder.

"It's for the documentary," he explained.

Karen laughed out loud. "You can't call a couple of eegits falling off their BMXs a documentary?"

Connor and Rick were both biking boys. But lately they'd come up with the *ingenious* idea to video their stunts and call it a documentary.

****

Rosemary fields or lavender dreams? Karen wondered as she rummaged through her bath salts. Deciding on the lavender, she stepped into the suds and steam. The bubbles welcomed her with their soft embrace and she slid shoulder deep into the tub. She was looking forward to a boy-free evening of relaxation. Lavender dreams, however, had other ideas.

Her dreams took her to the familiar fence. She wanted to hurl at the sight of it. Soon the screaming would start. The scene was so familiar now that she knew she was dreaming. She just had to endure it a little longer and she would wake.

But Karen didn't wake. Instead her dream took on a new form in a new place. Her eyes were drawn to the sky, where the moon hung suspiciously low. The other planets she didn't recognize, they painted the forest around her a gentle blue tone.

Though Karen wondered where she was, she knew where she had to be. She was lucid-dreaming now, her favourite kind. She needed to find the bright vaporous place. She could see it in her mind's eye and that was where she needed to be, she decided.

****

It was ten o'clock when Rick finally mastered the 360-degree fire flip and he wasn't sure if his shaking was from the adrenaline or the cold evening air. He was never good in the cold; he had goosebumps and bright-red cheeks when they finally went indoors.

He took a seat with Connor at the bar and ordered some cheap beer and chicken wings.

"I think we should *teach* the stunts, make it a bigger online hit," Connor suggested.

But Rick looked unsure. "I don't exactly know how to do them." he explained uneasily. "Different stuff works different times. Couldn't we just film me looking cool?"

Connor was about to respond when he noticed Rick's attention wander as he tried to flirt with two brunettes who had just entered the bar. But the barbecue sauce on his upper lip let him down.

Connor chuckled; it was a deep rumbling sound. He was feeling light headed. Connor liked to feel light headed, or numb at the very least, he hoped the walk to the station wouldn't ruin it by sobering him up.

"Wish I lived as close as you to Raptures," Connor complained.

"No you don't. Not with that four lane traffic magnet at Manion's Corner? You have to carry on the whole way down to the junction just to come back on yourself again.

The night was calm when Connor finally left. It seemed the sky had gotten the rain out of its system and the stars could now breathe. Connor stared up at them with admiration. When he crossed the bridge he could see the red brick of his house across the park and he wondered if Karen was still awake. But the thought of his sister brought a faint cold fear to his chest. He had to grab hold of the railings to steady himself as panic grasped him in a vice-like grip. It squeezed the air from his lungs and he almost doubled over.

Something was wrong, his body insisted, but his mind was still several steps behind, searching for physical danger. But Connor had never had much regard for reason so he began to run. He ignored the food rising in his gut and ran faster. His legs carried him like a silent motor across the park and into Ashton Estate. He cleared the fence of his garden in an effortless motion and let the front door be his brakes.

The house was quiet. There was no smoke and no damage. He listened intently but all he could hear was the rasping sound of his own breath. He checked the rooms one by one.

Finally three steps at a time he made it up the stairs to the bathroom.

"Karen?" he called in a choked tone.

****

Karen had been walking through the dark woods for hours but her feet felt no pain – another reason dreaming was so much better than waking. Eventually the sound of the crunching leaves beneath her turned to a softer sound; she'd reached marshy terrain. She smelt the water before she heard it and followed the sound of the stream until she saw two fishermen.

She stared in peaceful silence out over the water and regarded the men with interest. They wore sandals on their feet and long dress-like sweaters. Both sat with their rods perched on the bank.

After some time the larger of the two stood up and reeled in his rod, presumably to change bait. He turned to his trunk then, and Karen caught a glimpse of his face; handsome and chiselled. Then she met his eyes and they chilled her to the bone.

They had no pupils – completely blue, nothing but swirling pools of blue.

Karen would have thought he was blind were she not witnessing him searching through his bait box. He raised his gaze then, but he appeared to look straight through her. She was startled to hear her name loud and clear, but his mouth never moved, he sounded like Connor. In fact, he began to look a lot like Connor.

Now she was awake and it looked a lot like Connor splashing cold water over her face.

"Jesus, you scared me!" he exhaled.

Karen gasped loudly as she realized all the suds in the bath had disappeared. "This is awkward," she whispered.

"Awkward!" Connor agreed, letting go of her head so fast he almost drowned her himself. He was out of the bathroom quicker than she could take her next breath.

Karen stared down at her skin, which had shrivelled up like an old prune, and she began to shiver involuntarily. It must have been hours she'd lain there, asleep in the cold water.

Karen found it difficult to warm up after that. Even her heavy feather duvet felt threadbare against her skin. Connor brought her a hot water bottle and a cup of hot cocoa. He had poured himself a large whiskey in a coffee mug.

"Sorry I scared you," she said through chattering teeth.

"It's not your fault." Her brother shook his head. "I should have checked in."

Karen sighed at the thoughts of resuming a never-ending argument.

"You're not my father, Connor; you're my brother, not even my *older* brother."

Connor was rubbing his eyes restlessly. "I am by two minutes," he argued weakly.

Karen sat up straighter, hugging her water bottle between her knees and chest. "You need to stop seeing threats everywhere. If a child gave you ice-cream you'd probably check it for anthrax."

Connor thought about it for a moment. "Kids are crafty buggers," he said before turning his attention back to his mug of whiskey. "Besides, I think that's a bit harsh. Take Wayne, for example. I welcomed him with open arms when he started seeing Mum. That's trusting." He raised a finger in mock demonstration.

Karen sniggered; it stopped her teeth chattering for a few moments. "Mum's not seeing anyone; Wayne's just her *special friend*." she giggled. "You only like him because he taught you engines and gave you your first dirt bike."

They chatted some more until the shivering subsided and Karen finally dozed off.

Sleep didn't come so easily to her brother. He went to bed with a heavy heart as he thought of his father's last words to him: "You're the man now, Conaire." He'd used his Irish name and ruffled the hair on his head. Connor remembered thinking it was because he'd just beat him at football. How he'd welled up with pride as he'd puffed out his six-year-old chest. If only he'd known. At least he still had the twin thing with Karen, he consoled himself. It wasn't one of those girlie emotional connections you read about, but he always sensed if she was in danger, even if she didn't.

Chapter 4

On Friday Penbrook offices struggled to contain an excited workforce. The cafeteria was buzzing with the sound of people making plans.

"Jake and I are rehearsing," Zara chirped.

"*You're* in the band now?" Sam sounded incredulous.

"Well, not officially," Zara said. "But I do sound checks, make sure their outfits match, important stuff like that."

Despite its scalding temperature Will swallowed his coffee hard to stop himself laughing.

"You going out tonight?" Olivia asked as she munched on her salt and vinegar crisps.

"Just over s to Broderick's for beers," Will told her.

"Would you like to come?" Karen offered. Karen felt sorry for Olivia. She was a mum of two and didn't get out much, so people got used to not inviting her.

Olivia however didn't seem to notice. She was so obsessed with her children that nothing else mattered that much. Her favourite pastimes included talking about her children, talking to her children on the phone and talking about how sick of people talking about their children she was.

Karen and Sam had just finished making plans for lunch when Brenda bounced into the canteen. Ensuring she had everyone's attention, she did her usual irritating glance at her wristwatch, indicating that coffee break had ended approximately one minute twenty-seven seconds ago.

That was Brenda's management style; she favoured irritating little idiosyncrasies over making direct requests.

Karen knew it was just a product of her own insecurities, a way of avoiding confrontation, but Sam and Olivia hated it.

"I wish she'd just come out and ask us to get back to it, instead of pasting that patronizing smile on her snout," Sam fumed.

Brenda bounced back into the office. She had an unusual little strut, making it look like she had springs attached to the soles of her shoes.

Her tall and busty frame made the effect all the more noticeable. But it was the excessive field of facial hair that had earned her the nickname The Buffalo. It was cruel but it was accurate.

****

Lunch hour brought Karen and Sam to Henry Street.

They meandered through crowds of determined shoppers until they reached the large Georgian windows of Croft's boutique.

Sam would have no trouble finding something, Karen thought. She looked great in everything. Sam's hair hung in layers of golden strands across her small and striking face. Piercing eyes of crystal blue always ensured she got what she wanted. They were her greatest weapons and she knew it.

Karen was feeling disheartened, she had tried on an emerald-green silk blouse, a low-neck turquoise top, and a purple tunic, before Sam barged into the changing rooms with a black sequinned dress.

"Dresses make me look dumpy," Karen moaned.

"It's perfect!" Sam argued. "You're trying it on! You can wear it to Battle of the Bands next week, so you'll get your money's worth."

Karen complained until her reflection shut her up. It dampened the doubts in her mind and replaced them with a rare appreciation. Sam had chosen well; the dress was a chic little number with a studded pattern along the sleeves. The chiffon material felt cool against her skin. It was a bit shorter than she'd have liked but the black did go with the bags under her eyes. Sam picked her some red studded jewellery but Karen drew the line at the bag Sam kept shoving onto her shoulder.

****

Will contemplated the complexities of the female getting-ready process as he sprawled his long body on the leather sofa in his penthouse. He glanced at his watch for a third time. The girls always chose to get ready at his place. It was in the Docklands, near work and right in the city centre.

He was on his second can of lager when Karen and Sam strolled in, wafting the scent of perfume and hairspray around the room. "At last!" he said, and sat up.

It was a mistake that resulted in a serious scolding relating to men's incapacity to understand the female psyche that lasted all the way to the pub.

Broderick's was booming. Hordes of rugby enthusiasts were jam packed into every corner of the pub. Will looked smart in his jersey. He'd put a little gel in his hair, Karen noticed, but his face turned purple when he spotted his favourite waitress buzzing from table to table furiously scribbling down orders.

Just as it looked like they would never get a seat, they were waved down by none other than Brenda Butcher. "Please no." muttered Sam without moving her lips so much as a millimetre. Karen once suggested Sam look into ventriloquism. She had an extraordinary gift for disguising her disgust with a smile, while expressing it fervently under her breath.

"Tell me you didn't invite The Buffalo," she continued, through a set of clenched teeth.

"Sorry! She was admiring my new dress. She asked where we were going; I couldn't be rude."

Sam was appalled. "I swear you'd invite the devil himself if he complained about having no friends."

"Okay," Will interjected, "no need to be drama queens, we've got seats now let's get some drinks in before kick-off."

Brenda was perched on her seat with her shoulders back, intently scanning the room for Mr Right when the others joined her.

She wore one of her usual low-cut busty tops that left nothing to the imagination. Her black greasy hair was tightly pulled back and further neatened with her favourite hair band, making her face more severe-looking than ever. Her lipstick had been applied heavily in an inaccurate shape that made her lips look bigger than they were. It was a misguided attempt to follow a beauty magazine's instructions on how to achieve that Hollywood pout.

Those things should come with a disclaimer, Karen decided.

"Karen!" Sam clicked her fingers. "You're doing it again. Come back to earth."

"Sorry," Karen said, "what were you saying?"

"We're going to order." Sam was smiling at her friend's attention span.

Will wanted chicken wings and a bowl of wedges, but when Leslie approached, he appeared to lose his voice as well as his colour.

Karen liked Leslie. She was a chirpy friendly waitress with strawberry blonde hair and the whitest set of teeth she'd ever seen. When it started to get embarrassing, Sam ordered for Will.

Will looked totally dejected when Leslie left. His shoulders slouched and his frame collapsed as if he'd been holding his breath. He ignored his friend's attempts to lie and tell him it wasn't so bad and instead sought solace in his pint glass. Finally, his attention shifted to the game. It was a powerful start for England but a late score from Wales made them level. Will furiously tapped his smartphone to update his online bet. Another couple of pints later and his eyes began to glaze over as they danced happily across his betting account.

It was half time when Karen needed a toilet stop. Making her way through the crowds was like trying to complete a military obstacle course. She was pushing under the arm of a six-foot-tall rugby fan when a striking foreigner caught her eye.

He stared straight ahead like the Terminator, knocking shoulders with everyone in his way. His eyes were such a frosted blue they were almost grey. Karen quickly glanced away so as not to stare, but when she looked up again he was right in front of her making her jump.

"Excuse me!" he said to her. "It's just so crowded here."

Karen merely smiled in response. A smile she wore the entire way to the rest rooms and back.

The second half saw Will lose one hundred and fifty euro. But he appeared unfazed. Karen suspected he was more annoyed over making a fool of himself with Leslie. When Sam gave Brenda a gentle reminder that it was her round, she scuttled off to the bar. No sooner had she left than grey eyes took her place.

"Can I buy you a drink?" he offered. "Make up for earlier!" he added in an accent she couldn't place.

Karen learned the handsome foreigner's name was Marcus Savidis. When he said he was new to the city, Karen felt a pang of sympathy for him. The city was the hardest place to try to meet friends. Marcus however, showed no signs of loneliness or dependence, even after confirming he was out alone. In fact he seemed quite comfortable to sit and chat, he managed admirably well at ignoring the conjecture of the group. He answered all of their questions with ease.

"I'm from Piraeus, in Greece," he responded politely to Sam.

He returned Will's manly nod and answered "unattached" to Brenda's most obvious enquiry.

Karen found she had a lot in common with the stranger. Marcus was a teacher at St Anne's Grammar School, and teaching was a career path Karen regretted having not followed.

"The pay is atrocious," Catherine had warned her. "It can take years to get a permanent position." So Karen had contented herself by becoming a volunteer reading teacher at the community centre instead.

Soon the two were deep in conversation about their curriculums. Marcus favoured folklore as his reading material too. But Marcus had a theory that the world had only a few great stories and that each country had simply adapted them to work with their own culture. Before Karen could disagree her phone interrupted them.

"Sorry; my brother." She squinted at her phone. "He worries if I don't answer."

Karen regretted her decision to take the call outside. The rain was falling so hard it formed a mist through the streetlights. She could barely hear her brother over the downpour.

"I put off calling as long as I could." His voice came crackling from the other end of the phone. "We have a leak and it's like a lake in here. You might want to come home and salvage some stuff."

Perfect! Karen sighed as she hung up the phone. *Of all nights!* She took a deep breath and returned to bid everyone goodnight.

Will flashed a nervous glance her way when Marcus offered to walk her to the station. "I can call you a taxi," he protested.

"It's only across the street." Karen laughed.

Marcus could take her that far at least.

Outside, Marcus removed his leather jacket and placed it over Karen's shoulders. The wet weather suited him, she noticed. The rain played with his eyelashes joining them in saturated masses and spilling water from their tips. His dark hair was stuck to his forehead, while Karen's on the other hand frizzed out at the sides, making her look like a lightning-struck gerbil.

"Can I call you sometime?" Marcus asked in a tone so calm he made it sound like an afterthought. Karen's ego told her to match his nonchalance and she responded with, "If you like."

Karen was perhaps more cautious than her peers. She had learned the hard way and bore the scars to prove it. After they exchanged numbers Marcus caught her by the hand. He intertwined her fingers with his own and they ran across the street through the traffic, causing several hoots from angry motorists.

By the time Karen boarded the train she was soaked to the skin and still laughing. It had been dangerous and childish but that's what had made it such fun. She drew her knees in close to her chest to keep warm, and though she hated herself for it, she couldn't relax the cheesy smile that had fastened itself to her face.

Marcus finished waving at the carriage before he turned to face the eyes he'd felt boring through his back. Turning slowly he met Will's gaze full on. Shivering outside Broderick's, Will's jersey looked like a wetsuit from the rain that had drenched it. This time there was no manly nod and no social niceties and they both turned and went their separate ways.

Chapter 5:

Connor's leak looked more like a flood. Karen flung her belongings onto the phone table, afraid to go any further. A loud crashing and slamming sound echoed from the kitchen and a string of profanities ensued. The door had to be thrust open because Rick had laid so many towels beneath it.

Connor was like an angry dog – a dog that had buried his bone somewhere but couldn't remember where he'd put it. "I can't find the blasted stopcock," he growled. "It should be under the sink like in any other normal bloody house."

Water was gushing from the utility cupboard, forming a large pool on the kitchen floor.

"What's a stop clock?" Karen whispered to Rick.

"It shuts off the main water supply; it *is* usually under the sink," Rick whispered back. "I tried the water board but there's no connection."

"What about the fire brigade?" Karen asked.

"No!" Connor grunted. "They'll think we're idiots." He was barely audible over the dreadful hissing sound of the pipe. Karen looked imploringly to Rick.

"I'm calling them," Rick said.

By the time the fire brigade arrived the water had reached the hall, stopping at the local cupboard under the stairs and inviting itself into the skirting boards for afters.

Karen opened the door to two middle-aged men.

Larry was the first to enter. He was a tall blond-haired man with a decoration of evening stubble along his jawline. Karen was reassured to note that he looked a lot like MacGyver.

Did MacGyver ever solve flooding problems? She tried to recall a familiar episode but was distracted by the unlikely sidekick by the name of Frank who followed close behind. Frank wore a smug look on his face and Karen almost understood Connor's reluctance to call them.

MacGyver gave Connor a friendly nod and asked him where he'd searched for the stopcock, but Connor was busy staring at Frank who was heading straight for the kitchen sink. When he resurfaced, his face was red and sweaty. He swept three strands of hair back into his comb-over in an attempt to ignore Connor's told-you-so face.

"I'll try the pipe," said Frank.

"You fellas keep checking for the stopcock." MacGyver fumbled through kitchen cupboards while Connor went outside, running his hands through his hair in frustration.

Rick and Karen exchanged worried looks as Frank moaned and groaned with his head stuck in the utility cupboard.

Karen leaned forward to peak over him a couple of times just to make sure he was still breathing.

All of a sudden there was silence and the water stopped flowing. MacGyver had found the stopcock, behind the fridge.

"I knew you'd find it." Karen almost leapt forward to hug him.

Rick raised his eyebrows at her.

Frank surfaced a few moments later, coughing and wheezing as though it were all down to him.

Everyone took a moment to look around the room. The dining room was ankle deep in water and the carpet in the hall would need replacing.

"What happens now?" Connor asked the two men, looking forlorn. "Do you have industrial pumps?" he asked.

"Too shallow," Frank grunted. "You'll have to just get rid of what you can tonight and hire a wet vacuum for the rest. I know a fella who'd take that carpet off your hands though."

MacGyver gave him a look.

"What?" Frank shrugged. "I do!" It was almost 3.00 a.m. when the two men expressed their sympathies by slapping

Connor on the shoulder. The silence in the kitchen was deafening.

Rick hated silences. He missed the hissing pipe. "Anyone for tea?" he said.

"I'll open the back door." Connor got up from the table. "We can brush it out and get the wet vacuum tomorrow."

They set to work with buckets, brushes and bags until fatigue claimed them one by one. Karen gave up first. She looked at her little kitchen like it was a wounded animal, and trudged up the stairs with wet feet and a heavy heart. Her skin was damp and cold and she wrapped herself in a dressing gown before falling into bed for another restless night's sleep.

Chapter 6

When Karen woke the next morning the weather had broken. The sun was beaming through the curtains, proclaiming a rare and sunny morning. It tried to make its way past her squinting eyes but failed as she shut them tightly.

The next time she opened them she found her mother standing over her bed. For a moment she had that bizarre feeling where she couldn't remember if she'd gone to sleep in Dublin or Griffin. The aches in her joints and temples, however, reminded her exactly where she was as she remembered the night before.

"Connor said you'd be coming home today. I came to collect you both, unless you'd rather get home on the back of a motorcycle." Catherine threw her eyes up to heaven. She would never approve of the wretched thing.

Karen tried to get up to greet her mother, but found her head resolutely stuck to the pillow. Her forehead was pounding and her muscles ached. Her prayer for the flu the previous Monday had come back to haunt her. "Of all prayers to be answered," she whispered, "it had to be this one." That report she'd messed up couldn't have just *disappeared*? Zara's hair straighteners couldn't just *break*? No it had to be the flu.

"You're running a temperature." Catherine took her hand from her daughter's sweaty forehead. "I suppose lying in a cold bath for an evening will do that to you." She sighed.

Great! Connor had gone and blabbed because he was such a drama queen. "I'm fine," she lied.

"Well, you can't stay here! You need some home cooking, and God knows I'm not the woman to give it. We'll go to Esther's."

Karen tried to smile but it seemed like too much effort.

"Connor's giving a guy from work a call to sort out the kitchen. There's no need for you to stay. Andrew and Katie'll be there too."

Catherine scurried over to the wardrobe to pick out some clothes. It appeared that declining the offer was not an option. Catherine always got her way. "You know if I hadn't examined her myself I'd swear it was twins Katie is carrying."

Katie was Uncle Andrew's partner, and Karen loved her dearly. Everyone loved her dearly. She was bright and bubbly with a passion for life so inspiring it made Disney look depressing. She worked with St Vincent de Paul and spent her weekends doing charity work for Passing Paws dog shelter.

Karen made a painful move to get out of bed. Catherine took the opportunity to choose her only daughter's clothes.

She'd been denied years of flowery dresses as Karen discarded them for jeans and woolly jumpers. Catherine feigned a sulk when Karen ignored the top she'd chosen in favour of a Griffin Rangers hoodie.

Connor was still on the phone when they made it downstairs.

It was mildly amusing to watch him on his ancient mobile phone. It was so old and scratched it looked like he was speaking into a tin can. Connor was not an animated conversationalist but when he was on the phone he transformed into an avid communicator, complete with hand gestures, head nods and, on one particularly embarrassing occasion, Karen had accused him of winking. He took all his calls in private now.

The journey to Griffin took longer than usual.

Connor was talking about Fabien, the new plumber at work; he droned on and on about pumps and wet vacuums, but Karen couldn't pretend to be interested. Her throat felt like she was swallowing glass and she wanted to forget all about last night.

A welcome wave of relief descended when they pulled into Esther's pebbled driveway. Karen imagined Esther inside, pottering about the kitchen, her thick glasses resting so far down her nose they'd be in danger of being baked along with the cakes she'd be checking in the oven.

Neither Connor nor Karen could resist speeding up as they drew closer to the porch. They had been racing for the best cut of cake all their lives and even at thirty they weren't willing to give in.

Karen didn't even feel like food, she just didn't want Connor to get there first.

The low yellow glow from the kitchen flooded the dusky porch as Connor barged in first. A chorus of greetings sounded from the already full dining room. Katie was in the chair of choice by the range, looking annoyed at being pampered.

"The gruesome twosome," she said, smiling. "Come help me talk sense into these lunatics."

"What's up?" Karen croaked as she flopped into the armchair by the window.

"Andrew's insisting I don't go to the dog shelter today and Esther won't even let me make a pot of tea."

Esther appeared in the doorway, knitting in hand. "I think Dermott's a great name!" she was staring into space. "I know we don't know the sex yet but I get feelings in the bones about these things, and my bones are tellin' me it's a boy she's havin'."

Esther had started knitting a lemon-yellow cardigan to match a hat so small it could have been a tea cosy.

The afternoon passed with further conjecture on gender and baby names. Andrew liked Poppy but Katie said she refused to call her baby after a fart. Karen stifled a laugh because it hurt her throat. But Katie's stubborn and out-there views always made her giggle. Nobody could convince her Poppy would be attributed to a flower and nothing more.

Andrew remained quiet, but he was probably sulking over having no say whatsoever in the baby's name. Connor's suggestion wasn't well received either. Stanley was the first and last name anyone heard from him. He was in a world of his own, munching on bread and bacon.

"That's disgusting!" Karen commented.

But he wasn't listening, he tuned out on the fluffier topics of babies and knitting, so he was relieved when Wayne finally arrived. Esther, however, stiffened at his arrival. She would never accept him, whether it was because he was dating her son's widow, or because he was a few years Catherine's junior no one could tell, because all she would say on the matter was "Nothing against him".

Wayne cruised across the kitchen in his usual carefree manor, oblivious to any tension. He wore his usual dirty white vest and greasy blue jeans, filthy from the engines at the workshop. He'd had an eventful morning. "Old Mrs McCormack's just had another crazy rant down the garage." he told Catherine. "Apparently her Nissan Micra needs to be fitted with fuel injectors and turbo exhausts to make sure she can escape the screaming witches in the fields."

Connor laughed wildly but Catherine, forever the GP, looked worried and muttered something about KGV assessments.

"Well, you'd better get to her quickly," Wayne warned. "Ollie only wants to sell her air vents to make her more aerodynamic in the fields."

Wayne and Connor enjoyed a chuckle at this but the women (particularly Esther) were scornful at their insensitivity. Mrs McCormack was one of the few neighbours they had.

Griffin was a small town, homes on the Bellview road were popular, but there were few of them. The stream in the back fields ran parallel to the houses and made for an attractive summer's day walk. All that was needed was a summer.

The McCormacks had lived there for as long as Karen could remember. Bertha and Jim McCormack married in 1954 and settled in Griffin around the same time as Esther and her late husband, Seán.

Esther once spoke of their friendship back in those times, house stops for poker night and evenings spent down at the pub. Jim loved a good pint of Guinness and Bertha could drink whiskey for Ireland, which was a good thing by Esther's reckoning because it made her slower at the poker.

Bertha was desperate for children but Jim became ill with TB in the sixties and died. He was only twenty-six. Bertha was devastated. It appeared to all that she'd lost her mind in the months that followed. She recoiled from everyone, accusing them of being in collusion with the witches that had taken her husband before his time. Now she lived alone, protecting her dog, Rascal, from the same fate, and it broke Esther's heart to watch it.

"There's no getting through to her," Karen heard her grandmother cry one evening.

"The more I try, the more she thinks I'm part of it – some delusional conspiracy. She said I brought the witches with me. She said your father was the real target the night Jim died."

That had been the final straw for Esther and soon after she stopped speaking to Bertha altogether. It was a disturbing story to hear.

Esther never spoke about her son's death. No one did. It had almost torn them apart when he died the way he did; the endless conjecture, the rooting through files, the private detectives, and all for nothing.

In the end it was Catherine's scientific nature that saved her. "Sometimes you just have to know when to stop cutting," she resolved.

Esther took a little longer to come around.

"It's better to trust in the Lord than put confidence in man," she said, quoting one of her Bible passages to Catherine.

"What's that supposed to mean?" Catherine was bitter on anything God related.

"It means we have to dwell on his life and not on his death."

Whatever their sources of closure, it was acceptance that saved them both.

Karen wondered if the same acceptance might have helped Bertha through some of her pain. She was still thinking of the old woman when everyone else was gathering their things for home.

"Karen!" Catherine repeated. "You're in one of your world's again."

Esther was smiling. "You're just like your father, you know."

Karen returned her smile but without the emotion behind it. She couldn't remember a thing about the man.

****

"You look like crap." Connor passed his sister the remote control.

Karen's forehead was damp and pasty and her skin was as white as a sheet. "You're a good brother!" she told him as he switched on the television. She found an old movie but nodded off before she could comprehend the plot. It was a restless, fever-driven sleep, and in between dreams of Bertha and her father she found herself back in the dimly lit forest she'd dreamt of before.

Like before she knew she should head north to – the place was on the tip of her tongue now, teasing her – Aingeal Forest, that was it!

Karen knew she was dreaming but she had to pause to take in the wondrous intricacies of the world her mind had created for her. The forest was dark and eerie, full of sounds she'd never heard before, but none of them frightened her.

She recognized the sequence of breaking sticks as footprints close by, and she watched two female figures enter the clearing where she stood.

Karen was reminded of the fishermen she'd seen. These women had identical eyes, full of blue but no pupil to indicate where their gaze rested.

A set of demonic-looking slanted brows gave cause for consternation, but Karen couldn't decide if they were demonic or angelic.

The red-haired one looked as though her hair was spun from silk. Karen heard her refer to her companion as Sháya. She was attempting to convince her to take a shortcut to the banquet, but Sháya was adamant on taking the conventional route.

Karen bit her lip before deciding to ask for directions, but as she approached she noticed their complete lack of awareness of her presence. Like the fishermen before, they could neither see nor hear her.

Karen huffed in frustration before turning on her heels and heading in what she hoped was a northerly direction. She had barely made it out of the woods when her dream dissolved into the sitting room right in front of her eyes.

Catherine was nudging her gently and sending her off to bed. "You'll get a crick in your neck."

****

The next time Karen woke, it was to a loud tapping on her bedroom window. At first she ignored it. But when the knocking became more persistent she angrily gave in and pulled the curtains open to the morning light. Rather than snap at an unwanted intruder her heart exploded at the sight before her. There stood Katie, big as a house, wearing a grin spread like butter across her face. She was holding up the most adorable dog Karen had ever seen. It was a squirming, giddy, deliriously happy chocolate brown puppy, sporting what looked suspiciously like Esther's lemon, knitted baby cardigan. Despite her aching arms Karen shot open the window in glee.

"Wait!" ordered Katie. "There's more." Katie produced a woolly little hat and placed it over the unsuspecting puppy's head. "Open the door, then!" she squeaked in excitement.

Karen's was the only downstairs bedroom in the house and she raced through the hall to the great white doors to let them both in.

"I rescued him from Passing Paws this morning."

"Is he yours?" Karen asked, hopeful.

"Well, I was sort of hoping he'd be yours."

Karen took in the squirming pup.

"I hope it wasn't too presumptuous, you don't have to take him. It's just I knew you wanted one and this little guy's got no home."

Karen wasn't even listening; she was so full of joy, mimicking the pup's nodding head with her own. "What's his name?" she asked as they headed for the kitchen.

"I've been calling him Buddy," said Katie.

"Buddy it is!"

Buddy wasted no time inspecting his new surroundings. For a puppy with no home he was unusually comfortable with marking everything as his own territory.

"Andrew will be by shortly to take us to town," said Katie. "We'll need some supplies."

Katie was looking dangerously attached to the puppy.

"Did you not keep one?" Karen asked.

"I'm tempted, but Andrew wouldn't go for it."

They heard his truck pull into the drive after breakfast.

"Someone order a lift to Hanivan's?" he asked in his deep and husky voice.

"Can he come?" Karen nodded at the Labrador.

"It's not like I'm car proud!" Andrew shrugged.

Andrew's old red truck was always filthy. Coke cans and crisp packets littered the back seats. Copies of *Farmers Weekly* were so abundant they looked like seat covers (which turned out to be convenient since Buddy wasn't yet toilet trained.)

Connor had learned how to drive in this truck. He'd spent more time in it than he had on the farm. He even began to smell like it at one point, oily and grimy. He spent many evenings with his head stuck in the engine, even though there was nothing to fix.

Hanivan's was cold. Karen wore an old Aran cardigan of Catherine's, but still she shivered. Katie said a plastic bed with hay bedding was warmer and more hygienic than any blanket. But Karen had images of Connor spreading hay throughout the house.

"What colour goes with chocolate brown?" Karen asked. "I want all his stuff to match."

"Em, lemon yellow!" said Katie, shaking the oblivious pup with his home-knit attire.

There was no queue at the counter and the store clerk's face told them why, as he stared into the eyes of Bertha McCormack and her beloved Rascal.

"It's an outrage, is what it is!" Bertha cried. "Clearly a cover-up for your dodgy products, Hanivan. You should be ashamed of yourself. My Rascal doesn't even *mix* with other dogs," she said huffily.

"It's nothing to be ashamed of," Mr Hanivan tried to reason. "All dogs get fleas at some stage, Bertha."

Bertha looked even more outraged now. "Are you sayin' I got nits?" she hissed.

"Please, Mrs McCormack, of course not! All I'm saying is we've got products that will sort little Rascal right out."

"Ha!" cried Bertha. "It was your dodgy shampoo gave'd him this problem in the first place!" she spat and she stormed out of the store.

Even Rascal appeared to glare over his shoulder as they left.

"What can I get you ladies?" Myles Hanivan asked in a tone that suggested everything was as it should be and that he hadn't just been verbally assaulted by a woman twice his age.

Karen played along. She was always willing to help anyone out of an embarrassing situation.

Back in the truck, Buddy was ferociously licking Andrew's chin as though it were a plate of sausages and bacon. Andrew looked pleased as punch as he ruffled the dog's floppy ears.

"That's the happiest I've seen you all week!" noted Katie. "You sure you don't want us to get one too?"

Andrew looked resolute. "It's going to be hard enough with a new baby."

Karen was silent all the way home. She worried for Katie and Andrew; they'd never planned for a baby. Katie was forty-two and had always been fulfilled with her charity work, and Andrew, although great with children, had been happy not to have any of his own.

Karen was so deep in her own thoughts she hadn't noticed when they pulled up to the driveway.

"I smell dinner." Andrew perked up.

A pot of chicken soup sat simmering on the stove. It was the only thing Karen ever ate when she was feeling under the weather. Her nose appreciated the smell but her stomach threatened to throw out any trespassers, soup or otherwise.

"You're back!" Catherine ran into the kitchen and straight over to the stove, stirring the soup ferociously.

"*You* made that?" Karen asked with too much surprise in her voice.

"Esther's not the only one who can cook, you know."

Unfortunately Esther *was* the only one who could cook. Everything Catherine put her hand to ended up either overcooked or undercooked.

"I love your cooking," Karen lied, "but my stomach is on strike right now."

"Oh!" Catherine looked disappointed.

"I'll still sit with you though."

She watched her mother pretend to enjoy her soup from across the table.

She watched Esther through the window, throwing crumbs to the chickens, and she wished she didn't have to return to the city.

Andrew was elected chauffeur when Catherine and Wayne announced their intention to go to the Sunday motocross event at Currens' yard.

"Public transport's out of the question now I've a child of my own," Karen joked. When Andrew didn't reply, she decided to have it out with him on the journey home. He was like a grumpy old man of late. He had a beautiful girlfriend, a loving family and a baby on the way, and all he could do was moan.

Connor brought their bags to the car and Karen carried a very round-bellied Buddy close to her chest. She sat up front in preparation for the grilling she had in store for her uncle.

"That's one hyper hound." Andrew opened the driver's door. "You'll have some fun training him."

"We'll get him toilet trained first." said Connor. "If all else fails, we'll just borrow some nappies from you guys," he joked.

"Would you like a boy or girl?" Karen asked then.

"I really don't care," Andrew snapped.

"No, you really don't." Karen was staring out the window.

Andrew took his eyes from the road to flash her a dark look.

"I'm sorry," Karen said, "but I happen to care."

Connor squirmed in the back seat and suddenly became very interested in Buddy's little collar. If he could have covered his ears and started singing the theme to *Sesame Street* he would have.

"I know you never planned this, Andrew, but you'll be fine. You're great with kids, I know you are. I see the joy in your face when you play with them."

"Yes," Andrew answered after a pause, "but they're not *my* kids; I'm not responsible for bringing them into the world; I'm not at fault for anything bad that happens them."

"At fault? No one's at fault if anything bad happens them. Nobody lives a perfect life. They're going to have their ups and downs no matter what you do."

Andrew didn't answer but it wasn't in his niece's nature to give up. "If they never experience the tough times they'll never appreciate the good ones."

They were on the slip road for Dublin down the N11 before Andrew finally spoke.

"What if he hates me? What if I make mistakes and do the wrong thing and he hates me. Children are so pure they can see the bad in people, you know? What if he hates me?" Andrew shrugged like a lost and scared little boy.

Connor was now so focused on Buddy's collar that he looked like he might eat it, but Karen finally felt like she was getting somewhere

She shifted to face her uncle. "If you were a perfect person you'd have to name your son Jesus, and I'm not holy enough to be his auntie. Nobody's perfect, Andrew. All you can do is your best, and if you fall, then you just stand back up and keep on going. If you don't accept your own humanity, then you'll just stay on the ground for ever. And besides, I can hate you enough for the two of us."

Buddy seemed to agree as he pissed all over Connor, and even Andrew broke into laughter. Connor tried to be annoyed, but the sight of the pup's wide eyes asking him if he'd done good won him over.

It was dark outside when they reached Dublin. Karen was grateful because it meant no one saw the embarrassing bear hug her uncle bestowed upon her. Connor went straight indoors, either to avoid the same affection or to inspect Fabien's work. He appeared content with the result and he told Karen that Fabien would be coming to fit a new pipe soon. Karen didn't care; all she cared about in that moment was her bed. She'd done her job, given a right good telling-off to her uncle and she was feeling lighter now. Giving out always made her feel better.

Chapter 7

Karen woke to the motion of paws dancing across her chest.

A ferocious cheek licking told her an overexcited Buddy had been landed on her bed. Payback for having a sick day from work. Her brother looked like a drill sergeant, standing over her with folded arms.

"Of all the pups in the litter, we get the crazy one. He's pulled all the clothes off the radiators, shredded your scarf and pissed in my boot. And why is it always my stuff he urinates all over?"

Buddy ceased his cheek licking and stared at Connor expectantly, wondering if this particular rant meant he was getting a walk.

It was all too much commotion so early in the morning, and she had yet to phone in sick for work, a task she was dreading even more than cleaning up after Buddy.

Brenda's attitude to sick leave was: *Come to work unless you're in hospital.* And even that was a grey area.

Karen crawled out of her bed to make the dreaded call. "I'm not going to let her make me feel guilty, I will not feel guilty!" she told herself.

It was Zara who answered on the third ring. Naturally a story ensued involving her and swine flu. It ended nicely with her still making it in to work, before she connected Karen to Brenda.

There was a silence on the line after Karen explained her symptoms.

"So you'll probably be a bit late then," came Brenda's response.

Such a typically stupid Brenda reply.

"No I just won't be coming in at all." Karen deserted the passive approach. She was feeling too ill to be wasting any more energy on Brenda.

Karen had watched two episodes of *Murder She Wrote* when the front doorbell rang. Buddy leapt off the couch, dancing in circles, all the while keeping his eyes on Karen, just to ensure she knew he was doing his job. The light hurt her eyes when she opened the door to find the small man before her. He had the bright blue eyes of a much younger boy, making her second-guess his age. His wavy blonde hair was tied back, save for a few locks which hung all the way down to his cheeks. His face was angular and defined and he looked foreign. "I am Fabien," was all he said.

Karen couldn't place his accent. "What number are you looking for?" she asked, trying not to sound curt.

The stranger inclined his head slightly. "I believe you need me."

Then Karen registered the bag in Fabien's hand; she hadn't noticed it before. There was a Galford's van parked out by the lawn. "Oh, the kitchen!" She reddened. "Come in, it's through this way."

Fabien entered, not taking his bright eyes from her face.

Karen felt embarrassed and uncomfortable with her glowing red nose. She wasn't sure she liked this man. Even Buddy seemed uneasy. He lay before the stranger with his head bowed low until Fabien cracked a smile at the sight of him. It brightened up the room. He laid a steady hand on the dog's head and that was it – Buddy was back to his normal bouncing ball of energy.

Fabien went through to the kitchen.

Karen was getting cold watching the stranger fumble about beneath the sink.

"You have a single split in the pipe behind your utility press from a water freeze. You have insufficient pipe lagging, I think."

Karen felt like a scolded schoolgirl about to receive detention. "Will it take long to fix?" she asked.

"No. I have brought some couplers. I'll cut out the damaged one and repair; water should run by lunch time, I think."

"Thanks." Karen was relieved. "Are you lifting the carpet also?"

She was hoping everything would be done today so there'd be no need for any more visits from this wannabe dog whisperer.

"I will be back tomorrow to lift the carpet. Let me know when you have the replacement to lay."

Karen thanked him politely before retreating to the living room. Buddy, the traitor, remained in the kitchen to help him. Daytime television was worse than Karen remembered. Without the energy to change channel, she lay on the couch, listening to the sound of the saw coming from the kitchen. The rhythmical sound was strangely soothing and soon she was asleep. It was the calmest most peaceful sleep she'd had in months. The afternoon passed and she never stirred an inch.

It was three o'clock when Karen woke of her own accord – no bounding pups, no bath full of cold water, and best of all no alarm clock. There was nowhere she had to go and no place she'd rather be. She gave a satisfying stretch as her eyes refocused, but rapidly lowered her arms at the sight of Fabien slouched in the armchair by the fire.

"Your kitchen is complete!" he announced, as if there were nothing unusual about sitting on her chair, watching her television and drinking her tea.

"Why didn't you wake me or let yourself out?" Karen made herself ask.

Fabien looked rather taken aback. "Wake you?" he repeated, looking indignant. "I would never be so rude." Fabien pointed to the coffee table "I have made you a honey milk drink. It should help with your flu." He looked proud of himself. "Call me when you have the carpet." He placed his own mug on the table, and with that he was gone.

****

Connor was home early. Karen was frying his favourite dinner: potato cakes, egg and sausages.

"Wow!" he sniffed. "You're feeling better, then?" He gazed about the spotless kitchen.

"Much better thanks. Kitchen's not down to me, though. That Russian friend of yours cleaned it."

Connor looked bemused. "What Russian friend?"

"Okay German, then, whatever. The patronizing git who fixed the pipes."

"Oh, Faeb!" Connor laughed heartily. "Fabien's not Russian, he's Polish and he's certainly no git. I should have known he'd cleaned up. The guy's a neat freak in work. Definitely in the wrong job."

"Not sure it's normal to go through people's things, though," Karen said. "He even took out the bins."

"That's not exactly going through your things, though, is it?"

"Then what about making me a honey drink?"

Connor feigned outrage. "The cheek!" he said. "The sheer thoughtfulness of it; seems to have cured your ailment, though."

Karen turned the potato cakes she was frying just in time. "I didn't drink it, dummy."

Connor was shaking his head. "I can't believe you threw out one of Faeb's tonics. They're infamous at work; guy's got a cure for everything. Seventh son of a seventh son and all that."

Karen brought dinner over to the table, eager to change the topic of the marvellous Faeb. "Is Rick over tonight?"

Connor put a big dollop of runny egg yolk over his potato cakes before answering. "Nope, but he told me to tell you Roxy wants you to call her."

Roxy was Rick's younger sister. She was only twenty-six but she had her own hair salon on Cawley Street. Karen refused to have her hair cut by anyone else. The fact that she did home visits was an added bonus.

Roxy wasn't like her brother. She was driven and knew exactly what she wanted and more importantly, how to get it.

She was fiery to the point of confrontational and if she didn't like a person, they tended to know about it.

Karen suspected life had toughened Roxy.

Connor had mentioned before that Mr Brady had a drink problem. Karen had only met the man once. He appeared so jolly he reminded her of Santa Claus, with his swollen red cheeks and a round belly. Ironically, his name was Nick too.

"Well, aren't you a gem!" he'd said, when they'd first met. "When are you gonna marry this young lad of mine and take him off our hands?" he'd chuckled. When he laughed, his whole body shook and his belly had a laugh all of its own.

Rick had turned purple. "He always laughs at his own jokes." he'd mumbled.

Roxy lived in a flat above her salon that she shared with her boyfriend, but she was so fiery it was more like a war zone than a love nest.

Karen was glad to have her appetite back. She loved her food.

She swallowed two sausages before attacking her egg. The hot tea felt soothing as it trickled down her throat, and she almost decided to go back to work in the morning – almost.

Connor had agreed to take a half-day and choose a carpet with her.

House shopping was Karen's favourite kind, but she rarely had the cash. Connor knew a discount store some of the builders used.

"Do you think they'll give *us* a discount?" Karen asked but she didn't hear his answer. Her phone had buzzed and her heart did an embarrassing little flip when she realized it was a message from Marcus.

She'd been wondering if she'd hear from him before their date. His text was casual, bordering on educational, as he asked if she'd read the books he'd recommended. It was refreshing to talk to someone who shared her interests. There weren't many people she could discuss literature with. The only book Connor had ever read was *Soccer Legends of the Nineties*.

It was lunchtime the following day when Connor sped into the driveway, brakes screeching, before his van almost hit the front door. He'd always been a reckless driver. His motorcycle was a constant source of worry. Naturally, Esther blamed Wayne for introducing the wretched things to him in the first place.

"The carpet store is in a warehouse." He stared at Karen who was wearing only a T-shirt and jeans. "We'll be there five minutes and you'll be asking for my hoodie. Then you'll have it smelling all flowery and I'll never hear the end of it at work."

"I don't need your smelly hoodie." Karen told him.

She had brought one of Catherine's Aran cardigans back with her and was planning never to return it.

It was crisp and fresh outside. The air tickled her lungs as she inhaled and it reminded her of Halloween.

People thought it strange that Karen loved Halloween more than Christmas, but in Griffin it seemed to be *the* holiday. There was pumpkin pie and pumpkin soup, artificial cobwebs in frosty windowpanes and eager trick-or-treaters at every corner. It conjured many pleasant childhood memories for Karen, though perhaps not for her brother.

Connor had watched *The Silence of the Lambs* at Shauny Burke's house one Halloween and his obsession with mimicking Anthony Hopkins' famous tongue roll had landed him in piping hot water. The memory still evoked a giggle in Karen, after all these years. It still hadn't got old.

Tired of being excluded by the boys one Halloween, Karen had had a sleepover. Wayne had erected a tent in the back garden. Catherine had borrowed outdoor camping heaters from Andrew. They'd toasted marshmallows by the ditch fire and listened to the wood crackle. Everything had been perfect, especially the jealous look on Connor's face. He'd think twice before refusing her entry to his pathetic little tree house now.

Disaster struck at midnight when Connor unzipped the tent in the guise of Hannibal Lector, performing his terrifying tongue roll. It was the only excuse Patricia Maloney needed.

Later she would say she'd mistaken it for a *come on*. She was on her feet at lightning speed, brandishing her hurley, and she hit Connor with such force that she broke his nose.

Mr Maloney had taught his little princess to swing her hurley at any boy who tried any "funny business". Nobody dared inform him that his little princess would be quiet safe from any funny business for quite some time. Patricia Maloney was bigger and bolder than any other girl (or boy) at school. She had those beady little piggy eyes that could bore holes in your head, and she walked like a minotaur on a mission. Connor was so embarrassed he'd stayed indoors for a month.

He sat now, jaw set, same macho façade he'd always shown the world, and Karen decided not to shatter his shell by reminding him of it.

The carpet warehouse was dead inside. It reminded Karen of a factory with its long lonely aisles. A young weasel-like man was perched on a stool at the counter, looking over a stack of invoices. He had short spiky hair, which had recently been highlighted blonde – a cardinal sin for any weasel.

Karen watched his pale, pinched face tear itself away from the stack of paperwork. She half expected him to rise and eagerly rub his hands together before raiding their pockets.

"Afternoon Bernard, just having a quick browse."

Connor guided Karen by the shoulders down one of the aisles.

"He'd sell snow to the Eskimos," Connor whispered.

Karen's eyes widened at the vast selection of colours: crimson reds, deep-sea blues, bright greens and chocolate browns. Connor was absolutely no help. He stood with his hands so deep in his pockets he could have been scratching his feet. "That's grand," was his only contribution to any suggestion she made.

In the end it came down to soft beige and a rustic red. One look at Connor's stupid face and filthy boots told her to go for the red.

Bernard was disappointed. The beige one cost much more. He tried in vain to change her mind by trying to sell its durability and by saying it was easily washable. His squeaky little voice sounding more and more desperate.

****

That evening Karen was planning what Irish legends to read to Oscar next week at her voluntary reading group.

Karen would never admit she had a favourite pupil, but she certainly thought of Oscar more than any of the other children in her group. He always had a dirty little face and a runny nose and he resolutely refused to read for her. The best she could hope for was to capture his attention at least. Maybe then he'd want to read by himself.

She'd even bought him *Percy Jackson and the Lightning Thief*. Most children his age loved the story. She had to mess up the pages a little to make the book appear second hand.

Oscar's mother was a very proud woman. She was a single mother with mousy brown hair and a peculiar distant demeanour. Karen got the distinct impression that the woman didn't like her very much.

Her thoughts were interrupted by the doorbell. Connor's selective hearing activated itself and Karen huffed her way loudly to the front door. She opened the door to the bright and beaming faces of Sam and Will. Sam's nose was bright red from the chilly evening air, and it matched Will's big red ears. They came through the door, bringing with them the smell of the outdoors. Karen realized she hadn't enjoyed the isolation of being at home alone the past couple of days and found herself hugging them both with genuine affection.

Sam looked a little anxious. "You're not contagious are you? Because I can't go around looking like that." She pointed at Karen in jest.

Karen was embarrassed about bringing them into the kitchen. "We've had a leak," she explained. "It might smell a bit."

"So long as there's tea," Will said.

Karen brewed a large pot of tea and put a plate of custard creams on the table. "So fill me in. What's been happening without me?"

Will tried to open his mouth but only managed a twitch before Sam beat him to it. "Oh, it's been awful!" she blurted out. "Buffy's got Will doing audit," she said, using Brenda's nickname, "which leaves just me, Zara and Olivia. But Olivia has to leave early to pick up her 'precious children', which leaves just me on my own with Zara!"

Karen looked confused until Sam resumed: "Maybe you didn't catch that – me, on my own, with Zara."

"She's being more Zara than usual," Will said.

"With Jake's gig on Friday, she never stops." Sam sighed. "When she's not talking about it, she's singing about it, which includes a verse from his new song by the way: 'If you wanna talk lame, don't say my name, you wanna feel pain come play my game, but you'll be off side while I'm taken the fame.'"

Karen nearly sprayed them both with a mouthful of tea before burning her throat and swallowing hard instead. She laughed until tears streamed down her cheeks and Will and Sam joined in.

Suddenly Buddy bounded into the kitchen, afraid that he was missing something. He'd been left sleeping soundly by the fire but apparently couldn't pass up the opportunity for some attention. His clumsy demeanour worked like a charm on Will, so much so that he ventured into the living room to talk football with Connor.

"You're still coming Friday night, right?" Sam asked anxiously.

"Of course!" Karen said. "I'm back to work Thursday; just one more day of singing left."

"Have you heard from Marcus?"

Karen almost broke into a girlie giggle but managed to pull it back just on time. Sam was none the wiser. "He texted me yesterday. He can meet up with us on Friday night."

Sam looked pleased, as though Marcus had just passed a test.

The two girls were polar opposites in their approach to men.

Sam had a new 'follower' every week. Karen called them that because that's exactly what they were, 'followers.'

For Sam, a boyfriend was like a handbag – an accessory to make you feel good – but she always got bored and wanted a new one.

She changed her mind more than Rick changed religions, which was quite a lot.

Sam could often be found in a nightclub hiding from the same man she'd been chatting up earlier the same evening. Karen had a completely different attitude. Karen would never trust a man again.

Someone must have scored then because they heard cheers coming from the living room.

When the game ended it was followed by an old horror movie. It was one of the worst Karen had ever seen.

"I almost miss the footie."

"You were only half concentrating." Connor pointed out.

It was true; she had spent more time checking her mobile than she had watching the television. Would Marcus text her tonight? Would she be pleased if he did or would she think him too eager? A faint little buzzing from the phone in her chest pocket told her he would. Buddy tried to eat it.

She wrestled him for it before checking the screen. "How is the patient?" it read.

Chapter 8

The atmosphere in work was chilly when Karen returned.

Olivia looked worried. When Olivia looked worried she looked angry, and when Olivia looked angry, no one dared even enter her atmosphere. And so it was that she sat by herself, forehead frowning, staring intently at her keyboard.

Had she cut the crusts off Rex's cheese sandwiches this morning? She wondered. Had she packed his box of dead spiders for Show and Tell? What if someone commented on how they seemed to *sleep* an awful lot? But, what worried her most was that dreadful role he'd been cast for this month's play. It wasn't even March; a play about St Patrick seemed pretty inappropriate for October.

Someone should inform Miss Rivers! *Yes*, that's what she would do. She would make its irrelevance known and if they insisted on this play, Rex would just have to be recast. Niall of the Nine Hostages! What sort of an inappropriate role was that for a blond-haired, blue-eyed boy to play? The other children would tease and taunt him; she just knew it. The Bad Guy, they'd call him.

"Out with it, Sandy!" Karen demanded.

Olivia glanced up sharply, she'd become accustomed to the nickname. Her full name was Olivia Newton and her husband's name was John; she should have expected it, really.

It took a while to convince Karen of the problem at hand, and even now, Olivia wasn't so sure Karen understood it. Karen was nice most of the time but sometimes, like today, Olivia got the feeling she was humouring her. Like the time she'd discovered Rex's mathematical gifts; no four year old could have fit those blocks together in that amount of time; he obviously had a natural aptitude for trigonometry, but Karen hadn't appeared impressed enough.

"So who is Niall of the Nine Hostages anyways?" Sam piped up, revealing her talent for eavesdropping without being detected. "I don't ever remember him from school."

Karen brightened at the prospect of telling a story.

She read *The Life of St Patrick* to the children at the community centre every year. There was always a Patrick in the class, and every year that little boy would be the envy of the classroom. Most of the children were surprised to learn that Patrick wasn't even born in Ireland. He was born in Wales in the fourth century.

"His real name was Maewyn Succat," Karen told them.

"Maewyn Succat?" Sam repeated incredulously. "Isn't that some American singer?"

"No, that's Miley Cyrus," Olivia snapped. "Go on Karen."

"Not much is known about Maewyn's early life in Wales Most stories begin after he and his two sisters were captured by Niall of the Nine Hostages during a raid on his village. He was sold as a slave somewhere along the east coast where he remained for six years herding cattle, a post that would later earn him the title the Shepherd of Ireland.

"Eventually he had a dream that would lead him to freedom. It brought him to a boat on the docks that was bound for England."

"Rex should play St Patrick!" Olivia declared, but Karen ignored her.

"While in England he joined the Church, but after a time he began to pine for Ireland. It is said that he considered himself Irish because it was here that he found God.

"He used the Shamrock in his teachings of the Trinity: the Father, Son and Holy Spirit, together as one."

"Rex loves Shamrocks," Olivia interrupted again.

Sam was looking like one of the confused children at Karen's reading group. "So his name wasn't *ever* Patrick?" she asked.

"No, he got that name when the Pope made him bishop in Rome and baptized him Patritius. I think it means Father of his people."

"I'm betting he never banished any snakes, then, either." Sam sounded disappointed.

"Maybe it's metaphorical," Karen said, trying to cheer her up. "He used his wooden staff on a great hill to drive them all into the sea, and banished them forever."

"At least Rex wasn't cast as a snake." Sam turned to Olivia.

"And Niall of the Nine Hostages later became King," Karen consoled.

"King?" Olivia repeated. "Now *that* I could see." She gazed dreamily at an imaginary picture above her head.

As the atmosphere lightened, people were expecting Brenda to appear and quench all signs of life.

"Where's Buffy?" Sam asked what everyone was thinking.

"She was on Love Match when I dropped over the stats earlier," Will whispered and made a face.

Karen peeped up over Olivia's desk divider and sure enough, she could make out the bobbing head of Brenda typing ferociously on a keyboard that looked ready to break under the pressure.

****

Zara was sulking Friday when she learned Brenda was skipping Battle of the Bands in favour of a hot date.

Zara was a nervous wreck. "So much to organize," she sighed. "And so much for friendship." She glared in Brenda's direction.

Zara had at least forty T-shirts made with *Suns of the Underworld* plastered under a picture of a globe across the chest.

"You do get it, don't you?" She showed them to Sam.

"Of course, they own the world."

"Oh, for goodness sake, you're useless! Suns of the Underworld ... and they're *under the world,*" Zara stressed.

"Ah yes, now I see it," Sam lied.

"Well, artistic expression has always been my forte." Zara played with her hair.

****

Karen wished she had Zara's confidence. Maybe then she wouldn't feel like taking off with the butterflies she felt in her stomach. The thoughts of seeing Marcus again had her feeling anxious. She was sat with her head in her hands planning what she would wear when her train pulled into Platform 7, and she was so deep in thought she almost missed it.

The carriage was full. Karen shuffled through the aisle but there were no seats left. She was staring at the windows when she got the uneasy feeling someone was watching her. She glanced about her, finding nothing or no one suspicious. Just as she was about to give up, she caught the offending gaze. It was coming from a tall, well-dressed young man. He wore a suit and tie but had none of the tell-tale signs of a day at the office in Dublin. The collar of his shirt was crisp and fresh. His hair was neatly combed and lacking the hurried chasing-public-transport look. She watched him carefully while he sat back and blatantly continued examining her.

Karen rarely lost a staring contest. She had a twin brother after all, and had years of victories under her belt. But something about the stranger made her uneasy. She felt like an endangered species being examined under the microscope of a mad scientist.

Karen was relieved when the train pulled into Ashton Park.

She pushed her way hurriedly onto the platform, leaving the mad scientist behind.

****

Connor was on his third pint. It was getting harder to keep the camera lens focused on the rink, with Rick blubbering like a girl at every fall. His elbow bore the tiniest gash but he stared at it lovingly willing it to heal. They had only shot about three good stunts in the space of an hour and it was getting colder.

He was about to call it a night when he spotted three striking girls returning for a suspiciously frequent cigarette break. Connor noticed Rick's stunts become much less extravagant in his efforts to stay on the bike.

Connor was surprised to notice that the girls seemed genuinely impressed. They were puffing on their cigarettes in the cold evening air and shuffling from one foot to the other in an effort to keep warm, but all the while still looking at Rick.

Connor wondered if Rick was good-looking. He seemed to do all right with the ladies. This confused Connor. Rick had scruffy hair that sat in messy kinks at the sides. Whenever his own hair got too long Karen would taunt him about girls not liking blokes with pigtails. Rick just looked like an overgrown teenager. Connor wondered if that was a look girls went for. Then he wondered why these girls were throwing him dirty looks, before realizing that, with all this wondering, he'd been staring open-mouthed at three pretty girls with a video recorder.

"Shit," he muttered, quickly lowering the camera and shoving it clumsily into his bag. He was still zipping it up when he spotted his sister arrive through the windows. He barely recognized her. Her curly hair was styled up, with auburn strands curling down the sides. Her freckles were all but invisible under her makeup and she looked elegant in that dress.

He relaxed a little when he saw Will lead her to a table near the front. It sat directly in his line of vision. "Good boy, Will," he muttered and threw his bag over his shoulder.

****

Karen thought Raptures looked great; it was like stepping into a different world. Candles were wedged into old wine bottles, lighting up the tables and melting down the sides in rivers of hot wax. Crowds were forming in pockets around the venue. A couple of sound technicians were prepping the mics and speakers on stage and Karen admired anybody brave enough to perform in front of so many people.

A group of underage youths stood in a corner trying desperately not to look suspicious. But one particular hopeful was giving them away with an obvious display of poor coordination. Karen noticed a couple at another table arguing in an alcove. The girl's efforts at ventriloquism were as successful as the teenager's attempts to look sober. She would have benefited greatly from some lessons from Sam, Karen noted.

"Where do you go?" Will asked her suddenly. "When you stare about you like that, you get this hazy look in your eyes."

"No I don't I'm merely appreciating the aesthetics of the venue."

Zara was running around in a fluster, looking like a Hollywood movie star and Karen suddenly lost the self-esteem she'd come out with.

"I need to run backstage to work on some last-minute choreography," Zara panted.

Will was shaking his head into the pint he'd just bought. "I blame reality television."

"Someone should tell her rock groups don't have dance routines," whispered Sam from behind her hand.

"I disagree," Olivia said. "I'll be having a bit of a jig later myself."

Olivia looked like a different person tonight, a person radiating enthusiasm and excitement. She wore a white blouse with low buttons that revealed years of sun damage. Small brown pigmentation decorated her chest and neck and the lines on her skin lay in folds making her look much older than she was. "When does the karaoke start?" she asked the worried group.

****

Jimmy Reynolds was waiting in a state of sheer petrifaction backstage. His shaking hands pulled a chink in the curtains to reveal the crowds behind it. The place was packed.

It was Jimmy's band; he was the lead singer; it had all been his own stupid idea. How could he possibly have thought they were ready? His mother was to blame, really, he thought, always telling them they were brilliant. He should never have listened to her.

Jimmy's heart was hammering through his eighteen-year-old chest now and he was certain he'd swallowed his own vomit a few times.

"You all right, man?" Eddie asked, clapping a consoling hand on his friend's sweaty back. Jimmy tried to reply but his mouth was too dry.

"Just do exactly what you did in rehearsal and we'll walk it." Eddie was smiling. "Think of all the chicks."

Easy for Eddie to say, thought Jimmy. He was the drummer; he could sit and hide behind his drum kit. What could Jimmy hide behind now?

****

Karen had been watching the stage with anticipation when the first band came through the curtains.

The small and skinny frame of a pale-faced red-haired teenager took centre stage. He was followed by three other equally young and inexperienced band members. The drummer was waving his sticks so high in the air that his T-shirt crept up his torso, revealing a hairy milky-white belly. The bass guitarist had spent so many hours styling his hair over his face that he'd forgotten about the need to see and he almost tripped over the wires.

Once the intro was over, the band appeared to settle into their stride, a stride of shouting, clanging and banging, but a stride nonetheless. The vocals were drowned by guitar and bass and it was hard to make out the words.

It was a poor start talent-wise but the second act made up for it. The husky voice of Marcus Savidis was spellbinding. He sat on a high stool, with an acoustic guitar resting comfortably on his lap. Karen almost fell off the chair when he appeared on stage.

Marcus wore a pair of light-washed denim jeans, ripped at the knee, and a simple black polo shirt that revealed a line of dark curls creeping up his chest. There was a guy on keyboards, too, but Karen barely saw him.

Marcus's song was enchanting. He sang each note with such emotion it was hard not to feel controlled by him. He was like the Pied Piper only much better looking.

"You never said he was performing," Sam barked in surprise.

"I didn't know," Karen shouted over the noisy crowds. "He just said he'd meet me here."

"Smooth," said Sam.

"Arrogant," mumbled Will.

The audience was silent for the entire song. There was applause of sorts when he finished but nothing like what there should have been. They must still be in shock, Karen told herself. Sam quickly slapped her friend's chin back into position to correct her hanging jaw before Marcus joined the table.

Marcus immediately introduced his band member as Liam Tullon. Liam was tall and skinny with a shaved head, making him look like a pencil with no rubber top. He was bony and pale-faced, and his skin was mottled from what must have been aggressive teenage acne.

Liam was staring out the pub window where the concrete ledges of the adjoining arena dipped and slopped. He was watching a group of youths racing up the gradients. Karen spotted Sam staring at him. She was sure she must be misreading the signs, but Sam seemed smitten. Either that or she was wearing a particularly strong pair of beer goggles.

Everyone scooted up. Sam made sure Liam was tucked safely by her side. But Marcus stayed standing close to Karen, leaning lazily across the table.

"You never said you were in a band," said Karen.

"I wanted to surprise you."

Karen had forgotten about his accent – smooth and velvety. She noticed his smile then – cheeky and crooked.

Liam, they learned, was Marcus's elder cousin. Karen found it comforting to learn Marcus had *some* family in the city. Marcus revealed he was an only child, and like her he had lost his father at an early age. Piraeus sounded captivating. He described it as a bustling city with the largest harbour in Greece. "It means the place over the passage. A place with something for everyone," he explained. He described evenings spent fishing on the Corinth Canal. "It is better in evenings," he told her. "The fish come to feed on the wildlife hovering just over the water."

"You'd get on with my brother," Karen told him. "He's obsessed with fishing. Karen gazed into space for a moment or two. "Dublin must seem pretty dull," she said, thinking allowed.

"No, I like this city," Marcus admitted.

Everyone turned to the jeering coming from Liam. He was staring out the window enjoying the view of Rick falling off his bike and onto his backside. He was a jerk, Karen decided instantly. One of those people who loved to criticize. He would go to town on Jake's band; he'd devour them and Zara would devour him right back and Karen wouldn't lift a finger to help him. Karen made a point of running to Rick's aid, in the hopes of evoking some form of regret in Liam. It didn't.

Rick was hurt, Karen could tell. He wasn't limping or displaying any evident injuries, but he didn't have to. His eyes never lied. They were less round than was normal for Rick. He was putting up a front for the audience that had formed, but his bushy eyebrows were twitching. She couldn't help but hug him, inhaling the familiar scent of wood chippings and workshops. Carpentry was the only thing he'd ever stuck with and he always smelt like a forest, fresh and woody.

Marcus moved so quickly she barely noticed the motion. He was behind them in an instant helping Rick straighten up.

A moment later Connor approached. "You okay?" he asked a little too late. He'd been busy scrutinizing the stranger hanging out with his sister.

Joining their table wouldn't have been Connor's first choice, but Rick was feeling shaky. Connor ordered him a large whiskey and Will, ever the gentleman, gave him his seat.

"Did we miss anyone good?" Rick asked with a wince.

"No," Zara informed him before anyone could respond. "Suns of the Underworld haven't been on yet."

The distant tone of her voice indicated the lack of intention to offend anyone, and even Liam found it amusing. She almost fell off the chair when Suns of the Underworld finally did make it to the stage. Jake shouted his way through the entire song, completely out of time with the rest of the band. He winked at Zara so many times it looked like he was having some form of fit. They were easily one of the worst bands at the venue.

Nobody could look at Zara's face for fear of the embarrassment they might find there.

Rick was the first to break the silence. "I think they're great." he said, with glassy intoxicated eyes. Everyone exhaled freely as Zara exploded with elation.

"They are, aren't they?" She was positively glowing, speaking of record deals and Ireland's biggest agents.

Liam, with a face full of sarcasm, suggested bypassing Ireland all together in favour of breaking America. But his sarcasm was completely lost on Zara, who had an unshakable belief in the band.

Olivia was head-banging to "Jump Around" when Karen left.

Rick was showing his elbow to some unfortunate red-haired girl and Sam was distracting Connor while Marcus left with Karen.

"Would you like to get something to eat?" Marcus offered.

"Chips?" Karen was looking hopeful.

"I was thinking of something a little more palatable."

"Nothing is more palatable than chips."

Karen sat on the window ledge outside the chippers wondering if she'd emphasized enough just how much salt and vinegar to get. The streets were crowded with Friday night revellers. Many of them weren't sure where the footpath ended and the road began.

Marcus looked like the soberest man in the city as he emerged victoriously from the chip shop with a soaking brown bag.

"You have to work for them," he joked, shaking the bag. He took her hand then and ran across the road through the traffic. Karen caught her breath on the other side and whacked his shoulder mockingly. "Stop doing that," she tried to sound angry. "Last time it was raining; this time you've no excuse."

Karen stopped when they reached the taxi rank, but Marcus managed to convince her to walk. The night was cold and she would have preferred to engage in pointless conversation with a taxi driver, any driver, even the smelly one they'd gotten last weekend with the wonky eye that stared more at Sam's legs than the road.

"I'll keep you warm," Marcus promised putting his arm around her.

"You'll feel better for it in the morning."

"Do you drive?" Karen enquired hopefully.

"Not if I can help it. I like to be outside as much as I can."

Karen wondered how this might work for him in Ireland. She pictured his school materials: soaking-wet pages and saturated leather binders. He looked like the leather binder type, she'd decided, and all this she shared with him.

The walk was every bit as long as Karen had anticipated, but more enjoyable than she had imagined it would be. It was starry and bright, she was full of beer and chips and was almost disappointed as they approached the green at Ashton Park. They took the shortcut through it, where the grass had separated and given birth to a temporary track fathered by the residents of Ashton. The sirens of the city were distant and muffled and Karen was surprised when Marcus broke the silence. "Do you miss your father?" he asked out of the blue.

The moment lingered.

"Probably as much as you do," Karen replied.

****

Karen tossed and turned but she couldn't sleep. A thousand thoughts ran through the plains of her brain. She worried that Connor wasn't home yet. She wondered if Rick had had any luck with that red-head – probably not; she looked ready to keel over with the smell of whiskey on him.

She hoped Sam hadn't gone off with that Liam. And of course there was the kiss, how could she sleep after that kiss? That kiss had left her breathless on the porch.

Marcus had tasted of tangerines and cream, his stubble had tickled her chin and his lips were soft. There was something about how he had held her, his hands lay respectfully and protectively about her waist, making her feel like a precious jewel. With each motion of his lips he simultaneously moved his body rhythmically until it felt like they were dancing to a tune no one could hear but them. Karen played the memory over and over in her mind until finally she fell asleep.

Chapter 9

Rachel Donovan was running late. She brazenly edged her Corsa into the busy queue of traffic on Main Street. Oscar sat studiously in the back seat, licking a strawberry lollypop while intently examining his picture book. The pages were getting stickier and harder to turn.

Rachel sneaked through another amber light, determined not to be late.

It was bad enough Karen O'Driscoll thinking she couldn't afford a book for her own son, she wasn't about to give her the satisfaction of being late as well.

If only she were made permanent at the hospital, the financial noose around her neck might loosen. In the meantime, if her son needed a book, *she* would be the one to buy it. She didn't need anyone's help.

Despite all her efforts Rachel was almost half an hour late. Her shirt was damp with sweat and her make-up felt oily on her skin. But seeing the shape Karen was in instantly boosted her confidence.

"Morning." Karen winced through half-closed eyes.

"Hi," was all Rachel could muster as she examined her son's reading coach.

The tell-tale signs of a hangover were written all over Karen's face. She looked dazed and tired. Her lips were dry and swollen and she was slumped across the desk like one of her pupils. Rachel recognized that slump; she'd used it in Maths class many times herself. Perhaps Karen wasn't as high and mighty as the rest, with all their judgements and brilliant advice on how she should be raising her son.

Oscar smelled of strawberry lollypops and his fingers were so sticky his new book opened two pages at a time. He never noticed the massive gaps in the text. When Rachel had kissed him goodbye, she'd almost stuck to his cheek. As was usual for Oscar, he dodged making any effort to read and insisted on Karen reading the first chapter. But today Karen had a plan. She'd been working on it all week. "If you read the first paragraph, just the first paragraph, I'll tell you about the real Percy Jackson. Not many little boys know the real story, and it's not just anyone I'd tell it to."

Karen knew it had worked before Oscar did. His eyes were just as easy to read as Rick's were. She could see the cogs in his brain begin to turn, excited little cogs, unruly, easily distracted, inquisitive little cogs, weighing up this interesting new prospect.

He wiped his nose on his sleeve and began his endeavour.

Oscar surprised her, every second word was a challenge but he was trying, and that's all he needed, just to know he could do it. When he finished he was out of breath. He looked at Karen expectantly. His wide eyes stared unblinking at hers and she knew she had to deliver.

"Okay," Karen said. "Go switch off the light and come sit by the window," she instructed. "Now," she began when Oscar was safely sat next to her. "Do you see that great big berry bush out there near the car park?" she asked.

Oscar was nodding eagerly.

"Well, that used to be part of a row of hundreds of other bushes in a forest that used to be here. Birds would land on it, rabbits would run under it. And some say Percy Jackson ran past it," she said.

Oscar didn't interrupt until Karen finished her story. He was so impressed he agreed to read a page from the book. They were that engrossed with his progress that neither noticed they had run well over their lesson time. They read late into the morning while Rachel sat patiently at the back of the classroom. The pride was evident on her tired face as she made a fuss over the excellent reading she'd just heard.

Oscar's little chest puffed out with the sense of achievement that bubbled beneath. He probably thought he could behead a monster himself, and perhaps even do a better job of it than Percy.

Rachel promised her son an ice cream. "You're welcome to join us," she said to Karen. But Karen was looking a little green.

"Do come," Rachel insisted. "It's the best hangover cure there is; either that or more alcohol."

"Is it that obvious?" Karen asked.

"Only because I've been there and got sick on the T-shirt," Rachel admitted.

****

No one understood how the ice cream stand stayed open. It was always raining and it was always dark, but the children of Ashton Park must have been a persistent little generation, well versed in getting their own way.

The stand had been making Benjy a steady income since it had opened.

Benjy was his usual jovial self and smiled a toothless grin at Oscar, who was visibly put out by the gesture. If ever there were advertisement for why not to buy ice cream, Benjy was it.

Because she knew him so well, or perhaps because he was too scared to speak, Rachel ordered her son a choc chip deluxe, which he accepted open-mouthed from Benjy.

They strolled along together towards the swings, where Oscar tried to prove it possible to hold a cone in your mouth and swing at the same time. Karen and Rachel sat on the swings opposite him. Rachel was right about the ice cream. Its thick and creamy consistency lay like a soothing blanket in her burning belly.

Rachel was the youngest of three sisters, Karen learned, all more settled than she had ever been. One was a lawyer and the other a doctor. But while they'd spent their years in college, Rachel had chosen to indulge her wild side and go travelling. When she returned, pregnant and with no father in tow, she was greeted with a wall of parental judgement and I-told-you-so's.

The rift only deepened when Oscar was born.

"You spend your whole life quietly craving their acceptance," Rachel explained. "Then you have your own children and that approval that seemed so important becomes the final nail in the coffin of closeness."

Karen was confused. "Didn't it bring you closer? Having a child I mean."

Rachel was looking really bitter now. She screwed up her mouth as though she were sucking on a lemon, a lemon dunked in vinegar, perhaps, and then rolled in chilli. "You would think so, wouldn't you?" she responded and began to swing a little. "You don't mind being judged yourself, but when it extends to your child, it's an entirely different matter."

"My mum would love to be a nan." The words were out before Karen finished thinking them, and she lowered her gaze in tandem with her thoughts.

"I'm sure she will be some day, when you're ready," said Rachel in a jovial tone.

No she won't, thought Karen, silently swallowing her pain.

It was a hard thing to swallow – pain. It was lumpy and temperamental, constantly changing in shape and size. Sometimes it grew larger, making swallowing impossible, and choking more likely. She was watching Oscar swing higher and higher, knowing that she could never have an Oscar of her own.

The ice cream began to taste sour.

Chapter 10

Somewhere on the train lines of Dublin, a middle-aged man was sitting opposite to Karen O'Driscoll, with rivers of drool dripping from his chin. Karen wondered how he could remain so oblivious to his condition. Surely he would have noticed the translucent stains on his shirt in the evenings. Surely that would have been incentive enough to stay awake. Karen tried to keep her eyes focused on her book but she couldn't ignore the swine-like sounds that could only pass for snores if you lived as a pig on a farm.

When she could take no more Karen decided to stand and she made her way to the end of the carriage in a huff. Where had all her patience gone? Slimer wasn't the first hygienically challenged passenger she'd ever shared a carriage with. There had been countless before him, like that guy who used to take his shoes off and pretend he didn't notice the effect it had on other passengers' breathing. Or that girl who smelt like she'd eaten cigarettes for breakfast. Karen had never allowed them to cost her a seat before. But she had less patience of late. Perhaps she was getting old, or perhaps it was the lack of sleep.

It had been another restless night, cushy pillows, hot water bottles and a locker full of books and still she could not sleep. But here sat this human-swine hybrid in a stuffy carriage, snoozing from station to station.

Typically, getting off the train with the prospect of a day's work ahead of her depressed Karen, but today it was a welcome relief. She threw herself onto the platform and took a deep breath, cooling her mind and body with the crisp morning breeze.

****

Sam was feeling wonderful, and wonderful wasn't a word she used too often. Wonderful was a word she laughed at people for using. Wonderful was more of a Zara word really.

A couple of years before, and things had been very different for Sam. She had been two stone heavier then. She was out of work and living at home. Her mother was driving her crazy, but she couldn't afford her own place and wine was fast becoming her very best friend.

When she finally turned things around she felt better than she ever did in her life. She gave up drinking, she began running every morning, and she quit smoking (nearly). She'd felt rejuvenated. This was how she was feeling now. Liam had awoken something in her: a hope, and an excitement.

Sam second-guessed her decision to ask Karen to double date with her and Liam when she saw her friend arrive late again. Karen was looking dreadful. She'd lost weight and her cheeks were gaunt and colourless.

Sam scolded herself for thinking it, but Karen even looked like she could have used a shower. Sam toyed with the idea of avoiding her for fear it had something to do with Marcus.

She had really hoped he'd turn out to be one of the good guys. He didn't have to be *the* guy, just a good guy.

Sam had established some time ago that her friend had been hurt in the past. What the details were, were anyone's guess. If Karen were to confide in anyone Sam was sure it would have been her. But Sam thought sharing was overrated. Some things were better left buried. Buried deep inside and covered with layer upon layer. What's done is done! If you acted like you didn't care, then pretty soon you wouldn't! That was Sam's motto.

****

The appraising look on Sam's face made Karen feel like walking straight back out the door. She kept her head down until lunchtime, avoiding the judging eyes in the office.

Sam, however, insisted on buying her lunch. She also insisted on mushroom soup. "It's feel-good food!" Karen was unconvinced. Every food was feel-good food to Sam. But her heart was in the right place.

The best thing about Sam, Karen thought, was that she never pried. She never pushed or prodded. Regrettably, today Karen felt like she'd welcome a good old-fashioned push. She needed to talk; she just didn't know what about.

"Karen?" Sam repeated, when she realized she'd lost her friend's attention again. "Right, that's it." Sam slapped the table. "You need some chill-out time. We're going bowling, Thursday night."

****

Karen held a heavy lock of hair in her hands and said goodbye to her split ends before ringing Roxy's buzzer. She could hear Roxy yelling from upstairs. She was shouting at Niall. She was always shouting at Niall. It could have been over the mess in the bathroom, it could have been over the full-fat milk he'd bought when she'd specified low fat, or it could have been for not making the sun shine that day.

But one thing was certain; it was definitely Niall's fault.

Bickering aside, Roxy and Niall were the most passionate couple Karen knew. If they weren't arguing they were zealously making up. People said Niall had the patience of a saint to put up with his girlfriend, but secretly he liked her fiery side. He loved how she never put up with his moods, loved how she challenged him. He loved the emotional rollercoaster she took him on day after day.

Niall was looking very amused as he answered the door.

"I've hidden her credit card," he whispered with a cheeky grin. "I'd make sure she's calmed down before she starts cutting though."

The best part about Roxy's hairdressing (apart from the childhood stories she told about Rick) were the head massages. Karen thought if she could make shampooing feel that good she'd never get out of the shower.

Roxy had plenty of news to share. She always had the most up-to-date gossip from the salon. She'd had to suspend two of her staff. Sarah had been seeing Tanya's boyfriend behind her back and a nasty brawl had broken out in the salon.

"Ridiculous!" Roxy fumed, "Fancy letting yourself down like that in front of so many people. And not just any people, but customers! *My* customers." She sighed. "I suppose that's what I get for hiring teeny-boppers fresh out of college."

Karen was trying to remember the offending girls but her memory failed her. Roxy was using a strengthening serum on her split ends and she was feeling too pampered to care much about shop politics.

"That's terrible," Karen said sleepily and hoped Roxy hadn't said anything that constituted good news. Roxy had begun her head massage now and it was threatening to send her to sleep.

When Karen awoke a few moments later, Roxy and Niall were standing over her with worried expressions on their face.

"I thought I'd cut your ear off." Roxy's voice was shaking and she was patting her chest with both hands. "You were dead still, and then you just jerked your hands up to your ears like I'd cut them."

Karen was embarrassed. She felt a rush of blood burn her cheeks.

She couldn't tell them she'd just dreamt of a scream that burst her eardrums. "Better than sleep walking, I suppose." She had tried to sound nonchalant but wasn't sure she'd pulled it off.

"You called for your dad," whispered Roxy after subtly sending Niall to fetch a glass of water from the kitchen.

Karen's cheeks felt so hot now they could have insulated the room. This must be how Will felt, she thought. "I don't even remember dreaming of him."

Roxy gave her one of those awful sympathy looks. Unlike Sam, Roxy wasn't big on privacy.

"What's wrong?" she asked. "You look horrible."

Roxanne Brady was about as subtle as a baseball bat, but because her intentions were good, she usually got away with it. She once managed to convince a client to update her hair style by telling her the current one made her look like a mushroom. Amazingly she ended up still cutting the woman's hair, and even more amazing was the tip she received.

"I'd like to attribute your nodding off to my amazing head rubs, but we both know better. You were definitely having a nightmare."

"Nothing new there then. I always have them."

Roxy took a seat at the table. "You know, dreams often have a way of helping you with conscious problems. Like a portal or something. What's bothering you when you're awake?"

"I don't know!" Karen was being honest. Weeks of frustration bubbled beneath her skin, seeping through cracks formed by its suppression.

When Karen spoke again she was shocked to hear the shake in her own voice. "My eyes burn." she heard herself say in an unfamiliar voice. "All I want to do is sleep. But when I do, it's just nightmare after nightmare. Everything seems like a mission. My job annoys me. People annoy me and I just want to cry all the time."

Roxy looked on in dismay as her friend burst into tears. Niall returned with a glass of water but turned expertly on his heels when he realized a girl was crying at his dining room table. Roxy stared on in helplessness. She was fond of Karen. She had even attempted to set her up with Rick and make her a sister-in-law. She was forced to neglect the endeavour, however, when she saw nothing but friendship between them. And they didn't fight nearly enough.

Unlike her brother, Roxy was *a fixer*. She was determined there had to be a simple solution, a remedy, a plan of action. She exhausted ideas from PMS to repressed childhood memory syndrome before finally resting on fatal familial insomnia. In the end, the only constructive advice she could offer was that the very best way to sleep was by not trying to.

"By not trying to?" Karen repeated with a sniffle. "I haven't tried that yet," she hiccoughed.

Karen's heart felt lighter; she had a plan now. She would not *try* to sleep, not even go to bed, just stay up and enjoy some telly maybe.

Nobody was home. Connor had Buddy out walking and Karen put on a movie – *Babe: Pig in the City*, it was one of her favourites.

The most relaxing movies were always those you'd watched a trillion times over, she thought. Maybe it was the familiarity or the predictability. Either way they required less attention.

If Roxy was right, and our dreams are formed by our conscious environment, then Karen would be dreaming of friendly farms and little pink piglets in no time.

Roxy was wrong. There were no cute and cuddly farm animals and no country pleasantries. There was only dread.

Predictability lost its appeal as Karen climbed the familiar fence knowing what was on the other side.

To say that she heard the mystery screamer would have been inaccurate. Hearing, no matter how unpleasant the pitch, was a human sense. But there was nothing human about this feeling. It lifted her out of her body.

Karen was reminded of a story her mother had told her many years before. They had come across a car crash, and Catherine being a doctor was obliged to stop and assist. Karen had gotten out of the car to follow her. It was one of the only times she regretted not doing as she was told. What she saw caused her weeks of sleepless nights. It wasn't until her mother explained how the brain numbs the body from great pain that anyone got any sleep.

Karen felt that way now; like her out-of-body experience was protecting her from the pain by projecting her somewhere else.

When her senses finally returned, she could almost make out a name. It was softer than a whisper, impossible to make out but definitely female. It was then Karen saw it – the silhouette of a hooded figure shaded a colour she couldn't quiet identify. She could have been smoke in the wind, so pale and wan she seemed to blend in with the descending dusk.

Karen and the mysterious figure stared at each other for a time before Karen's eyes began to burn. Stinging hard, they began to bleed, floods of blood seeped down her cheeks before she woke in the arms of her brother. Connor was shaking her gently attempting to waken her. The tears he shed matched the flow of hers. Suddenly Karen's pain felt halved. It was like he had taken a chunk of it and swallowed it whole for her.

The following morning came and went without anyone mentioning the night before. Other more pleasant topics were discussed instead. Topics like Buddy; Karen and Connor made up a roster of who would take him for walks and when.

Karen envied Buddy as he lay curled up in a comfortable brown ball sleeping the morning away. He had chosen the most inconvenient spot in the kitchen as his favourite – right in front of the cooker door.

Connor said it was because food magically appeared from this enchanting place. Rick said it was for the heat, but Karen had the feeling he just liked to be in the way.

Thursday came quickly and Karen was excited about her double date.

Sam she remembered to be hopeless at bowling.

She may have looked like a tough cookie, slim and toned, but she could barely lift a bowling ball.

Chapter 11

Marcus lived in a bedsit. It was old and the air smelled heavy of must and old newspapers. Being on the main street, it had witnessed the lives of many passing residents. It had been home to numerous stories over the ages, Marcus could sense it. The walls whispered their secrets to him. Marcus liked it. It was devoid of any elaborate furnishings or trinkets. Liam called it The Abyss but Marcus didn't care; he was a minimalist.

He stood now, applying his aftershave in the poky bathroom mirror with no light. It was dusk and the last of the sunshine revealed playful pieces of dust dancing together in the final rays of light.

He would have time to feed the cat before Liam picked him up. The old Victorian window creaked as he opened it onto the street. Loose white paint fell onto the window ledge as he looked for the stray.

Cats were his favourite animal, his creature of adoration even.

He liked their self-sufficiency, admired their ability to take what they needed and yet somehow make you feel grateful. He left some tuna in a bowl on the mossy rooftop below before leaving.

Liam was puffing on a cigarette when Marcus pulled open the passenger door. His long arms lay across the steering wheel as he stared ahead appraisingly. He sipped the contents of the silver flask he kept inside his jacket pocket.

"You're late," he said, smacking his thin lips.

"I was feeding the cat."

"Cats are for girls; you need a bull dog to match your face." Liam laughed at his own joke.

The traffic was heavy and Liam swore and banged at the steering wheel the entire journey. The car was stuffy and smelled of cigarette butts and cheese and Marcus was relieved when they finally pulled into the car park.

The bowling alley looked like an old rundown factory. Marcus laughed at the large decrepit sign hanging sadly over the entrance.

He read it aloud, "The Bowling Alley. Very innovative!" He sniggered.

"Well, what did you expect in this crap hole place?" Liam asked.

They continued their argument inside until they spotted Karen and Sam sneaking in some practice runs without them.

Sam looked like she might have mastered the complicated art of picking up the ball, if they returned perhaps next week. The little black waistcoat she wore flapped over her short legs drawing attention to her slender frame. She looked dainty, Liam noticed appreciatively.

Karen was in the middle of a demonstration when Marcus planted an unexpected kiss on her cheek. He smelled of sweets and aftershave, or perhaps just a very sweet aftershave, she couldn't quite tell. Her bowling skills went downhill rather quickly after that. It didn't matter; Marcus was equally as bad, although Karen suspected he was holding back. Unlike Liam, who was intent on displaying his superiority with every throw.

Karen tried hard, but she couldn't see the attraction Sam did. Not even if she squinted, not even if she covered one eye. She watched Liam swagger in his dreary green army T-shirt and wondered how he even managed to lift the ball with those bony white arms.

Karen went to get another beer, just so she didn't have to witness another sickening strike. Sam followed her with starry eyes.

"I think I might manage to keep it in our own lane next round," she announced. "Owing to Liam's expert training of course."

"Of course," Karen said. "Don't you find him a little … peculiar?"

Sam looked surprised. "I know he's not my usual type. But maybe that's a good thing. Where has my usual type gotten me so far?"

Karen thought about it but she realized that Sam didn't have a type. Dark, fair, tall, small, male, female, and Karen admired her for it, but she said none of this to her friend. Instead she chose to criticize Liam's stinginess at bringing his own drink in a stupid little flask. It was the only concrete thing she could think of.

Sam looked affronted. "It's just root beer. Not even alcoholic. They make it in the army. You still take your grandmother's scones to work and no one laughs at you." Karen felt her face sting. "That's different! And I never see you complain when you're filling your face with them either."

Sam did improve in the next round. She was certainly more aggressive, and she even managed to knock a pin. Karen sat out the last game.

It was only ten thirty but she was tired and her legs were failing her.

The night was turning into more of a chore than a joy, and the argument with Sam had upset her more than she cared to admit.

They never fought, especially not over a guy. Karen wondered if she had been a little insensitive. She wouldn't have liked it if Sam had criticized Marcus, but then, how could she? Karen realized then just how much she liked him and it scared her.

Marcus appeared then at the table, armed with a box of jam doughnuts.

"Some sugar might help," he said. But the later it got the blurrier the lanes became. Finally Karen gave in to exhaustion and Marcus brought her home.

He also brought her back to Griffin the next morning.

His embarrassment at Liam's car was obvious as he smacked the stereo ferociously trying to locate a signal. Karen spent the entire trip trying to convince him she was just grateful for the lift. Buddy had made it impossible for her to take the train.

"They're a lot of work." Marcus nodded at Buddy in the back seat.

Karen stared at the dog lovingly.

"They're worth it. He finds excitement in everything."

Socks were no longer just socks – they were funnels full of fluffy bits, snout catchers and soft toys all in one. A clothes horse was a particularly intriguing thing; fabrics dangled enticingly and tickled your ears. If you lunged at them they moved, and if you tugged them hard enough they made the lights go out.

Buddy growled when Marcus kissed his mistress goodbye.

Karen worried that her boyfriend was expecting an invitation inside.

He stared past her, eyes almost greedy with enthusiasm, asking question after question about her family. She awkwardly thanked him for the lift but it was definitely too soon to introduce him to anyone, she decided.

On her way into the yard Karen met Andrew, however, who insisted on introducing himself to Marcus before he left.

"Have you no shame?" Karen spotted his dirty overalls tucked into filthy old wellington boots.

"But they're this season's!" Andrew lifted his heels mockingly and headed for the car.

Catherine would still be on call so Karen made her way into Esther's. Her grandmother was bustling about the kitchen preparing breakfast. Her glasses were all steamed up and falling down her nose as usual. Fat sausages sizzled on the pan over the gas stove, spitting oil at anyone who had anything to say about it. Most of the meat Esther bought was local. Brackens was the local butcher's but it was forced to close when their youngest emigrated with half the family funds. Robert Bracken was an alcoholic and had likely drunk every last penny of it. Esther liked to remind everyone now and again that Wayne had been close to *that Robert Bracken boy* at school.

"One of the ewes is lambing," Esther told her granddaughter.

"Fancy watching a lamb being born?" Karen asked Buddy. It looked like he said yes. But he always looked like he was saying yes, so they made their way across the fields, Buddy chasing butterflies.

Karen found Katie in pen eleven, inspecting Rosie the ewe.

She lay the towels and hot water down before kneeling next to Katie who looked closer to giving birth than Rosie did. Her cheeks were bright red and she was sweating. Her hair fuzzed out at the sides like two wild and fuzzy horns.

"I'd say we've jumped the gun with this one," Katie panted. "She's gonna be taking her time, she is."

Rosie appeared unfazed by Buddy's presence; he was behaving quite well under the circumstances. He sat with his inquisitive head tilted slightly to the side as he looked on with what appeared to be a professional interest.

"Why don't we go in for a pot of tea?" Karen was worried Katie would go into labour before Rosie.

When they reached the back kitchen Katie finally agreed to put her feet up. Andrew was naive enough to think he would be allowed dab her forehead with a cold facecloth but came away looking dejected when she waved him away irritably.

Chapter 12

Back in the City, Connor and Rick were in Hoopers Festivity Store.

Rick's parents were going down the country for the weekend and he was planning to host a Fright Night party for Halloween. Rick's mother was too ill to spend another Halloween jumping at every firework that came through the letterbox.

Connor admired how Rick took such care of his mother. She was so ill so often with her ME that it made her husband's addiction even harder to tolerate.

Rick never spoke much about it but to watch someone make himself ill while someone else tried so hard not to be must have been frustrating. Rick had paid for his parents to stay at a hotel by the sea in Wexford. He couldn't give them spending money because Nicholas would only drink it all. Rick learned a long time ago that vouchers were a much safer option where his father was concerned.

Connor bounded up to his friend with a *Scream* mask covering his face.

"Very original!" Rick commented. "But what about this?" He held up a Hannibal Lector mask.

Connor's face fell. "That's just stupid; you're not getting that." He snapped it out of his hands.

"I think someone's afraid of Hannibal Lector."

"I think someone else should get a move on and make sure their parents leave."

They made it back in time for Rick to have one last argument with his father. Connor stood kicking stones in the driveway while he pretended not to hear. Connor liked to *not hear* and he liked to kick the ground as he did it. His boots never lasted more than a couple of months.

"You know our place is a three-bed," Connor offered.

"Thanks man, I'm happy where I am, though. Until someone can cook like my Mum, I'm going nowhere."

The evening turned cold and frosty. A dense sheet of fog descended on the city and it was beginning to feel like Halloween already. Cotton-wool cobwebs were strategically placed around Rick's house. However, precision suffered more and more with each beer consumed. The horror theme got a little lost when Rick stuck up his alien paraphernalia.

"I hope they don't take this as an invitation." Rick believed in alien abduction.

"Because of your posters?" Connor asked. "We'll just throw them next door if we see any bright lights, okay?"

"No." Rick looked worried. "Next door have kids. What about MacEntie's across the road? That John MacEntie's a right old git. I saw him check out my mum once."

"Ew," said Connor before the dagger looks Rick threw him educated him of his insensitivity. "I don't mean it like that of course."

"Just stop talking."

Connor knew when to shut up. Rick was idealistic and a little naïve but he was also ferociously loyal.

****

Rosie had been in labour over an hour now. It was dark outside and Karen stood back while Andrew examined the ewe. Lambing was a job she'd never managed. She knew what to do; she just couldn't bring herself to do it. Andrew washed his hands in the soapy water she'd prepared. He generously applied some lubricant to his gloved arm before Karen decided to wait outside; she swung the lantern by her side as she walked into the chilly night air and laid it down by her side.

She should be using a torch; most people used torchlight.

They were safer and they were brighter but they didn't keep you company in the dark the way a lantern did. There was no energetic eager little flame exploring the night with you. A couple of moths seemed to agree. They were drawn to its flame and began head butting the glass repeatedly. She watched them dance around the glow until she fell sleep.

Karen saw Connor whacking his fishing net off the logs at the back fence. She climbed it in slow motion. The atmosphere was hazy and the scream was muffled. She squinted persistently through the pain, determined to hear the words this time. Her efforts were rewarded.

Karen heard her father's name. It came slowly and deliberately, like a summons and it left behind an empty feeling, like the world had been stripped of something significant. Karen noticed a second figure then. A saddened defeated little figure watching the events unravel before her. It was Bertha McCormack.

Andrew carried his niece next door. She stirred in his arms while she slept. He watched the curls fall from the sides of her face as she mooched. She looked like her mother. He smiled. He could see none of his brother in her, except perhaps her stubborn nature.

Catherine was reading by the range when Andrew came in. She jumped to her feet.

"It's okay," Andrew assured her hurriedly, "she's just sleeping."

"I know," Catherine lied, protecting her cool demeanour. "This way," she whispered and guided him past the great white doors to Karen's bedroom.

****

Connor liked spending nights at Brady's. Rick had built an extension that any bachelor could be proud of. A short corridor led out of the house and formed a studio-style dwelling. There was an excessively large widescreen television with movie collections from floor to ceiling.

Video games and consoles littered the floor surrounding two beanbags and they'd played on every one of them. Connor had drunk too much and was falling asleep now.

"What do you think about black holes?" Rick asked. "Why are aliens so hard to believe in if black holes exist? Couldn't they simply live on the other side?"

Connor wasn't answering, but Rick went on, "You know time travel is possible don't you? Not to the past of course, but to the future. If you go faster than the speed of light then you go forward in time; I saw it on Discovery."

Rick realized he'd spent the night talking to himself when he saw the first shades of light peeping through the trees. He stared about him lazily. Empty beer cans lay on the floor and pizza scented the air.

****

"I thought you were staying at Bradys'?" Karen was surprised when she arrived home to find both Rick and Connor watching football in the living room.

"It's too messy!" Connor yawned.

"Did you get us something?" Rick asked spotting the shopping bags. "Is that a pumpkin I see?" He got up to help her.

Karen rolled the pumpkin onto the countertop. "Knock yourself out."

"Aren't you going to help?"

"Sure!" Karen opened another bag. "As soon as you've gutted it, I don't like the gloopy feeling on my hands." She made a face.

"That's the best bit!"

But Karen wasn't listening. She was reminiscing about Halloweens in Griffin, before her world had come undone around her. She and Connor would spend it at Burkes' playing Halloween games. But no one ever mentioned Burkes' any more.

****

Karen was absently hammering away on her keyboard. The letters were beginning to fade from the billions of words it had been used to create over the years. There were twelve policies that needed uploading by lunchtime and it was already noon. Had she been more organized earlier in the week there wouldn't be such a last-minute rush.

The keyboard jammed and stiffened in protest. The tiny protruding lines of the home keys were all but faded away, but she didn't need them anyway.

Karen could do her job with her eyes closed. She could probably do it with one hand while hopping on one leg. She knew exactly how many tab spaces lay between each field off by heart. It was embarrassing.

Field one was Policy Number, automatically populating Client Details. If you hit the tab key seven times it took you to the next updatable field. This worked if you were too lazy to use the mouse and wanted to look busier than you were.

"How's my favourite gal?" Will wheeled over on his office chair. "Don't tell Sam I called you that!" he added quickly.

Will was looking particularly smart this morning, Karen noticed. "Why are you in such a good mood?"

"Why are you not?"

"Policies!" Karen waved her hand over the intrusive bundle on her desk but immediately regretted it.

Brenda had clearly been eavesdropping and she entered the cubicle.

She raised her eyebrows, circling them both like a tiger. She stared at the offending paperwork with a look of horror that would have been more appropriate for a murder scene.

"What are … Is this … Are these all for today?" She finally asked. "You know the system can't apply the discount if they're later than fifteen days."

Karen felt a bead of sweat form on her forehead. She hadn't even begun to think of an excuse when Will was on his feet taking half the bundle.

"Actually these are mine. I wanted Karen to do half since I've been swamped with the audit. I can do them if you want to help with the audit, though."

Brenda looked deflated, disappointment written all over her face.

"Well I'm very busy with appraisals, you know how much have you left?"

"Just a few more pivot tables."

Bingo, thought Karen. Everyone knew Brenda couldn't do pivot tables but liked everyone else to use them.

"All right," she conceded, "you continue. Karen and I can update the policies for you."

Will manoeuvred past the girls as quickly as possible, hiding a cheeky smile.

"I love you," Karen mouthed.

Later it transpired that Brenda had an ulterior motive for visiting Karen that morning. She had already been around everyone else's desk displaying the direction of her Claddagh ring, which now indicated she was no longer single.

Brenda sifted through policy after policy, elaborately waving her hands just to draw attention to it.

She pointed at problem fields on Karen's computer screen where there was no problem, sometimes no field either.

Karen gave in after she almost had her eye poked out by an impatient finger. "Wow! Who's the guy?" she made herself ask.

Brenda beamed and blushed at the same time. "How did you know?" She giggled.

"The ring," Karen answered trying not to sound too bored.

"Well, aren't you the little Sherlock?" said Brenda, before launching into a tiresome tale which told of one Lawrence Lavin from Canada.

"Canada?" Karen echoed. "What brought him to Dublin?"

"Well, he's never actually been to Dublin," Brenda confessed.

"You mean you've never met the guy?"

It was too late to back track now that the thunderclouds had descended on the plains of Brenda's sweaty forehead.

A lecture on the success of online love matches ensued, before Karen was finally left in peace to catch up on her paperwork.

"And I thought I had problems," Karen muttered.

Chapter 13

Alarge blazing pumpkin sat on the windowsill of Number Five, Ashton Park. It looked like someone had tried to turn it into an alien. Dangerous-looking almond-shaped eyes embellished its face leaving room for nothing else. Several oranges stood on the fireplace gutted and carved into pumpkin-like tea-light holders.

A bowl of sweets lay on the phone table near the front door. There were Chewits and apple drops, toffee pops and jellies. Karen had thought better than to include any fruit in the mix after last year's ingrates had thrown them back at the window.

Karen had spent hours cleaning the house. It would be Marcus's first visit. He was due to arrive any moment. Karen bounded down the stairs two steps at a time when she heard the doorbell.

She checked her reflection in the mirror and puffed up her hair before answering. When he wasn't there, she lowered her gaze to the duo stood before her. One was Darth Vader and the other an overexcited storm trooper.

"Trick or treat!" they yelled simultaneously.

The storm trooper was hopping from one foot to the other as though he were trying not to wet himself. Karen hurriedly chucked some sweets into their baskets in the hopes of keeping her doorstep dry.

She stood smiling as she watched them skip down the drive before closing the door, but a large intrusive boot wedged itself menacingly in the gap. Her heartbeat quickened in her chest before she realized it was Marcus.

"You scared the life out of me," she gasped. "Where'd you come from?"

"It's Halloween; I'm allowed to scare you." He rattled a bag full of cocktail mixtures.

Marcus apparently prided himself on Halloween concoctions. "Tonight, my love, you shall have a ghostbuster, a red witch and a pumpkin spice, all rare delicacies of the underworld."

****

Rick's party went off with a bang. Every firework in the poky back garden was completely illegal, which meant they were completely brilliant. Niall had done the station the great service of disposing of the confiscated explosive items. Having a sister who was engaged to a police officer had some perks, Rick noted.

The crowded family home hadn't catered for this many visitors since Roxy's twenty-first birthday party.

Rick was hoping Diane, the pretty red-head from Raptures would show. She had seemed impressed with his elbow injury, he thought. She'd kept pushing him away like his scars were so impressive they made her squeamish.

Connor was already pie-eyed in the kitchen from the punch he was mixing. "Very important to taste your brew," he informed the guests. He added more cinnamon sticks before spilling the mixture into some plastic cups. Connor had remembered his friend's instructions.

The normal family china was not to be used; it was safely tucked away in the back cupboard to avoid any embarrassment. Rick remembered the Christmas Roxy had purchased a new set for her mother. Watching her expression was like seeing Cinderella presented with her glass shoe. Mrs Brady loved intricate designs and china. Her Christmas present lasted until New Year's when Nicholas knocked the entire shelf down after one of his quiet ones down the local.

Rick had worked hard not to hate him that night, but he failed.

"... Gonna wanna see you with a face like that man." Connor interrupted his thoughts.

"What?" snapped Rick, unfolding his arms.

"I said she's never gonna wanna see you with a face like that," Connor repeated. "There's the door now; it might be her."

But it wasn't Diane. It was two of Connor's work colleagues, Dan and Fabien. Fabien had a bottle of red wine tucked neatly under his arm.

He was a little overdressed, which appeared to embarrass the tall and gangly Dan, who shifted uneasily by his side.

Fabien was wearing black slacks and a white dinner shirt.

His patent-leather black shoes were so shiny they reflected the light like disco balls. Dan looked scruffy at the best of times, but next to Fabien he looked like a down-and-out. They sat uncomfortably on the little green settee, sandwiched between Niall and Roxy until Connor's punch melted away the social inhibitions.

Niall told them the excuses he'd heard for the fireworks he'd confiscated during the week. One boy said they were a message for his mum down the grocery store. "Milk and fireworks!" she'd ordered.

Later in the night Dan told ghost stories.

"Now he's a brilliant storyteller!" Roxy nudged Niall in an accusatory fashion.

"Not good enough to shut you up," Niall muttered.

Dan's voice was deep and husky. His facial hair looked like whiskers twitching around the sound effects his mouth made.

Roxy had no ghost stories. Her conversational contributions were of the more feminine variety as she shared her concerns about Karen.

Rick's opinion was that Karen was a good person and karma would take care of her. But it led to an elaborate explanation of a newfound religion he'd been trying out.

"We should turn our backs on conventional living," he said. "Only then can we can be saved."

Fabien was enthralled. "Is this what you believe?" He sipped his red wine and looked rather out of place on the little green settee. "You believe you will be forsaken should you not follow rules?"

"No," Rick corrected with confidence. "God forgives all who repent; it says so in the Bible."

Roxy piped up at the opportunity for a good argument with her brother. He was her second most favourite person to quarrel with after Niall. She swayed drunkenly, waving her wine glass threateningly.

"So you're saying that chauvinism is acceptable just because it's in the Bible, then, are you? Homosexuals are doomed to hell, too, I suppose?"

Rick was looking a little more rattled. His sister was not a woman to be trifled with, especially with a glass of wine in her hand.

"Like they say, it's Adam and Eve, not Adam and Steve. God made man to be with woman; that's why only a man and woman can conceive."

Fabien looked confused now. "I am wondering," he began patiently, "procreation cannot be the sole function of love. Surely love has no function. God did not create Adam and Eve to conform to a society of rules they fabricate for themselves in his name. He created them to be a vessel of his love and in doing so, he lives in us all."

Rick sniggered. "I like you Fabrilly! You think God is in us all because love is in us all, so we're all just walking Gods really."

"God left us a plan," Rick continued. "The Bible tells us how to live, what is and is not a sin. You either follow it, or you don't. That's all I'm saying."

Fabien's perfectly neat eyebrows came together in thought, like he'd just been introduced to algebra for the very first time. "I thought the bible wasn't written until hundreds of years after the death of Christ? Doesn't that make parts of it largely the word of man?"

Roxy enjoyed a good giggle at the look of horror on her brother's face. Fabien noticed it too and quickly backtracked.

"Please don't misunderstand!" he added. "The Bible is an undoubtedly a brilliant source of wisdom and guidance. But God's true feelings are portrayed in the stories he told and the meanings behind them. Why is it, do you think, that the greatest prophet recorded never wrote his own testament?"

Nobody answered.

Dan seemed uninterested as he swirled the whiskey in his glass. He looked a little perturbed that his ghost stories didn't evoke such emotion, and Niall was pretending not to think about it.

It was Roxy who finally attempted a theory. "Because tools like Rick would twist it!"

"Perhaps," Fabien admitted. "Or perhaps it was because you must search before you can find. One person's conclusions may not be another's. God must have known of man's tendency to institutionalize everything; to create a hierarchy empowering people and calling priests heirs to the apostles."

Rick was done. He had nothing left and he was feeling too drunk to win this argument.

****

"Don't you have anything scarier than an old Freddie Krueger movie?" Marcus looked surprised.

"I do," Karen admitted, "but you wouldn't be able for the gore."

Marcus sniggered as he popped the movie into the DVD player. He liked to be challenged. He liked Karen.

Karen followed him into the kitchen, eager to witness the cocktail preparations he'd bragged about so much.

"This one's a ghostbuster," he told her, lining up some Bailey's, Kahlua and vodka. He mixed in some crushed ice before emptying the contents into a highball glass for her to try. Karen swallowed it down in two thirsty gulps, licking her lips for the aftertaste. She was impressed but held off admitting it until she'd sampled another, or perhaps ten.

"Next up, we have the exceptional pleasantry that is a pumpkin spice." This he poured into a cocktail shaker before showing off with a professional shake.

Karen was feeling content as she lay comfortably in Marcus's arms on the sofa. Her stomach purred in appreciation for the cocktails and crisps. The last thing she expected in that moment was taxing conversation. But Marcus wasn't known for his predictability.

"Where do you see yourself in ten years?" he asked out of the blue.

Karen thought carefully before responding. She dreamed of owning a cottage and rescue centre in the country. She would have a great big wooden panelled door and a range in the kitchen, like Esther's. The backyard would be full of chickens and there would be a pigsty where pigs would be *clean*, sort of like Piglet in *Winnie the Pooh*. "Karen?" Marcus asked. "You still with me?"

"Sorry, yes!" Karen shook herself. "A high-flying executive, of course."

When he raised his eyebrows sarcastically she knew she hadn't fooled him.

"What? I could be a high-flying executive."

"I have seen your company's definition of high flyers, and I must tell you, the future is not bright."

"Being Brenda could have its perks." Karen tried to think of some.

"Don't you have children in your future?"

Ordinarily Karen would freeze at such a question, change subject or perhaps lie and say she never wanted any. But the secrets that wound themselves so tightly around her heart were beginning to come undone.

"I can't have children," she blurted out.

And there it was, out in the open, words that had haunted her, words that escaped her mouth with such force she had to take a breath.

Marcus didn't say anything. She stared up at him, and still he said nothing.

Karen was relieved. She hadn't known she needed to talk about it until he'd left her space to. She told him how she lost a baby when she was just twenty-one. She told him how they'd always been close to the Burkes but that everything changed when Shauny's cousin came to Griffin.

"Corey was a heartthrob," Karen explained.

"Define heartthrob." Marcus finally spoke.

"He had sooty black hair and grey eyes like yours. We spent the summer together, feeling all grown up just because we could get served in Razors. Connor wasn't so overprotective in those days." Karen smiled and shook her head at the memory. "He covered for me on the farm and we even double-dated with Molly Maloney. Then everything changed."

Karen's smile faded and Marcus began to feel uncomfortable.

He listened to her descriptions of morning sickness and pregnancy tests until finally she got to the part that interested him. "How did Corey react?"

"Like any immature boy I guess," Karen sighed. "But he came around, He told me his own dad had been such a let-down he was afraid of making the same mistakes. I said it could be an incitement for him to do better.

"And then?"

"Then he just up and left. We fell asleep together one night, and woke up apart the next morning. He went back to England; I lost the baby. There were complications and I can't have another."

Marcus said nothing. Karen didn't expect him to.

She stared blankly into the fire instead. It always brought her peace, staring at the flames like they were alive and moving with a purpose as simple as just to burn.

"Funny!" Karen finally admitted. "He wanted to do better than his own dad and he didn't even make it to the birth."

Marcus sat up and joined in with her trance-like gaze at the fire.

"Maybe that *was* him doing better, maybe he thought you'd be better without him."

Karen hadn't the energy to argue. The effects of releasing so much pain had taken its toll. Her body felt raw and tender, but something else too. She felt lighter.

"Can I fall asleep with you tonight?" Marcus whispered.

"Connor would kill you." Karen tried to make it sound like a joke, even though she was serious. "He doesn't even know you."

"What is his problem? You are all grown up now, no?"

Karen finished the story Marcus thought had ended. "Corey didn't just disappear. When I lost the baby Connor followed him to England and beat him to a pulp. He always blames himself when things go wrong. Then he makes things a million times worse when he tries to fix them. He beat Corey so badly his family pressed charges, leaving him with a criminal record following him to every job interview he ever gets."

"They shouldn't have done that," Marcus said. "They are assholes."

Karen laughed a little at his pronunciation of the word.

"If I stay I can be gone before you wake."

"Fine." Karen was too tired to argue. "But you better not snore."

****

Marcus was gone by morning just as he'd promised he would be. Karen dreamt of him. He was holding her tightly to his chest, but she couldn't make out his face. Each time she tried, he would tuck her head gently back into his chest. She felt a grazing on her forehead from his stubble, which surprised her. He was usually clean shaven.

It was then she noticed it was no longer Marcus, but Rick.

His shape changed then to a slimmer frame and she found herself looking at Will. Will dissolved into Andrew, and through it all she felt suffocated. The air was heavy and her mind felt cloudy as she fought to regain her senses.

Chapter 14

Will was worried. It was ten thirty and Karen was a no show. She always called ahead if she was running late.

He sometimes felt like a shepherd, a shepherd on a hill overpopulated with a flock of accident-prone sheep.

Some of the blonder variety needed transport lest they went home with the barman. Others squealed and head-banged at the rare excitement of a night out, and then there were those who lost weight, slept late and didn't show up for work.

It was times like these he wished he had a little sister. Maybe then he wouldn't fill the void with all these reckless sheep. He shook his head. He didn't like being the youngest of three boys. He felt more like the eldest; he should have been the eldest.

If he were he'd have kicked the other two into shape by now. Steven was thirty and John was two years older. They still lived at home, which was fine in Will's eyes. He didn't understand the stigma some people attached to still living at home past thirty. Why not live with the people you loved rather than living alone? But the fact that they left their dirty clothes lying about and never prepared a meal grated on him. A sister would have been nice.

Karen was kicking herself. She'd gone back to sleep after that bizarre and suffocating dream and now she was paying the price, running out the door and skipping breakfast again. Her stomach growled in protest as she ran.

A heavy mix of vodka and rum was fighting over who would make an appearance first and Karen fought to keep them both down. She had to stop and take a breath for fear of announcing the winner.

She glanced at her wrist only to find a patch of pale skin where her watch used to be. Last night was probably the first time she'd removed it in years. Marcus had laughed at its boyish appearance until she removed it to reveal the etching at the back.

"It was a gift," she defended. A gift she'd chosen when she was just ten. "I guess fashion's changed a bit." She frowned.

"It is cute." he had chuckled. The memory of him put a smile on her face, a smile she kept there until meeting Brenda at the office.

Brenda Butcher had one of those fish mouths, Karen thought; a mouth that naturally sat like the letter *n* just above her chin. The sides dipped down at either side. Pouting with a mouth such as this portrayed a very intimidating effect.

Karen knew that if she wanted to turn things around that day she would have to ask how Lawrence was. But she didn't. She couldn't. She wouldn't give old trout mouth the satisfaction. Instead she put up with all the jibes about how being late could interfere with everyone else's schedule. She accepted all the extra filing landed on her desk and she powered through her policies.

Will found her rubbing her temples by evening. "Come on, you're coming to Broderick's. We'll have a pint and a game of pool."

Socializing was the last thing Karen felt like doing. "Maybe another time. I'm not great company right now."

"But it's been ages since we knocked a few balls around."

It was true they hadn't played for ages and pool might be a good distraction. People didn't have nightmares about pool pockets. Broderick's was quiet and Will led Karen to the pool table. Pool was their *thing*. Karen liked it because of the sounds it made. The clinks and clonks of the balls, the scraping of the chalk on the cue tips. Will liked it because he could call it a sport without having to break a sweat.

"So Roxanne Brady tells me you have fatal familial insomnia." Will blew the excess chalk from his cue.

"I'm sure you'll disagree find something a little more logical, no doubt."

"Of course." Will was still examining his cue. "Usually when someone can't sleep they have something on their mind. Find out why your mind won't rest and you'll find a good night's rest." He looked proud of his assessment.

He'd made it sound so simple, standing there, all six foot of him, idly furrowing his brow.

"Thank you, Dr Freud, but the problem isn't getting to sleep, it's the sleep itself." Karen broke the colourful triangle of balls with too much aggression. Yellows and reds went firing about the table. Two reds sank into the corner pocket with a satisfying keplunk.

"If I win you have to upload my policies for a week," Karen perked up.

She always did that, Will noticed, conveniently forgot to make a bet until the odds were in her favour.

"No way, you've already two down." He laughed at the expectant look on her face.

"Fine." She shrugged her shoulders, sank two more balls and snookered him with the third shot.

Will looked around him, subtly checking that no one was watching.

He spotted Leslie behind the bar and his cheeks went a Ribena-red colour. When he turned his attention back to the game, Karen was staring at him.

"Ask her out, Will. What's the worst that could happen? If she says no, big deal."

"That's not the *worst* that could happen, the worst that could happen is she tries to resuscitate me because my colour tells her I'm choking."

"That's *good.* You get the kiss of life and everyone's happy."

"I'm hungry," Will said, changing the subject. "Can we eat now?"

"What about your previous girlfriends?" Karen ignored him but followed him to a table. "How did you ever ask them out?"

Will thought of a sorry sequence of failed attempts at romance. He'd really liked Amy Butler in college. It seemed like a good idea to ask her out in a tracksuit and trainers so she'd assume his red face was the effect of a really manly work out. He'd marvelled at the ingenuity of it all until she chose the college triathlon as their first date.

Will was probably the most unfit person at the college. He sweated like a pig the entire way through and even Lorna Simpson beat him. There was no second date.

"Well?" Karen pressed.

"I guess I've always just been friends first," he lied. "Anyway, it's your issues we're here for today. *You* should be telling *me* what's wrong."

"Why does everyone keep asking me that? I don't know what's wrong."

Will looked sympathetic. "Then maybe you should pray." There was no smirk and Karen was sure she'd heard him correctly.

"You don't even believe in God. You told me before. You said, and I quote, 'When you're dead you're dead.'"

Will shifted uncomfortably in his chair and stroked his beer glass. "That doesn't mean I don't believe in prayer. As an atheist it always fascinated me why prayer works for so many people."

This was typical Will, thought Karen: thinking, thinking, always thinking, trying to apply logic where no logic existed. "You think too much. You need a date."

Will ignored her. "I think it's because we're honest in prayer," he went on. "You lay your heart bare and verbalize what you never knew was there. Then when your desires are clearer you're in a better mind-set to achieve them."

Karen was feeling patronized. Why did men always think they had the answers to everything? Maybe her expressions weren't as guarded as they ought to have been because Will looked hurt and embarrassed.

Catching his hand seemed like the right thing to do.

"Sorry." He responded to her touch. "But if you don't know what's wrong it might be a good place to start is all."

****

Karen's rosary beads were ancient. They even smelled old. Made from tiny wooden beads they had the simplest of detail. Not even a depiction of Christ himself occupied the little wooden crucifix.

Thoughts of what prayers the little beads held at their core comforted Karen: her father's prayers, her grandfather and maybe even his father before him. Karen's father had specifically left them to her.

Will was right about one thing: most people only ever prayed when they needed something. Not that he was much better. Will believed in ghosts, he believed in evil spirits, yet he didn't believe in one good spirit. She wondered why it was easier for people to believe in bad than it was to believe in good. It was a sombre testament to mankind's mentality, she thought.

Chapter 15

Evening tea breaks in the building trade were notoriously long, sometimes longer than lunch.

Galford's were working on an office block just outside the city. It felt good when your destination lay in the opposite direction of morning gridlock and the absence of frustration over traffic was having a positive effect on morale.

"Why don't we go camping?" Fabien asked.

"Because it's the middle of winter," Connor responded.

"We could rent cabins," Dan suggested. "We could invite your sister. Only because you don't like leaving her alone," he clarified when Connor threw a vicious glance his way.

"Humph." Connor chewed his sandwiches suspiciously. "She's seeing someone anyway." he said after a while.

"I know," Dan admitted. "I'm not interested in her like that, but I am interested in the someone she's seeing. Your sister's dating a prize A-hole, you know."

Connor was uneasy to learn about the origin of Dan's scar.

Marcus got the blame for producing a smashed bottle in a bar brawl.

Probably the result of someone chatting up someone else's girlfriend, Connor thought; these things always got out of control when mixed with alcohol.

Dan was a bruiser; he was always in fights, too difficult to tell what was an attack or self-defence. If Connor ever wanted to feel better about his temper, he would compare it to Dan's. Even now Dan's veins were popping on his temples. It wasn't until Fabien mixed him a brew that he calmed down.

It was Connor's turn to clean up. He collected Dan's cup and stared at the little leaves congealing at the bottom. They looked like little green people nestling together to maximize the heat on a cold winter's night. Where did Fabien learn all these handy little brews, Connor wondered. He knew the myth: being the seventh son of a seventh son qualified you as a healer. Ryan Fox's cousins from Donegal said the infant's mother would place an item in the child's hands. When the child grew up this would be their item of choice in healing. The item would be placed on the wounded area to provide the cure. But Fabien had no item, he had no ritual.

****

As the sun set on another day, Connor saddled his Yamaha Thundercat. This was his favourite part of the day. The rooftops glowed amber through the settling dust of the work site, and all that was left was the open road home.

Connor caught the gear with his foot several times yanking the throttle but to no avail. The leather of his jacket groaned in protest as he fumbled over the side of the bike to inspect the crankcase. The nasty little oil spillage he'd been expecting stared glassily back up at him. He was going nowhere.

****

Karen was resting comfortably on her boyfriend's chest when yet another text caused his phone to vibrate intrusively in his shirt pocket. Marcus's expression was unreadable as he stirred beneath her. "I have to go."

Karen was alarmed. Go where? She wondered. She didn't want to be one of those controlling girlfriends, and it was so long since she had a boyfriend, she wondered what was and wasn't normal to worry about.

"Why the urgency?" She couldn't help asking, it was out there before she could stop herself. "Not that I mind," she added hurriedly. Before he could answer they were disturbed by a set of headlights illuminating the driveway.

Karen hurried downstairs and peeped through the sitting room window. Marcus followed close behind to see Connor and Fabien exit Fabien's small green car.

Karen noticed their frosty reception to Marcus. Even Marcus, who always seemed unperturbed by other people's opinion seemed on edge and it made her glad he was leaving.

"I'll walk you some of the way," she offered.

Marcus kissed her forehead. "Stay inside and be warm." He smiled. "I will call you tomorrow." He gave her brother a suspicious look before leaving, but Connor didn't seem to notice.

"Will you stay for tea?" Connor asked Fabien.

****

Karen was embarrassed. They hadn't done the shopping and the fridge was all but empty. A few sorry-looking bread rolls and some tomatoes stared back at her from the middle shelf. There was a cut of honey-roast ham but it was out of date. Maybe Fabien could have that?

"Can I help?"

Karen jumped with a start from Fabien's voice behind her.

"You could throw this out." Karen indicated the ham. "I am vegetarian." Fabien smiled warmly. "I can make you a meal, I am good at food."

"You can prepare Buddy's if you like?"

The little chocolate Labrador was staring at the cut of ham like he'd just found God. A trickle of drool flowed steadily from the sides of his mouth.

He'd gotten big in the past weeks. His legs were long and dangly and they almost tripped him up, even though he had four of them to balance on.

"Come," said Fabien, and the little Labrador followed like a devoted young soldier.

Karen waited until she heard the back door close before rummaging desperately through the cupboards. *Soup* she almost shouted in a moment of inspiration. You could make soup out of anything. She buttered some bread rolls and cut some tomatoes.

Karen was mixing some herbs into a boiling saucepan when she felt it. It was an icy chill that spread through the air like a virus. It descended on the room stealing all the oxygen in its path. The radio began to crackle and fizz like it was choking. Karen steadied herself against the counter, and then it was gone. It disappeared so quickly that she wondered if she'd imagined it.

"Something smells good." Connor appeared from behind her and tried to interfere with a clove of garlic. He smelled of soap and aftershave.

"I was considering a camping trip earlier today," he told his sister. "Would you be interested?

Karen loved the outdoors just as much as her brother did. "A camping trip or a fishing trip?"

"Both?" Connor chanced.

"You won't kill the fish?"

"Only behind your back."

Connor suggested bringing Sam along for some female company, but they weren't on the best of terms after Karen made her feelings clear about Liam. She tried to put the memory out of her mind as they sat down for supper. It made her squirm and she couldn't work out if it was from annoyance or guilt.

"What about Lough Corrib in Galway?" Connor suggested.

"Can we go somewhere more historical?" Karen didn't want the trip to revolve around fishing.

"The Holy Mountain?" Fabien offered.

"Somewhere not in Jerusalem, mate." Connor patted his friend's back.

"He means Croagh Patrick, dummy."

Karen remembered every story her grandmother ever told her. Unless it was about the Fianna, a sword or a battle, Connor did not.

"St Patrick and his pilgrimage up the Holy Mountain," she reminded him.

Later that evening Karen attempted some internet searches on log cabins. She opened her laptop but Connor slammed it shut again. "We'll organize it. Call it an early Christmas present."

Instead of feeling grateful Karen was feeling fretful. Men never got it right. What they described as *character* usually meant *missing a wall*.

Maybe bringing Sam wasn't such a bad idea after all.

****

Karen slept right through the night without any appearance from the screaming woman she fought to keep from her mind. She had been reading *Eragon*, Rick's favourite book, and its detachment from reality settled her. The words had danced across the page like distorted sheep jumping fences of black and white paragraphs and daring her to follow.

But her imagination was stubborn and led only to the dark stellar land of her dreams. Something was different. Karen didn't feel the same drive to be somewhere that she had before. There was nothing she needed to find and nowhere she had to be so she sat by the bank without purpose.

After a time, the faint sound of crackling sticks drew closer, melodic and thumping. Karen recognized it as an approaching horse. It arrived with two men on its back. Both dismounted together. One of them went to the stream for water while the other tended to the horse.

Karen knew she was invisible to them. She was surprised a lot more wasn't invisible to these people with their strangely coloured eyes. They were like puddles of blue on an otherwise human face.

"Are your observations ready?" asked the man returning from the stream. Karen could make out glistening drops of water shining through the hairs of his beard and he wiped them with a dirty sleeve.

The second man was leading the horse to the stream. He stroked the horse's nose gently. "Almost." He pressed his forehead to the horse's when they'd reached the bank. The huge animal nudged him gently and began to drink deeply from the river. It could have been swallowing light itself as its nose broke the beams that bounced off the current. Karen found herself wonder what was making everything shine in such a dark place.

The horse remained still while its master withdrew a thin piece of what looked like stiff paper from the saddle pocket. He paused and studied it. "Tomorrow I may not be with you my friend."

Karen watched them leave and sat back down on the bank.

She gazed out at the river. It called to her with sounds of swollen secrets, rising and falling with the waves. Karen found it thought-provoking. It showed her her own curious reflection, it showed a yearning in her eyes and finally it showed her the howling spirit of her nightmares. The spirit her conscious mind had been pretending not to know. But everybody knew her; everybody knew the banshee.

Chapter 16:

To the untrained eye Karen would have appeared busy at her desk.

Her eyes were glued to her computer monitor and she'd barely spoken a word all morning. But none of the internet searches she did had anything to do with insurance.

Poems, texts and extracts on the very specific subject matter of the banshee flooded her screen. She sifted through the information she already knew: the word *banshee* came from the Irish Bean Sí. She could appear in many guises, Karen sped read, from a haggard old woman to a stunning young lady with long flowing hair. Karen took a quick look around the floor to make sure Buffy wasn't en route, then whipped her head back to her monitor. Sightings of banshees had been reported as recently as 1948, she learned.

There appeared to be two schools of thought on the banshee's intentions, however. One was that she came to forewarn of a death in the family, that her cry was one of grief and sorrow and she could be seen washing the blood-stained clothes of those who were about to die. It is said she once walked the earth as a beautiful woman, before suffering a violent death. Her death was so brutal she now walks the earth as a haggard old woman, following her descendants to escort them to the afterlife.

Not such a bad thing, Karen thought.

The second interpretation was more disturbing. It said that rather than warning of a death the banshee was the bringer of death.

Karen minimized the window on her screen. Her lips were moving almost as fast as her heart.

This banshee is said to relentlessly pursue certain families. Once targeted, she would drive her victims to insanity and finally death. She follows noble Gaelic descendants, namely the Macs and the O's

Karen read the text of a poem she'd never heard before.

By Mac and O

You'll always know

True Irishmen they say

But if they lack

The O and Mac,

No Irishmen are they

"Cursed be to hell," Karen muttered. She had never been so sorry to be an O'Driscoll. "Why couldn't we have been soupers?" She wished for the first time. *Soupers* was a term Esther had taught her. Its relevance went back to the famine. There was conjecture that some of the English charities that ran soup kitchens only provided aid if one dropped the *O* or the *Mac* from their name, making their names more *Anglicized*. Karen saw no shame in it, and she was pretty sure she'd have changed her name to feed her children.

Zara was watching Karen's vacant expression. She had noticed the head sweeps protect her computer screen. She knew that sweep. She'd invented it. Zara was intrigued. It was mid-month – quiet time – so why did Karen look so busy? Maybe she was updating her CV. Zara gasped. It could explain the lack of interest lately. Maybe she didn't care if her declining performance got her fired.

Zara had two operating lenses by which she interpreted the world about her. Those were, *good for Zara* and *bad for Zara*. The initial analysis of the situation indicated *good for Zara:* Karen leaves and Zara gets promoted. Further analysis revealed, however, that Karen's role was level with her own, so in fact no advancement and the possibility of extra workload. Bad for Zara, very bad for Zara!

"Would you like a cup of tea?" Zara offered Karen out of the blue.

Karen accepted suspiciously and cautiously closed her internet searches.

She'd seen enough for one day and returned her attention to the office. Olivia was revealing her *X Factor* plans for her youngest. Kiera was five but already showing promise for a life of stardom.

Karen took a steaming cup from Zara gratefully. She noticed Zara loitering before delicately placing her large bottom on the edge of Karen's desk.

"So," Zara began, "how are you?" she sang with a chirpy tone, before gently slapping her colleague's arm.

"Em, fine." Karen lied, as she looked around suspiciously. She could see Sam in the corner of her eye appraising the situation, a testament to just how un-Zara-like this behaviour was. "I've just got a lot on I guess."

"Let me take some off you then." Zara dug into Karen's to-do pile that had spread like a fungus across her desk. "You know I could hook you up with a really good hairdresser that could sort out your curls."

It was hard to overlook the insult but since this was Zara being nice there was no point in arguing. Normally, now would be a good time to email Sam with a *WTF*. It felt so wrong not speaking.

When Zara finally left, Karen turned her attention to Sam. It was time to eat some humble pie. Karen had never understood the expression. *Eat rancid fish* would have been more accurate. She swallowed hard and drafted a very carefully thought out email:

Lunch at Mario's?

Seconds later the small flashing image on her screen told her that Sam had replied.

I've already made arrangements with Liam.

Karen scrolled down but there was nothing else.

No *Why don't you join us*, no *Maybe tomorrow,* nothing.

Suddenly Karen wished she'd taken the humble pie and smeared it all over Sam's face instead.

She would go out for lunch anyway, she resolved. There was only one person she felt like seeing right now. And she punched Marcus's number into her phone.

****

Starbucks was quiet for a lunch hour, save for the group of teenagers experimenting with how loud they could get without being thrown out.

Marcus hadn't answered his phone; Karen left him a voicemail. This was the closest coffee house to St Anne's. She hoped now that it wasn't also his students' local lunch venue.

Karen had time to develop her theory on Bertha McCormack. She had been thinking of the old woman ever since she appeared in her dream. She wanted to talk to her. But it was madness, what would she even say? *Hi, Bertha, do you believe in banshees? Coz I think I saw one in my dream and I think you did too.*

But Bertha's eyes were too yielding to ignore, they knew something. They were hiding a similar torment as hers. What if this kindred emotion meant something more? Karen began to fret. What if she was going crazy like Bertha was? What if her father had been crazy and now it was her turn? Karen wiped the sweat from her brow. Next she'd be calling Buddy Rascal.

Marcus still hadn't called and these were definitely not his students, Karen decided. St Anne's was a posh school and she was pretty sure they didn't allow hot pants and belly tops. It was obvious the young girl they called *Shazzer* was the ringleader.

Shazzer was scantily dressed in denim hot pants and a belly top. Her gold hooped earrings were bigger than the ears they clung to. Several others appeared to be copying the trend. They all looked cold and underdressed but they still managed to snigger at everyone through chattering teeth.

Karen kept her head down and sipped her latte, grateful she wasn't a teenager any more. But she couldn't help feeling a sting of embarrassment at being stood up. The more time passed, the more awkward she felt. Her fingers played with the locket on her chain in what she hoped appeared to be a carefree manor. But even Shazzer could see through the façade and she afforded her a look of sympathy by way of female solidarity.

****

Rick had gotten through an entire evening's work in just under two hours. This always happened; every time he had something on his mind he would power through it with work. Now that he was working for himself Rick could see why Reece was so reluctant to let him go. Rick must have made half the profit in the first few years of his trade. Business was booming, even in the recession. Rick didn't fit the common perception of the tradesman. He called back when he said he would, he finished contracts ahead of schedule and he was punctual.

Standing there now, with a hammer in hand, he was angry at himself for not going solo sooner. It was fear as usual that had stopped him. The final decisions rested with him, no one to check with and no name to hide under. He'd been such a fool, fretting over nothing.

Rick carefully examined the beading he'd just laid, and took a second look around the property. It was a four-bed dormer with woodwork throughout. He stared out the front bedroom window. There was no more work left and nothing to occupy his mind, nothing but that familiar feeling of fear.

Rick began to peel flakes of fresh paint off the window sill, unable to stop moving his hands, unable to stop thinking, remembering. He was dreading the fishing trip, terrified of being on a boat.

He recalled a summer's evening over twenty years ago. It was so fresh in his head he could almost smell the lake. Nicholas had rented a small fishing boat. Neither he nor his son expected to catch anything. In fact, Rick privately hoped they wouldn't. He couldn't stand to kill a living creature. But being on the water, rowing through the currents with the noise of the water splashing against the oars was a novelty.

Nicholas had brought his cans of course. He always brought his cans. He sank one after the other while Rick cast and recast his line.

"Drat," mumbled Rick. He had peeled off too much paint and a piece of plaster had come undone. He gave a loud sigh and resumed staring out the window. He folded his arms in annoyance.

Children don't understand when it's time to go home, he realized now. He remembered his eyes feeling heavy, his A-Team T-shirt no longer warm enough for the chilly breeze on the lake. Nicholas was snoring when Rick felt the pull on his rod. His heart thumped with fear and excitement and he called out to his father. But Nicholas was out cold, too intoxicated to hear him.

The slender rod began to bend and contort. Rick tried to reach his dad with his foot. What if it was a shark? He panicked; he'd seen *Jaws;* everyone in his class had. In a frenzy he'd stretched too far behind with his leg and was thrust forward into the lake with a yank of the rod.

The same friendly water from earlier was now a cold and hostile place. It was like it had turned on him. It hurried around his body, contracting his ribs and his breathing came in short rasping pants. The water was dark about him and his legs jerked wildly in fear of what lay beneath. Then he began to sink.

His very short life flashed before him. His mother's face was first; it was always first: waking him for school, kissing him good night. He saw his sister next. She had his Transformers; she was always stealing them. His father's face didn't feature at all. Eventually he gave in to the urge to breathe and swallowed a large mouthful of the water.

It burned his lungs.

Rick saw his father when he opened his eyes and realized he'd just resuscitated him. Nicholas was pressing his chest and tapping his son's little blue face in a frenzy. Nicholas's eyes were swollen and puffy and he squeezed Rick close to his chest.

Rick could see those eyes now in the reflection of the window. He hated having his father's eyes, he hated that he looked any way like him at all.

Rick hadn't been on a boat since. Who was he kidding thinking he could go on a camping trip? Of course they would rent a boat, no one was ever happy with fly-fishing on the banks. Karen would think he was a wuss. Fabien would love that, but then what would Fabien have to fear? He could probably walk on water anyway.

****

Marcus kept a watchful eye on the building where Karen worked. He was in trouble; he knew he was by her text – something about how he should check his phone more often.

People were emerging now in dribs and drabs. He chewed on some spearmint gum while he waited, appraising every employee he saw exit the building. Men with umbrellas made him laugh. Marcus didn't think any man should use an umbrella, or wear a scarf. And as for gloves, they were just ridiculous.

Will emerged with an umbrella. Karen was underneath it. They almost passed him until Marcus stepped away from the lamppost he'd been leaning on. "Remind me why I came to Ireland." he joked, looking up at the rain. "I had my phone on silent. It's dead now so I said I'd come meet you instead."

"I'll see you tomorrow." Will made the very bold statement of kissing Karen's cheek before leaving. Marcus spun on his heels like a tornado. He thrust his chest forward and caught Will on the shoulder. Will recognized the irrational response he'd anticipated. He had exposed Marcus's animalistic rage, a rage brought on by disrespect. Marcus had been eating from his bowl and Will had deliberately interfered.

Marcus recognized something too, it was a look ofexpectancy in Will's eyes.

A smug look telling him Will had anticipated such a reaction, a reaction Marcus would make sure didn't materialize. "Sorry man, I slipped," Marcus lied. "Not used to these slippery pathways."

Will chose not to answer and left his umbrella with Karen.

"He's a little overprotective," Karen consoled Marcus when Will had left.

"Afraid he'll be left on the shelf, no?" Marcus replied cruelly. "Never mind. Where would you like to go?"

"How about Broderick's?"

"Hmmm, too full of suits."

"Copper's?"

"Too full of cops." he teased and played with her hands.

Karen suggested at least two more venues which he declined based on the fact that people didn't like him there.

"I thought you didn't care what people thought of you?" Karen said.

Marcus took her hand and led her down the steps onto the street. "Somewhere quiet, just us," he decided.

There was a new steakhouse on Cawley Street, not too far from Roxy's salon. It was small and intimate and you could smell the steak from the street. Marcus requested a table near the open fire. He didn't feel the cold, but Karen did. The fireplace was shaped like a cauldron and the tables were made from old oak.

Marcus appeared satisfied as he scanned the menu. He ordered a bottle of Merlot, which Karen used to pluck up the courage to talk about what was on her mind.

Marcus didn't seem the sort of guy to believe in banshees or fairies. As an English teacher he was of course interested in stories and fairy tales, but believing them was an entirely different matter.

A young waiter of about sixteen came to take their order. Karen ordered nachos and Marcus a blue steak.

"So how does it get blue?" Karen asked. "Some kind of sauce?"

This made him smile from ear to ear, he smiled like a cat Karen noticed, albeit she had never actually seen a cat smile before, but he was definitely more a smirker than a smiler.

"Blue is how it is cooked: rarer than rare. They basically just put in on the pan and turn it. You can try it if you like."

Karen had drunk too much Merlot before eating anything. "So do you believe in banshees or what?" was her next question. This sometimes happened when she'd had too little sleep or too much to drink. The boundaries between subconscious considerations and verbal deliberations became muddled, and she had trouble distinguishing between what she was thinking and what she was saying.

For the first time since she'd known him, Marcus looked rattled. He turned around to check it was him she was addressing.

"Why would you ask that? Halloween is over if you're thinking of dressing up." He crossed his legs and sat back in his chair giving her an appraising look.

Drunk as she was, Karen could tell by his reaction that the truth would be too unnerving for him. "No reason," she lied. "Just something Sam was saying in work, about growing up near a fairy fort."

Karen quickly changed the subject by inviting him camping, but before he could answer, a waitress arrived with dinner. Karen looked around; she had been expecting the sixteen year old, but the waitress's motivation soon became apparent as she ogled Marcus like he was her favourite flavour lollipop.

She was small and busty and the blouse she wore looked two sizes smaller than it ought to be. One of the overworked little buttons held on for dear life as she put Marcus's steak and chips before him.

She gave an inappropriate wink before leaving. But her flirting went unnoticed. Marcus only had eyes for the disgustingly bloody steak on his plate.

Perhaps Esther was right, Karen thought, the way to a man's heart *was* through his belly. Esther attributed successful matrimony to a good meat loaf.

"Wouldn't you rather a hotel break?" asked Marcus breaking her train of thought. "I can take you somewhere plush, just us."

"No. I want to go."

"And who else is going?"

"My brother, in case you're interested in getting to know him, and a couple of his work friends."

"What friends?"

Karen raised a finger and clutched it in a counting manner. "Dan Leavy, never met him, Fabien something or other, right old prat, and Rick." She counted on her third finger.

Marcus looked uneasy. It wasn't a look he wore well; he looked like a child sulking. "I have classes. But I can spend the nights with you."

Karen leaned over and kissed him then. He tasted of steak and red wine. He was truly gorgeous, she thought. His grey-blue grey eyes stood out wildly on his handsome sallow face.

"You get cold at night," said Marcus all of a sudden, as though it had just occurred to him, and he pulled out a wad of cash from his inside pocket. "You will need warm gear."

"But we'll be in a log cabin."

"But this log cabin is in Ireland, no?" Marcus slipped the money expertly into her handbag.

His persistence should have made her feel special, but it didn't. It made her feel awkward and uncomfortable but she couldn't fathom why. Perhaps it was the loss of independence; perhaps it was the fear of a change in the status quo, but he so obviously wanted for her to accept it that she couldn't refuse him.

"Someone's feeling flush today," Karen commented on the over-generous tip.

"Tax back." Marcus draped his leather jacket over her shoulders, deliberately dismissing the umbrella Will had left her.

Chapter 17

Dr Kenna was covering at the surgery for a couple of days. Catherine couldn't recall the last time she'd been off for an entire weekend.

It was stressful being one of the only doctors in a town inhabited by a population of hypochondriacs. Every head cold was flu, every headache a tumour. Catherine wondered where they'd all got their medical degrees or why they even needed her at all.

She missed her husband. Daniel may have been a farmer with no medicine degrees but he was always interested in her work and the welfare of the town's people. Catherine missed how he mispronounced *Hodgkin's* and *lymphatic,* she missed how he left his muddy boots in the hallway, and she missed how he used to visit Bernie Bracken after her son left.

"Are you really going to Bingo?" Wayne interrupted her thoughts.

"It's for Esther," Catherine snapped. "She hasn't been since Bernie's been bedridden.

Wayne felt a familiar pang of guilt at the mention of Bernie Bracken's name. He knew he shouldn't. It wasn't his fault his friend had skipped the country with his mother's life savings.

"I could call around to visit Bernie," he offered. "I just wouldn't know what to say. It's not like we'd have much in common, expect Robert of course, and I'm pretty sure she wouldn't want to talk about *him*."

Catherine was on her feet and kissing his cheek before he could finish. "I think she'd love it, including any mention of Robert. Your son is always your son."

Wayne grinned broadly. He loved to see Catherine smile. He thought she was the most beautiful woman in the world. She was way out of his league, he knew. He remembered the shock and disbelief the day she'd finally agreed to go out with him. He'd fixed her car – well, half fixed it – so she would have to come back the next week.

She was angry with the service. He remembered how distracted she was, staring out across the yard. The wind throwing her chocolate curls onto her face, and he thought she looked like a Hollywood movie star.

Of course she refused his initial advances. He had expected as much but he would be happy just to have her in his life in some way, any way at all. "What age are you?" he'd asked her.

The look she gave him could have shattered the glass of every windscreen in the garage.

"It's just the older we get the harder it is to make friends. I'd just like to be your friend, that's all." It was all he could offer. He could never move in her circles or hold an intellectual conversation with her but he could be there for her and maybe one day she would love him.

****

Bingo was held at the community hall. As Catherine took her seat, she was reminded of the years she'd spent studying. The great big hall bulged with cheap chairs and desks decorated in graffiti.

The high ceilings threw people's voices back and forth to each other like it was a game.

The small man calling tonight's numbers was Henry Harris.

He was a round-bellied red-faced old man and everyone knew him as a hot tempered wheezy old wife beater. Henry had anger issues for as long as he could remember.

As a boy he would trash his bedroom when building blocks didn't work the way he wanted them to. As a teenager he was expelled for thumping an older boy who had made the horrible mistake of complimenting his girlfriend. And now, as a sad and lonely old man, his wife had finally left him, presumably for that goodie two-shoes Malcolm down the women's centre.

Mary would often go there after he'd lost control and beat her out of the house. He didn't mean to, Henry told himself. She just wound him up, having that Agnes around filling her head with all sorts of garbage: garbage about getting out more, maybe joining a class. Probably just cover-ups for meeting a new man and leaving your husband. Her family had always been poisonous.

"Legs eleven, number eleven," Henry bellowed.

He was one of those people who could have a conversation without truly focusing. His mind could be in overdrive resolving some internal conflict while he communicated convincingly enough to others, like tonight.

"Unlucky for some, number thirteen." he roared. Bert was right – he'd get her back. She always came back. It was that Malcolm who was the problem. "All the fives, fifty-five." He had a headache now, and the balls in the drum were like hammers on his temples, but the worst was yet to come.

"Pay attention, woman!" Esther whispered. "Fifty-five, you have it there," she added, as if it were a matter of life and death.

"No I don't!" Catherine countered staring bleakly at her book.

"Two and four, twenty-four."

Esther lunged forward then, frantically circling a number on Catherine's booklet.

Karen was amused to notice her mother sulk for the rest of the round. She understood now why her presence had been so vital.

It was halfway through the next round when the doors rattled against the weather outside. The wind was howling and whistling beneath them, and they began to shake. Someone was trying to get in, someone with a grudge against door handles.

Finally the doors burst open to announce the arrival of a disgruntled and dishevelled-looking Bertha McCormack. Bertha wore a battered old purple shawl with green stockings and layers of other mismatched clothing. Her frock was down to her shins and her black wellington ankle boots were trailing mud tracks across the floor. She waddled from side to side with the weight that she carried until she appeared to have found the noisiest spot she could to sit down.

The atmosphere had changed in the hall and Karen spent every spare moment peeping over at Bertha. Karen saw her squint at her booklet, covering with her large arm what she must have thought were the answers.

When the interval was called, the kiosk opened in the corridors, selling a variety of refreshments. Karen was queuing to buy a drink when she saw Bertha chase a very flustered looking Henry down the hall.

Now was her chance. Karen edged out of the queue to pursue the pair. She needed to talk to this woman. She knew something about her father; she just knew it. Karen found them both near the registration desk, where Henry was pretending not to hear Bertha.

"You can't trust him," Bertha persisted. "He's not what you think, can't you see? Listen to the good in you, man. You have a choice; you always have a choice."

"Listen, woman, that man's been a tower a strength to me; been like a brother, he has. Now away with ye." Henry waved his hand dismissively. Bertha looked livid and Karen abandoned her plan.

****

Connor had replaced the O-ring on his bike and was tightening the nut with his wrench. The oil return line to the tank was dry and he was eager to take it for a spin. He knew exactly where he wanted to go.

The traffic on Main Street was heavy and it was hard to find parking on Saturday nights. Generally when people had a few too many they thought it acceptable to just hop on a parked motorcycle for a bit of a laugh. The bike usually ended up on the ground with a few new scratches.

Connor parked at a loading bay; he didn't imagine he would be long. Marcus's bedsit was just two blocks down as far as he knew. He shoved his hands into his jacket pockets and made his way through the busy street.

"Have ya gor any change fur the bus?" A toothless junkie stood in Connor's way. He recognized him and he stared up at the bus sign. "Seventeen?" Connor read it aloud. "The number seventeen is your bus?"

"Yeah!" the junkie looked impatient.

Connor leaned down closer to the man's face. "Then why are you always frightening the women, looking for change at the fifty-eight stop? Forget your bus money a lot do you?"

"Ah Jaysuz, forger it." the junkie waved his dirty hand.

Connor knew he should have just ignored the man but sometimes the city made you do stupid things and he stared about cautiously, in fear of getting jumped.

Marcus answered the intercom on the first ring. He didn't appear surprised or put out by the visit. Connor declined the whiskey Marcus offered him. He didn't want to stay any longer than necessary.

"This is about your friend Fabien, no?" Marcus began.

"Not just him, Dan too. He told me how he got that nasty gash on his face."

"Informed or misinformed?" Marcus asked calmly. He lit a cigarette.

"I didn't know you smoked."

"There are many things you don't know about me, which is why you are here, I presume."

"There's two sides to every story. I'm just here for yours."

Connor looked around the bedsit. It was spotless. It would be comfortable if it weren't so polluted by the noise of the street outside.

"You find nothing unusual about your friend Mr Fabien, no?"

"I find him unusually nice," answered Connor.

"Unusually nice indeed." Marcus inhaled the smoke deeply.

He crossed his legs and lay back smugly on the settee. "I think I would be unusually nice too if I had the curative assistance he does."

Connor was growing impatient, and he didn't know what curative meant.

"Get to the point."

"Drugs, of course," said Marcus smugly.

Chapter 18

It was cold outside and Karen could see her breath in the evening air. She pulled her collar around her neck and folded her arms tightly across her chest. She had told her mother she was going out for the evening.

Buddy howled from inside but Karen knew Bertha would not welcome another dog into her home. McCormack's was the last house on the Bellview road. It lay across the stream, further back in the fields than the rest of the houses, and it was hidden by the very driveway that used to show it off.

The long, wet grass announced the entrance to Bertha's driveway. It was overgrown with bushes and brambles. It had never been paved, Karen noticed, and it was hard to imagine anyone lived in the rundown cottage it led to.

There was no doorbell and Karen rapped loudly on the door. She was about to knock again when a shuffling sound came from inside. It was followed by a sequence of crashing sounds and finally the door was opened.

Bertha squinted out through her shawl.

"You!" she said. "Are you alone?" She poked her head out of the doorway and grabbed Karen inside at the same time. Karen almost tripped over the mess in the hallway. Large picture frames and pot plants littered the floor and Rascal was peeping down from between the banisters at this rare interruption from the outside world.

Bertha took one last suspicious sweep of the garden before locking the door tightly behind her. She kicked it a couple of times, as if were part of a ritual.

Karen had been wondering all afternoon how to open a conversation with this woman. What would she say? How would she introduce herself? Now it appeared no introduction was necessary and it stumped her. Her rehearsal thwarted, she just stood there dumbstruck.

Thankfully Bertha was not. "Been wontherin when you'd show," she said. "Spose ye better come through." She waddled into a small and messy little living room.

The best way to describe Bertha's home was as a kind of home to the homeless, though not in the literal sense. It was just that nothing in it *had* a home. There was no table for the knitting magazines that lay on the floor. There was no cabinet for any of the old books that were stacked from floor to ceiling, and the coal for the fire was kept in an old flowery cooking pot. A ruffling sound coming from under some old newspapers stocked in the corner told Karen that rodents shared the house with Bertha.

"You sit there on the couch." Bertha shoved Karen's shoulders down until the acquired effect was achieved. "I'll get us some hot milk." Bertha wore an encouraging smile. "There we go now," she said.

Karen was surprised to notice Bertha's eyes were round and bright now; quite the opposite of the scrutinizing squint she wore in public. Karen sat a little stunned while she waited for Bertha, who left her to go and heat the milk.

"Great day for it," Bertha called out.

"Shit," Karen whispered frantically to herself. Great day for what? What was she doing here? This poor woman was clearly ill.

Rascal arrived in the doorway then, probably to make sure he wasn't dreaming and there was an actual visitor in his house. Karen got the distinct impression that he might even have his own bedroom.

She tried to relax by watching the little portable television in the corner, but she couldn't concentrate because an old radio was humming away to itself in another corner. When Bertha still hadn't returned after ten minutes, Karen made her way out to the kitchen. She fell over several videos and a record player before she found Bertha leaning over a saucepan.

"You don't have a microwave?" Karen said, more to herself than to anyone else.

"No I don't hold much with them ole things," she said. "Puttin all that electro magneticness into your body, you never know what it might attract."

"Except for in the sitting room?" Karen couldn't help but clarify.

"Ain't no microbox in the sittin room," Bertha said.

"No, I mean electromagnetic waves from the TV and radio. Together."

"That's different," said Bertha in a more serious tone. "A radio is like an alarm bell, it is. There'll always be signal interference when she's near. Best keep it on, I find."

"When who's near?"

Bertha didn't answer and continued to stir the milk, but Karen was afraid she already knew the answer.

****

"Where's Karen?" Wayne asked.

"She's gone out. I think to Maloney's," Catherine answered.

Wayne opened them each another beer and put his feet up on the coffee table. He generally had to drink quite a few bottles just to endure the documentaries. But Catherine enjoyed them too much for him to admit how much he hated them.

"I hope it is Maloney's she's gone to." Catherine seemed concerned. "It's good for her to talk to some female friends; I'm not sure about this boy she's been seeing."

"Why not?" Wayne swallowed another mouthful of lager.

Catherine turned away from her documentary to face him.

"You know the growing drug problem in Dublin?" she asked. "A lot of young foreigners over with new dealing methods, dozens of new 'drop-in centres' opening, and I'm worried this Marcus might be mixed up with it in some way."

"Why would you think that?" Wayne asked sitting up, already planning how to fix this.

Catherine tried to pacify him. She explained that it was just a hunch, but the trouble with Catherine's hunches was they were rarely wrong. "It's just little things," she went on. "She admits he's a bit aloof, picky about where he goes and who sees him there. He seems to have a lot of money, too, for a teacher."

"But that sounds like just about anybody." Wayne was surprised at the lack of evidence.

"She says he spends a lot of time on the phone and is quite secretive about it, too."

"That could be anything, babe." Wayne placed a lock of Catherine's hair behind her ear. She sighed as she contemplated this new threat to her only daughter. Karen had had enough suffering in her young life. "I don't like him." she decided.

****

Bertha sat on the settee across from Karen, who sipped a mug of warm milk gratefully. Bertha seemed to be enjoying hers too, though this was probably due to the large amounts of whisky she was regularly adding.

Rascal sat obediently in front of the fire, like the guest of honour. Bertha was quiet now for the first time since Karen had arrived. The onus was now on Karen to talk and she found herself lost for words again.

"You knew my father," was all she could think to say.

"I did." Bertha nodded.

"Did you like him?" Karen asked innocently.

"Grand lad. Used to cut my grass and bring me butter; not that his mother knew, of course."

"Was my father ill?"

"Ill?" Bertha repeated. "You mean did he see things that others didn't?"

"I guess so." Karen swallowed the lump of anticipation she felt in her throat.

Moments passed before Bertha answered, "No. He didn't see things others couldn't. He just knew they were there."

"What things?"

Bertha's composure seemed to break a little. "Night-time things," she whispered. The fire flickered casting shadows across Bertha's weathered face. It made her look haggard and exhausted. "Things that only come here at night; things that walk among us, pretend to be like us, but they're not." Bertha raised a finger. She ignored the milk now and just drank the whiskey instead.

"I don't understand," Karen confessed eagerly.

"You see things at night too, don't you?" Bertha whispered. "Just like me."

"Only in dreams."

"Humph, you're lucky so. Like your daddy was. You see *their* world. It's those that cross into *our* world that I see. The beasts that walk among us. You don't see them. They whisper things, try to make us the same as them."

"I need you to be very clear, Mrs McCormack," Karen interrupted. "What beasts?"

"Oh, people try to romanticize them." Bertha waved a hand. "Call 'em fancy names like vampires and creatures of the night, draw nice neat little fangs on 'em and think that fits the bill." A silence passed before Bertha continued. "They appear charming, that much is true, but I see their real form. I see their foreheads distort when they detect vulnerability. I see their jaws grow and their teeth protrude. They are sons of the Gorgon. Children of Neptune, they call themselves. It is not blood they feed on; that's just a metaphor."

"A metaphor?" Karen attempted to correct her.

"Yeah, one a those. Oh, they like the blood don't get me wrong, but it's the bitin they enjoy. Suckin all the goodness outta ye."

"I'm sorry, I think I was mistaken," Karen got up to leave.

"Ye think yer mistaken coz I haven't gotten to *her* yet."

Karen stopped in her tracks.

"Oh, you know who I'm talkin about. You seen her all right and she's spent all her life just tryin te see you. You and yer family – whichever wan of ye has what she wants."

Karen gasped and wheezed in the night air as she shut Bertha's door behind her. She stood at the doorstep clutching her chest but she couldn't get enough oxygen into her lungs. "Move." she told her feet.

They finally complied and she hurried down the bumpy driveway.

"You're early!" Catherine said as Karen banged shut the great white front door.

"Molly wasn't in," Karen lied. "Is Connor home tonight?"

"He's staying in the city," said Catherine. "I wouldn't call him either. I just spoke with him and he's in one of his moods."

Karen wished he was there. She would probably tell him nothing of the evening's events but she still wished he was there.

****

Back in the city Connor was slouched on the settee with his arms folded, feeling perplexed. The Premiership was on but he barely registered the television. He was more confused now than he had been when he left to see Marcus.

He had gone to visit him with the intention of clarifying the contention between him and Dan, and now he was faced with the possibility that both Dan and Fabien were into something more sinister. This was hard to believe of Fabien. And it was harder to believe that Marcus was the unlikely hero, attacked for reporting their drug abuse at a club. Why was he even entertaining such a notion?

Marcus was just so damn sure of himself he could convince you of anything. In the end Connor went with his gut and put the whole thing down to a misunderstanding.

Fabien was probably adding some tonic to his water; he'd seen him do that before – it was no biggie. Marcus must have got the wrong end of the stick. A drunken argument on a night out, everyone had them. It just happened that this argument involved Dan, who was one of the most unforgiving people Connor had ever met.

****

Rick lay on his bed browsing the internet. AC/DC were playing on the radio and he was tapping his feet in harmony to the music. He had volunteered himself to organize the trip in the hopes of finding somewhere close to a river rich enough in trout that no boats would be necessary. The River Erriff, he read, was good for brown trout. The only log cabins within their budget were miniature rundown little shacks on a campsite. Their dark and dingy exterior threatened poorer conditions inside, but the owners had cleverly chosen not to post any interior snaps. He wondered briefly if he could book one of those for Fabien.

After upping the budget he found an exclusive little development in the forest by the Erriff. It was clearly marketed at fishermen but he imagined Karen would like it just the same. Most girls wouldn't; most girls would prefer a sun holiday. But Rick didn't think Karen was like other girls. He suspected she'd been one of those children happier with the wrapping than the present inside it. She always made the most of things and he admired her for it.

Karen wouldn't have to do that on this trip, Rick decided. He would find her lots of activities she'd enjoy and she wouldn't have to make the most of anything. Rick liked history more than the others so he could take her on a day trip somewhere. "Crap," he said to himself, "I need to brush up on my history."

****

"Who left me these pastries?" Karen asked when she arrived at her desk on Monday morning. Zara had started a new diet plan and had offloaded all her carbs onto her colleagues' desks. In her time at Penbrook, Zara had done every diet plan written, none of which her fitness instructor boyfriend agreed with.

There was the Cabbage Soup Diet, which had made everyone gag from the smell. The Raw Food Diet, which made everybody's bladder ache from avoiding the toilets so much. And everyone's favourite, the Apple Cider Diet.

When Karen switched on her computer she was excited to find a message from Sam in her inbox. It was short, true, but it was inviting her to lunch. Karen wondered if it had been Olivia's influence.

Olivia sat next to Sam and liked to remind the girls that she had seen and learned a lot more in the extra ten years she had on them. "No man should come between you and your friends." she had reminded Sam. "Unless it's John," she muttered under her breath.

Karen thanked her at morning coffee break, but Olivia seemed miles away.

"Have you seen Brenda today?" Olivia asked.

Karen watched her miss the cup with her teabag and spill sugar across the counter before finally scalding herself with the kettle.

"What is it?" Karen pressed.

"Just something I heard." Olivia was wide-eyed. "Might not even be true. You know what this place is like for gossip."

"Don't say the R-word," Karen pleaded.

Cannacord Marketing had laid off seventy staff the previous month and one of the investment banks was in the middle of putting together redundancy packages. Karen's heart hammered hard at the thoughts of meeting her mortgage repayments.

"More like the B-word. I heard Brenda tell Zara she was bringing you in over your work and timekeeping." Olivia bit on a fingernail.

Karen was silent. She must have heard wrong, she told herself. This had never happened before. Never in her entire career had she been brought in over her work. She could tell

Olivia was waiting for a reply by how hard she was biting her lip, but still she couldn't speak.

"I might have got it wrong," Olivia said. "You know those two are thick as thieves, always moaning about something."

Karen felt embarrassed. She wondered how many other people knew.

The advance warning did nothing for the shock Karen felt as she sat in the boardroom in front of Brenda. Even Brenda looked uneasy and embarrassed. She was shifting around on her chair and sifting clumsily through papers.

"It's not me you see. It's the powers that be, you know. They've noticed the time keeping and I have to be seen to be doing my job."

Karen felt her face burn. *How could I have let this happen?* she wondered. The last thing she needed was to be unemployed. There would be serious reasons not to sleep then. "I've just been dealing with some personal issues recently, that's all." Karen was proud she'd made it to the end of the sentence without crying.

"Well, you know you can trust me!" Brenda's eyes were eager with anticipation. She sat forward in preparation for information that would never come. Her eyes were bulging. *She would just love that*, Karen thought; *to be the really cool boss and know everything about everyone.* No sooner would she leave and the entire office would know her personal business.

"It was nothing, it's all fine now." Karen gave her best fake smile to Brenda before leaving.

****

"What a cow," spat Sam at lunchtime.

Karen could barely hear her over the noise in Mario's. The only seats left were the high stools by the window and Karen stared miserably out at the drizzle hitting the windowpane.

"Nobody takes Brenda seriously!" Sam consoled.

But Karen wasn't listening. She was thinking about Bertha again.

"Do you remember your trip to Egypt?" Karen said, changing the subject.

Sam was confused and wondered how it had anything to do with Brenda. "Yes."

"Can you tell me more about all that Gorgon imagery you saw?"

Sam was beginning to worry. This lack of attention was unusual even for Karen.

"They look like vampires, don't they?" Karen continued. "I mean with the fangs. Maybe they're not the teeth of a serpent at all but the teeth of a vampire."

"Do you want to change Brenda's nickname or something?" Sam tried to make the connection.

Karen saw the worried look on her friend's face and decided to put her mind at ease. "Yes," she lied.

Sam laughed with relief and began a new list of potential names for Brenda. "Super Gorg," she tried. "Gorgomania? Gorgantua? How about the Gorgie Monster?"

Karen did her best to engage and eventually she told Sam she was going away for a few days. "Can you come?" she asked.

Sam looked elated. "Liam was just saying the other day that we should get away."

It was an awkward moment but there was no getting around the fact that Liam wasn't invited.

"It's only for a few days, Marcus and Liam could join us on the Saturday?" Karen offered. She was happy at her diplomacy and thought Sam would go for it, but the look on her face said otherwise.

"I can't," Sam said, picking her jaw up from the floor. "Liam has the week off and I promised I'd spend it with him."

****

134

"Maybe it won't be so bad," Will said after lunch. "So you're the only girl there. Big deal! You're a bit of a tomboy anyway."

They were in the large cold archive room in the basement, where Will spent most of his time these days. The trouble with the audit, Will explained, was all the old documents you had to collect, and the trouble with that was they were never where they were supposed to be.

Karen handed him one of his beloved beef sandwiches and he sat on one of the cardboard boxes. She wondered how he managed to stay so slim as she watched him devour the entire sandwich in just a few swallows. It had barely touched the sides when he was reaching for the second one

Karen sat on a box next to him. "No offense, but guys really know how to get in the way of a friendship."

"Not if we're the friends in question."

Will kicked the box from under her then, and caught her before she hit the floor. Karen laughed like a child at the shock it gave her and marvelled at his ability to make her feel better.

Chapter 19

Rick was feeling sick. He wasn't a very good traveller and Dan was driving too fast, whistling at the wheel as though it were his own private disco. The roads were narrow and winding and he held on tightly to his stomach around the bends.

"Dude, I think you're making Karen nervous," he tried.

Karen, who was staring out the window, didn't even hear him; she was too busy trying to recall where she'd seen Dan before. He made her almost as uncomfortable as Fabien did. She'd caught him watching her in the mirror several times now.

"Are we nearly there yet?" asked Rick.

"We are near Aughagower." Fabien sounded like a tour guide.

"You might want to stop here," Rick told Karen. "It's a medieval village St Patrick passed through on his way to Croagh Patrick, you know."

Karen was impressed. "How do you know?"

"I know there's round towers and a graveyard dating back to the famine." Rick sounded proud. "I was good at history in school," he lied.

Rick regretted mentioning it as he entered the graveyard. The rusty old gate snarled at him for making it move. It reminded him just how disturbing he found these places. Everything was old and it made him imagine what lay beneath the soil.

Headstones sprawled onto neighbouring plots where strangers in life rested, together forever in death.

"I hate graveyards," he complained, just as Karen was contemplating how interesting she found them.

She wondered how old the graves were. She touched the cold hard surface of one just to feel connected to the thousands of hands she imagined touched it before her. When she raised her eyes, Karen found Fabien watching her from a set of ominous-looking rocks. He turned his back so as to show them to her.

Karen fumbled through the long grass to get to them. She was surprised to learn they were not rocks at all, just slabs of fallen headstones.

"McDermott," Fabien said quietly. "Six of them." *Maybe from the famine,* thought Karen.

"Maybe," said Fabien, startling her. Karen had been certain she wasn't speaking aloud but she must have been.

"Elizabeth McDermott," she read. "Born 3rd March, 1830. Died 14th December, 1852. Miriam McDermott, died at just fourteen. Paul, Damien, Niall."

Fabien was watching her again. The sunlight bounced off his blond curls so they looked like sparkling bars of gold. He would be attractive if he didn't stand so poker straight and speak like he'd swallowed an encyclopaedia.

Her mother would like him, Karen thought. He always looked so smart. He wore a simple black round-neck T-shirt today and the short sleeves showed off impressive biceps; not 'I live in the gym' biceps, just strong and firm.

"O'Sullivan." Fabien pointed at a neighbouring grave. "Five all before the age of thirty." None of these were from the famine years.

"Some families are so unlucky." Karen sighed.

"Maybe they are too powerful," said Fabien. "Maybe they have what dangerous people want."

"Sounds a bit paranoid to me, Mulder." Karen chuckled.

"Don't you think it is strange? All these families with common surnames killed before their time?"

Karen felt the familiar flutter of fear stir in her stomach.

Surely he wasn't referring to her. How could he be? No one knew she believed in banshees. Fabien couldn't know her fears. And if he did he certainly wasn't exploiting them; he had no reason to.

"Ah yes, the famine graves." Rick appeared behind them. "1845 to 1852. I don't suppose you covered this in Poland, Fabien." Rick took off his baseball cap.

"This is not a famine burial ground." Fabien's tone was polite. "There is of course a famine monument twenty minutes away. It remembers those who died on their way to Delphi. We can stop there also if it pleases you."

Rick looked like he'd been punched in the gut. "Well, y-yeah I know *this* isn't the graveyard, of course." He shoved his hands deep into his jeans pockets in a fruitless attempt to hide his embarrassment. "I'll check what the others want to do." He turned on his heels and left.

"Have I upset your friend?" Fabien asked sincerely.

Karen was still staring after him with fondness. "No, he'll be fine." She watched him hurry down the hill.

"I like your friend," Fabien said.

And in spite of herself, Karen found herself liking Fabien in that moment, too. He helped her down the slope of rocks and his hands were warm and soft. The sun was still shining when they left the graveyard.

Dan drove a little slower now much to the relief of Rick, who was looking a little green. The road narrowed as they turned left at the sign for West Winds Campsite.

"It's like a scene from *Wrong Turn*." Rick complained.

"I was thinking more *Scooby Doo*," said Connor. He was in unusually high spirits, but the outdoors always had that effect on him. He wiped a circle clear on the misted-up window to get a better view.

Giant evergreen trees grew on either side of the road like a protective shield. The track was soft and green. It was like a place lost in time, the tarmacadam and concrete of the city left far behind.

****

Sam had drunk too much. The room was spinning and she wasn't sure where exactly she was, her place or Liam's. The only thing she was sure of was how much she wanted him. She dug her nails into his back and wrapped herself up in him completely. Nothing mattered when she was with him. She never worried about the future or got caught up in the past when he was there.

Sam laid her head back to lose herself in his eyes, but they were foreign to her. She squinted to refocus and find the familiar brown pools she'd come to adore, but she couldn't see past his brow. It was furrowed and uneven.

Liam's familiar face was lost. His skull seemed grotesquely large for his body. Sam thrust herself back immediately, trying to wake from what she thought was a dream, and it worked. Panting, she found herself staring wide-eyed into his familiar but startled face.

"What's wrong?" he whispered.

"Nothing," Sam muttered, shaking herself back to reality. "I must have drunk too much, that's all." Sam wanted to ask him to hold her but those weren't words she could speak. Pride forced her to hold herself instead, and she drew her knees in close to her chest.

Liam put a skinny white arm around her shoulder and she eventually succumbed to nuzzle into his chest. His bed was warm and familiar and she fought to stay awake.

"Why does your friend not want me on her trip?" Liam asked suddenly.

"She thinks you drink too much and laugh at other people's expense."

"Indeed." Liam sniggered. "She does have ideas about herself, your friend."

Sam was too tired to argue but she mustered enough energy to issue a warning for Marcus to treat Karen right. "Does he like her?" Sam pressed.

"More than he should," was the last thing Sam heard before falling asleep.

****

"It's beautiful." Karen looked around her as she took in the charming little cabin. "I could *live* here." She was holding her hands together tightly to her chest and poking her head into every nook and cranny. A flat screen TV stood proudly in the living room alcove. The furniture was wooden and handcrafted from locally felled trees. Rick examined it with professional interest.

"Can you make me one of these tables?" Karen asked him eagerly.

"I'll have one too if you can," said Dan before laying his size-eleven tennis shoes on its surface. It was just a couple of degrees over freezing outside and all Dan wore was a baggy T-shirt and a pair of long shorts, showing off a pair of monstrously hairy legs.

Karen stared at them sprawled all over the table and she decided she didn't want one any more. She began to question her sanity, choosing to spend five days in a confined space with four boys. They would belch and they would pass gas, they would leave dirty towels on the floor and clutter up every surface they could find. She consoled herself with the knowledge that it would bother her brother just as much as her. He was used to living with women who cleaned up after him.

Outside, Rick was sat feeling queasy on the back porch. He tried to concentrate on the view. He watched the clouds chase each other over the mountaintop, tipping its surface as they played. A couple of swallows chirped loudly to each other in the leafless trees, keeping his senses stimulated.

He would have been content here if Fabien hadn't volunteered to stay behind while the others went for groceries.

"Where are you going?" Rick was watching Fabien stroll into the forests without a care in the world.

"I won't be long," Fabien assured him. "You need some herbs for that stomach."

"I'm not eating leaves some fox has been pissing all over!" Rick yelled after him.

Fabien didn't respond and Rick was left stunned. He remained motionless until the sound of crunching twigs and branches faded into the distance. He was wearing the same stunned expression when Fabien returned with a small bag of ingredients.

"Fox urine happens to be very good for sweaty hands, by the way." Rick followed him reluctantly into the kitchen.

"I'm not eating anything I haven't prepared myself."

"Very wise too." Fabien was searching the cupboards busily and gave a satisfying grunt when he'd found what he was looking for. A pestle and mortar sat beside the spice rack and Fabien began to unravel his bag of goodies.

"Nettles!" Rick proclaimed. "You want me to eat nettles!"

"With peppermint and milk thistle, yes." Fabien handed Rick another bundle, these ones looked like purple-headed weeds.

"What am I meant to do with these?"

"Boil the roots," Fabien instructed.

Rick surprised himself by filling a saucepan full of water, if only out of curiosity. "I'm only doing this to prove a point, you know. A bunch of weeds won't do anything for me."

"You know the more negatively you think about things the worse you are likely to feel."

"We'll see." Rick was resolute. He watched Fabien carefully tear the leaves into little pieces; he didn't even flinch as he broke up the nettles' heads with his fingertips.

Rick watched him grind the little leaves together in the mortar. Then he peeled the stems from the milk thistle and left them to soak.

"Here you go." He passed Rick a glass of thick green liquid and smiled at his expression. Rick swirled it around a couple of times before downing the entire concoction in one gulp.

"That's the most disgusting thing I've ever tasted," he said and coughed several times.

"Or is it just the newest thing you've ever tasted?" asked Fabien.

"Stop talking about it or I'm sure to throw it all back up. Tomorrow, talk about tomorrow," he pleaded. "What's on the agenda?"

"Rent a boat on the lakes I suppose."

"Boats are a bit dull though, aren't they? Compared to the banks; you always catch more on the banks."

The front door of the little cabin flew open to reveal Dan armed with a crate of beer, followed by Connor with a bottle of whiskey and Karen with, rather oddly, a *Dirty Dancing* DVD.

"You look better." Connor examined Rick. "Better for *you,* I mean."

"In that case you can share your whiskey with me."

Karen was relieved to hear Connor wouldn't be guzzling the entire bottle by himself. His quests for intoxication had been known to last days at a time. Karen recalled the time when he attended Peter Maloney's stag do and nobody heard from him for three days, until he turned up at the hen do. It would have been mildly amusing had it not been for what it led to.

Connor had gone through a period of binge drinking, during which socializing was no longer the priority. The more he drank the further he withdrew into himself. He no longer kept his promises, he ruined Rick's birthday party and his mood swings were intolerable. No amount of common sense could reach him.

"You have to want to get better. You need to have commitment to get better," Catherine had droned on and on. "But if you're in denial you have none of that. That's why addiction is so frustrating." she'd explained to Karen. Esther dismissed this as a load of psychobabble. There was only one way to deal with an alcoholic and that was to lock them in the pantry. "Just ask your Uncle Andrew."

In the end it was Rick who reached Connor. "You're just like Nicholas," he'd told him. "I'll give you his number if you like and you can be *his* best mate."

"You do look better," Karen said, looking at Rick.

Rick's cheeks were back to their rosy complexion and his eyes were bright as buttons. He took the bottle of whiskey from Connor and poured himself a generous glass. "Let's see what we can do about that, then," he joked.

****

Rick's heart was racing; a rather unfortunate game of blackjack forfeits had lost him his sweater. This didn't bother him; he'd never been embarrassed about his physique. Years of lifting heavy planks and doing manual labour had left him toned and muscled. His shoulders were arched and defined and his collarbone protruded like the hilltops of a pretty valley. What did bother him, however, was the pair of green five-year-old threadbare underpants he'd chosen to wear that morning.

Rick was praying his next forfeit wouldn't involve him losing his jeans. He swept a glance around the table. Karen's score was nineteen. She was looking a little green after consuming a raw egg as her last forfeit. Connor and Fabien both had fifteen and Dan's face, as dealer, was unreadable.

"Hit me," said Rick and Dan dealt him a king.

"Bust!" yelled Connor. "Forfeit time."

Why? thought Rick. Why hadn't he thrown them out years ago?

Images of the offending green underwear were racing through his head. *Please not my jeans; please not my jeans.*

Somebody answered his prayers but with an evil condition. Dan bestowed a forfeit involving him jump off the boat the following day instead. Rick hung his head in defeat; there was no way he could accept. He would have to surrender and down another shot of whiskey.

"Stuff it, I'll down the shot."

His stomach begged him not to and so did Fabien. "You are already drunk," he said, confusion in his tone. Fabien watched in silent miscomprehension as everyone else appeared to follow suit and he was the only sober one left. He found Rick later in the kitchen attempting to eat the thistle stalks he'd been soaking.

"These aren't bad you know." He pointed one at Fabien. "They sort of taste like rhubarb."

"Why are you afraid of boats?" Fabien asked.

Rick's mouth suddenly tasted bitter and he decided he didn't like rhubarb very much either.

"I'm not afraid of anything!"

Fabien lowered his gaze at the scorn. "I am!" Fabien confessed before leaving.

Rick stood staring after him feeling quite silly, before finally slouching into a chair at the kitchen table. He put his head in his shaking hands and tried to massage the pain away. How did he do that? Stand there and admit to fear like that. And why did it evoke respect rather than pity.

Chapter 20

Liam was becoming impatient. "Where is she?" he asked.

"I told you; she's camping," snapped Marcus down the telephone.

"With *them?* I will not fail this assignment because of you."

"They won't get it first. I'm close now."

"You better be. Sam almost saw me the other night."

"Saw you what?" asked Marcus.

"I mean *saw* me."

"That's impossible. There are no seers in her family tree. You're just being paranoid."

"Perhaps," said Liam. "She was intoxicated; it may have altered her state of consciousness."

Marcus was pensive as he hung up the phone. He shuffled the potential items together in his hands with disappointment. He could touch them now the banshee had returned them to him.

An old watch Karen had been given as a present – he had been certain that was it. It even had the added significance of being a gift. Then there was the small gold locket she wore; this too yielded nothing. Áine had been livid. Neither was the portal key and she was already enraged by Karen's knowledge of her existence.

Marcus put the locket around his neck. He fastened the delicate little clasp with a gentle click and he lay on his bed attempting to focus. He could detect her scent on the chain. Everyone had their own scent. Not the ones they purchased in little bottles from behind the counter of chemist shops, but an authentic core odour from the earth, always from the earth.

Most humans smelled of bark and ash, some of foliage and soil. Some smelled of fruits and greenery. Karen smelled of apples; of red apples that had basked in the sunlight from dawn until dusk, apples in which you could taste the sunshine.

Marcus tried to focus, tried to recall every conversation they'd ever had, every family photo, and still nothing. He decided that if Karen had been left the portal key, she was unaware of it. She was unaware of the pivotal role she was to play in the balance of life.

Dawn was descending and Sublimina was calling. He closed his eyes to return there, leaving another fruitless night behind him.

****

Karen awoke reluctantly on the sofa. Someone had placed a blanket over her body and she stirred beneath it.

"You slept well." Fabien spoke softly, from the kitchen. He looked like he'd been up for hours.

"What time is it?" Karen asked.

"It is 9.00 a.m. I tried to raise the others but they threw something green at me. I'm afraid to contemplate what it may have been."

Remnants of the night before littered the cabin lounge.

There were cigarette butts that had been trying to reach the ashtrays but missed. Beer bottles lay at the side of the couch and an empty bottle of whiskey was overturned in a corner, rays of sunlight bouncing off its surface.

Karen was expecting to feel nausea at any moment but the hangover never came. Instead she felt fresh and alive and she admired the weather outside. Fabien was looking out the window, too. He looked statuesque sitting on the broad windowsill.

Karen felt sorry for Fabien; he didn't really fit in and he must have been bored. "We could go for a walk if you'd like?" she offered.

"I do like to be outside." He perked up, making her smile.

Karen pulled on one of her baggy sweaters and met Fabien on the porch. He was watching a spider web with scientific interest. The morning dew revealed the detail of its intricate pattern.

Karen watched him. "You really are a nature boy."

Fabien smiled his sunshine smile. "It is what binds us, I think. People forget they are not separate from it, but so intrinsically part of it that they lack the objectivity to see it." He touched the web with his fingertips. "People probably wouldn't feel such a need to belong if they opened their eyes. "I don't think people are as lost as you think they are. I don't see this need to be part of something."

"Then why do you like history so much?" Fabien asked as they began their walk. "Is it not to feel part of something lasting?"

Though she was warming to him, Karen couldn't help the occasional urge to smack Fabien. But instead she linked his arm.

There was a faint sound in the distance, the sound of running water splashing over rocks. Parts of the forest floor were frozen solid and every step sounded like they were crunching icicles with their boots.

"I like this weather," Karen said. "I know it's freezing but it's fresh and bright. What's the weather like where you're from?"

"Not so dark and cloudy."

Karen couldn't imagine ever leaving Ireland, it was true it was dark and dismal but it smelled like home – water and mud, a depressing smell for a home, really, she thought.

But Karen hadn't always felt that way. There was a time she'd wanted to travel. She remembered a foreign exchange programme in France in her third year of secondary school, but it had been one of the worst experiences of her life. However, looking back it had been a necessary one.

Karen had found her temper in France. She had been looking forward to sunny mornings and long evenings, eating croissants and stealing wine with the rest of the class. The reality, however, proved to be much different.

She was landed with a military family, ordered around by a man who insisted on being addressed as Général Dupont. Their thirteen-year-old son, Jean-Claude, was just as arrogant. He taught her fake French and then laughed about it with his spotty teenage friends.

Karen spent hours crying down the phone to her mother. It continued no more than a week when Jean-Claude got a little more than he bargained for in the form of an unexpected punch to the face. Général Dupont declared his son's nose broken and Karen found herself happily extradited from the dreadful country.

"What are you thinking?" Fabien interrupted.

"How uncomfortable I find it away from home." Karen confessed. "Connor said you have six brothers. Do you miss them?" she asked.

"Yes, and my sisters, too."

"Six brothers and you have sisters, too?"

"Yes. I miss all the people. Where I come from people don't get so angry when you tell them the truth."

Karen wanted to help Fabien but she didn't know how without offending him. "Not if you wait for them to ask for help first, they don't."

"I am waiting for your friend Rick to ask. He has trouble trusting himself, I think. He looks outside himself when the answers are inside; most likely attempts to regain control over something he can't, I think."

"Hmmm, maybe best leave that one till he asks all right."

"It's not a criticism! More an observation."

A sharp, whipping breeze interrupted them, lashing across their cheeks, and they huddled closer together.

"I see he relentlessly faces his fears in an effort to become free of them. It is a commendable strategy, I think."

Karen wasn't listening; she was worried about going fishing with the wind so strong.

****

148

"It's not the greatest day for it," yelled the little old man at the lake. Everyone watched him, shin deep in water, wading through the boat chains. "Spose ye could keep this side a that there island and ye might be all right. Can't say yez'll catch ought at this time, though."

You needed to be up really early in the mornings or very late at night for fishing, Karen recalled. Connor went through a craze one summer, and Andrew had collected him every morning at 4.00 a.m. during the holidays.

"We don't have to go," Fabien said.

"Yes we do!" said Rick. "We have to catch the lady a fish." he added when everyone stared at him with suspicion.

The old man smiled a toothless grin. "Right ye be." He coughed roughly and removed the chain holding the boat nearest the dock.

"He's so cute," Karen commented about the little man waving from the shore. All four looked her over suspiciously.

"He stank," Connor exclaimed.

"So do you! But we still hang around with you."

No one really expected to catch anything. No one but Rick, whose skin had turned a pasty white colour again. Karen tried several times to get him to sit and relax but he cast out the hook over and over again.

By evening it seemed one suicidal fish, bored with life on Lough Moher felt sorry for him, and took the bait just to end his embarrassment. Rick passed the rod to Karen so she could feel the pull. His hands were red and sore-looking. Karen took the line and was surprised by her own excitement. She watched it bob up and down on the surface of the water and waited for the fish to appear.

Karen wasn't sure what she was expecting; it wasn't like it was a shark or a swordfish that would surface. She handed Rick back the rod in a fluster and noticed the amused contentment on his face. He chuckled slightly as he brought in the fish. Fabien caught his eye and smiled at him.

"And now we have dinner," declared Rick.

It was pretty disgusting, thought Karen, as she stared down at the flapping scaly body of a large rainbow trout. She desperately wanted to ask Rick to put it back. She knew he would but she couldn't burst his bubble.

As the evening went on the atmosphere on the lake changed.

"Red sky at night, shepherd's delight." Fabien stared at it. Grasshoppers chirped in the distance and a low humming sound surrounded them.

Dan was breaking the waves with the oars; they knocked heavily against the boat's hull like an impatient neighbour telling him to turn down the music. Karen thought she heard a growling sound as they neared the shore only to realize it was her stomach. The ugly giant fish began to look surprisingly appetizing.

Karen watched Dan jump into the water like it was a hot bath. He effortlessly dragged the boat to shore by its creaking chain and whistled with indifference all the while. Karen had the annoying déjà vu feeling again. She definitely knew him from somewhere.

But the gruff raw look was so similar to all of Connor's construction acquaintances it could have been anyone.

"Impressive," Fabien muttered to Rick as they jumped onto the muddy shore.

"And not an ounce of milk thistle," Rick joked. "You look like you could use some though."

Fabien looked awful. His normally bouncing curls lay deflated and sweaty on his forehead and there were black bags under his bloodshot eyes. "It is the weather. It is so dark, with so few hours' sunlight."

"Yeah well, welcome to Ireland," said Rick. "How 'bout I let you have first cut?" Rick held up the slimy fish and Fabien almost threw up.

Connor and Rick resembled a couple of boy scouts gathering sticks and kindle for the fire. Karen was relieved to find some bread rolls in the cabin refrigerator and she buttered them gratefully. When she returned there were two separate fires, both welcoming her with their embracing warmth.

Karen took a seat next to Dan, who was guzzling a can of beer with his feet up on a bed of rocks. Fabien was drinking … well, she wasn't quite sure what Fabien was drinking, probably raw eggs or something, she guessed.

Rick split some green wood down the middle to hold the trout. He was like a wood wizard, Karen observed. It bent and shaped at his will. He made a jagged fork out of a stick; he made skewers out of twigs. His large hands crafted an outdoor kitchen in minutes.

Karen felt very uncreative settling down with her plate of bread rolls. Connor sprinkled pepper and butter buds over the fish before placing it carefully over the fire which had now settled to a bed of glowing embers. He presided over it like a father watching his toddler take his first step. His black hair was standing poker straight on his double crown and his face was freckled with overnight stubble, he looked nothing like the gourmand that he was.

Chapter 21:

Rick felt proud. "Did Fred Flintstone provide or what?"

"You're really more of a Barney," Karen corrected.

Rick ignored her. "Tell a story or something."

Karen thought for a moment, playing with a piece of fish that had got caught between her teeth. She used it as inspiration.

"Once upon a time there lived a little fish," she began. "One day, while out with all his friends, a mean old man came and ate him. The end."

"Well, that was crap," Rick complained. "Anyone else?"

"I have one," Dan volunteered. "It's a true story from back home."

"Those are the best ones." Connor produced a bottle of rum out of nowhere.

"Well, it's an old legend from Glenkeel, where I grew up. I heard it when I was ten, but it's always stuck in my mind, probably because I couldn't sleep for months after." He chuckled.

Karen poured herself a generous helping of rum. It tasted sweet and syrupy after the peppered fish fillet. The heat from the fire felt like it had extended two flame-like arms and was now cupping her face with its fiery palms.

Dan had a deep hypnotizing voice, sort of like a younger less sophisticated Morgan Freeman, she thought.

"We lived on the banks of the canal. It's a small community, and everyone knows everyone. Seán O'Donoghue told us about the spirit of the banshee. You know who that is." He nodded at Karen.

Karen felt an uneasy feeling spread like a fever through her blood. Why did he ask her that?

"Seán's grandfather, Ivan, was a blacksmith. He was an impatient bad-tempered old man who spent most of his life in his workshop, with only his tools for company. Ivan relished their incapacity to answer him back or annoy him in any way.

"Seán was helping him shape hammerheads for the hardware store that night. They hammered and punched the hot iron rods until it was past bedtime. The old grandfather clock Seán thought to be broken chimed ten o'clock and Ivan grew uneasy.

"Seán said he was hungry and wanted to go in for supper but his grandfather wouldn't let him leave until the order was complete. Seán told us the hammerhead he'd been trying to mould was beginning to look more like a banana, but when he looked up for guidance he found his grandfather staring silently out the cobwebbed window.

"There's a storm coming,' he told Seán. The rain was splashing in the yard outside when they heard it, low and broken: the sound of a wailing woman. Seán thought it was a baby at first, a baby alone and crying in its crib. But it grew louder and shriller, too deliberate for a child.

"The great propane fire of the forge roared as steady as it ever did but still the air grew chilly.

"'I think it's Mother calling me for supper,' Seán chanced. He winced in expectance of his grandfather's wrath. He had heard it all before. He was a lazy uncoordinated boy with woman's hands. He would be better off baking bread with the women. But what he found in Ivan's face was something that disturbed him much more; it was neither impatience nor disappointment. His eyes just looked imploring. 'Yer a good lad,' he'd said. 'Now go get yer supper.'

"The sound was getting closer now and Seán had second thoughts about leaving the workshop. Ivan unmounted his old rifle from over the door and ordered Seán into the house while he locked up. He waited to see his grandson go in the back porch before he headed into the rain.

"Seán took his muddy boots off and headed straight for the kitchen. He could hear the high-pitched voices of his mother and grandmother, pottering about making the tea. Suddenly he realized he no longer felt hungry. He headed back down the hall to stare out the window.

"There he saw his grandfather, walking down the lane way. He was unmistakable with that limp he'd developed from his arthritis-riddled legs. There was a faint blue light flickering at the far side of the fence. Ivan was probably going to turn it off, Seán thought.

"But as he peered through the frosted window pane he could make out the shape of a woman. She appeared to flicker on and off like a faulty light switch. The rain grew heavier, impairing Seán's vision and all that he could do now was to listen. Seán heard a single gunshot, and he never saw his grandfather again."

"It was the banshee?" Connor stated the obvious.

"So Seán says."

Karen got up from the fire and ran towards the banks. Connor got up to chase after her, until she threw him a threatening glance that stopped him in his tracks.

"I'll go." Fabien stood up. He found her by the lake leaning against a tree trunk for support.

"Are you all right?"

"I never thought he'd betray my trust like that."

"What do you mean?"

"Connor, of course! Telling people my dreams, my fears. *My* fears, nobody else's business, certainly no one else's tool for amusement." she huffed.

There was a pause before Fabien responded. "Connor never shared anything private about you with us. Surely you must know this."

"Then how come everyone knows?" Karen spat.

"Not everyone knows," Fabien assured her. "Come and sit down; let me explain."

Karen ignored him and stared out across the lake but Fabien continued regardless, "Dan doesn't know of your dreams, but he does know of the banshee. He knows she is a being permitted to enter this world both in darkness *and* in daylight."

Karen had barely sat down on the log next to him when she considered leaving again, but her jelly legs warned her she would only get so far.

Fabien was still talking: "She searches this country to find a portal key. A portal key allows other beings from her world to enter the waking world during daylight, just as she does."

Karen was desperately hoping this was just his country's interpretation of the legend. "I'm not in the mood to debate legends right now." she warned him. "I'm not interested in what you think she is, or where you think she's from. I'm interested in knowing why you care. What's your involvement in all of this?"

Fabien buried his head deep in his hands, grasping his curls in his palms before facing her again. "You're in danger." His voice almost broke. "Your family is in danger. Dan and I are here to protect you."

"From a banshee?"

"The white portal key is guarded by one family here, passed through generations with secrecy and protection. The banshee didn't even know what form it was in. She knew nothing of its whereabouts, only that it was in Ireland. But now they have it narrowed down to a family with the surname prefix Mac and O'."

"One possible key keeper was traced to a small town in rural Ireland – a clever man who spent his life waiting, preparing, a man who distorted the trail by choosing to die in another country, under another name. Your father was a hero Karen. I was his guardian angel, and now I am yours."

Many thoughts raced through Karen's mind, all fighting for attention, half-thoughts, fleeting thoughts jumbled up inside her head. This could be a sick and twisted joke.

Halfway through this thought was a consideration for what had happened to her father. Her father guarded an object; was it a secret? Did her mother know? Most likely not, when he'd gone to such lengths to hide it. The second thought was one of disbelief. How was any of this even possible?

Insanity! It was simple – it was insanity. Yet how did Fabien know where her father was found? Before she could finish the question she was already formulating an answer she could be comfortable with: Connor. Connor could have told him.

One thing Karen didn't feel, however, was anger. She was sure she would have been angry with anyone who would attempt such manipulative lies, but not Fabien. As quickly as she decided none of this was true she decided Fabien believed it to be true.

He believed what he was saying. He had to be very sick, Karen decided. An overactive imagination had become his reality. Everyone mocked crazy people, but Karen thought them brave. How must it feel to actually believe the devil was after you, that aliens were abducting you or any other fantasy full of fear. These people believed their nightmares and faced them daily. Braver still were those who were educated about their illness and accepted that their minds could not be trusted. She wondered if Fabien were one of these people. Fabien, she noticed, was still waiting for a response and so it was frustration he felt when she touched the side of his face with a gesture of empathy. It told him she thought he was crazy.

Fabien traipsed behind Karen, deflated, as they returned to find Rick embroiled in an argument with Dan over his choice of story. They both shut up abruptly when they noticed Karen and she quickly saw a gaping hole in her theory – Dan. The chances he shared the exact same delusion as Fabien were practically non-existent. Karen knew about mental illnesses and each patient's delusions were individual.

Chapter 22

Katie was becoming more and more uncomfortable as the days went by. Andrew watched her from his armchair. He couldn't get her to rest. He caught Catherine smiling to herself from behind a newspaper. *Fool for the ladies*, that's what she'd say.

"This is different," Andrew told her. "She's pregnant."

"I never said a word," replied Catherine. "Daniel told me about musical chairs, by the way." "Stupid story." It had been a great source of amusement to the family when Andrew lost every game of musical chairs on his seventh birthday. He couldn't be reconditioned to understand the object was not to give up your seat for the girls. His father and brother may have laughed but Esther beamed with pride. Andrew loved his mother. She was the only one to look at him and see just him. Not the second son, not the younger brother, just him.

He shifted in his armchair and watched the flames dancing together to a silent tune and he thought of his father. He knew that he'd loved him, but he also knew that he had been second. He would always be second.

Andrew understood now the necessity of it, and he was grateful he had not been the firstborn, not destined to hold that cursed object. Their difference of opinion on the portal key would be what drove an unmovable wedge between the two brothers. Andrew saw it as a curse, inviting demonic forces to pursue its keeper. He would rather have no children at all than put them in danger of having to carry it. Daniel on the other hand saw it as a divine obligation. He saw it as the thread that held the universe together. Left in place, it protected the very borders of existence, but pulled by the wrong hands, everything would come undone.

Daniel had felt that giving up the key would be killing all that was good in the world, thereby killing his children anyway. Entrusting the perilous task to them might endanger them now, but it would protect them in the long run.

Andrew disagreed. "There is no long run," he'd argued. "Not everyone believes in life everlasting, some of us believe in the here and now."

Daniel was lazy, thought Andrew. He accepted things instead of trying to fix them. He should never have had children. He was selfish, just like their father.

Chapter 23:

If Marcus's heart could beat it would have exploded through his chest. He sat in the Gorgon temple awaiting his mission review. The altar had already been set. A great stone slab stood ominously in the centre of the room lit by a single candle that flickered menacingly. It appeared to watch him through the flame. He had to look away. The sconces in the great marble recesses had not been lit tonight and allowed the lonely candle to throw whatever shadows it chose across the floor and up the walls.

Marcus heard her before he saw her. The hissing was unmistakable. He wondered which of the sisters it was, until Stheno slid into the room. Her movements were fascinating; wild and unpredictable. Having the lower abdomen of a snake and the torso of a human produced some captivating movements. Her body moved and contorted until it came to rest behind the altar. Marcus knelt on the concrete floor before her.

"Seven nights since you last sat before me and still no key!" she hissed.

"She doesn't even know she has it, let alone what form it's in," Marcus whispered. He chose his next words carefully. "The mission has been compromised by the angel and his wolf. To make matters worse, her eyes have been opened to the careless banshee who seeks her."

"You dare blame Áine for your short comings?" hissed Stheno from high above him.

It was a clever move. Marcus knew of the power struggle between banshees and Gorgons, particularly between Stheno and Áine. Marcus thought any attempt to denigrate Áine would buy him time. But he was wrong.

"Would you like to drink from my left hip?" Stheno asked him mockingly.

These were the words Marcus had been dreading; words that sent spasms up and down his limbs. He remembered Liam's teachings the night of his resurrection: *Blood drunk from the right side of Gorgon would heal you; blood from the left could kill you.* That, more than any other teaching, had shocked him. Marcus hadn't thought he could die again. Drinking the blood of a Gorgon he imagined to be similar to the sound of a banshee roar on human ears: insufferable.

"Remind me again, converter, what is your function in all of this?"

"To find what form the key has taken so we can inform the Great Banshee Áine."

Stheno sniggered down at him, finding amusement in his change of tactics. "Oh, the *Great* Banshee Áine, is it now? A moment ago you labelled her careless, did you not?"

Marcus swallowed hard and closed his eyes tightly. He was sure this would be the end of him. "You need to learn respect, converter," Stheno spat. "Converters cannot use portal keys. They cannot even touch them without combusting. What good is finding the key if you don't have a banshee to seize it?"

Marcus opened his eyes slowly, grateful his life had not been taken.

"We have to find the white key before their prophet is born," Stheno whispered through teeth too large for her mouth. "We may not be able to use their key, but the banshee can seize it. She can prevent the next prophet from claiming it."

Marcus wondered if Stheno was speaking directly to him or to herself. No one could use a portal key without consent from the human prophet foretold to use it. Curiosity almost got the better of him and persuaded him to ask what the banshee would do with it, but he refrained and chose a safer response instead. "I understand."

There was a long uncomfortable silence, the sort of silence that grew and congealed the atmosphere into a thick and sticky paste, an atmosphere in which expectancy breeds anxiety.

"You understand, do you now? You, whose conversion figure lies at a mere twenty-three mortals. You have influenced their decision process to do our will by a mere few degrees and you tell me you understand."

Stheno laughed, an evil soulless sound, and Marcus fought to resist the urge to cover his ears.

"He understands," she repeated. "Tell me, who was the last prophet to use a portal key?"

Marcus was confused by the question. Which portal key did she mean? There were two portal keys – he knew that much – the black key and the white key. Stheno could be referring to either. Marcus thought about it. It was the black key that was last used for evil but that had been lost for centuries. He hoped this was the one she was referring to when he answered. "Rahoul Metzger, the dark prophet from the 1400s used the black portal key to invite vampires to the waking world in daylight." Marcus had chosen the right answer; he knew he had because his head was still on his shoulders.

"And how many conversions were he and his vampires responsible for?"

"Nine million deaths," bragged Marcus. "He is responsible for the ideas which led to the publication of *Malleus Maleficarum: The Witches Hammer,* which in turn led to the great witch hunts of the fourteenth century."

"It is not the deaths that are significant," spat Stheno. "Nine million deaths means nine million mortals with the capacity for pure unadulterated hatred." Stheno's voice softened as she tilted her oversized head in an attempt to flick her snakes behind her shoulders. "The ability to breed hatred," she said dreamily, "to nurture and cultivate it until it is strong enough to spread its glorious wings and fly all by itself – it's beautiful."

Stheno returned a spine-tingling gaze to Marcus with a directness and severity that seemed to shake the room. "The children of Neptune *will* overpower the children of the moon! The black portal key may have been lost when Metzger disappeared but theirs is still out there. I am giving you one week to find it. Otherwise you will be replaced."

Stheno's eyes seemed to flicker like those of a reptile. A transparent slippery film whipping across her eye slits seemed to open the great stone door behind her. At first, Marcus thought there was no one there, until through the darkness he could make out the shape of a curvaceous and captivating young female, leaning against the doorframe. Marcus continued to stare in awe as she peeled herself from the doorway and entered the room.

Her presence was profound.

The air became charged with energy so intense it made the un-beating heart in his chest want to pump blood again. He felt his body react, open itself completely to her. His nostrils widened, his eyes dilated and he was sure he could feel the pores of his skin open.

When the candlelight revealed her face her eyes were exposed, and he saw the savage hunger that lay behind them. She wanted something; wanted it so badly she was panting.

"This," Stheno explained, "is ambition. If you fail to find what form the white key is in, Amelia will replace you."

Just then the flame of the candle exploded and died, the wax split down the middle and revealed a piece of thin bark that Stheno now presented to Marcus.

"Liam has converted the friend to a Sprite. You will assimilate the information and report back to your banshee."

Marcus was on his feet in seconds, he spun around so fast his heels burned. He was almost out of the temple when he heard her call to him.

"Stop by Hamied's Hub before you leave. I've ordered a more potent glamour tonic. And pray to Neptune you do not disappoint me again!"

Chapter 24

Rick was feeling nervous but he couldn't work out why. He sat up and propped up his pillows for the third time that night. He glanced at the clock. It was 4.00 a.m. He lay back down with his hands behind his restless head and stared at the ceiling. What had he to be anxious about? he asked himself. He'd done it. He'd gone out on the boat and nobody had detected the faintest hint of fear from him. So why did he still feel so nervous? It must be a build-up of adrenaline, he told himself.

There was a creaking sound coming from the corner of the little bedroom. He shot his eyes over to the door and saw the handle slowly moving downwards. He bolted upright.

"Are you awake?" came a gentle voice from the doorway.

"I am. Are you?" he whispered back before kicking himself at the stupidity of the question.

Karen merely giggled. "Can I come in?"

Rick moved over and threw open the duvet cover. "You have another nightmare?"

"Yes ... No ... Well, sort of." Karen was nervous. "I need your advice."

"That's my middle name."

"No it's not. It's Nicholas." Karen lay next to him.

A few moments passed and they both lay staring at the ceiling, neither speaking a word.

Karen had always found it hard to ask for advice; especially when there was a risk it made you sound crazy. Karen may not have believed all of Fabien's story; he wasn't an angel, Dan wasn't a werewolf and Marcus certainly wasn't a vampire. However, had she not already been contemplating the existence of the banshee? Karen wondered if banshees were only visible to those who suffered mentally. It would make sense. It would be the only sane explanation.

Rick was ever patient. Karen knew she could take as long as necessary without being pressed. "Do you remember the dream I told you about before?" she finally began.

"The one with the walking whales?"

"No. Not that one; the one with the woman screaming."

"Yes."

"I think I know what it means now."

Rick listened attentively to the description of her dreams. He listened to Bertha McCormack's deliberations. He silently evaluated the possibility that Karen's father knew he would be killed by the banshee.

Karen shared nothing about Fabien with him. "What do you think?" she asked. "Do you believe it's possible?"

"I believe in aliens. What makes banshees any more implausible? Anything is possible, the vast majority of people who don't believe that are simply afraid to try."

Karen felt relief and fear at the same time. She was relieved at having shared her troubles and fearful because now it was real. Now it had been verbalized and someone else agreed that it was possible.

Rick wanted to warn Connor but Karen was adamant that they didn't say anything.

"He's like Andrew that way," she explained. "He doesn't believe in anything supernatural. He calls my dreams *night terrors*. If I go shouting my mouth off about what happened to Dad and Bertha then he'll only have one theory – that I'm losing the plot. He'll get worried and he'll tell Mum, just like he always does."

They talked until dawn approached and the sound of birds chirping filled the little bedroom. Karen felt the loneliness she had been feeling dissipate, replaced with the warmth of friendship instead.

Rick fell asleep first and was snoring lightly. Karen watched his large muscled chest rise and fall, steady and even. Eventually she, too, drifted into a peaceful sleep.

Chapter 25

Fabien didn't know whether to be offended or not as everyone gawped at him in his walking gear. "What?" he asked. "I like to be prepared." He stood poker straight on the porch with his hiking stick and gaiters. A warm woolly hat covered his curls.

"If we are climbing this mountain we may as well do it properly."

"I agree," said Dan, "but the reflective armband might be a little over the top."

"I like it. It is bright," Fabien traced the stitching with his fingertips.

****

"Wow," Connor stood at the foot of the mountain, "maybe it's us who looked foolish and you who had the right idea after all." He glanced sideways at Fabien.

"Hindsight is easy." Fabien shrugged.

Swarms of people were making their way up the mountain. They looked like ants with rucksacks on their backs. Some were making the trek as a religious pilgrimage and others were there just for the challenge.

Karen noticed a small visitors' centre right at the base of the mountain. "I say we start off easy." She smiled at the prospect of spending some money. The door made a ringing sound when they disturbed the wind chime that hung above it. Its dangling feathers tickled Karen's shoulders as she entered. Ornate miniature megalithic sculptures decorated the shelves and windowsill. Charm stones and gems were on display.

Karen picked up an onyx stone. She raised it to the light shining through the window. There was a pretty picture of a gladiolus flower etched on its surface, she noticed.

"The symbol for the festival of Lughnasa," said a voice from behind her.

"People celebrated the harvest season in pagan times by making the pilgrimage to the top of the mountain." The voice belonged to an older woman with piercing blue eyes that drew the attention away from the lines on her face. Karen saw her name printed in bold on her staff badge - Winnie. "The gladiolus symbolizes love, marriage and family." she explained. "Some call it the fertility stone."

"Isn't onyx a birth stone?" Karen twirled it in her hands.

"The August birth stone, and August is the month the harvest season begins."

"Lúnasa," said Karen, suddenly making the connection. "Lúnasa is the Irish for August. Is that where the name came from?"

"Who's to say?" The woman shrugged her delicate shoulders. "No one really knows how these things get mixed together over time, Perhaps Lúnasa was named after Lughnasa; it's called Lammas Day in other countries."

"That's nice." Rick stared over her shoulders. "Let me get it." He put his hands into his pockets to retrieve his wallet.

"Just this?" Winnie asked. "Sure 'tis only a mini little thing, you keep it," she said to Karen, folding it into her hands and pressing it into her chest.

****

During the first hour of the hike the least fit members of the group began to reveal themselves. Karen and Connor were already panting and guzzling bottles of water. The breeze felt intrusive, sweeping under their collars the steeper the mountain became.

"This is *your* fault," Karen wheezed. "All those creamy sauces you like to make so much."

Connor had in fact put on quite a few pounds since they'd moved house. Karen stared back at the ground they'd covered and it looked barely more than a field. She wiped the knotted strands of hair from her face but the wind seemed to like them better where they were.

Through her curls Karen could make out Fabien up ahead. She wondered briefly why he didn't just spread his wings to fly to the summit, and she chuckled to herself.

Karen found her phone when they reached the statue of Saint Patrick. Cleaning the screen with her sleeve, she snapped several images of the great white sculpture.

The statue included his signature tall hat and his shepherd's staff stood steadfast in his right hand.

"Down with snakes!" Rick chanted. He, too, was snapping happily on his phone.

Chapter 26

It was dusk and Karen's legs were burning. She could barely make out the souvenir shop they'd visited earlier. Suddenly she got the uneasy feeling that someone was watching her.

It was Marcus, finding her eyes as he always did. Marcus didn't break his gaze, not even to acknowledge anyone else.

Later on reflection Karen would recognize this as impolite, but not today. Today she was happy to be the centre of his universe. She was the only one that mattered, the only one who counted in the eyes of someone so magnificent and mysterious.

Marcus flashed a mischievous smile as she approached and Karen threw her arms around his neck. He smelt musky. Marcus appeared to be inhaling her scent too, which embarrassed her given the mountain she'd just climbed.

"You smell like apples," was all he said as he opened his eyes.

Everyone had trailed ahead except Fabien.

He was staring at them both with a confused expression on his face.

He appeared to remember himself suddenly and hurried to catch up with the others.

"I missed you." Marcus put his arm around Karen's shoulder as they walked. "Did you miss me?"

"No," Karen joked.

Marcus didn't see the funny side. Perhaps sarcasm was lost on the Greeks, she mused. She couldn't deny he was hard to read. He had so many sides to him. There was the confident side that cared nothing for anyone's thoughts about him except Karen's. There was a jealous and nasty side she chose to ignore. And then there was her favourite side, a side that appeared only when they were alone, a side that made him smile with his eyes.

"Let's leave the others and go to the Village Inn later," Marcus suggested.

"I can't leave. Everyone will think they're just second best."

"And are they not?" Marcus raised a dark eyebrow.

"It would be nice to get to know them."

"I understand." Marcus nodded pensively. "You are unhappy I came, no?"

Karen sighed, it wasn't what she'd meant, and she got the feeling he knew it. "You love to twist things."

"If saying things how I mean them is twisting them, then yes. Saying things you don't have the courage to."

Karen stamped down hard on his foot.

"Don't ever tell me I've got no courage." She stormed off with a swing in her arms that rivalled that of a soldier.

Marcus stood in amusement and admiration as he stared after her. He caught up with her in an instant and turned her in a single sweeping motion. He kissed her passionately. By the time they unlocked their embrace it looked darker, and they both had swollen lips.

"You're an asshole," Karen whispered.

"I know." Marcus was smiling.

Karen was relieved to see the soft glowing lights through the log cabin windows. They were almost there. Marcus gave her a piggyback through the forest. It took longer to reach the cabin because he kept doing three-sixty-degree turns in an effort to delay their return.

"This way, let's go this way," he'd say and dart off in the opposite direction.

When they finally reached the porch there was a smell of Indian cooking and savoury spices. The scent wafted into the evening air as they opened the door.

"In honour of our guest." Dan raised his glass to Marcus. "Compliments of our good chef, Mr O'Driscoll here." He nodded in Connor's direction.

Marcus stood in silence before remembering himself. "We were actually going to go out."

"Oh, nonsense," Dan waived a hand in a gesture so effeminate for him that it confused everyone in the room.

"I wouldn't want to trouble you all; I really can't stay." replied Marcus, with what he hoped was a convincing smile.

"I insist!" Fabien made himself heard from the kitchen doorway.

Marcus stared him down. "Okay."

Karen breathed a sigh of relief. She hadn't the energy to go anywhere and all she wanted to do was eat and be merry, just for tonight. After all, tomorrow was another day to worry about banshees.

"What are you drinking?" Karen asked Marcus.

Dan sniggered rudely under his breath and Karen shot him one of her most evil looks.

Dan was behaving like Connor did with her boyfriends. She wondered briefly if he'd been put on duty to free Connor up for cooking.

Karen went into the kitchen to find her brother. "What's up with your asshole friend?"

"What? Dan?" Connor whispered. "I guess he's not good with new people. Or maybe he's jealous," he said. "Don't worry, I won't poison your boyfriend, now make yourself useful and pass me some nutmeg, would you?"

"Ha!" Karen sniggered. "And leave Marcus to the wolves? Not bloody likely."

Karen returned to the lounge, where Rick could be trusted to be the only one conversing. "All I'm saying is it's a money racket, that's all."

Karen handed Marcus a bottle of beer. "Are we talking about the driving test again?"

"Of course!" Rick continued without so much as a glance her way.

Rick had failed his driving test for the fourth time the previous week and was taking it very badly. Karen suspected it was because of his sweaty palms. She couldn't imagine how anyone could steer properly with them. It would have been like trying to steer a ship with a helm made out of butter.

Rick, however, had come to other conclusions. "I finish the damn thing and he shows me some form full of ticked boxes. I asked him when I'd made these mistakes he'd ticked and the bloke couldn't even tell me. He said I stopped at a yield sign instead of just slowing down. Well, that's bullshit, I said, when did I do that? And he couldn't even answer me. Money racket just like everything else in this country. I'm happier cycling anyway." He was talking so fast that he was out of breath.

Nobody appeared as outraged as Rick had been expecting.

"Very unfortunate," was all Marcus muttered.

Connor served up a steaming curry with condiments of chutney and Indian mint sauce.

Fabien, who, Karen had noticed, lit a candle at every meal, had outdone himself putting numerous little tea lights down the centre of the table.

Karen sat protectively by Marcus's side as Dan sat opposite them. It would be an interesting evening she decided. She had one man who thought he was an angel. Another who would start a fight with his own reflection, and a boyfriend arrogant enough to take them both on.

To her surprise it was her brother who brought some semblance of normality to the table. "Naan bread?" He offered everyone.

Connor was amazed to learn that Fabien had never tasted Indian food before. "What? Never? What do you get for take away?"

"I only ever prepare my own food," Fabien told him.

"I agree with that," Rick interrupted. "I read all about those additives and preservatives and it does your insides no good."

It had become apparent that Rick's envy of Fabien had turned into awe. Karen was glad she hadn't told him of their conversation. Telling someone their newfound hero was crazy wouldn't make for a pleasant conversation. She contemplated telling Marcus before quickly deciding against it. Karen ignored the voice in her heart that told her she should be able to share everything with her boyfriend.

Marcus was pouring her a large glass of wine and staring at her in his captivating way. It was like he could talk without speaking. He gave Karen the slightest of nods, which she understood to mean that everything was okay.

"And how are you finding Ireland?" Fabien asked.

Marcus finished chewing on a piece of meat and took longer than necessary to reply. "It is not my first time here."

"Ah yes, I had forgotten," said Fabien.

Karen left her ears wide open for any minor accusations such as *Are you the vampire? Because I told your girlfriend you were working for the banshees*. But Fabien was well-mannered as always.

"So how is it you know each other?" Karen asked

"We used to perform at the same gigs," Dan told her.

"So you all know each other and never bothered telling me as I introduced you. Thanks a bunch!"

"Only as acquaintances," Marcus corrected her. "We've just been to the same events."

Just then Fabien went through all seven colours of the rainbow and began coughing and choking uncontrollably.

Marcus leapt up in defence before realizing Fabien was merely reacting to the food he'd swallowed.

"What in the name of the heavens above is this?" Fabien looked like he'd been scalded. He was half standing now. "It has burnt my gums. I cannot feel my tongue"

"Dude, it's just chilli." Rick clapped him on the back. "It's supposed to feel that way."

"Why would you want to feel this way?" Fabien asked. "I will never understand this place. You're supposed to like potatoes and cabbage. What's wrong with potatoes and cabbage?" he asked as he ran from the table.

Karen found herself smiling. He really was a character, but a dangerous one if he couldn't keep his imagination in check.

Chapter 27

The night was quiet. Marcus nuzzled into Karen's slender frame. It was a single bed, the only drawback to the cabin so far.

"Are you awake?" Marcus whispered into her ear, so that if she wasn't, she would be now. "I have something to tell you. I'm in trouble. I think I'm dying."

Karen turned with a start. "What are you talking about?"

"Boredom!" Marcus replied. "I'm going to die of boredom if you don't get me out of this place." Karen laughed in spite of herself.

It surprised him. She was always at her grumpiest just after she'd woken up. She dug an elbow into his ribs.

That's more like it, he thought. "Let's check out the Westport night life: me, you, the owls and the moon," he suggested excitedly.

Karen thought about it and changed her mind a couple of times before answering. "One condition! We sneak out and we're back before dawn. I don't want to wake anyone or cause any upset because we left without them."

"Deal!" Marcus jumped up to reveal his magnificent torso.

Karen felt like a teenager quietly sneaking across the floorboards with the exaggerated jerking motion of a chicken. Marcus was sniggering behind her. The quieter she tried to be, the more noise she seemed to make. She almost fell over removing her nightie. Marcus helped her take it off, his hands brushed against her skin as he lifted it over her head and she shivered. He traced his hands back down the sides of her body feeling the bones of her ribs and the curves of her hips.

Karen pressed her lips to his in the darkness and he pulled her close. She wished they were alone in the cabin. "We should go," she whispered.

They rummaged through piles of clothes before Karen finally chose an outfit with the loudest shoes she could have selected. Her logic made him laugh. *She* made him laugh; not just smile, but laugh – something he hadn't done in a very long time. It was a pity, he thought. Maybe she could be converted. If only he had more time.

"Marcus! Marcus!" she half-yelled half-whispered. "Stop standing there gormlessly and come on!"

"You're the only person I've ever met that could shout and whisper all at the same time." Marcus hurried out the door.

"You have a plan, I'm assuming?" Karen asked in the cold night air. She could see her breath forming shapes in the black night. "Because I haven't the foggiest idea which direction the town is."

Marcus flashed her an arrogant smile before zipping up his jacket. "I always have a plan!" he bragged and took her by the hand.

"This is stealing," Karen protested.

"No it is not. Not if you're going to return it." Marcus fidgeted some more with the lock of the mountain bike outside one of the cabins. "Keep an eye out will you!"

Karen glanced uneasily over her shoulder and Marcus took the opportunity he'd created to snap the chain with his hands. "Hop on, M'Lady."

"Imagine the mortification if we get caught." Karen reddened.

Marcus looked her squarely in the face and his voice changed to a very low and serious tone. "I don't get caught!" he said. "And you're with me, now. You won't get caught."

To her own amazement Karen jumped up on the cross bar.

"I can't believe I'm…" She never got to finish the sentence. The wind came and swept the air out of her lungs leaving the words unspoken behind her.

They were going at an uncontrollable speed now down the forest hill. Marcus weaved in and out through the evergreens. He foresaw the uneven terrains of rocks and mounds at just the right moments, avoiding them with expert precision but never reducing speed.

Flashes of green and brown sped past in a blur. Karen was going to either really hate him or really love him when she got off that cross bar, he thought.

Marcus's body hung low clutching the handlebars in a way that cocooned Karen and kept her in place. Up in the air the bike ramped over a mound of grit and they were out on the open road, leaving the sleeping forest behind them.

Marcus didn't have to wait for Karen to get off the bike to see her reaction. Her body was shaking and he saw that she was laughing – a liberated, infectious laugh. He joined her and couldn't help himself from planting a kiss on her cold red cheek, swollen by her smile.

The absence of a forest hill didn't slow their momentum. Karen's laughter encouraged Marcus to pedal all the faster. Marcus raised himself up into a standing position and pedalled ferociously in the middle of the road. He sped around corners with a reckless regard for what might be coming towards them. It was almost a disappointment to reach the town centre.

Not many pubs remained open. After a period of wandering down dingy little side lanes they found what they could only assume to be the only nightclub in the town. The entrance was tall and narrow and the only part in view from the outside was a set of steps.

Irritating garage music was blasting from the entrance on to the empty little street. Marcus and Karen passed the round-bellied bouncer and made their way upstairs.

Everything inside appeared so dead by comparison to the trip they'd taken to get there. Karen wondered briefly why anyone would ever do drugs when such natural highs existed in the world.

"I think cocktails are in order." Marcus decided.

He ordered them both a red drink that smelled of strawberries and Karen took in her surroundings. The club was full of drunken Saturday night revellers, locals who had just been paid and were eager to spend their earnings on getting themselves as sick as possible.

A couple sat entangled with each other at a high table near the window overlooking the street below.

"Hold these a moment!" Marcus handed her their jackets.

****

Michael Wall couldn't believe his luck. This bird was hot, he thought. She must have been wearing beer goggles, because he'd never scored a chic this hot. His racing thoughts and libido were interrupted by a heavy tap on his shoulder. Marcus leaned in close to whisper in his ear.

"Take your girlfriend and get up from this table or I'll smash this glass into both your throats. If you don't smile and nod to my girlfriend on your way out I'll find you and you'll beg me to kill you."

Michael sobered up like someone had thrown a glass of cold water in his face. He examined Marcus, who was standing over him. He wasn't overly buff; he could probably take him on a good night. But there was something about the guy that told him to get as far away as possible. Every muscle in his body told him to leave and leave fast. Michael grabbed his companion and scurried past Marcus, giving Karen an overfriendly smile, and with that they were gone.

"What was that all about?" Karen sat down.

"Oh, I just paid him for their seats. She obviously doesn't mean that much to him," Marcus joked.

"*You* wouldn't sell *me* out then?" Karen asked.

"Everyone has a price." He winked at her.

Several cocktails were consumed before they finally began to fit in with the environment around them.

"How's work?" Karen asked.

"Dull, to say the least. Half of them couldn't be bothered and the other half I couldn't be bothered *with*."

Karen was surprised. "But you must be bothered. What about all those stories you'd prepared?"

Marcus shook his head. "They're not interested, so why should I be? They can fail if they want to, that's their choice." He sulked.

"Don't you care what happens to them?" Karen asked.

"Not really. And I don't know why you do, either."

"Because I do."

"You don't know them! They're nothing to you. Caring so much about total strangers is just a waste of time. You're better just taking care of yourself. Take that couple over there." Marcus nodded toward the bar where a young girl was desperately trying to hold her boyfriend back from pounding two other men. "He thinks they stole his girlfriend's phone, but it's right under there!" Marcus pointed at the little crevice between the tables.

"How do you know?" Karen asked.

"I can see it flashing."

"So why don't you tell them?" Karen asked in surprise.

"Exactly!" Marcus clicked his fingers. "That is exactly what I'm talking about. You're trying to right wrongs that have nothing to do with you. Why not just let matters unfold? Don't bother yourself with it and just enjoy the show."

Karen sighed. "We're very different people!" She shook her head and got up to retrieve the phone.

Marcus huffed as he watched her. "We certainly are." he mumbled under his breath. He already regretted his honesty. What had he been thinking? He would never convert her, there wasn't enough time, and now he would have to work even harder to get her to trust him again.

Marcus let them both back into the cabin without so much as a sound. He carried Karen to bed since her heels appeared to have gotten louder as the night had progressed. She was asleep within minutes.

There was time to look around. Marcus knew there was. But what were the chances the key would be here? It would be a personal object, something she would keep at home, he convinced himself. He would come back tomorrow. He would probe her about her father. The timing was right. She could talk to him now, or at least he hoped she could. All he needed was to create the platform for the discussion, and Marcus was good at that, good at creating opportunities.

Chapter 28

Karen woke to a sharp uncomfortable feeling in her ribs. She rolled over and fished out the little onyx stone she'd been given.

"How did *you* get there?" She groaned and threw it on the floor.

Connor was knocking loudly on her bedroom door.

"Where's Marcus?" he asked finding only Karen.

"He's working."

"Never mind; he'd be bored waiting around anyway."

Horse riding! Karen had forgotten they were horse riding today. She rummaged through her case to find the old pair of riding boots she'd packed. She'd forgotten them the last time she'd been horse riding with Sam. She'd had to rent a smelly old pair from the instructor's equipment room and they were two sizes too small. Her feet were pinched and cramped the entire session and Sam said they were smellier than the rear end of her horse.

Karen missed Sam. She wished she were there to talk to. Rick had believed her too readily and she longed for Sam's logical mind to dismiss her theories as rubbish and return to the black and white in which she saw the world.

Karen found Dan in the kitchen. He was lifting sizzling hot sausages from the pan. He was swallowing them before they even had a chance to cool, Karen felt ill just watching him. She turned her attention to Fabien who was eating a yogurt.

"Is it hard being a vegetarian?" she wondered out loud.

"Not at all." Fabien smiled at her with a look of relief on his face that told her he was grateful she was still speaking to him.

"I couldn't live without meat."

"Me neither." Dan was examining a sausage like it was a precious specimen, before swallowing the entire thing. Karen was glad it was their last day; she wasn't sure how much longer she could spend with Connor's friends.

Rick had never been horse riding before but had convinced himself it was simple.

"Just be careful that's all I'm saying," warned Connor as he locked up. "Tell the instructor you're a beginner. So what if you have to go a little slower."

"I'm not sitting around on some pony while you guys get to go down to the lakeside." He slowed down and hung back to talk with Karen. "I didn't get to catch up with you yesterday with Marcus around. Are you okay? Did you have any more dreams?"

Karen could see anxiety in Rick's blue eyes. "You're making me nervous."

"Just checking!" He raised his hands. "You didn't tell him, did you?" Rick was trying to sound casual but it wasn't very convincing.

"What if I did?"

Rick whipped his head around abruptly. "You didn't! Did you? He's not even Irish! He wouldn't even know the legend!"

"Relax! I'm not stupid; he'd only think I was crazy."

"Exactly!" Rick agreed, and dug his hands into his pockets with satisfaction. "We must be close now."

The forest path before them had emptied, telling them everyone else had made a turn off.

An energetic sheep dog materialized from the bushes and escorted them the rest of the way. He danced over and back almost tripping them up. They followed him until they came to an opening and they found themselves at a great old farmhouse. It was a dull grey-washed building, and its large Georgian windows appeared to be watching them with silent interest. The air smelled of silage and hay mixed with something else – cigarette smoke. A small man with a heavy moustache emerged from a little outhouse in a cloud of cigarette smoke. "Ye rang for the horses?" he asked in a tone that suggested he didn't really care one way or another.

Rick looked longingly at the cigarette.

Karen intervened before he could give in to temptation. "You don't want one!" she assured him.

Rick tore his eyes from the cigarette. "That's us. It was Faye I spoke with, I think."

"Yeah, that's the mother," said moustache man throwing the smouldering cigarette butt to the ground. "I'm Tommy," he rasped. "Got 'em ready for ye."

Tommy led them back into the little outhouse. The shelves were stacked full of riding hats and old muddy boots of every size. Tommy tilted his head to examine their footwear. Satisfied with Fabien's he looked to Connor, who wore his usual Timberlands, and finally to a flatfooted Rick with his size eleven Vans and multicoloured laces.

"What?" Rick asked defensively.

"You'll need something with a heel," Tommy informed him. "What size are ye?"

"Thirteen!" Rick said, glancing shadily around the room and making eye contact with no one.

Tommy fumbled around on the floor behind an old table before resurfacing with a dirty pair of size thirteen cowboy boots.

Karen could just about make out the horses through the filthy windowpanes. Fabien was kitted out already and stroking them lovingly. *Angels indeed,* she thought

"You ready?" Connor asked, picking his sister up.

"What are you doing?" Karen struggled to escape as he threw her over his back. It knocked the wind out of her lungs and the heaviness out of her heart.

When Rick was finally ready, Tommy brought around the last available horse. It had the hugest rear end he had ever seen. "Bloody typical," Rick murmured as he pulled himself up onto the large animal.

Karen got the feeling her horse was feistier than the rest. It shoved its way impatiently to the front directly behind Tommy's. Karen patted its great muscular neck. The mare was black and she was beautiful.

After a brief assessment of their capabilities, Tommy allowed them trot ahead to the shores of the lake. Fabien took off like an accomplished jockey, with Dan and Connor a little behind. Karen found Rick desperately kicking his horse but the animal seemed more interested in the bushes at the side of the road.

"It's obvious why this one's called Chomp!"

"Pull on the reins!" Karen called to him. Rick did as he was told but chomp merely raised his head and took a large steaming dump at the side of the road. "Aw, for fuck's sake." Eventually Chomp seemed satisfied with his deposit and followed the group at his own pace.

"Step up and sit down in time with his movements," Karen told Rick.

Chomp obliged with a trot and Rick managed him faultlessly. He knew he did because he could see the awe in Karen's face.

"You *have* done this before." Karen sped up.

Rick chased after her. Fabien was watching him. He was watching the effort on Rick's face as he tried to keep up. Rick's demeanour had changed. He needed to be near her. She'd told him, Fabien surmised.

****

After a couple of hundred yards of riding along the stony lakeside, Tommy veered right into the surrounding fields and back in the direction from which they came.

It was a quiet place, with nothing but the sound of birds in the sky and hooves on the ground. The sun had set but Karen could still make out the energetic sheep dog playing with a man watching them by the fence.

Karen's horse slowed for the first time during their trek. It wasn't until she got closer that she recognized Marcus. His hair was tangled and knotted and he was sweeping it from his eyes. Karen dismounted swiftly and began leading the great black horse to the stables.

"You're like Batman," she told Marcus. "Always turning up out of nowhere."

"I like to rescue you," Marcus joked.

"Karen!" Rick called impatiently. "We've got another circuit."

"You go ahead; we'll meet you back at the cabin," Karen called back.

"You're earlier than I thought," she turned to Marcus.

"Study group." Marcus shrugged. "Languages aren't subjects they struggle with at the grammar school. It's more maths and chemistry. Probably down to my good teaching," he boasted.

"See – you do care. I knew you did."

"Of course I do. I was just fooling around the other night."

They began to walk and Marcus flattened the long grass impatiently with a stick.

"You don't like the countryside," Karen said.

"I prefer the city," he admitted. "The hustle and bustle, I even like the traffic."

"No, you like running *through* the traffic," Karen corrected.

"Yes, that too, but I also like the lights and the masses of people, and the music."

"You can have music in the country. That's what a céilí is for."

"A what?" Marcus laughed.

"A céilí. It's like a gathering or a sing-song. I wish we'd brought some instruments now."

"You can borrow my guitar." A voice came from behind; Dan was just a few feet away.

"You need more than a guitar for a céilí." Connor appeared behind him.

Dan looked disappointed. "Come on, Conaire," he pleaded.

But Connor looked like he'd been punched in the gut. "Don't call me that!" he said.

Karen reddened. The only other person ever to use her brother's Irish name was their father. It meant *little wolf,* he'd explained.

Karen was disappointed Connor seemed to remember a lot more about their father than she did.

****

Karen and Marcus were warming their hands by an outdoor fire Marcus had managed to light. Karen almost burnt her hands she held them so close.

"You're shaking." Marcus pulled her under his shoulder.

"So when do I get to meet your family?" he asked out of the blue.

"You barely know my twin brother."

Marcus was making her nervous. The random questions he asked her out of the blue made her uncomfortable.

"Would you ever leave?" he asked next. "Leave this place and start over?" Was he asking her to move back to Greece with him? Karen wondered. If so she needed to make things very clear.

"No, never."

"Then you would not have done as I did? Leave your homeland?"

"Is that what this is? Are you missing home?" She placed her hand in his. "Why don't you go back and visit?"

"What if you couldn't?" He glanced at her sideways. "What if you could never return and never learn of your family's fate. What would you do?"

Karen thought about it. "I would pray," she told him. "I would say every decade of the rosary until I felt them close to me."

"Rosary beads. Those little wooden beads you use."

"Yes, those little wooden beads I use."

Marcus turned to a knocking at the cabin window behind them. "Your brother is calling you."

Connor managed to open the stiff cabin window. "Can you fetch Butch Cassidy and the Sundance Kid for me?" he asked, referring to Rick and Fabien. "Supper's nearly ready."

Karen got up and brushed herself down. "Aren't you coming?" she asked Marcus

"No, I'll stay here."

"Can't believe you'd rather stay with my brother than me," she teased.

"And I can't believe I'm not important enough to introduce to your family." Marcus sulked.

Karen shot him a dark look. She didn't like to be blackmailed or manipulated and Marcus was very good at both.

Chapter 29

Fabien and Rick were nowhere to be seen. Karen climbed the fence onto the shore but couldn't see or hear them anywhere. She wandered past the trees so they couldn't obstruct her vision. After pulling back the branches of an old ash tree she saw them. They were performing some sort of kata.

Rick was a brown belt in karate but Karen had never seen him train before. It was the only thing he practised quietly. But Karen didn't think it was karate. It looked like yoga or aikido. She'd never seen men move so gracefully before, at least not any of the men *she* knew. They moved their arms in unison into their chests and back out again. Fabien appeared to be showing Rick the sequence. After a time, Karen decided to interrupt. She stepped out from the trees and approached them.

"What are you doing?"

Rick's concentration broke first and he turned to face her. His gaze was so full of sadness it almost knocked her over. It came at her in an invisible heavy wave of melancholy.

It was Fabien who answered. "I'm trying to encourage Rick to take up karate again."

"That's great," said Karen. Rick still hadn't found his voice.

"Rick," she called.

"Sorry," he answered shaking himself. "I was miles away."

"Well, come get something to eat before you fade away."

The more they walked the more suspicious Karen became. Something had happened, she knew it had. What if Fabien told Rick he knew about the banshee? What if Rick believed him about being a guardian angel? Surely he wouldn't, she told herself.

"What is for dinner?" Fabien asked.

"I don't think you'll like it," Karen said. "It smelt like homemade burgers."

"Never mind. Where there are burgers there are salads." Fabien smiled.

But Karen wasn't listening; she was contemplating the hopelessness of her situation. She was stuck in a forest with a man who thought he had divine powers and a friend who was gullible enough to believe him.

"I smell rosemary." Fabien flared his nostrils.

I smell bullshit, Karen was tempted to say but she held her tongue.

Marcus was still sitting by himself at the fire when they returned and Connor was heading towards them. "About time." Connor called. "You almost missed supper. Go get some plates and we can eat out here."

"I'm not hungry," Rick said. "I'll just make some toast."

Karen followed him inside hoping to catch him alone long enough to discover what had upset him. He was dragging his big feet clumsily up the cabin steps like they were weighing him down.

"What's wrong?" Karen caught him by the arm.

He stared past her shoulders and down to the fire. Only when he appeared satisfied they were alone did he look at her again. "Why didn't you tell me?" His tone was imploring, and disappointment was written all over his face.

Karen had to take a step back, as if to protect herself from its force. "Tell you what?"

"About Fabien! Someone else has actually seen the banshee you see in your dreams." Rick was shaking his head. "I can't believe you have a guardian angel and you didn't tell me!" Rick laid his head against the doorframe as if holding it up by himself were paining him. "You never mentioned anything about a portal key or vampires being sent to find what form it's in – none of it."

Karen grabbed his arm to take him inside where she could raise her voice. She couldn't help it. She always raised it in desperate situations. Not because she was angry but because of a desperation to be heard.

"That's exactly why I couldn't tell you." Karen slammed the door shut behind them. "You'd have believed it too readily, and it's not true."

"Why isn't it? You believe in the banshee! She's an evil spirit."

"According to who?" Karen argued. "Fabien?"

"Well, what do you think then?"

Karen took a deep breath before launching into her explanation that Fabien was suffering from delusions, just like Bertha McCormack. Whatever was clouding their vision of the real world gave them clarity in another. There were no vampires or werewolves and there certainly wasn't an all-important portal key.

Before she could finish, they were disturbed by a crashing sound at the door. Connor had dropped a bottle of beer on the porch and was cursing his own clumsiness.

Karen huffed as he tried to clean it up. "Just leave it," she told him rubbing her temples. "I'll clean it later."

Connor really picked his moments, she thought. He'd linger stupidly now for another long spell sensing nothing of the tension around him. When he'd finished cleaning, he began rummaging through the kitchen cupboards. "Have you seen the mayo?" he asked.

Karen gave another threatening sigh. "In the fridge where it always is." She clenched her teeth.

Connor gazed into the fridge for another few moments but seemed to suddenly forget what he was looking for. "There's only a few beers left. Here!" he called to Rick and threw him one.

Rick missed and the bottle smashed on the floor. Only then did Connor appear to join them in their reality. He saw the agitation on his sister's face. He noticed the silence in the room and Rick's distracted gaze. "Ah, I'll clean that," he said.

"Oh, just get out!" Karen snapped. "Just give us five minutes to have an adult conversation, would you? Five minutes!"

Connor's face reddened and Karen regretted her outburst instantly. "Sorry, I'm just having a bad day."

"You're having a lot of those," Connor muttered as he left.

Karen flopped down into the sofa, cursing herself.

"He'll be okay." Rick sat next to her. "He'll just go lick his wounds somewhere and he'll be right as rain." Rick began rubbing Karen's shoulder. "I get it. It's hard to believe when you have no proof but have you actually asked for any?"

"What do you mean?"

"Have you asked Fabien for proof?"

"Actually, yes. I told him I was never left any key. And do you know what he told me? He said it was in a different form, and that it was too dangerous for me to know what it was yet." Karen raised both eyebrows in a gesture that indicated her suspicion.

Rick sat forward then and put his large hands on hers. "I'm not putting pressure on you, but maybe you're finding it hard to believe because you find it too scary to believe."

"That's not it." Karen curled her thumb around his fingers. "If that were true then I wouldn't believe in the banshee, would I?"

Rick shifted a bit on the sofa as though choosing his words carefully.

"You didn't at first, though, did you? It takes time to process these things. Maybe our brains need to accept things at different stages. You know, to protect ourselves."

"Yours doesn't," Karen pointed out.

"Well, I'm a bit different, aren't I?"

Connor chose that moment to storm back in the door. "And what do you mean an adult conversation? I'm plenty capable of an adult conversation. Why don't we have one right now? I have some great food and drink arranged for any adult conversation, only it's all going to waste because you two are sulking over God knows what."

"We'll be right there." Rick looked guilty.

Connor lingered for a few moments as if processing the answer. "Right then," he muttered when he appeared satisfied.

Karen felt like she was babysitting a bunch of sulky toddlers when she arrived for supper. Marcus was sitting cross-legged holding his knees and conversing with no one. Not that she blamed him, among such an unfriendly bunch. Karen broke a bread bun and drenched it in tomato ketchup before floating a smoking burger on top. She brought it over and sat next to Marcus by way of reconciliation. "I chose the least cooked one I could find. Can't say its blue but it might give you salmonella." She peered down at it.

Marcus broke a smile and accepted her peace offering.

"You look tired. Are you okay?" Karen asked.

"I will be," Marcus answered.

They huddled together in a comfortable silence. Karen's hand draped across his knee. He held it there with his own as they listened to the fire. The wood snapped and crackled like a bowl of Rice Krispies.

Connor was still waiting for everyone to compliment his burgers. Subtle as the bricks he laid, he decided to take matters into his own hands. "So, the burgers, eh? Ye like the burgers?"

"Burgers were good." Rick patted his friend's back.

Karen offered to help clean up to make up for her earlier outburst.

"How well do you really know Fabien?" she asked her brother after dinner. The others were having a nightcap in the lounge and it was one of the only moments they would have alone together. Connor passed her a dripping plate.

"Rinse it, will you!" Karen scorned.

"God, you're turning into Mum," Connor moaned. "I know Fabien as well as anybody."

"Do you trust him, though?"

"Sure." Connor shrugged. "He gets things a little muddled sometimes but his heart's in the right place." Connor was thinking of the time Fabien accused Marcus of assaulting Dan.

"What do you mean?"

"Nothing really. Just innocent stuff."

Connor chose his next words carefully so as not to reveal his investigation into Marcus. "He thought a guy I knew was some sort of loose cannon, it got me worried, especially with my record. Anyway, I checked into it and it was all a big misunderstanding."

Karen glanced into the living room to make sure no one was listening.

"Do me a favour and don't tell him anything personal will you?" she pleaded.

"Is this about that story Dan told earlier?" Connor asked. "Cause I had nothing to do with that. There are millions of banshee stories. I didn't even know you were having nightmares about a banshee."

"No, not just about me, about our family. Don't tell him anything else about Dad."

Connor looked confused. "I never mentioned Dad; why would I?"

"Because you … well you might have … because …"

Connor raised his eyebrows. "Because it's just the sort of thing I usually slip into friendly conversation?" Connor shook his head.

The kitchen seemed to swirl then, or was it the ground? No it was definitely the kitchen, Karen decided, because she could see the walls closing in.

Was this what happened when the brain was finally ready to accept things? Was this what Rick had been referring to? "Where's that Whiskey?"

Connor smiled mischievously. "Really? You really think there'd be any left?"

Karen was in shock. How would Fabien possibly have known such details about her father? Where Karen had grown up, the only thing for shock was a good stiff whiskey. Her mother used it after coming across road accidents. Esther used it when Evelyn Maloney beat her in the tidy gardens competition and Connor used it for Mondays.

"There might be some of that prissy wine Fabien drinks in the cupboard," Connor offered.

Karen poured herself a large cup of red wine and sat slowly down on the sofa.

The liquid rolled rhythmically down her throat as she gulped, promising a satisfying sting to follow. She swallowed harder on the second gulp just to feel the burn that would bring her back into the room.

Marcus found her there later with an empty bottle of wine in hand. "I wanted to talk to you but you look ill."

It seemed an eternity before Karen answered. "I have a headache."

Marcus wrapped her in a dressing gown and took her to bed. He propped up the cushions and stood motionless for a moment. They smelled of her, of autumn apples. He counted seventeen hairs on the pillows. Marcus could smell each and every one of them. He placed her gently on her side and he lay next to her. Eventually her breathing changed and he knew she was sleeping.

Chapter 30

Niall was patrolling Main Street. He had forgotten to pick up the milk Roxy had ordered him to bring home and now the stores were shut. It had been a quiet night by city standards and he was about to wrap up.

The cold winter wind tickled his lungs and told him it had been considering snowing but not to tell anybody. The ash trees that lined the pavements had loaned their leaves to the kerb. Had it not been for these leaves Niall may never have heard the scuffling coming from the alley behind him.

He wandered over expecting to find someone drunk, but he was wrong. The alleyway was long and it was hard to make out exactly what he was watching. A small but livid man full of rage landed the final blow on the head of his victim, knocking the life clean out of his body. The attacker was panting now. His chest was moving rapidly in and out in frantic rhythms.

Niall caught him from behind with a body blow and brought him down. Now the man was lying on the cold grey ground right next to a man he'd just murdered. He fought against the handcuffs Niall was trashing against his wrists but the adrenaline that had empowered him earlier was gone.

Niall was strong. He'd played rugby for the senior cup team in college. The situation was under control, he told himself. His victory was evident as he sat astride the savage little man's back and clipped the handcuffs.

It would have been a clean arrest if a blow to the skull from behind hadn't knocked him out.

Liam dropped the stone. "Rise, my friend." He smiled slyly, and the vicious little man stood up. Blood stained his jaw from an earlier thump. Liam broke the cuffs. "You have done well," he whispered. "Now give me your neck."

****

Liam was feeding. Marcus could taste the blood in his mentor's mouth. He felt the gloopy sensation at the back of his throat. It tasted different. He felt like his tongue was swimming in a pool of liquid metal. It reminded him of how it tasted as a human, when he was like *her*.

Marcus turned to look at her now. Karen was resting peacefully. He had to get a move on. When Karen awoke the bed was empty. She stretched out a hand to find the man who had betrayed her, but he was gone. She still felt drunk from the red wine but she dragged her legs out of the bed and made her way to the kitchen. She felt the breeze instantly and noticed the front door was swinging open.

Outside she found a bottle of her favourite perfume on the porch; a bottle of Chanel she kept in her handbag. She squinted to see her bag lying open on the forest track.

Her eyes felt sticky and full of sleep but still she wandered down to the lakeside. She had to find Marcus; she wasn't afraid of him.

The grass tickled her ankles as she made her way down the track. As she neared the shore she heard a crashing sound, echoes of movements and activity storming ahead of her. Suddenly she was awake, wide awake.

Karen had watched boxing on television before. Andrew had bored her enough with it that she knew all the rules. The only thing she never understood, though, was the fighters' huddle: the moments when two opponents huddled together half wrestling, half lying on each other's shoulders. Andrew said it was to do with stamina – a preservation of energy or a moment's recuperation. Karen now saw another explanation. It was to remove the perilous space between them that if utilized would allow the lethal blow.

The creatures fighting before her were demonic. One swipe was all that was needed. If one gained the ground to attack, the other would inevitably fall; and so they crouched and scuffled, pushing each other in every direction.

One of the figures, with bulging muscled legs, smashed his opponent into one of the boats on the shore. Karen noticed his thick and leathery skin, dark and deep brown in colour. The little fishing boat smashed in half, sending sharp pieces of wood high into the air.

The creatures rolled and trashed about the shore until one of them doubled over in pain and the other rose. Karen could just make out its facial features. They were twisted and contorted. His skull and his teeth were oversized and gruesome as he stared down at his adversary. They did look like Gorgon offspring, Karen noticed, snake-like with venomous razor sharp fangs.

Karen tried to scream but nothing came out. Her lips remained tightly together as though terrified to leave each other's company. The creature seemed to lose his footing then as an ankle sweep brought him down faster than a sinking stone. He hit the water with a heavy splash and the fight continued amidst the waves.

Karen never got to see who resurfaced; a vibrant light from behind her forced her eyes to look away. A power had arrived. It was a presence that dominated the lakeside and suddenly Karen no longer felt afraid.

Now that the light-bringer had stepped out from behind her Karen could see it was Fabien lighting up the lake with his eyes.

She watched him raise both hands from his hips and pour a blazing ray of light in their direction. It looked like shooting orbs soaring through the air and blasting into the chest of one of the creatures.

Karen saw the creature's eyes as it fell and they looked familiar, but not from the demonic face now before her. It went under the water and didn't resurface.

Karen could feel her body on the light-bringer's radar and thanked God quietly for the guardian angel he had sent her.

Fabien turned to face her but she couldn't meet his eyes, they were swirling in pools of light too bright for her to withstand.

Chapter 31

Katie was watching the wildlife channel in bed while munching on a large bag of crisps. Andrew lay sleeping beside her. He was used to the little bits of salted crisps that littered his bed, biting his knees and itching his feet. Katie rubbed her belly and continued chomping. She was addicted to these kettle chips, so much so that she questioned whether they had anything to do with pregnancy cravings. She was disappointed (but not discouraged) to learn that they were harder to swallow tonight. She wondered if it was indigestion and contemplated kicking Andrew to fetch her some water. But instead she persevered and went back for another handful.

Andrew awoke to an elbow in his back; it kept prodding him over and over.

"Can you get me some water?"

The whisper dropped delicately into his ear. Andrew wasn't annoyed at being awoken. He loved to hear her voice. He pulled his large tired body out of bed. The timber floor was cold on his bare feet as he made his way to the kitchen.

When he returned Katie was sitting up and looking distressed.

"Did you spill the one you had?" Andrew noticed the wet bed sheets. She didn't have to answer him. He already knew, or he thought he did. "Oh, mother… that's the waters, isn't it, the ones that come before the baby?"

"Get your coat!" Katie ordered. "The hospital bag is in the wardrobe. My phone is charged in the spare room." She was about to give another order but Andrew was already having trouble with the first few tasks.

Andrew's heart was hammering and so was Katie's, no matter how much she tried to hide it. She was nervous and anxious, but she was excited too. She was sick but she was hungry. She wondered briefly if she had time for more kettle chips.

Andrew thudded back into the bedroom. He seemed to have pulled himself together a little bit. "The car's loaded," he told her and he helped her from the bed. She put her arms around his broad shoulders. It was a welcomed surprise for Andrew not to be pushed away for helping and it dawned on him why. He stopped to look in her eyes, and time took a break from its busy schedule to afford them a moment. "We're really going to do this, aren't we?" he said.

Katie stared back at him in a daze, holding his hand to her chest. All the anxiety that had wedged itself between them the past few months evaporated and all that was left was love. "We really are!" she told him half giggling, half crying. They made their way downstairs like two teenagers let loose on the nocturnal world.

****

Robbie King was nineteen and working at the hospital to earn the money he needed to drink his summer holidays away. He hated the maternity wards: creepy places with creepy howling women. He'd been called down to bring one up now.

He leaned his arms on the handles of the wheelchair he was rolling down the corridors. His patient seemed as reluctant to get in it as he was to wheel it. Robbie met his patient in the atrium. She was agitated, fussing and picking bits of fluff from her cardigan and mumbling. Her husband looked embarrassed but Robbie couldn't make out what she was saying, except "overkill" – something about wheelchairs and overkill.

Robbie warmed to the woman. Maybe this one wasn't a howler. He hoped she would have an easy birth, that her baby would pop out, just like on television.

Katie continued to pick fluff off her jacket, just for something to do, just to ignore the terror she felt. She knew she was an older mother. She knew the complications that might bring. She'd spent the past nine months worrying about them.

Please let it be okay, please let it be okay, she prayed over and over.

Robbie wheeled Katie through a set of double doors and onto the maternity wards. He left her with Andrew in the examination room and quickly ran away.

The lighting in the little room was low and dim. This was good, Katie thought. It meant she was processing the environment again and out of her own head. She was good at pulling herself together, she reminded herself. She closed her eyes and took deep breaths.

A heavy pressure was mounting against her pelvis. It felt like her body was detaching at the hip. Shooting pains exploded through nerve endings she never knew she had. *This is okay,* she told herself; *this is just pain. Pain can't kill you. You eat pain for breakfast.* "Where's the doctor!" She wanted to shout, but she swallowed the words instead.

Andrew was playing with his rosary beads in his pocket. He'd lost track of whether it was an Our Father or a Hail Mary he was on so he went straight to a Glory Be to The Father instead.

"You're doing great! Can I get you anything?" he offered.

Katie wanted to say "The doctor!" She was sure she should be pushing by now but she didn't want to be dramatic, especially not this soon into labour. She thought of Rosie the ewe. She'd been in labour for ages, and she wouldn't be outdone by a sheep. Suddenly she leant over and almost fell out of the wheel chair. To hell with drama, she thought. "Get me the doctor!"

****

Karen was resting her head against the rain-stained window of the back seat. She was staring up at the sky, in an almost hypnotic state, and she felt safe. Everything was going to be okay now she told herself. Fabien had placed his palm on her chest. She had felt the peace, or was it love? Karen had nothing to compare it to. Of course she had experienced love before but this was different. Perhaps it wasn't the love itself but the absence of anything else.

Love as Karen knew it was always associated with something or someone. This wasn't. This was just the pure and concentrated emotion in its truest form. She wondered then about the science of emotion. She was sure it had something to do with chemicals. But why was that in itself not a miracle – that it could work in such ways to allow us the ability to heal each other. Karen had read that science and religion did not have to be mutually exclusive and for the first time she felt she understood why.

Connor snorted like a pig in his sleep causing the rest of the car to giggle. *He must sense pivotal moments like these in his genes and become compelled to interrupt them*, Karen thought.

The city was sleeping when they returned, save for the usual suspects on the road who hadn't work the next day. Dan pulled into the driveway at Ashton Park and helped Karen with her bags. Rick watched him through the window with admiration. "A werewolf!" he mouthed.

"Freaking amazing."

"He is not that amazing," Fabien said. "And he is not a werewolf. He doesn't crouch on all fours, nor does he turn into a wolf. That's just how you've portrayed them here."

"Well, what do they call them where you're from?"

"Children of the Moon." Fabien lay back, resting his head on the seat.

"So *where you're from* …" Rick probed.

"You do not need to know this, you know too much already."

Rick waved back at his friends as they shut their front door.

"So if you're not from *here* that must mean there must be a *there* – somewhere else, right? Does Karen know that?"

"Karen will know after she has rested. She is involved and she needs to know. You, however, do not."

Dan pulled open the door and drew his lanky body back into the driver's seat. He shifted in his seat until he was facing Rick who was sitting in the back.

"What?" Rick felt like he was being studied.

Dan shook his head. "I can't believe you told him." he said to Fabien.

Fabien gave a tired sigh. "He already knew, I could tell. All I did was fill in the gaps."

Dan remained unconvinced.

"Ask yourself!" Fabien pressed. "Where would we be if I hadn't? Karen would still be picking and choosing what to believe and what not to. It is easier to hear the truth from someone you trust."

Rick stuck his chest out smugly.

Dan was still staring at him. "I don't like it!"

Fabien's tone changed. "It is better than upsetting her with banshee stories! What were you thinking?"

"I was merely letting her know what to look out for. She doesn't need to know the rest. The more she knows the more danger she's in."

Fabien was quiet for a moment. Then he said, "I think you must come to accept that we are nearing a time where we have no choice."

****

Esther's phone echoed throughout the old farmhouse. It filled the hallway and right the up to the landing. It did this several times before Esther woke properly.

She listened carefully to the joyful tone of her son the other end of the line. It was a tone she hadn't heard since he was a boy. Esther had just become a grandmother again.

"A baby girl. Seven pounds seven ounces!" he told her. They would call her Darcy, on account of the thickest, blackest head of hair the hospital had ever seen.

Catherine's phone rang. She wasn't on call and she was tempted to ignore it until she registered the time. It was after midnight; something could be wrong. She bolted to answer it just in time, to hear the good news.

Evelyn Maloney's phone rang; she was up anyway. It might be *juicy* she thought and she picked up the phone in a hurry. She was almost sorry she did. That Esther O'Driscoll showing off. Had to get in there before our Shane, she thought.

Bertha McCormack's phone rang. She attacked it with a shoe.

Chapter 32

Karen lay in bed staring at the ceiling. A faint ray of sunlight was peeping through the curtains and drew her attention to the window. It didn't encourage her to get up. She wasn't sure if anything would. The euphoria she'd felt the evening before had left her. What would it be replaced with now Fabien wasn't here? What would it be like to face a new day knowing what she knew?

Everything had changed. *Everyone* had changed: Fabien, Dan and worst of all, Marcus. None of them were who she'd thought they were.

So what? Karen heard a fearless little voice inside her. It almost perked her up. Karen recognized it. She'd heard it before in times of self-pity. It sounded like her mother's voice, like her grandmother's, but it wasn't. It was the rebellious part of her soul that always made her fight.

Screw you, Marcus! Screw you and your bastard banshee!

Karen made her legs move and got out of bed. *Don't you go feeling sorry for yourself!* She told herself. Self-pity was the curse of the twenty-first century, Karen decided.

It was easier to be brave, easier to just meet things head on. Karen's senses agreed; they smelled coffee and brought her downstairs to the kitchen.

Buddy greeted her with sloppy jaws and dirty paws. He'd been running in circles around the back garden again. Karen smiled; not everything had changed. "I don't think Mum's walked him much. I'll take him out after breakfast," she said. This would give her a chance to meet with Fabien. There were so many questions she still had.

Connor was busy pouring hazardous amounts of oil into a frying pan.

"What happened to the Fry Light?" Karen asked.

"This tastes better!"

Karen took in the swell of his growing belly.

"You won't make it up that mountain next year." Connor ignored her and brought his oily breakfast over to the table. Karen poured herself some coffee and worried about what would happen to him if she wasn't around anymore. He'd become so used to his bachelor lifestyle he'd never make the effort he needed to with a girl.

He had a job, she consoled herself; he had friends he cared about and who cared about him. But what good was that if he didn't confide in them or accept their support?

Karen made a decision. Connor needed a girlfriend!

"You're getting a makeover!" she blurted out.

"What?" Connor barked with onions hanging from his mouth.

"It's decided!" she said with conviction, as the onion fell from his mouth.

"I'm not wasting my money on some poncey shirts," Connor warned. "This is a recession."

"A recession? So if I ask you what page you've been examining I won't find the horses, will I?"

Connor shut the newspaper in a sulk.

"Don't be like that! This can be your Christmas present."

Connor's lips began to move but Karen couldn't hear him. She was already planning a shopping trip. She was going to get him out of those dingy little pubs he drank in and introduce him to new people. Then she began to think of many more loose ends she should attend to in preparation for the worst, but this line of thought depressed her, so she focused on meeting Fabien instead.

"Karen?" Connor interrupted her. "You haven't listened to a word I just said, have you?"

"Absolutely I have! Next week it is."

****

206

Karen tried to control her mind and stay focused as she took a shower. But thoughts of things she should do were all fighting for attention. She would have to make up with Sam, one part of her brain informed her. Another thought climbed impatiently over this one and began shouting about the mortgage. Had she the right life cover? Would Connor be left with any debt?

Karen threw her head back, letting the water splash over her face; that always relaxed her. *What about Buddy?* A little thought snuck up and whispered mischievously in her ear. *Oh, for crying out loud!* she fumed and stepped out of the shower. *Focus!* She told herself. *Prioritize!* The most important thing right now is information. Knowledge is power, she told herself, and she would have that once she'd talked with Fabien some more.

Connor was watching football when she got back downstairs.

"Makeover!" she shouted as she left the house with Buddy.

Buddy still hadn't managed the art of not chewing the lead while walking. Karen tried to discipline him but he was too excited to care. It was noon and the sun hadn't run away yet. It was hard to be annoyed with the little pup.

Karen's heart quickened with anticipation as she crossed the bridge. She took the steps down to the canal where she was meeting Fabien at a derelict stone cottage. It would have been glorious in its day. Karen often wondered who'd lived there. Who had built it? When had it been deserted? She could see the tip of its chimney now, getting clearer and clearer until finally she reached it. She was early. Fabien hadn't arrived yet. She sat at the doorway looking out at the water.

Neither Karen nor Buddy, with his acute sense of hearing, heard Fabien arrive. He smiled his sunshine smile. "Interesting meeting point," he said as he looked around the cottage and its missing walls. "How are you feeling?"

"Do you already know?" Karen asked.

Fabien looked out across the calm unmoving water and casually placed his hands in his trouser pockets. He still hadn't sat down. "You have spent the morning worrying about everybody else, I expect. You are worried about your brother. You worry who will take care of your dog if you are gone. It is hard for you to stop thinking."

Karen followed his gaze out across the canal.

A robin was perched on a branch that was kissing the water's surface.

"So do you have like a third eye or something?" she asked. "Am I being watched?"

Fabien looked down at her sitting vulnerably in the doorway.

"No, not a third eye and no you are not been watched. Your body told me everything I need to know."

Karen shook her head and sniggered. "I'm sitting down stroking a dog, Fabien!" she pointed out.

"You are not stroking the dog, you are clinging to it. You are not sitting down you are sprawled uncomfortably in an exposed posture, suggesting your worries are peripheral and not personal."

Karen relaxed her shoulders. She surprised herself by realizing she was more comfortable knowing he'd used nothing more than observation to draw his conclusions.

"So do all angels know psychology now?" she asked.

"All *humans* do!" Fabien corrected. "You've just forgotten how to use it. You associate speech with evolution but I'm not so sure."

He gave a long sigh. "Sometimes I think you were more intelligent as you were."

Karen suddenly wondered just how long Fabien had been around for. How much had he seen? Buddy began to squirm in her arms, begging to be set free to roam the banks. She let him go. "So banshees don't like me very much then?" Karen decided she would open light.

"You have something they want, something they need to get and hide before you give it someone who can actually use it."

"You said before that banshees could enter the waking world at any time of day or night, unlike other beings from the world of slumber. Did you mean nightmares are coming true?" Karen asked. Karen had been mulling this over during the night. She'd barely slept, analysing what Fabien had already told her and it was the only conclusion she could draw.

"No." came the abrupt response that left her feeling deflated. "You know that another world exists. You've been dreaming of it. What you don't know is the importance of that world. Your world could not exist without it."

Fabien picked up a shamrock and rolled it thoughtfully between his fingers. "Consider this shamrock. Now, instead of looking at it like the Trinity from St Patrick's teachings, let's look at it and suppose it represents the world. Three parts," he explained and stared at it intensely. "Two leaves exist side by side. One is the conscious, the other the unconscious. Yours is the conscious leaf. The unconscious leaf we call Sublimina."

"What about the one on top?" Karen asked.

"That is the divine leaf. Even I don't know much about that one. My only contact with it is through meditation."

Karen took a moment to try to understand. "What's the point?" she shrugged. "What's the point of an unconscious realm, I mean?"

"Because consciousness feeds subconsciousness; one cannot exist without the other." Fabien tore one of the leaves off. "There is no longer balance." He showed her by tipping the shamrock on its side. "It will no longer stand."

"I see." Karen stared hard at the shamrock.

"Do you?" Fabien sounded hopeful.

"No."

Fabien didn't lose heart. It was what made him such an exceptional angel. "Sublimina wakes when you sleep. While you are all tucked-up in your bed, while your eyes are flickering and your body is resting, your mind is awakening in another world in another form."

"The decisions you have made during the day determine the form you will take that night. As a human, there are only two forms you can take, a Sublim or a Sprite."

"What's the difference?" Karen interrupted.

"Sublims have been influenced by virtue, Sprites have been influenced by malice."

"So if I'm a good girl today, I live as a Sublim tonight and if I'm naughty tomorrow, I'm a Sprite?"

Fabien smiled at her. "Essentially, yes," he said.

"How does that work? Population-wise, I mean."

"Eighty-twenty, of course."

Karen was familiar with the rule. "I assume you mean eighty per cent Sublim and twenty per cent Sprite." Karen's experience to date was that most people were good-natured. If she could have guessed a ratio it would have been just that.

"Actually, it's the opposite," Fabien said. "Eighty per cent of those you meet will take the form of a Sprite in Sublimina."

"Eighty per cent of people are bad?" Karen was shocked.

Fabien looked wounded. "Sprites aren't *bad,* merely misguided." His tone was soft and clear. It delivered the effect most people hoped they would achieve by shouting.

She listened.

"Good and bad is part of what makes us human. You must accept them both in order to embrace your humanity."

"I know that!" Karen recalled a similar lecture she'd given her uncle. "I know it's our choices that define us."

Fabien knew he had been spending too much time in this world. He knew because he felt an old feeling he hadn't felt for decades: frustration. "It's not so black and white," he said. "People make mistakes all the time. It's the intentions behind the actions that matter. If one person lies to protect their children, does that make them a bad person? If a young man leaves his pregnant partner for fear of being a bad father does it make him a bad man? You must let go of your hate, Karen."

"Humph, sounds a lot like a Get Out of Jail free card to me," she muttered. "Everyone would simply say their intentions were good."

"I know," Fabien sighed. "This is why humans make such bad judges."

He found her eyes so he would not shock or surprise her. When he had her attention he leaned gently across her arms and put the palm of his hand on her chest.

She felt a heat like she'd never known before, a heat that moved and folded inside her.

"Only God can see what's in a person's heart," he whispered. "Nothing saddens him more than seeing his children extradited by the misguided judgements of others, others who are not without sin themselves." He removed his hand and Karen coughed.

"God must be sad a lot, then."

"Never more than when such judgements take place in his name."

"Do you mean the Church?" Karen asked in a steadier voice.

"I mean the word of God getting lost in the word of man."

Karen felt as though her entire race was being scorned because they'd all gotten it so wrong.

Fabien awaited the next question but there was none. He was troubled to see that she had now withdrawn. She was gazing intensely at the gravel beneath her, as though the little pebbles there would give her the answers she needed.

"I didn't mean to patronize," he said. "I just wanted to explain that Sublims and Sprites reside in us all."

Karen did not answer; she was now watching an old married couple approaching, hand in hand. She envied their ignorance. The old man's cheeks told her he spent most of his mornings outdoors; they were red and veined like someone had splashed ink across his face. Karen wondered what form he took in Sublimina. She couldn't imagine him being anything but a Sublim no matter what Fabien said. "Why?" she suddenly asked. "If it's not such a big deal whether you project into a Sprite or a Sublim, then why the two separate forms in the first place?"

Fabien liked her train of thought; she was getting there all by herself. "Balance." he told her as he took her by the hand to walk with him. "The information they collect from your mind is reported to converters in Sublimina."

"What are converters?" Karen found herself confused again.

"You must know what converters are by now!" Fabien was surprised. "Converters will use the information of Sublims and Sprites to convert a soul to seek love or hate."

Karen didn't want to have to verbalize it, but Fabien was offering no answers and eventually she gave in.

"Vampires and werewolves," she said and watched him smile at her as if this were some great situation to be in, as if any of it was.

Chapter 33

Marcus checked his lunar dial. It was dusk: dawn in the waking world. He thought of the waking world now and his body ached. His limbs and shoulders told him he needed a muscle tonic. Staying up all night writing a letter that should have taken mere minutes hadn't helped matters.

Marcus took the stairs up to the great timber trap door above him. His footsteps sent a lonely echo through his pit. He pushed the door outward but it barely budged. He heaved against it a second time before it grudgingly groaned open, revealing the night.

Marcus was out of breath by the time he dragged his body out onto the soil of the forest. He looked to the sky. It was a bright night but it was warm and it was sticky. There was no breeze and the wildlife in the trees that usually had so much to say were silent.

Something was coming. He could sense it, just as he could sense there was something profoundly wrong with him. His throat burned but he couldn't drink. He hadn't fed in days. Human blood was beginning to taste like a liquid metal. He added a plasma tonic to his mental list for Hamied's Hub.

Marcus walked at a slow pace to sooth the burning sensation in his lungs. The air no longer fed them the oxygen they needed but burned them instead as though it were withdrawing his welcome to the world. He wasn't far now from Nixon Valley, he consoled himself.

Marcus passed several Sprites peeling the bark from a messenger tree, getting ready to report the opportunities they saw in the waking world. He envied them. He passed more and more until finally he came to the hustle and bustle of the Hub. There were always stalls outside the Hub. It was the only tonic-manufacturing site.

The shouting in the markets aggravated him horribly tonight.

This is worse than being alive, Marcus thought as he recalled Saturdays in Covent Garden. He still hadn't gotten used to his Greek accent after spending his waking life as an Englishman. But Greek was more alluring, Liam told him. It charmed the right kinds of people for this assignment. They had done their homework, the elder converters. An English accent wasn't something that conjured happy memories for the subject.

"The subject!" Marcus muttered to himself. It seemed so inaccurate a description. She was the key keeper. Surely she deserved a better title. Other than a prophet, she was the only living being who could use the key. They underestimated her. He would not make the same mistake. These so-called higher sentients weren't as clever as they thought. Marcus was clever. He knew he was. He had a plan; he always had a plan.

"Thunder Whiskey, sir?" A Sublim chanced his luck and stepped out in front of him. "That furrowed brow tells me you need it."

"I am a Child of Neptune; I always have a furrowed brow." Marcus snapped, and pushed the Sublim aside.

They still disturbed him, Sublims and Sprites, how could you tell where they were looking when their eyes had no pupils? Liam said it was because their eyes belonged in the waking world. It's what allowed them to see through the subconscious.

****

Marcus pushed his way through the great double doors of Hamied's Hub. He cherished the silence he found there. It was cold in the great stone atrium and not without reason. The temperature in this place was meticulously monitored and no room was heated to the same degree. The atrium was always cold, a natural deterrent for those impatient enough to wait for their orders on site.

Marcus's footsteps echoed as he approached the treatment desk. There was never a queue; most people made their own tonics. It was only the higher sentients who requested made-to-orders and they were done monthly.

"I need a couple of plasma and muscle tonics." Marcus said in a crisp tone. The Sprite behind the desk looked up but she could have been staring at the ceiling for all Marcus could tell.

"Outside the monthly order?"

Marcus never flinched. "Yes, we underestimated this month and I am newborn." He made himself appear busy by rummaging through the journals on display. He was searching to see if he could find any issues relating to the symptoms that plagued his once-powerful body.

He found nothing of significance as he sifted through the titles. *Pallas - The New Nixon Valley* read one title. Marcus put it back on the shelf and sighed. "Boring!" he huffed. "I'll be back to collect those."

The library was the only place he'd find any sort of credible answer, he decided. He took a shortcut through an alley behind the Hub and enjoyed the sound of the waterfalls. It made him pause momentarily. It was a thundering sound, the roaring sound of speeding water pouring into the dark river that separated Nixon Valley from Liekos Park.

He took the stone steps up the bridge two at a time and stopped in awe at the view beneath him. It was the only place that reminded him of being alive in this dark world. The water hitting the river below was forming massive mists that climbed up the darkness, determined to be seen. It began to look hazy and Marcus had to refocus his eyes, but everything still appeared blurred.

He huffed in annoyance at his deteriorating condition and continued to the library. He needed to find out what was happening to him and he needed to do it in secret. Every cell in his body told him sharing this with anyone would be dangerous.

Marcus liked the library. It was built in such a way that only one would ever be needed, a one-stop shop with titles on everything from human anatomy to doctrine, laws of the land and parliamentary scrolls.

"Excellent!" whispered Marcus. Elaina was working today; she had eyes for him. It was obvious. He walked right past her. He didn't want to use up any favours until necessary.

He went straight to the Higher Sentients' section and searched until he found an aisle on converters. *Great Converters of Our Times* he read and placed it to one side. *Mission Assignments 101*; this too he dismissed.

Interpretation the Tool was also pushed aside. Then he found what he was looking for: *The Transition*. Every converter would have read this at some point. He'd read it several times himself before, but now he was looking for specifics. Marcus browsed the table of contents in search of vampire illnesses but found nothing. Vampires didn't get sick. There was a section on common newborn experiences but nothing of importance to his situation.

He searched several other texts before Elaina came to offer assistance. "What happened to your arm?" she asked.

Marcus stared at the skin beside his elbow. It was raised and bruised. "Just a bit of a brawl on a mission."

Elaina took his arm in her hand. "Surely it should have healed by now. You should bear no marks, should you not?"

Her entirely blue eyes looked into his face with what he could only assume was concern. He would never learn how to read those eyes.

Marcus made a decision. "Exactly!" he said. "I should have healed by now." He looked around to make sure they were alone. "I'm worried it could be an attempt to sabotage my mission." He lowered his voice. "You know the consequences that would bring the perpetrator, don't you?"

Elaina gasped. "It is forbidden! No feud from the conscious realm should continue in Sublimina. Has a Child of the Moon threatened you?" she asked with motherly concern.

"No," whispered Marcus. "But I'm not feeling myself." He held up the black hardback book in his hand. "According to this, vampires don't get sick, but I'm off my game. I'm sluggish, I've lost my appetite and my lungs burn."

"You have to tell someone! If a converter is responsible for this, it is a crime punishable by death."

Marcus pulled her close. "That's exactly why we should keep quiet about this. Not until we're absolutely certain a Child of the Moon is responsible. If we're wrong then an innocent converter could be put to death. We need more information. Can you do this for me?" he whispered.

"Of course." Her breath was quickening and Marcus let her go.

"There's something else. I need you to find a Sprite who works in passport control in the waking world and I need her to get a fake passport issued for this person." Marcus handed her a picture.

Elaina examined it closely. It was creased and the edges were torn in places but she could still make out every detail, every freckle on Karen's nose and curl in her hair.

Chapter 34

Karen was thinking of her rosary beads. It made perfect sense now that they would be the key. Her father had left them to her. She thought of Connor and she wondered if their father knew she was destined to carry the key, or if he had chosen her to carry it.

Fabien broke her train of thought. "I think he's getting tired." He nodded to Buddy who had indeed fallen behind.

Karen picked him up and looked around her. She wondered how long they had been walking. "Where are we?"

"I think you call it Manion Park. It reminds me of Sublimina here." Fabien peeled some loose bark from a tree.

"I think I've been there – Sublimina, I mean. Is it possible for me to dream of it?"

"Quite possible." Fabien returned to the walking track. "You are of the Key Holder clan. You have no projection in Sublimina; you can visit it any time you like and still remember it when you wake. I would be surprised if you hadn't been dreaming of it. You've been looking for me whether you know it or not."

Karen recalled her wanderings through the familiar moonlit forests. "You spend most of your time in Aingeal Forest," she told him.

Now it was Fabien's turn to look frazzled. "I do." He raised an eyebrow. "Most angels do. It is bright and we can meditate there. Not like here." He sighed as he looked about him.

"I asked for directions," Karen continued, "but everyone I met ignored me."

"They can't see you. Not unless you were wearing the key and intended to go there. The key allows you to exist in both realities whether it is day or night."

Karen saw an opportunity to redeem the intelligence of her race and she grasped it gratefully. "So we didn't get *everything* wrong then. All our stories call vampires and werewolves night walkers, which would be correct considering they can't come here in the day."

Fabien was surprised at her compulsion to defend her brothers and sisters of the waking world. He realized that he had blasted her reality apart and made her feel like she'd been living in ignorance all her life and it saddened him. "Of course you didn't get everything wrong." His voice was gentle. "On the contrary: people have been in tune to something more for centuries now."

"I don't think reading *Dracula* counts." Karen was looking forlorn.

"What about the concept of yin and yang?" Fabien asked.

"That's something the human race has been in tune with for centuries. You may hold the white key and *they* may hold black but we both fight for balance. Isn't that what yin and yang are about? Isn't that something humans have discovered alone?"

Karen found no solace in his words. She thought of the key. She thought of the dusty drawers they'd rested in over the years.

Fabien appeared to be thinking of them too. "Can you imagine how the balance would be in our favour if we had someone to convert souls by day?

"Not really." Karen shrugged. "So they could create more Sprites? Not such a bad thing according to you."

"Not such a bad thing in manageable numbers," Fabien corrected. "Did you ever wonder how one man could convince entire nations that women were evil?"

Karen wasn't sure she'd heard correctly. "Nobody ever thought women were evil."

Fabien raised one of his sandy coloured eyebrows; it lifted a curl his fringe had left there. "So thousands of women weren't tortured and burned at the stake in the 1400s?" he asked.

"*Shite!*" Karen couldn't help the word from escaping her mouth. She was sure cursing in the presence of an angel wasn't a good idea but Fabien didn't seem to notice.

"Do you see now the power a prophet with a key can have? How one man can influence millions?"

"What happened to the black key?" Karen was frightened of the object ever turning up again, frightened of another dark prophet using it to bring forth the most dangerous converters.

"No one knows, the dark prophet disappeared shortly after the witch hunts ended."

"Was he killed?" Karen was hopeful.

"A prophet with a key cannot be killed, unless they wish it of course."

"Or unless they give it up," Karen added.

"Why would they do that? No I suspect the prospect of immortality appealed to him. Metzger was renowned for his indulgent lifestyle. I expect he still has it but doesn't use it so as not to draw attention to himself."

"Bummer for the dark side!" Karen sniggered "But if the white key can only be used by a pure soul, then why is the banshee chasing it? It's not like she can use it, and neither can I, at least not to convert people anyway."

"She wants it so she can hide it," Fabien explained.

Karen was beginning to shiver. Buddy was warm and she held him close but even he was losing his heat.

Fabien placed his muscular arm around her and she felt safe.

"Why hide it?" Karen asked. "Why not just destroy it?"

"She can't destroy it. She can't even hide it in Sublimina; she can only hide it in the waking world where all battles are fought." Fabien dug his free hand into his jacket pocket and retrieved the tired-looking shamrock he'd used earlier. "Do you remember the divine leaf I told you about?"

"The top one?"

"Yes." Fabien looked impressed. "Well, it is from the divine leaf that prophets are chosen.

"Was our white key ever used?" Karen felt like she already knew the answer; there were millions of possible names floating around her head.

"Of course!" Fabien flashed a knowing smile and put his hands behind his back as he walked. "It was used with much greater success too. A young Roman by the name of Saul." Fabien spoke like a scholar, a scholar on a subject Karen had never taken. He kept his hands behind his back and his head to the sky as he spoke.

"Never heard of him."

"Of course you have." Fabien smiled warmly. "There isn't a man alive who hasn't. Ancient texts refer to him as Saul of Tarsus. In Greek they know him as Saulos, and in English you will know him as St Paul."

Chapter 35

Connor knocked at Bradys' front door. It stood out from the rest of the terraced houses in the neighbourhood. It was solid varnished oak. Rhetson Court looked like an estate made out of cheap Lego pieces, the ones you had left over after building the main station. Bradys' was the main station in this Legoland and it looked out of place.

Connor knocked again. He knew Rick was home. There were no cars in the driveway but he could hear music from the back extension. A fumbling came from inside and he could just make out a figure through the long panes at each side of door.

"Hey," Rick greeted him half-heartedly when he opened the door. It looked like it was all he had the energy to say. His long and scraggy hair was stuck to his forehead with sweat and he was perspiring through his sports top.

"Aw, not you too!" Connor moaned and threw up his hands dramatically.

"What?" Rick was struggling to catch his breath.

"Working out, staying in shape, needing a makeover, needing a girlfriend."

Rick watched his friend make imaginary air quotes with his hands in amusement. "Jeez, relax! I'm going back to karate. I'll get hammered if I don't train."

"What's got you back into that?"

Rick never finished anything he started. He'd surprised everyone by staying long enough to earn his brown belt. "Maybe you should join." Rick pointed to his friend's growing belly.

Connor stared at him open-mouthed. Why was everyone picking on his abs, or lack thereof? "You know I was gonna see if you wanted to come down the bookies with me. Got us some hot tips, but you can go back a donkey now for all I care."

"Give me two minutes." Rick ran back inside for a baseball cap to cover his sweaty head. "Are we not taking the motorbike?" He noticed Connor had left it in the driveway.

Connor patted his stomach lovingly, "No, no, let's walk."

The sky was grey and the forecast was for snow. It was a dark December afternoon and it was beginning to feel like Christmas.

"So what's all this about a makeover?" Rick asked, shoving his cold hands into his pockets.

"Karen!" Connor spat with semi-annoyance.

Rick waved a hand in dismissal. "That's just what women do. Your sister always tells me my clothes don't match. You're not meant to listen."

"Yeah, but yours don't. Even I can see that. You'd wear pink and red together *and* you wear multi-coloured shoelaces."

"Least I wear some colour. All you ever wear is black and grey. You look like a walking photograph from the sixties."

"Ah ha!" Connor cried in victory. "So you *do* think I need a makeover. You're such a woman!"

Rick went quiet for a little while. "Let her have her fun," he told his friend.

****

Makeovers were far from Karen's mind as she pushed her way in the front door, almost falling over Connor's boots again. It would have been polite to invite Fabien back, she knew. They'd spent hours walking in the cold but she had no more left to give, not even to Connor, who she was hoping was out.

Karen was relieved to find all the lights off. She called to her brother, hoping for no answer. There was none; she called again. He was definitely out. She heaved a heavy sigh of relief and marched upstairs and straight to her bedside locker. She opened the drawer and began mooching. She shuffled through books and train timetables until she found them. They were exactly where she'd left them. She expelled a puff of air from her lips in relief. *"The Key!"* she whispered and held it close.

Downstairs Buddy was passed out in front of the fire. Karen lay on the rug beside him with nothing to do but think. Why, when there was so much to digest, was Marcus the only thought in her mind? Marcus had been lying all this time. He had been sent to find out what form the key was in. He had never cared for her. This was the part Karen was having the most trouble with. Why had his eyes told her different? Vampires were supposed to be immortal but it seemed that was just another thing she'd got wrong.

Karen relived the final moments of Marcus's life in her head. She saw him hit square in the chest with a blast that sent him below the murky waters, never to resurface, and she cried. Tears poured in hot streams down her face. Their salty flavour reached her mouth and she ignored it. Wiping them would somehow be admitting her grief and she could not mourn him. It would be a betrayal of her father and of Bertha and the life that was stolen from her.

Fabien had told her Bertha was a seer. Those who have heard the scream of the banshee will always see her and her world.

Karen laid another stick on the fire. An angry spark jumped out and burned her hand. She dropped the stick like a hot potato. Buddy woke and came rushing over to see if it was in fact a hot potato. Disappointed, he sat back down.

****

Connor found his sister staring at the fire when he came home. "Guess where I've just been!"

"The bookies?" Karen guessed without taking her gaze from the fire.

"Yes, but after that. I went clothes shopping."

"That's not how a makeover works. I have to be with you and help choose."

"Who needs help?" Connor pulled a black hoodie from the bag.

Karen reluctantly took her gaze from the fire. "Another black hoodie that looks identical to all your other black hoodies."

Connor stared at it intently. "How can you say that? Look at these green stripes down the sides, none of my other ones have that. And look, there's a crest at the back."

Karen stared at the cheap and tacky logo. "Oh, brother." she whispered, rubbing her eyes. "What else did you get?"

"Just something for the baby." Connor pulled out a red baby grow for aged nine to twelve months

"What baby?" Karen was confused.

"Darcy, Andrew's baby."

Karen sat up, indignant. "Katie had her baby?"

Connor looked pensive for a moment. "Oh, yeah, sorry; Mam rang this morning. Now I think of it she *did* say to call her back too."

Karen snapped the baby grow from his hands.

"Oh, you're useless. I could have gone to see her. I'm working tomorrow, so I'll have to wait till the weekend now. And could you not have gotten something pink?"

Connor snapped it back and held it up to the light. "That *is* pink!" he looked confused.

"And is she a giant?" Karen asked. "Nine to twelve months!" she muttered, half laughing.

Chapter 36:

Penbrook looked like an alien planet to Karen as she entered the office on Monday morning. She recognized everyone but she knew no one. She'd been gone only a week, but everything had changed in that week.

The last time she'd walked these floors she had been living in ignorance, blissful ignorance. Now all she could think about was who was a Sublim and who was a Sprite. Not that it mattered much according to Fabien. It was the volume and degree of change that mattered. But still, she couldn't help herself.

"Welcome back!" Brenda greeted in a tone too enthusiastic to be genuine.

She was definitely a Sprite, Karen decided. In fact, there may be another creature entirely for Brenda's category. She wondered briefly if bullfrogs had any part to play in Sublimina.

Ronan from IT bade her a more pleasant good morning and she found herself imagining how he might look in Sublimina. She tried to imagine his pupils replaced with nothing but the colour blue, but she failed and ended up embarrassing him instead. *Great! He'll think I fancy him now*, she thought.

Karen's desk was exactly how she had left it. A mountain of paperwork that had seemed so important last week now seemed meaningless.

"How was the trip?" Zara asked as she passed by her desk.

Karen coughed on the perfume she left lingering in the air as she passed. "Good," she said. She watched as Zara threw her coat on the rack and rummaged through her bag for some lipstick before settling in for a long day of doing nothing.

Olivia and Will arrived together but there was no sign of Sam.

Karen opened her inbox to see if there was an absence profile but hundreds of other emails were screaming to be read. Later she would thank them for giving her a focus, for showing her life wasn't over, that it had just changed. Policies still had to be issued, people still needed insurance and Brenda still needed to feel in charge.

Karen learned at lunch hour that Sam had been off sick for the past week. She had been snappy and short-tempered before her absence.

"Nothing to worry about," Will told her. "You women get like that sometimes, don't you?"

"I don't know," Olivia said. "She even told Brenda that Lawrence was only using her for a visa. Something's definitely not right."

"That's not like her," Karen admitted. "She'd normally at least have the decency to say it behind her back."

Will shook his head. "How is that any better?"

Olivia and Karen responded in unison, "It just is."

****

Galford's had many office blocks under construction. Dan and Fabien had been residing in one of the more developed suites. It was thirteen stories high and the view stretched the length of the industrial park.

Dan was looking down at it now. Evidence of his turmoil lay scattered about the place. Coffee cups were stacked by the sink and a couple of newspapers lay open at the crime pages. A young policeman had been left concussed after coming across a senseless and violent murder. The article occupied his mind for a brief few moments but not enough to distract him completely.

Eventually he gave in to the tears that had been threatening to fall all afternoon. They ran down his cheeks, meandering through fields of stubble until they met his lips and seeped into the corners of his mouth.

He was still standing there when Fabien returned. Dan cleared his throat so as to disguise his distress. "How is she?" He asked without taking his gaze from the window.

"She will be okay," Fabien answered. "She is your daughter after all."

Chapter 37

"It's snowing." Olivia sounded disappointed. Karen turned to peer outside, and sure enough, gentle white flakes were tossing themselves in icy eruptions against the window.

But not even the snow could make the offices at Penbrook look pretty. The pretty white flakes turned to brown mush as soon as they fell on the concrete. Karen was unaware that Penbrook held in the depths of its bowels a more disturbing force in the form of a sulking Brenda Butcher. Brenda was standing, arms folded, staring out the top window at the late arrivals trudging into her midst. They were taking advantage of her good nature, she decided, just because she was an understanding boss. She still had targets to meet. She had to meet Lawrence for lunch. Had anyone even considered the fact that he was only here for another few days?

Brenda heard the lifts open and quickly made up her mind on how best to deal with her staff. She felt she was gifted in the area of communication and diplomacy; she knew just how to handle them.

When her team finally made it back to their seats, Brenda huffed in frustration as she wrestled her jacket onto her shoulders. "I'm late now!" she muttered to herself. "Hope he's still there."

Brenda made sure everyone was on edge for the rest of the afternoon. She hinted relentlessly at the mayhem that resulted from extended lunch breaks. Olivia found blood in her mouth from biting her lip so hard. Will busied himself with archiving and Karen struggled not to message Sam. Fabien had forbidden it. Sam was being influenced by a converter now, a vampire, or a Child of Neptune as he called them. Either way she was being used to collect information.

If they found out Karen knew about the key then it was game over. Right now Karen supposed ignorance was all that was keeping her safe. She popped her phone back into her bag, feeling less tempted to contact her friend, and finished her reports instead.

****

The train station was dirty and smelly and full of people impatiently brushing shoulders. Public transport was always delayed in bad weather. You could bank on it being late more than you could rely on it being on time. Karen shivered a little into the collar she'd rolled up about her face but it wasn't keeping her warm. The digital clock told her there was a twenty-minute delay. Karen knew it was a lie. Twenty minutes meant forty. She imagined a mischievous group of engineers programming it just so and giggling at her expense.

Karen let out a heavy sigh as she stared out across the tracks. Hundreds of freezing faces stared back at her and her heart stopped when she recognized one. It was Marcus. They stared at each other in silence until the train arrived and tore through the invisible line that connected them. A moment passed and he was gone. People were already filling the gap he'd left. Karen felt her knees wobble but she made them move.

Her delayed reactions cost her a seat on the train but she didn't care; standing was better than falling. Her breath was short and she wasn't sure if her shaking was from cold or shock. She held on to the cold metal rail and tried to make sense of her feelings. There was anger, definitely anger; there was fear and anxiety also, but something else was lurking beneath and she fought to convince herself it wasn't relief that Marcus was okay.

Hordes of commuters moved in waves towards the door when the train finally stopped at Ashton Park. Karen fought her way through them with more aggression than usual. She would have to call Fabien, she decided. Her cold blue hands found her mobile phone at the bottom of her handbag and she dialled in his number.

Karen could hear drilling the other end of the telephone. She could hear her brother's voice in the background. Fabien said he would arrange for Connor to work late. They could speak in private with Dan. Karen felt guilty, leaving her brother in the dark again.

Chapter 38

Fabien snapped shut his little flip phone, thinking this disconnected the line. He would make this mistake several times a day, which infuriated Dan, who had shown him a million times already how to use the damn thing.

Dan watched him end the call from across the room and read his eyes. He went straight for the door and threw his jacket across his shoulders.

"Where are you going, princess?" Connor asked.

"There's some place I have to be!" Dan responded without looking at him.

"Yeah, welding this," Connor called after him. "Where's he gone?" he asked Fabien.

"I can weld," Fabien assured him. "He needs to get back to the apartment."

"Do you find it hard?" Connor asked after a while.

"What?"

"Living and working with the same person."

"No," Fabien replied truthfully, but he wasn't paying much attention. His eyes were scrutinizing the framework of the build for an opportunity. He found what he was looking for in the hallway. He took a look behind him before placing his hand over the wall bracket. He held his hand over it until it melted into a pasty gloop and then turned to dust. He opened his eyes. He twisted and elevated the brace until it looked like it might threaten to fall. Then he called Connor.

"Come and have a look at this." *This will keep him busy for hours*, Fabien mused.

"What?" Connor sounded impatient.

"There's no bracket for this brace." Fabien showed him. "Is it okay?" he asked innocently.

Connor touched the surface, as if his eyes were deceiving him. "Paul put this up yesterday. I watched him. We'd never miss a bracket."

"You are only human. Perhaps it's the supporting block you are thinking of."

Connor shook his head. He was hungry and he just wanted to go home for some dinner and a hot shower. "This will take hours!" he complained. "Not to mention getting home. Have you seen the weather?"

"I can come back and collect you?" Fabien offered. "Cars are safer in this weather."

"Not yours!" Connor joked.

"I don't mind coming back for you." Fabien insisted.

But Connor wasn't listening. He sat, deflated, on one of the crates.

"It's okay," he ran his hands through his dusty hair. "The evening's a write off now, no matter what time I get home."

****

Karen's hair flopped in layers of sudsy strands onto her face. She left it there and stood under the spray of the showerhead. She kept her head down and watched as the water turned from creamy white to crystal clear. Her skin began to thaw out and the numbness in her fingers and toes dissipated.

Dan was waiting for her in the living room. "What did he want?" He launched into his inquisition. "How did you get away?"

"I didn't have to," Karen explained.

"What do you mean?" Dan furrowed his bushy brows.

"One minute he was there and the next he was gone. He didn't hurt me."

"Probably too many people around and he got nervous."

233

Fabien looked pensive. "Whatever the reason, we need to rethink our strategy. Everything has changed now he's aware you know about the key."

Karen wasn't used to seeing worry in Fabien's eyes.

Dan stopped pacing all of a sudden. "We could move in!" he exclaimed. "You need twenty-four-hour protection and we can provide that if we're all under the one roof. We could say our place was flooded, burnt down, broken into, anything."

The look of expectancy on his face indicated the conviction he had for his plan but Fabien appeared unconvinced. "We need to accept the possibility that Karen may need to come to Sublimina for a time."

Dan acted like he hadn't heard him. He took a gulp of the coffee Karen had made him and began pacing again. "Connor will agree if you say you don't mind us moving in. You just have to sound convincing." He looked imploringly at Karen.

"Yes, but we need a Plan B," Fabien insisted. "We need to talk about this."

"Not yet we don't," Dan argued. "Think of the consequences."

"It will appear to everyone that she is in a coma. It will kill her mother. And what if they turn off life support? It's too risky. You can't just sleep for a couple of weeks and expect no one to notice." He finished by slicing the air with his hands by way of final protest.

"It's too risky not to," Fabien countered. "It will remain as a last option."

Karen wasn't sure how she felt about going to Sublimina. Another world, a world she would now have contact with. It had been enjoyable as a dream but to actually be somewhere else while her body remained here was disconcerting and she found herself agreeing with Dan for once. "I like the moving-in idea."

Dan looked elated. "I won't let anything happen to you," he promised.

"I know that." Karen was surprised by how much she trusted him.

****

By the end of the week the house felt crowded. Connor moaned about falling over Dan's boots. He moaned about the whistling that kept him up at night. Karen hoped it would make him more house-proud when they left. But she didn't want them to leave. She hadn't realized she'd felt so lonely before.

Dan played cards with her late into the nights she was too frightened to sleep. He taught her how to play solitaire for the times he wasn't there. He said it calmed his mind. "Nobody dies if you lose," he told her.

"How many others have you guarded?" Karen asked.

"Converted," Dan corrected her.

"But you're not here to convert me," Karen clarified "You're protecting me."

Dan fumbled uneasily in his chair. "These are exceptional circumstances. Angels like Fabien don't normally appear for such lengths in the waking world. I'm just here to assist when he needs to recuperate."

"How long do they usually spend here?"

Dan was losing concentration. She had been cheating the entire game, picking up three instead of four and he never noticed.

"Not long." He sighed. "Angels only appear when the need is great, or if the subject has potential to change things radically. Converters can be too slow sometimes."

He scratched at his stubble and rubbed the back of his neck. He did this when he was nervous, she noticed. It reminded her of her uncle and she didn't want him to leave.

Chapter 39

It wasn't often the twins brought home guests and Catherine had sent Wayne down to the grocery store for food. Darcy mooched in her arms. She was a perfect little thing. Catherine kissed her head and worried about her own daughter. How would she react? Would it be too painful for her? Karen loved children; she was one of those maternal people Catherine had never understood.

Catherine loved her own children but she had never yearned to have them, not the way most women did. Nor had she the desire to stay at home all day with them as babies. It caused a guilt that shadowed her heart. She had never spoken of it to anyone but Daniel. She'd shared everything with him; not by choice – he could just read her that well. He was the only one who knew her completely and still loved her, and then he left her.

A fumbling sound echoed down the hall from the front door; someone was trying to get in with the wrong key. "That would be my son." she whispered to Darcy. "You will hear some profanities shortly." she warned the sleeping baby. Sure enough Connor could be heard entering with his guests.

Karen's was the first face Catherine searched for and she felt like someone had punched her in the gut when she found it. She looked horrendous. Her curls had lost their bounce and black bags puffed up from beneath her eyes, but they brightened when they spotted the baby. Catherine watched her daughter melt as she took the infant. Karen's body sank down with her on the armchair, like a yearning had been satisfied.

"Wow!" was all she said and she looked like she was breathing for the first time.

"This is Dan and Fabien." Connor interrupted the moment by introducing his friends.

Fabien produced a bottle of merlot. "You have a lovely home." he said looking about him.

Dan fought to keep his composure and urged the muscles in his neck to form a nod of courtesy. The voices around him seemed to fade into nothingness as he watched the only woman he'd ever loved treat him like a stranger. Of course he was a stranger to her. She had no way of recognizing him in his current form. She hadn't changed, he noticed. Time had been kind to her. She still commanded a room, still made it appear that she was the only one in it. Dan fought the instinct to hold her.

Fabien stepped in front of his line of vision – on purpose, he suspected – and he was grateful for it. He'd tried to prepare him, but Daniel had never been very good at meditation. So he held on to what he *was* good at – determination. He would not let them down again. Nothing or no one would harm them.

He turned his attention to his only niece, the daughter his brother swore he'd never have. She looked like Esther, he noticed. Same slim face and bone structure; she was beautiful.

Karen felt Dan's gaze upon her but she didn't care, she was losing herself again, or was it finding herself? She wondered. She had that same floating feeling she'd experienced when Fabien laid his hand on her chest. The feeling told her she wasn't Karen O'Driscoll anymore; names weren't important, this place wasn't important, only what you felt in it. She felt like a floating soul, holding another floating soul and they would always be connected.

Connor mistook his sister's tears for sadness and tried to take the baby, but the smile he saw on her face enlightened him, and he laughed with relief. Then he laughed at Darcy's tiny hands and her curling little toes.

Andrew startled them all. He took everyone in from the doorway before his eyes finally fell on Karen and he froze.

"Give her to me!" he instructed. "I'll take her now," he added in a futile attempt at sounding more polite.

"She's fine," Catherine assured him. "You're meant to be taking a break with Katie."

Andrew gave an unconvincing smile. "New mothers – you know what they're like. She misses her already."

****

Connor listened to the mumblings of the guests downstairs.

He splashed a handful of cold water on his burning face and stared at his reflection in the mirror.

He was feeling dizzy, and he sat on the edge of the bath in frustration. He looked down at his belly and wondered if the pains in his chest had to do with the excess weight he'd been carrying. He was tempted to go to his mother's study and look up his symptoms, but he was afraid of what he might find.

"What's wrong?" Karen appeared from behind the door.

Connor almost fell into the bath. "You scared the life out of me." He grabbed his chest. "I thought you were all downstairs."

"I was." Karen sat beside him. "But I felt you might need me."

A thought occurred to Connor then that seemed to cheer him a little.

"Do you think they might be sympathy pains?" he asked hopefully. "Like when each of us knows if there's something wrong with the other?" he asked. "You've been ill recently; it could be a twin thing."

Karen looked doubtful. It was probably more likely to do with the amount of whiskey he'd drunk while they were away.

"I'll try feeling better." She gave him a reassuring smile.

"Well, try feeling great, will you?"

Chapter 40

Catherine was trying to prepare a lasagne in time for Katie and Andrew's arrival with the baby. She'd forgotten the layer of white sauce and she was now shoving it awkwardly under each pasta sheet and cursing under her breath.

Dan's acute sense of hearing meant he heard every muffled word. He noticed Fabien shaking his head at him from the doorway but he ignored him.

"Can I help?" Dan asked in his husky tone.

Catherine was silent. The depth of his voice had stumped her.

"I'm a surgeon. I mean I'm a doctor," she said awkwardly.

"I'm sure you're very good." Dan smiled.

"No," Catherine said feeling stupid. "I just mean this should be easy, but I found med school easier than I find this."

"I'll bet it's fine."

Dan took a slicer in his hand and raised the sheets to allow her to spread the sauce evenly. Her scent wafted its way through the narrowing space between them and he inhaled it deeply.

Fabien had seen enough. He raised his eyes to the heavens and left.

"Humans!" he muttered as he went to answer the front door.

As soon as he opened the door he regretted it. The muscles in his face tightened in an effort to mask the impact he felt from the negativity in the air. He looked to each of the guests to pinpoint the source. Esther was holding a baking tray; it wasn't coming from her. Katie was holding her baby, and exuded nothing but exhaustion. Andrew was definitely the culprit. He was smiling politely but his eyes were twitching against the emotion they hid. His aura was infected with a blackness that drained the light from Fabien's spirit.

Fabien winced as Andrew stepped past him. The air thickened further when Dan entered the same room as his brother, and Fabien began to feel overwhelmed.

Dan was harbouring a bitter disappointment. He watched his brother let everyone hold his child but Karen. Each time she extended her arms he would find some feeble excuse to take her back: to change her bib, or to fix her hair, even though she only had three strands.

****

Marcus was watching them through the blacked out windows of the car he'd stolen. It was still bright outside and he was counting the minutes until sunset. He knew if he got out now it would be the end of him. But every muscle in his body was twitching to get out of the car. He rooted through his pockets in a frenzied effort to find a lighter and then lit a cigarette to distract himself.

He watched as trails of grey smoke puffed from between his lips in frantic formations. It reminded him of his own direction in life – bursting with enthusiastic certainty only to be met by nothingness and then dissolve into emptiness.

Time passed as he watched the orange cinders creep up the cigarette with every drag he took. He was feeling a little calmer now. He sniffed the air. It was time.

The last rays of sunlight had died and he opened the car door. He crossed the yard and made his way to the back door of the large farmhouse. It had looked much bigger when he was alive, he noticed. There were no lights outside; no one would welcome him here. He didn't care. He'd only come for her.

But even *she* looked horrified to see him.

Karen was speechless; she had to look twice before she recognized Marcus. His cheeks were drawn and hollow and the bones of his face accentuated like craters.

"Who is it?" Catherine called. But Karen couldn't answer.

"Get inside, Karen!" Dan appeared behind her. The tone of his voice brought her back to earth.

Marcus peered over Karen's shoulder to get a closer look at her father.

"Oh, I don't think so, Daddy." He smiled politely. "We have things to discuss, Karen and I. We can do it in private or we can do it inside with the whole family. I'm sure someone will offer themselves as dinner." Marcus raised his head slightly. "Is that Esther I hear? I do like a bit of mutton."

A pulsating vein was threatening to pop through the skin of Dan's temple and he was sure he would have torn the vampires head off if Fabien hadn't appeared beside him.

Fabien looked steadily at Marcus. He looked to Karen's body language for guidance.

"If we give you five minutes with her, you will give us the word of Neptune that you disclose nothing to the people inside this house."

Dan looked like Fabien had just suggested they all go skinny-dipping, but he didn't argue. Fabien's eyes had seen something that Dan hadn't and Dan had learned to trust the angel.

Marcus's face changed the moment the door shut behind them. The confident in-control demeanour he'd flaunted had all but disappeared and panic and uncertainty was all that was left. "Are you ready?" he asked. "Where's your stuff? I suppose you don't need anything. New start, new stuff, right?"

He grabbed her hand and turned toward the car he'd parked across the yard. "You got my letter!" he continued, dragging her along by his side. "I knew you'd understand. It's because we belong together, you see!" he told her. "We did ten years ago and we still do now, even when I'm dead." He laughed crazily.

"What happened to you?" Karen was shaking her head in disbelief. "You're making no sense, even for you."

"You know what happened. It's in the letter. I messed up, I admit that."

"What letter?" Karen was still shaking her head.

"We don't have time for this!" Marcus sighed and scratched at his head. "I know you got it. You took it from the floor as I slid it under your bedroom door. Now we have to get going if we're to have any kind of life together."

Karen watched him check his chest pockets for his keys. He seemed so familiar to her, even his clothes. The grey linen jacket he was wearing was her favourite, but the last time she'd seen it she knew the person beneath it.

Marcus sensed her hesitation and for the first time since his arrival he realized they were on two very different pages. He looked around him to check no one was pursuing him from the house and when he turned to her he wore a sincerity that almost reached her. "I love you!" he said. "And I know you love me too. You stole my heart and I stole yours."

Karen watched the hope in his eyes swirl with anticipation. She thought carefully before answering. She thought about the night they'd met. She thought about how safe he'd made her feel in their little bubble. "The only thing you ever stole from me was a watch and a locket." Her voice was steady and even. "And the only reason I'm giving you these five minutes is to protect the people inside that house. I'd sooner be caught, and rot in the ground than go anywhere with you. You disgust me."

Marcus darkened. "Oh, you think so, do you? You think you'd be better off caught by her than elope with me?" he asked threateningly. "You think you'll be saying that when your ears are bleeding and your heart stops, do you?"

Karen was stepping back to match the steps Marcus was taking forward.

"You think she'll just politely take that key from you and be on her merry little way, do you?" His voice was getting louder and harder. He was so close to her face now that she could feel splashes of furious spit hitting her cheeks. "She'll rip the bloody womb right out of you just to be sure there'll be no more key keepers after you. Did you know that?" He grabbed both of her arms in a tight grip.

Karen didn't hear them coming but Fabien and Dan were by her side before she even tried to break free. Dan went to grab her but Marcus was too quick. He thrust her body behind his own and she found her head in a vice-like headlock. She couldn't move and she struggled to breathe. He had looked so skinny and harmless only moments earlier; she would never have thought him capable of such strength.

"Step the hell back or I swear by Neptune I'll crack her neck like a nut," Marcus threatened.

Anger swam dangerously in his eyes and Dan looked like a hurricane was tearing up his insides.

But Fabien never flinched. "No you won't!" "Don't test me!" Marcus produced a knife out of nowhere and pressed it to the throat of the woman he loved so much that he hated.

Karen never felt it, it pricked the surface of her skin but she had lost consciousness from the stranglehold he had on her.

"Why the knife?" Fabien asked. "*You:* the son of a Gorgon? Is it that you're feeling more like your human self, perhaps?" Fabien inclined his head with interest. "Your accent is returning," he added. "I suspect you will lose the appearance you chose shortly."

Marcus appeared to flinch, as though Fabien's words were cutting him.

"Soon she will recognize you, I suspect."

Marcus shot a look in Dan's direction. "She doesn't recognize *him*!" he spat. "Not even his own family does."

"Of course not, the form he chose here isn't fading like yours."

Dan wasn't looking at either of them; he was watching his daughter and silently counting the seconds she'd been without oxygen.

Fabien had exactly two and a half minutes left to execute whatever little plan he was concocting, and then it was his turn. He was already planning how he would dispose of Marcus.

"Leave!" Fabien advised. "You don't want her to see you this way."

No one saw it coming. Marcus was fast; he had plunged a knife into many necks in the past year. It felt like piercing butter with a pin. But this one felt better than all the rest. He felt like he was back on top again.

Blood poured from Dan's neck onto his shoulders and all the way down his chest. Fabien caught him as he fell, when Marcus released the knife from his jugular.

Marcus had Karen in the car before anyone realized what was happening.

When she regained consciousness she thought she was dreaming. The only things she could make out were colours, colours blurring and blending together as they whizzed past her eyes, and she realized it was a forest speeding past her through a car windscreen. She turned her head to the driver but her neck ached and she cried out in pain.

"You're awake!" Marcus took his eyes from the wheel for an instant. "You shouldn't make me angry, you know; it's stupid. You can be really stupid sometimes, you know." He was blinking erratically like there was something in his eyes, and he wiped them ferociously.

When Karen regained her senses she realized it was blood. He was bleeding from his eyes. It made a red river down the sides of his nose and smudged across his cheeks in messy shapes where he'd wiped it.

"Jesus!" Karen was horrified. She wondered how long she'd been out for.

"Seconds!" Marcus told her. "He's not the only one who can read you." he clarified when he saw the look of horror on her face.

Chapter 41

Connor looked about the kitchen. "Where is everyone?" he asked.

He was feeling better after a very cold shower. The water felt like it sizzled as it met with his sweaty skin.

"Catherine?" he shouted.

Catherine shook herself. "Sorry!" she turned to her son "I was miles away. They went to Fox's when Karen's boyfriend arrived."

"Marcus?" Connor asked, surprised that Dan and Fabien would go anywhere with him.

"Is there another boyfriend?" Catherine raised her eyebrows.

"No that's the one all right." Connor sighed.

"Why did he have to come here anyway? Could he not give the girl some space?"

"She likes him, you know," Connor muttered.

"I know," Catherine worried.

Connor felt uneasy when he noticed his mother shake. He hadn't known she was so upset. He looked away uncomfortably but then realized that it wasn't her who was shaking but the kitchen itself.

Everything his eyes rested on swayed. He blinked hard but nothing would stand still. He had to hold on to the countertop to steady himself. *I will not fall!* he told himself and shut his eye tightly.

When he opened them again he prepared himself to focus but there was no need. Everything was clear and crisp, too clear and crisp. His vision was heightened as though he were looking through binoculars. Everything seemed so close he had to take a step back. He backed into the hallway before anyone could notice his peculiar episode, but the claustrophobic feeling there was worse. The walls were closing in on him. They were so close now he could make out the brush strokes. He could see the colour they used to be. He hadn't seen that yellow since he was a teenager, and the green before that. He realized that this was probably the last colour his father had seen in the house and he felt sick.

What would his father have thought of him now? Some man of the house he'd turned out to be. The only manly thing he'd managed in the last five years was to call his mother by her first name. He would probably be turning in his grave to see his son now. Connor winced.

****

But his father wasn't turning in his grave; he was turning in a bed of green rushes while an elderly Sublim lay a dark plant across his neck.

"When can he return?" Fabien asked, his arms folded.

Daniel shot up from the herbaceous bed, spilling the healing fluid down his neck and chest.

"Hold still!" the Sublim shoved him back down with force and leaned hard on Dan's wound.

Daniel fought to free himself. "What the hell are you doing here? Tell me you've stopped that idiot boy taking my daughter."

"Oh, don't worry about him." Fabien waved his hand dismissively. "He's not going to hurt her."

Fabien dodged the surprisingly swift lunge to his torso and transported himself back to Griffin before Dan finished expressing his anger.

****

"Marcus!" Karen whispered.

Marcus was shaking violently at the steering wheel. His chest was rising and falling rapidly and a grinding noise came from his mouth.

Karen watched as blood began to bubble from between his lips and he raised his hand to his mouth to catch a tooth.

"Marcus!"

"It's fine," he insisted, with a lisp born from the gaps where his teeth used to be. "I can still protect you. We'll be okay."

A blanket of melancholy descended on Karen when it dawned on her that all that was left of the man beside her was spirit. It was the only thing left in a body that was mercilessly deserting him. She wondered what would happen if he were to stop and accept his fate.

"Stop the car. I know what to do; I know how we can be safe and still be together."

Marcus looked sceptical. "You cannot trick me."

"No tricks!" Karen assured him. "If you don't like what I have to say we can keep going."

Marcus glanced at her in suspicion until he found her eyes. He knew they couldn't lie to him, and he recklessly slammed hard on the breaks.

Karen caught her breath. "Look at me," she whispered.

But Marcus kept looking straight ahead. He looked nothing like the man she'd fallen in love with either time, and he knew it.

"You're lost," she whispered. "You are so lost!" she began to cry.

Marcus looked down at her uneasily when he noticed her tears.

"I *was* lost." He cleared his throat. "I know where I am now. I know I need to save you."

"If you want to save me you need to let me go. You need to let me back to those who can protect me."

Karen watched him swallow hard and shake his head. "They don't …," he began, but he swallowed his words and tried again. "They don't …," he wheezed to force his words out and Karen felt her heart might break at the sight of him.

"They don't feel, how I feel about you!" he pushed the words from his mouth.

"If you love me, let me go."

"I did!" Marcus wheezed. "Over ten years ago! I thought you and the baby would be better off without me and you've hated me ever since."

He watched her burst into tears at the confirmation of what she already knew.

"I'm no good." His voice quavered. "Dead or alive I'm no good to anyone." He realized this as the final moments of his life descended cruelly upon him.

Karen thought her own eyes might bleed with the sorrow she felt for him. "What can I do?" she asked.

"Don't let them have it." He tried to take her hand but his focus deserted him and he missed.

"I mean for you." Karen sobbed. "How can I make it better for you?"

"Talk to me," he answered. "Just talk to me the way you used to. I like trying to work out what you're saying."

Karen closed the gap between them and stroked the side of his wet face. She tried to find his eyes but they were no longer visible through the pools of blood that had taken them. "Mo chuisle mo chroí," she said.

Marcus tried to look at her but she swept her fingertips down his eyelids.

Karen felt him take his last breath and lost him for the second time in her short life.

****

Grief-stricken, Fabien somberly made the trek across the grass toward the car. It stood out like a foreign object contaminating the greenery around it. The soil beneath seemed to sink with the weight of grief upon it, and Fabien sighed deeply.

He didn't make it in time before the passenger door swung open. Karen climbed out and immediately began walking. He stared after her as she passed him but she never made eye contact or looked back. He wondered if she'd seen him at all.

Karen had tunnel vision, and in this particular tunnel, time appeared to have slowed. She was focusing very hard on putting one foot in front of the other and there wasn't much room for anything else.

****

Connor answered the front door. "Where have you two been?" he asked.

"Karen and Marcus have gone their separate ways. I think Daniel and I should make our way back tonight. Our apartment is habitable again," Fabien lied.

"Oh." Connor managed to sound disappointed as he watched his sister brush past him.

"I don't think she wants to talk about it," Fabien whispered.

Fabien was right, Connor learned.

Karen wasn't speaking. She was sitting on her bedroom windowsill rocking gently with her rosary beads around her neck. He watched her twirl the little cross in her fingertips.

"Where's your locket?" he asked from the door. But that just made her weep even more.

Chapter 42

Darcy had been crying all afternoon. Andrew was paranoid in case she sensed the weight of responsibility she'd been born into. He wondered if babies could sense such things.

He helplessly flicked his lips with his fingers by the fire while his family slept upstairs. Eventually he gave in and packed a bag. It was a small bag: some money, a change of clothes, and a torch.

He made his way to the derelict barn across the fields. The night was eerily silent, with only the nocturnal wildlife for company. The battered wooden door of the barn drummed against the ground as he shoved it open. It hadn't been challenged like that for some time. Andrew thought of the most memorable time he'd passed through it. He was only eleven and his father had warned him it was out of bounds, which of course made it all the more appealing. All that industrialized machinery and dangerous equipment was too tempting for a small boy.

The spiteful old door avenged itself by presenting vivid flashbacks to the offending intruder.

"Grian Clindna, Aebinn, Cleena and Áine."

Andrew heard his brother's voice like it was only yesterday.

"Again!" his father's voice instructed authoritatively.

Daniel had sighed but dutifully repeated the five names again.

"Relevance?" their father questioned.

"The five banshees presiding over Ireland."

"Appearances?" their father went on.

"Most prevalent in Ulster in the 1500s, Leinster in the 1600s."

Andrew would have been interested in hearing more had it not sounded so much like school. But he'd stayed long enough to watch Seán and Daniel replace the heavy book under the floor boards. They had spoken at length of *Áine* – the one closest in her search.

Now the years had passed and he still knew the exact board to lift. It had a rusty old screw head on its border, which was now warped from years of disturbance. Andrew knelt down on the boards beside it. He raised it from its slot and sat back down on his hunkers. The sight of the thing made him sick.

Hundreds of stories compiled to educate his forefathers on the banshees, their strategies and the sightings of them, all in a futile attempt to help predict the future. He opened the dusty hardback cover. The familiar scent of the yellow pages wafted up his nostrils and he sneezed.

Andrew swept his big hands over the family tree as though it would somehow connect him to the names he saw. Daniel, Seán, Ivan, Thomas, and now there was Karen the anomaly that had broken the father-son cycle. Andrew missed his brother.

Chapter 43

Karen's cheek felt hot and wet when she woke. The heat was from Buddy's hairy body on her pillow and the moisture she learned was from the tears that had escaped while she slept.

Karen fidgeted beside him, she'd had all night to think.

At some point in the early hours she'd realized that the core of the storm inside her came from ignorance. It was the undercurrent that prevented her grieving until she knew what had happened to Corey. After all, Marcus could not have existed had Corey not died. He would have to have left this world to exist in another. *If you died as a Sprite with potential, you could be chosen to rise as a vampire,* she thought, recalling Fabien's teachings.

Karen toyed with the idea of contacting Shauny Burke to ask about his cousin. She had played with the idea of quizzing Connor on where he'd found Corey all those years ago. But all that had the same problem. It was an insult to the men who protected her.

Dan had been stabbed and left for dead. Marcus had been plotting against them all along and Karen doubted they would care that he'd had a change of heart at the last minute. Karen rolled over and covered her shoulders with the duvet.

It was lonely concealing your feelings. She'd never had to do it before. She was sure she'd go crazy if she didn't confide in someone soon. There was only one person left she decided, one person who lay firmly and objectively on the outside. Karen lunged for her phone.

****

Rick watched drips of sweat fall from his face and onto the mat beneath him. "Fifty six," he counted, raising himself up for the last of his press-ups. His parents were away again and it surprised him how good it felt. It had been days now since he had last had to fight the losing battle of trying to fix his father.

The music escaping through the speakers spurred him on. *Four more days,* he told himself as he confronted the punch bag before him. It would be his first fight in six years and he was nervous. Dust fell from the bag as he pounded it frantically.

"Breathing!" a voice called from behind him.

Rick turned to find his new trainer, all five foot four of him. It was hard to believe he was a fifth dan black belt, but Evan Richards was lethal as a bullet. Rick had never hired a trainer before and he was excited. Evan was from London but he'd trained all over the world.

"Breathing!" Evan repeated. "You won't last five seconds inhaling while you punch."

Rick moved over and Evan stepped in front of the bag, lowering his stance. He snapped his arm out and back in a whipping motion and released an exaggerated puff of air from his mouth as he did so. "Exhale when you strike, mate."

He stepped around the bag and held it straight for Rick. "Try again!"

Rick began pounding again, this time blowing out with every strike. He felt no difference. "I still feel knackered," he complained.

"You just haven't found your rhythm soon you won't even have to think about it."

Evan held the bag for Rick but they were interrupted by the theme from *The A-Team* echoing from Rick's mobile. "I have to get that!" Rick pointed to the buzzing device.

Evan's butty little body appeared from behind the bag. He looked like a football hooligan. Black hair follicles spiked out from his scalp like living creatures. "Ain't going to be any telephone breaks in the ring mate," he called. But the only voice Rick was focused on was Karen's.

****

Rick walked confidently into one of Griffin's more mature estates.

He didn't know the town very well at all.

"The Willows" was etched in black writing on an entrance stone.

The gardens were all well-kept, save for one or two whose owners were rebellious enough not to have any flowers.

Rick didn't feel nervous. He was in character now; he had a job to do and Karen's peace of mind depended on it.

Fort-nine, forty-nine, he searched. He stared with distain when he realized it was the one with the army of gnomes outside. They were hideous-looking things but someone had taken the time to paint them lovingly. Rick still thought they looked like deranged little killers, just more colourful. He did a double-take as he passed two oversized stone eagles on the entrance pillars and he worried about the sanity of the woman inside. Still he made his way up the garden path and rapped on the rose shaped knocker.

Rick readied himself and straightened up as the door opened. He had to close his mouth. He couldn't ever remember seeing so much make-up on one woman. She looked like one of the gnomes from the garden.

"Hello?" Her posture softened at the sight of the handsome stranger.

"Is this Burkes'?" Rick asked in a convincing London accent.

"Yes," the mother gnome opened her green door a little wider.

"I'm Spencer Smith." Rick extended a hand.

"Jessica Burke," the woman responded.

Her blatant examination of him was starting to make him feel uncomfortable but he didn't let it distract him. "I'm looking for Corey," he announced. "He said he spent the Christmas holidays here with his favourite aunt."

Jessica Burke's face appeared to collapse in on itself. It was awful to witness and a feeling of guilt consumed him. "I told him if I were in Ireland I'd look him up. He said he'd show me around." Rick held his friendly smile.

"You better come in." Jessica gestured with an extended arm.

Rick followed her down a narrow hallway leading to the kitchen.

Jessica opened the corner cupboard and mooched around returning triumphantly with a bottle of rum.

"I thought you were tea drinkers like us?" Rick joked.

"You'll need something a little stronger," Jessica warned as she poured.

"Has something happened?" he asked innocently.

"How long has it been since you spoke with my nephew?"

"College, I think. We were in LCU together before he left the course."

Jessica appeared to be counting in her head. "That was over ten years ago."

She swallowed her drink and began rotating the empty glass on the table in a trance-like manner. "Corey passed away, I'm sorry you had to find out this way." Jessica looked sympathetic.

Rick stayed quiet as he played out the role of shocked stranger.

"We thought we'd contacted all of his friends."

Jessica's apologetic look made Rick lower his gaze in shame. He'd never even met Corey and here was his aunt apologizing for his death. Eventually Rick gathered himself enough to stare about the little kitchen. "Is that Shauny?" he asked when his eyes rested on a picture of a handsome boy in a university hat.

Rick had no idea what Corey Burke had looked like when he was alive. He'd only ever known him as Marcus Savidis, the vampire form he'd taken after he'd died, but he took a chance. "He looks just like him!" he commented.

It seemed to work. "Yes, people used to think they were brothers."

Rick watched Jessica produce a box of cigarettes from her handbag. If he didn't deserve one now he never would, and he eagerly accepted one.

Jessica had finished another drink and a second cigarette before she felt ready to go on. "Corey joined the army after he dropped out of that course ye took together." She flicked her cigarette and waved the smoke from her face. "Promising soldier, his sergeant told us; only been there six months when he went on one of those two-month camp things. They go to Winchester, you see, for training exercises. Do well at those and you can come back a sergeant."

Rick nodded sympathetically but said nothing.

"They were only there two weeks when the sister Maggie called. She sounded like she was asleep, all hazy and distant. Well, I didn't think anything of it, of course; she's like that the best of times. Anyway, turns out she had reason to be. Corey wasn't coming home. None of his platoon were. They'd all been shot during some other soldier's mental breakdown. Shot all his colleagues, he did, six o'clock and they were sitting down for the dinner."

"All of them?"

"All but the standing sergeant."

"Do you remember his name?" Rick sat forward.

"I remember everything about Corey's death." Jessica flicked another piece of ash into and overflowing ashtray. "His name was Liam Wilkins. Had a soft spot for our Corey, I think; couldn't have spoken enough about him."

Rick tried not to gasp as he recalled Liam's surname.

"He was in line for that promotion, you know?" Jessica pointed her cigarette at Rick by way of demonstration.

"Well, he was always a leader," Rick replied with what was expected of him. "Was there an investigation?"

"No need!" Jessica squashed out her cigarette butt. "Crazy, wasn't he? Some Harris kid, I think his name was. Just lost it and started shooting. Shot himself last."

Rick finished his own cigarette and blew out lines of blue grey smoke. His muscles relaxed a little and he realized he'd been holding his breath. "I'm so sorry for your loss."

"And I for yours," Jessica replied with mild surprise.

"Thank you." Rick got up uncomfortably.

Jessica led him back through the narrow hall that was crowded with pictures of a young boy. Rick stopped suddenly in his tracks, surprising Jessica.

"Mrs Burke, do you think it would be possible to get a photograph of Corey? I mean if you have one to spare that is."

Chapter 44

Karen was glad to be back in the city. She was also glad to have her home to herself again. Fabien and Dan had finally moved out now Marcus was no longer a threat. They would have to send some other converter to find their precious key, and they would be ignorant to the fact she would be expecting it. Karen smirked at the thoughts of getting one over on the banshees. Even Fabien seemed to shine a little brighter at the realization.

The city hummed with Christmas bustle. Normally Karen walked Buddy at Ashton Park but there was something soothing about being carried in a wave of random people on the high street. Nobody knew her here, no prying questions about Marcus or their break-up, no one checking to see if she was okay (except Dan whom she suspected was following her).

Buddy didn't share her newfound love of the streets. He jumped and jerked awkwardly at noises, and seemed to have launched a personal vendetta against cyclists.

They stopped at the end of O'Connell Street, and sat on the great monument overlooking the quays. The sky was heavily pregnant with snow and Karen wondered when it would deliver. She was learning, she realized, that she could get swallowed up inside if she spent any more time in her head. So she tried spending some time in others' instead. Everyone she set eyes on had a story to tell. A young mother's tired face pleaded in lonely silence for peace while her children competed for her already-stretched attention. A group of hyperactive teenagers, high on their yearning to establish themselves, emerged triumphantly from their first department store theft. Karen watched them drape their arms across each other's shoulders in exaggerated laughter. She recognized a look of inner conflict on the face of the youngest. She couldn't have been more than fourteen, her furry boots shuffling clumsily through the puddles to keep up. Karen watched her try to inhale the cigarette she'd pretended to want.

Sometime after ten o'clock the night sky gave birth to a healthy delivery of fresh white snowflakes and Karen decided to make her way home, all the while looking around for ways not to think of Marcus.

****

"Inhale properly, will ye!" the group of teenagers had entered a nearby alley to examine their free products.

Jasmine sucked hard and blew out before anything hit her lungs.

"That's it girl. We'll learn ye!" Chantelle winked at the dubious looking teenager staring about her nervously.

"I got these wicked bangles." Jenny shook her wrist in demonstration and blew a bubble so large that the gum almost fell from her mouth.

"Wicked," Chantelle nodded. "What about you, Jaz?"

Jasmine pulled out several sticks of make-up, triumphantly holding them high like a trophy. "I got these wicked lip glosses."

Jenny lunged to claim one.

"Me ma wears these. She goes mental when I use 'em. Nice one, Jaz."

Chantelle went to grab her share but Jasmine leapt backwards.

"Give us one, will ye!" but Jasmine was staring about her wildly.

"Did you *see* that? There! By the trash?"

Jenny and Chantelle stared behind them suspiciously, their pencilled eyebrows climbing up their foreheads as they scanned for security men.

Jasmine's body crumpled against the wall, her boots filling with water from the puddle she stood in. She was terrified to look, terrified she would find the creature those glowing red eyes belonged to. Their vibrant crimson colour lit up the darkness they scanned.

"You've just got the jitters," Chantelle told her.

Jenny was ready to back up her friend, as usual when she was interrupted by the echo of high heels emerging from the darkness. The owner didn't stop to acknowledge the three dumfounded youths. She walked straight past them in pursuit of a young woman with a brown dog instead.

****

The evening had gotten colder and Karen suddenly realized she could no longer feel her hands. They were numb and icy and she wondered how long she'd sat at the base of this statue watching the world go by. She made Buddy drop the stones he'd been trying to munch on and headed back down the quays.

"Stop pulling!" she ordered, as he played his part in tidy towns by hovering up cigarette butts and discarded mounts of chewing gum. Karen bent town to tighten his collar but as she crouched on her hunkers she got the eerie feeling that someone was watching her. It wasn't Dan; she knew because it felt like holes boring into her back and she quickly jumped to her feet. There was no one behind her.

The street was wet and dirty, with retail punters doing their rounds of the high street shops. A couple of college boys were running for the bus. She continued to check behind her but nothing stood out.

A tall dark figure closed in on her near the Luas stop. The streets were busy and everyone was caught up in their own hectic lives. No one noticed when a pair of large arms wrapped themselves around her waist and lifted Karen clean off the ground.

Rick let go in an instant when he realized how frightened he'd made her.

Karen didn't know whether to punch him or hug him, so she tried both at the one time, which caused some confusion.

"You okay?"

"No, I think I'm being followed."

Rick glanced around. "Let's get off the streets." He took her hand.

"Where are we going?" Karen half jogged through the puddles to keep up.

"Somewhere crowded. A café, there's something I think you'll want to hear."

Rick ordered them two black coffees and wondered if they would have been better off going to the pub considering the revelations he was about to deliver. But Caffuccino's was the only all-night café around and they allowed dogs.

When Rick returned to their table Karen was examining her blue hands and twirling on one of the high chairs. He sometimes wondered how she managed to hold it all together. She was so practised in escaping into her own world that an elephant could have brought her order and she would probably just have tipped it.

"How do you do that?" he asked with genuine interest.

Karen shook a sachet of sugar gently before spilling it into her cup. She leaned over to peer in, as though something magic were about to happen.

"Do what?"

"Escape the way you do? In your head, I mean."

Karen gave a deep sigh and gazed dreamily into her cup. "You wouldn't be saying that if you spent the night with me." They both reddened. "I mean tonight!" she clarified uncomfortably. "Tonight I've been a wreck, so I practised really hard on focusing on everyone else, staying in the real world."

Rick flashed her a smile. "Overrated, wouldn't you say?" He raised his mug to hers. He wondered how to tell her he'd tried to resolve her frustration about knowing what happened to Corey. He hoped she wouldn't be mad at him for going behind her back. But how could she be? "I know what happened to Corey," he blurted out.

Karen swallowed the mouthful of coffee she'd been savouring and wondered if she'd heard correctly.

"When you called the other night, I think you were right: knowing what happened will help you grieve properly."

Karen closed her hands around her mug to heat them for a moment. "How could you know that?" Rick was a sweet soul but she couldn't risk believing a lie fabricated to make her feel better.

But as soon as Rick described the gnomes Karen knew he'd been to Burkes'. Learning how Corey died stunned her. It was much harder to hear that he'd been murdered. Karen examined Rick's demeanour. He was uncomfortable. "What are you not telling me?"

Rick glanced around the table quickly. There were a couple of lap top geeks and some students nearby, just the regular clientele you'd expect late at night, and none of them appeared interested. Their waitress on the other hand was looking very interested indeed. *Linda* her white and gold name tag read. When Linda realized she'd been spotted she began cleaning down the cappuccino machine with unrealistic enthusiasm.

Rick lowered his voice. "Guess who the commanding sergeant was?"

Karen didn't have to think on it too long "Liam," she hissed.

Rick nodded. "You were right about him. He was a vampire; he was the converter who got inside an innocent man's head and made him shoot Corey and the rest of his unit."

Karen raised her eyebrows, and Rick began to look uncomfortable again. He squirmed uneasily and leaned down to pet Buddy who had finally fallen asleep. He kept his eye on the sleeping dog until he heard her voice again.

"We both know it wasn't Liam who got inside the killer's head. It was Marcus. It would be just like him, turning one man against another in an attempt to get a promotion. Liam only ever intended to convert a few soldiers, but Marcus was so good at influencing people he got himself and everyone else killed."

"We don't know that."

"Oh, come on!" Karen insisted. "We both know a vampire's goal isn't to kill, it's to convert. What would be the point of killing all those men?"

Rick didn't answer. He didn't want to taint her memories of the dead. But she'd come to the same conclusion he had and she'd come to it a little louder too. Linda's ears were cocked again.

"What a pleasant surprise it must have been for Liam!" Karen curled her lips in disgust at the thought. "To learn the man he'd been sent to convert would be so devious and influential that he'd cause a massacre and become a converter himself."

Rick appeared to be deep in thought. "Do you have to die to become a converter?" he sat forward.

"Yes." Karen's voice was strong and firm, "So don't even think about it."

"I wasn't!" Rick lied. Vampires and werewolves intrigued him. Converting people to do good or evil sounded heroic.

Linda's eyes were bulging with enthusiasm.

"No wonder he ended up a vampire."

"Eeeep!" A mousy voice came from the corner.

Karen whipped up her head and Linda realized how blatant she'd been. A few other customers noticed too and she fled, red-faced to the kitchen.

"Calm down," Rick whispered.

Karen ignored him. "You know what we should do?"

"What?" Rick was nervous.

"We should get drunk. We can drink to closure at last."

Rick watched her slam a decisive hand down on the table, but he remained dubious. "What exactly are we celebrating?"

"The truth," Karen answered.

Chapter 45

Connor had his feet up on the coffee table. It was nice not having anyone tell him to put them down. He rolled his tongue around his mouth tasting the last of the homemade burgers he'd devoured. A bottle of beer sat fizzing on the table while he flicked through the television channels. He gave a stretch and a long sigh escaped from his mouth. He felt healthy again. Things were better now, he assured himself. His leg vibrated and he realized his phone was ringing. He struggled to save it from his increasingly tight pockets. The cracked screen hid the caller I.D. "Hello!" he answered grumpily.

"Have you seen Andrew?" It was his mother. She sounded annoyed and he could make out the cries of a baby in the background. Andrew had been missing for three days now. No warnings, just an emptied pot of savings and a missing truck from the yard. Connor sat forward and rubbed his eyes in frustration.

"Idiot!" he sighed.

"Idiot," Catherine echoed. "Probably sprawled across a bar somewhere after spectacularly falling off the wagon."

"Where have you checked?"

"All the bars in Griffin. Can you go further afield? Any city bars you know he likes to visit?"

"There's a couple in Temple Bar we used to go to. I'll get on it!" He hung up the phone.

The weather was busying itself laying sheets of ice on the road and decorating it with snowflakes. Connor examined it thoughtfully through the curtains and decided to cycle. He zipped up his old leather jacket and pulled up its grey hood tight around his head. *What are you playing at, Andrew?* he thought, before leaving.

****

Connor was still out when Karen and Rick returned.

"Can I have his spring roll?" Rick asked as he laid two plastic bags of food on the countertop.

"Looks like it." Karen was searching for a note from Connor but there was none.

"Red or white?" Rick held up two bottles.

"Ew." Karen winced at the memory of the last time she got drunk on red wine at the log cabin. She had just learned that Fabien had been telling her the truth and she was in shock. How far she'd come since then, how much more she'd learned.

"Karen?" Rick was still holding the bottles at arm's length and shaking his head.

"Definitely white!"

Rick almost let both bottles fall when his phone rang. He seemed frazzled. He put his finger to his lips in a gesture for silence and he answered in an exaggerated sleepy tone.

"Hey."

Karen tried not to listen but Rick's suspicious behaviour made it hard not to.

"Been in bed ages," she heard him say. "Like you said, need to conserve energy for the fight."

Karen brought their food into the living room and straightened the rug by the fire. "Your mum?" she asked.

"No. Mum's not too keen on the old sparring tournaments."

"Why didn't you mention you'd entered?"

Rick shrugged his shoulders and swallowed a mouthful of wine. "Fewer distractions, I guess. It's hard enough to get beat up without inviting people to watch it."

"That's rubbish. We're your friends; you've nothing to prove."

Rick watched her pour a sea of vinegar over her chips and he scrunched up his face. "That's disgusting."

"So is not inviting me to your fight."

"Fine, you can come." Rick shrugged his shoulders. "You can get a lift with Fabien."

"You invited Fabien before me?"

"Of course I did – divine intervention!" Rick raised his hands in mockery.

"So tell me more about these Sublims and Sprites that reside in Sublimina." Rick wasn't sure he understood them completely.

Karen downed her wine in one gulp. "Sublims and Sprites are human projections."

"I don't get it,"

"When you sleep you will wake in the world of Sublimina, where you will take the form of a Sublim or a Sprite. Sublims are people who have been converted by werewolves. And Sprites are people who have been converted by vampires."

"I'm definitely a Sublim," Rick declared.

Karen gave him a mischievous look. "I'd say you've spent many a night as a Sprite."

"What about the key?" Rick's tone changed. "Fabien keeps saying some prophet will claim it and you'll be free of it. But how do they claim it?"

"By touch," Karen explained. Rick was asking all the questions she had asked Fabien, and she tried to be as patient as Fabien had been with her.

"If the prophet has physical contact with the key, then that's it – it's theirs. That's why the banshees will only seek it while it hasn't been claimed."

"What if the prophet lost the key? Or had it stolen? Or it fell into the wrong hands?" Rick tried to keep the panic from his voice.

"It would simply return itself to its rightful owner." Karen swallowed the last of her food. "I kind of wish Connor had one to be honest. Imagine how much money we'd have saved on spare keys."

"Yikes." Olivia squinted at Karen's bloodshot eyes. "Hangover?"

"The worst." Karen groaned and reached for the coffee pot.

"Hope he was worth it." Olivia winked.

"Actually we broke up."

Sam raised an eyebrow then and came over to join them. "Ditto." she shrugged meekly.

Karen's hangover temporarily subsided and was replaced by a surge of elation, which she quickly tried to mask with disappointment. "Really? Sorry to hear that."

Sam smiled wryly. "You're a terrible liar."

Olivia nodded and stirred her tea. "You are, you know ... a terrible liar," she clarified, missing her cue to leave. She stood gormlessly between her colleagues and stared from one to the other.

"Parent-teacher meeting tonight." She sighed. "Dreadful things, full of deluded parents."

Sam stared into her mug and tried not to laugh.

"Must be terrible." Karen tried to sound sincere.

An atmosphere of unease descended when Brenda entered the kitchen. Everyone got ready to leave, until Brenda informed them that Lawrence would be departing for Canada in the morning. It soon became apparent that it was okay to spend long periods in the kitchen provided Brenda's interests were the topic of conversation.

Karen and Sam took the opportunity to retreat to their cubicles for some privacy and left the others to suffer alone.

"I'm sorry." Sam touched Karen's arm as they sat. "I should have come to my senses sooner. I should have realized what was important." Sam hung her head in shame so that all that was visible was a head of sandy blonde hair that seemed to beg forgiveness.

"Don't be a fool; there's a pair of us in it." Sam's dainty face emerged from behind a curtain of shiny hair. "It just hit me, you know. We were at the bar and I noticed another couple. They were so ... I can't think of the word." She huffed and shook her hand frantically to trigger an invisible list of options. "So ..."

"Happy?" Karen offered.

"No. Supportive! That's the word I'm looking for. It was like they encouraged each other's independence."

Karen tried to keep up but Sam was talking too fast.

"So the girl was saying, 'I'm going to Stacy's later,' and the guy was like, 'Yeah, you haven't seen her in ages.' And then it dawned on me."

Karen wondered how all this related to dumping Liam.

"That's when it hit me. That's what decent guys do, isn't it? Encourage their partners, not isolate and smother them."

Karen clenched her teeth hard, realizing the amount of control Liam tried to exert, the ownership he tried to take on, and he'd almost gotten away with it. He must have been pleased with himself.

Karen indulged her mind with pleasurable images involving his face and a shovel, until Sam shook her out of it.

"Karen?" she repeated meekly. "Did you hear me? Can you forgive me?"

Karen spent the best part of the afternoon convincing Sam there was nothing to forgive. She needed a peace offering to prove it, she decided. "Do you want to come to a sparring tournament this Saturday?" she blurted out and almost smacked her hands up to her mouth. She remembered Rick's reluctance to invite anyone and she cursed her inability to keep her mouth shut. She would have to eat an entire humble pie for this, she knew.

****

Rick wasn't thinking about making anyone eat humble pie; he was too caught up trying to slow his breathing. The old badminton hall where the tournament was being held was smaller than he thought, with just four courts in total, and it was hard to find space to prepare.

Karen was watching him from the large wooden benches around the hall. The temperature here felt no warmer than outside and she huddled against Sam and Fabien's shoulders for some heat. She wondered how Rick was managing with nothing on his feet and couldn't imagine the karate suit holding much warmth either. She watched him shaking his arms out while Evan held up a white boxing mitt.

"That guy looks creepy." Sam whispered. "I'm sure I saw him on *Crimeline* robbing that post office in Kerry."

"Really?" Karen ogled Evan until Fabien's expression told them they were being childish.

"Who made *him* Mister Miyagi?" Sam inclined her head toward Fabien.

After the warm-ups the hall began to come to life, trying to communicate through a sequence of squeaks and thuds as contestants pounded the floors and tussled on the mats. Two fights had already ended on the far courts and Karen was learning that the tournament was far different from what she had imagined. There were no fancy moves like on telly and the fights didn't last very long.

"They're not very good, are they?" Sam leaned over.

Karen stifled a grin and looked guiltily to Fabien, expecting another dirty look, but he wasn't there. Her eyes caught him make his way down the centre aisle but she lost him in the crowds.

"Not really a place for children, is it?" Sam glanced around. "Especially not rough looking ones like those." She nodded down at some youths who were filling the contestants' shoes with chewing gum.

Karen looked around again for Fabien and this time found him talking discretely to a couple of people at the doorway. The man was attractive but the woman was stunning. Her blonde wavy hair curled about her shoulders. Her eyes were big and bright and the men around her were staring.

"That's them!" Sam shouted and pointed at the same time.

Karen almost fell down into the rivers of people before her. "You will be the death of me!" she scorned.

"There!" Sam ignored her. "Look!" she pointed again to Fabien. "That's the couple I was telling you about, from Raptures."

Karen was still lost.

"The ones who made me realize what a creep Liam was after watching them together."

Karen finally smiled at the realization. She had wondered when she'd get to see more converters.

****

Karen watched Fabien's little green car pull out from her driveway and waved good night to her friends. She stood in the porch longer than was necessary and pasted a convincing smile on her face. She kept it there until the headlights dimmed and the muscles on her face released it like it had burnt her. Something was wrong. Even more wrong than was normal of late.

Karen's bones whispered eerie words of caution and she listened to them. She caught her reflection in the mirror and a pale frightened face stared back at her. Her big brown eyes had always held a sparkle but now they just lay dead in her head. "Keep it together." she whispered to her glass self. It was too hard to imagine the impact her failure would have on the world.

Up until now she'd confined her fears to those closest to her. But now other people were beginning to spill into her mind too. The two little brats at the karate tournament, the children at the youth centre, even the Lawrence Lavins of the world. "Don't lose it!" she ordered herself out loud, but her voice broke and hot tears fell down her cheeks.

Buddy trotted into the hallway at the sound. He watched his mistress flop in a heap on the bottom step of the stairs and offered himself as comfort. And when Karen could no longer ignore him he buried his snout under her arm. "Something is coming." she told him. Buddy listened carefully. *Dinner* was the only word he knew and he was disappointed not to hear it.

Karen put her rosary beads around her neck. It was ironic that something that endangered her so much gave her such peace. If she fell asleep now while wearing them she would wake in Sublimina she knew – the key to existing in both worlds. It was a frightening thought, to lose consciousness and awaken somewhere else, yet still she put them around her neck. There was no fear of her sleeping while her mind was so tormented.

Chapter 46

Steve had worked at Quinn's long enough to know when to stop serving. He shook his head sympathetically at the down-and-out before him and took the empty glass from him.

Andrew didn't argue; he merely rubbed the growing stubble on his jaw and blinked hard. The bar moved slowly, his vision tried to catch up with his head as he leaned back to peer outside. It was raining hard and it was time to go. He settled his tab and turned to leave.

"Your jacket!" Steve called, but Andrew couldn't hear him. There were too many other voices shouting at him. His conscience was the loudest and he'd just silenced that with as much alcohol as he could get served.

He stumbled over several potholes and got into a row with a wheelie bin before the lights of the hotel caught his eye. They were bright and burned at his eyes as he squinted at them through the rain. He watched them merge and blend together as he stumbled backward to see the sign.

The Holiday Inn, it read.

So this is where it all ends! he thought.

The young and fresh-faced receptionist stared after him as, dripping wet, he passed the elevator and took the stairs instead. His backpack lay limply off his shoulder. Every step he took was like a step closer to hell. Andrew took the key from his wet pocket and wiped it dry. Room 203. He would remember that number for ever. From now till the day he died, it would be the number of betrayal for him.

The room was chilly. Andrew's wet T-shirt was stuck to his skin. Leaving a trail of footprints in his wake he approached the window and locked it tightly. His tired eyes looked around the room for anything else he could do to distract him from the ritual ahead.

Andrew was good at getting jobs he didn't like done. There was a very simple formula he'd learned. Don't think about the consequences and get on with the actions. Moral dilemmas could only be considered once the job was finished. Otherwise decisions wouldn't get made. Regular people wouldn't understand this of course; they had the luxury of not having to.

Andrew practised this method now by filtering his thoughts, allowing only the most basic instructions through.

A towel was the first image to emerge. He'd need a towel to sit on, he decided, and made his way to the bathroom. One of the bulbs was missing; it softened the lighting to a subtle yellow glow. Andrew was grateful, as it allowed him slink past the mirror without catching his own reflection.

After laying the towel neatly on the centre of the floor, he knelt down and tried to open his backpack. He watched his numb blue fingers like they were someone else's as they tried to yank open the zip. After several attempts he saw his hands bleed as they ripped it open instead.

Particles of muddy brown earth spilled onto the carpet and he heaped them up into a pile before him. Next he felt around the bottom of the bag and brought out a little box. He spilled the pebbles it held around the pile of earth. He did it several times over until pebbles from the graves of three of his forefathers surrounded the soil they'd been buried beneath. Daniel's were the newer emerald-green ones. They seemed to glare up at him with distain and he had to look away.

Seán's were older and a paler whitish colour, and time had stolen all colour from Ivan's. Andrew felt no emotion, having never met the men.

Almost ready, he told himself as he opened a little black pouch. He sprinkled dead wasps on the earth as though they were fertilizer.

The last and final item he swiped out of the bag as quickly as he could, without thinking about it. It was one of Karen's scarves.

He remembered the night he'd taken it. He'd been pacing her bedroom when a note was slipped under the door. He thought he had been caught until he took it from the floor. It seemed to be enough, and the messenger left. He thought of the letter now for the first time since he'd crumpled it up and carelessly threw it in the bin.

He barely handled the scarf at all before he tossed it straight on top of the pile. He couldn't afford to smell its perfume or feel its texture. Instead he lit a match and set the whole thing alight.

Andrew was confident he hadn't missed anything but he checked *The Book of Bean Sí* just in case. The book hadn't seen the outside of the barn in over a hundred years and the air around it seemed to sense it. It rippled like the fumes of a fire.

Andrew went to the relevant chapter and readied himself. He crossed his legs before him and closed his eyes.

"Bean Sí, éist leis an gceann a lorg agat," he began. "Bean Sí, Tá mé anseo." He rocked.

****

Josie Rattigan was the cleaner on duty at the Holiday Inn. She'd clocked on just under an hour ago, in time to notice the soaking wet guest make his muddy way up the stairs.

"No shame," she hissed.

Josie liked hotel work, even after twenty years at the same hotel. She prided herself on being the first to know all the local gossip. She'd been first to know when Kevin Devine was having that affair with his secretary. She knew that Jessup girl had one-night stands with older men, and her father, a solicitor, had the nerve to look down on the Rattigans?

Josie passed the mucky man's room now and put her ear to the door. She heard a lot of mumblings. A little disappointing but mumblings meant he wasn't alone. *Or is he?* She wondered. What if he was into the drugs and having the hallucinations?

Josie pressed her ear closer and began to feel a heat at her ankles. Smoke! She stood back. There was pale blue smoke coming from under the bedroom door. Definitely the drugs, she decided. She hurried off, thinking of all the psychotic killings that the drugs had caused and she was damned if she was to become someone else's topic of tragic conversation.

Chapter 47

Karen plugged in the radio for some company. The DJ was hosting a talk show on misleading insurance policies, and she tried to listen.

"Contents insurance! It either covers the contents or it doesn't," moaned the caller.

"Yes, but items covered are listed on your policy document," argued the insurance rep.

"If you have ten hours to read the bloody thing," the woman snapped. Her name was Betty, Karen learned when the DJ tried to interrupt her in vain.

"The television is insured but the screen isn't," Betty continued. "Landslides are covered but only in Monaghan. Next you'll be telling me the cat's insured but only if it's dead." Karen chuckled quietly to herself as she pottered about the kitchen.

The kettle whistled from the corner. She emptied a pile of ground coffee beans into the cafetière and filled it with water. The rich smell filled her nostrils and she inhaled deeply.

Before she could take a sip, she was alarmed by a rapping on the back door behind her. Karen froze and wondered whether she would answer it. Only family knocked at the back door; and they weren't in the habit of calling in the middle of the night.

A second round of knocking began and Buddy began barking frantically. It was a strange sound that seemed too big for him.

"Karen!" she heard her name.

Karen's shoulders relaxed once she recognized the voice, and hurried to let her uncle in.

"Jesus, Andrew! What are you doing out in this?" She pulled him indoors.

The stench of stale alcohol hit her immediately, but she said nothing.

Andrew stood uncomfortably in the kitchen rubbing the back of his neck with his palms.

This was bad, Karen thought. "I've just made coffee." Karen placed a cafetière on the table and waited for him to sit. Eventually he seemed to remember where he was and slowly Andrew pulled out a chair with such caution he seemed to be afraid of it.

"It's okay," Karen told him and placed the cafetière between them.

"Stop!" It was a barely audible whisper. "Stop being nice to me!" he told her.

Karen waited for him to compose himself and began to worry. Was Darcy okay? She felt her mouth go dry at the thoughts of the delicate little face she'd cradled only days before. Was Andrew merely having trouble adjusting? Was Katie? Karen tried to control an imagination that frequently got her into trouble.

Andrew shifted from one side of the chair to another. He looked uncomfortable, putting his hands on the table then back to his knees again.

Karen tried to find his eyes but they were doing their best not to be caught, so she gave up. She looked out the window instead, and hoped this would make him feel less scrutinized.

After a time he finally spoke again.

"The least I could do is be with you when it happens."

Karen fought not to look at him and kept her gaze on the window. She couldn't lose him now. "When what happens?"

"When she comes," Andrew whispered.

Karen wondered briefly if this was her uncle's bizarre way of asking her to babysit.

"You know if I could just give it to her I would," Andrew continued. "But *you're* its keeper."

Karen stiffened at the word *keeper*, it chilled her bones and she'd come to hate the wretched word.

"She needs *your* life to claim it and I don't even know what form it's in."

Andrew was waffling now. Karen stayed mute hoping he would somehow just stop talking so she could pretend she had imagined the entire conversation. But on and on he went. "It's better this way. Why guard an object that will choke you and every living descendant you ever have."

Karen had heard enough, "You gave me up, then?"

"For Darcy!" Andrew's voice broke. "I can't let her inherit this."

Karen could see his back rise and fall with emotion from the corner of her eyes.

He had betrayed her, her own flesh and blood. He knew all this time and he'd betrayed her. The man who had cared for her all her life had a new focus now, and she didn't matter anymore. She should hate him, she knew, but she didn't. She made herself look at him and realized she'd never seen a living thing in so much pain before, and hate just seemed so pointless.

"She doesn't have to inherit it!" a prophet will claim it and alleviate us of the responsibility. We won't need to protect it anymore."

Andrew merely shook his head. "The prophet!" He laughed at the idea.

Karen didn't blame him for being cynical; she was beginning to question its existence herself. Andrew tried to look at her but her face seemed to burn him so he winced and looked away instead.

****

Rick threw his sports bag in the hallway; he hadn't the energy to empty it. The house was quiet but the lights were on in the dining room. He found Nicholas at the breakfast bar with teary eyes and a glass of whisky.

Rick searched the cupboards for some food. There was nothing.

Eileen had taken one of her turns and the shopping hadn't been done all week.

"Didn't Mum give you the shopping list?" he asked his father. He knew he should have gone himself; the man couldn't be depended on for anything.

There was a box of cornflakes lost in the back of one of the cupboards and Rick grabbed it gratefully. But he almost cried when the milk he poured fell in a series of congealed lumps. "Jesus, not even a carton of milk."

A loud smashing sound from the back wall made him jump. Splashes of whiskey sprayed the wall and shards of glass flew across the floor.

"Will ye shut up about your blasted food, boy," yelled Nicholas.

Rick was alarmed. His father was a drunk, that much was true, but not an aggressive one. He'd never been violent or abusive and the only time he broke anything was by knocking things over as he fell or passed out. Rick stared at him for a moment. He saw his father's lower lip quiver. His face was red and his eyes full of tears. He was fighting not to let them fall.

Rick swallowed hard. "What's wrong?" he made himself ask.

Nicholas seemed to gather himself again. He took out a fresh glass and poured himself another drink. "Nothin," he said, wiping his eyes.

Rick relaxed a little, realizing it didn't relate to his mother. He poured himself a drink and sat next to his father. They never drank together. Rick made a point of it.

Nicholas's delight at the company was evident on his red face. He glanced sideways at his son but then looked away quickly in case he left. Rick downed his whiskey in one go and poured another.

"So, what's wrong with *you*?" his father asked.

"Nothin!" Rick sighed.

****

Buddy was getting distressed. There was tension in the air. He could sense it, along with something else; something was different in the wind outside. The house was silent and no one was speaking. The clock was ticking on the wall. The visiting man had his head in his hands and his mistress got up from the table.

She was pawing at the chain she wore around her neck and she began to pace. The man began making those sounds that humans did, but his mistress was ignoring him. Buddy followed her until he sensed the static in the air alter. It felt funny against his fur. Nobody else seemed to sense it so he started barking. None of the humans paid heed until the radio signal died. It crackled and hissed until eventually it delivered a deep and steady whistling frequency. The lights flickered and the air grew heavy.

Buddy hid under the table and wondered why no one else was joining him there.

Karen clasped her hands over her ears.

Andrew's knees buckled. He had hoped to be standing when she came, to at least hold his niece's hand. He reached for her now, but his body convulsed when he removed his hands from his ears. The air rippled and warned that it couldn't withhold the weight of the presence upon it. It made good its promise when the glass of the windows caved in helplessly.

It was time, Karen's heart told her. This was it.

It was true what she'd heard – life did indeed flash before your eyes in your last moments. Her mother was the first face she saw. She had an eighties hairdo and was brushing her hair by the fire. She could feel Connor beside her, climbing the furniture. Memories of Esther then flashed in and out of her mind. She was picking her up from school, standing at an old blue Ford Fiesta, waving her small hands at her.

Then she saw him. For all these years she'd wished she remembered her father's face, and now it finally made an appearance in her mind's eye. It was serious and it was handsome. She felt him kiss her forehead and felt the scar along his chin as he bade her good night.

"Sleep," she heard a soft voice and she fell.

****

"Rotten sly disease, it is," Nicholas declared.

Rick had never heard his father talk about his mother's illness before.

"Do you remember when they hadn't diagnosed her?" he asked, raising a bushy grey eyebrow.

"Yes," Rick admitted. He remembered very well the pain on his mother's face from her joints, and all the while she kept smiling. Fatigue the doctors had called it.

"The woman couldn't even look at the light without it paining her." Nicholas shook his head. "Took them four years to take it seriously! Useless shower of snotty-nosed self-obsessed little wankers!"

Rick hadn't known his father capable of stringing such a sentence together at all, much less do it while intoxicated.

"You don't know what it does to me!" his lower lip began to quiver again and Rick felt very uncomfortable.

"Then why don't you help her more?" Rick made himself ask.

His father gave him a mocking look. "Sure what can *I* do? Only watch it. There's nothin I can do. Do you have any idea what that's like?" he asked.

"Yes! I know exactly what that's like." Rick looked accusingly at his father who appeared to miss the jibe.

"This is a bad spell boy." Nicholas was shaking his head. "This is one where she's given up."

"Given up?" Rick repeated nervously.

"Not like that." Nicholas waved his whiskey-free hand. "It's just she has no fight left and that's when it takes hold of her. She gets quiet you know. Smiles at you longer than necessary so you won't suspect. But I know."

Rick already knew this about his mother, he just hadn't realized his father did. Eileen was a lot like Karen, he realized.

He thought of her now, waving goodbye at the doorstep, smiling and waving until the headlights dimmed. She never did that. She was covering up.

She was giving up.

"I have to go!" he told his father.

Chapter 48

Connor was angry. "This is ridiculous," he moaned as he traipsed in and out of pubs and clubs. He was feeling ill again and it was all Andrew's fault; making him search the city for him, just because he couldn't handle a bit of responsibility.

Well, he'd had enough. He was going home! Connor spun on his heels to turn back for home but dizziness caught him by surprise. It gripped his shoulders and seemed to rob his consciousness like a pickpocket on the busy streets. Connor forgot for a moment where he was and everything seemed foreign to him.

He shut his eyes tightly and squeezed his lids together; it had worked for him before, he thought.

Taking a slow and deliberate breath he opened his eyes again and recognized Manion's Corner. There was a shortcut he could take through the sloping park above it that would take him by Rick's house. If only Rick could drive he'd be home by now. His thoughts were interrupted by a series of tooting horns and shouts of protest on the road. Some adrenaline junkie maniac had ridden his bike over the park incline above Manion's corner, landing in the middle of the traffic. The bike sped off westwards, the rider only narrowly escaping with his life

****

Rick barely registered the danger he'd just caused as he sped west to Ashton Park. He had always wanted to make the Manion Park jump and clear the traffic. But now he felt like he'd never care about silly stunts again, not when there was so much else in the world to worry about. He jumped curbs and skidded over pathways until he saw the red brick houses of Ashton Park.

Rick threw his bike carelessly on the lawn and banged at the front door. There was no answer so he knocked again frantically. Slowly a window from a neighbouring house opened. *Oh no,* Rick thought, *not Cat Woman!* He shook his head.

A blond curly-haired figure poked her sleepy head out the window, and sure enough an ugly sphinx cat peeped out too. It looked like an evil gremlin.

"Sorry!" Rick called before digging his hands into his pockets for the spare key Connor had given him. He steadied his hand and unlocked the door. Carefully he stepped inside. The house was dark and he could hear Buddy whimpering from somewhere deep inside. He found him in the kitchen licking Karen's face, who lay motionless on the floor.

Rick could make out Karen's face by the moonlight that spilled through the kitchen window. It was sad and empty. A crashing sound caught Rick's attention. His head jerked at the noise like it had called him.

Later Rick would regret not staying. Perhaps he could have done more to help his friend. But there was rage brewing inside him. It burned at his insides and told him to give chase, so he did.

He ran out the back door and through the garden, where he saw a dark figure jump the wall. He followed it through the neighbour's gardens, in and out of slides and swings. He threw himself over wall after wall, but his target was fit and fast and he closed no distance.

When they crossed the park and the dark figure climbed the bridge it became clear that his destination was the railway tracks. Rick slipped through the fence of the station hoping to gain some ground and meet him on the tracks. His plan worked.

****

Andrew thought he had lost his follower but this boy was persistent. Under any other circumstances he would have been happy to know his niece had such friends.

But Andrew was persistent too. He had more determination than anyone. His body may have been polluted with alcohol and his mind tormented by demons but even still he knew he was uncatchable. He darted through the station barriers and onto the tracks, as Rick followed.

Andrew was over six foot tall. He bounded in long strides along the tracks and Rick had trouble keeping up. Rick lost his footing several times and Andrew gained distance again.

Eventually Rick's body caught up with a mind that told him he could no longer go on. He'd fought in a three-hour tournament, cycled across the city and chased a stranger along train tracks, and all with nothing in his belly but whiskey. His arms gave up first and fell by his sides. A sharp stitch stung his sides and his lungs were making the wheezing sounds of a dying dog. He was beaten. He couldn't even raise his head to watch his target disappear from sight.

The night was silent save for the sound of fleeing footsteps fading into the distance. Rick listened to his breath; only when it steadied did he think of Karen. He'd left her behind. What was he thinking?

****

The door of number twenty-five was still open when Rick returned. He could hear a shuffling sound inside. Connor was in the kitchen. He was checking his sister's pulse. He looked every bit as bad as she did. His lips were blue and he wasn't speaking. Rick swallowed hard and slowly approached his friend. He could see his boots taking the steps, slow and blurry like an astronaut struggling with gravity. He barely recognized them; they didn't feel like his own

This wasn't happening to him, it couldn't be.

Connor rose from his hunkers and seemed to find his voice. "I think it's beating." He tried to take the phone from his pocket but his fingers were like butter and it smashed to the floor.

"Give me yours!" he ordered Rick.

Rick dug deep into his pockets and dialled for an ambulance on his phone.

****

Karen's ambulance sped across Dublin's northside making its way towards the city centre. As it manoeuvred in and out of bus lanes and breezed through red lights, Connor and Rick were thrown around in the back. Neither could offer the paramedics any useful information on Karen's condition.

"Did you move her?" they asked Rick.

"No!"

"Did you check her vitals?" the other asked.

"*I* did!" Connor saved him.

"She was attacked!" Rick kept repeating over and over.

The piercing sound of sirens slowed and then ceased as the ambulance pulled into the Mater Hospital on Eccles Street.

Karen was taken in on a hospital trolley.

Connor caught Rick by the shoulder before they entered. "Did you see him?" he asked, with a dangerous look in his eye.

"It was too dark."

Connor merely nodded in acceptance. "Don't worry we'll get him!"

Rick watched helplessly as Karen was carted away from him. Connor followed her through shiny white double doors and Rick waited near reception with everyone else.

What had happened? His mind began spinning questions.

Was it Marcus he had chased across the tracks? Maybe he wasn't dead at all? Then he remembered the silhouette of the six-foot figure darting across the tracks and dismissed the idea.

Chapter 49

Esther was restless. "Please let me take the baby?" she asked for the third time.

"I said I'm fine!" Katie tried not to snap.

Darcy was screaming down their little cottage. It was a new skill she'd been practising all afternoon. Katie shut the windows with her free hand as if the noise were disturbing some imaginary neighbour.

"Maybe she senses her daddy is missing," Esther offered.

"Maybe she senses he's an asshole."

Esther pretended not to hear. "I'll put on the kettle." she offered, but she was distracted by the front door bell. Esther was surprisingly fast as she shot to the front door.

Katie cursed herself for following in hopeful desperation. Her heart sank when Esther yanked the door open.

Joy to the world, a new born King, came the chorus, loud and intrusive.

Esther flung the door shut like it was on a spring.

Catherine and Katie stared open mouthed; even Darcy quietened as though somehow sensing the tension.

Catherine eventually broke her shock-induced silence. "I can't believe you just did that! It's Christmas Eve! I know those people." She pointed to the door as if they were still there. "How will I ever shop in Heffernan's again?"

"Humph." Esther was unperturbed. "Didn't see Bridie Fox and Evelyn Maloney, did you? Poking their heads in to see if Andrew was here?"

"So what if they were?" Catherine said.

Esther acted like she hadn't heard. She tightened the bun in her hair and took a seat at the edge of the sofa. "The neck of them, and all in the guise of praising our Lord."

The door bell sounded again. "I'll get it," Catherine declared, preparing all sorts of apologies in her head. But her voice failed her when she saw Andrew at the door. He looked like he'd been dragged through a field by a tractor. His facial hair had grown into a fully formed beard and a nasty lump was forming on the side of his head.

"Esther!" Catherine called. "I think we should go."

"Is this about Bridie Fox?" Esther came marching to the door but lost her composure at the sight of her son. She ran to him and touched his face as if making sure he wasn't a ghost. "Oh, Andy." she whispered.

Andrew couldn't meet her eyes and lowered her hands with his own.

"I'm okay, Mother."

Chapter 50

An icy cold sensation encased Karen's body. It moved in ripples over her skin. She saw nothing but cloudy fluid about her, but instinct told her to kick her legs. She kicked until she broke the surface of Loch Gliese. Gasping for air, she wondered if she was dead or alive but her instinct not to sink below the water's surface told her she was very much alive.

She was in Sublimina, she had to be.

A silver shoreline, lit up only by the moon, beckoned her. She tried to swim but soon realized there was no need. Waves were thrusting her forward, as if the lake was trying to spit her out. Karen swam anyway and by the time she reached the shore she collapsed with exhaustion, her face buried in the shore.

The night was silent save for the sound of the water washing over the rocks. Karen's hearing was heightened. She thought she could make out the sound of water filling the uneven terrain; like the shore had several punctures and she could tell which ones were deepest.

"Welcome, key keeper!"

The clear and confident voice startled her. Karen raised her tired head and particles of soil and bark rained down from her cheeks.

The voice belonged to a slender-framed female with dark hair and piercing blue eyes that shone through the darkness. She wore a robe tied at the waist with something that looked like plaited rope. Her legs were bare and long as she unfolded them beneath her.

"I know you." Karen found her voice.

The woman raised a defined eyebrow in surprise.

"I saw you in a dream arguing about directions."

"I am Sháya." The stranger nodded. "Where is your guardian angel?" Sháya looked around them. "You must be in danger if he brought you here!"

Karen watched her scan the shores intently. She had a confident posture and the moonlight showed her angular jaw clenched in contemplation.

Karen tried to recall the circumstances surrounding her arrival but the details were hazy. "Fabien wasn't there." She was shaking her head as if to remember more clearly.

"I heard the banshee roar and then ... then I heard a whisper! It told me to sleep. Going unconscious while wearing the key brought me here."

"Impossible! You must have imagined it. There is no sound that could drown the call of the banshee."

"You mentioned my guardian angel ... Is there some way I can contact him?"

Sháya regarded Karen with intense interest before answering. "We will send him a message by bark but he will receive it only when he lights a candle."

Karen was confused. "Why would he light a candle?"

"To get his messages." Sháya looked equally confused. "Don't you put your messages in candles when calling a higher power?"

"Prayers... not messages." Karen was beginning to shake. Her legs were unsteady and she didn't have time to try to understand Sháya or the customs here. "Surely there's a faster way." She tried to keep her voice steady but failed.

Sháya noticed the shake in Karen's hands and it touched her. "I will have one of the angels contact him telepathically." She gestured for Karen to sit. "Perhaps you should rest a while; take some steady breaths." She laid a hand on Karen's shoulder.

Karen realized Sháya was trying to calm her, but how could she be calm, knowing her body lay unconscious at home?

****

Fabien's head hurt. A lead in Budapest had yielded nothing. He hadn't meditated all day and his eyes grew weary examining the text before him. Interpreting prophecies had never been one of his strong points but many held his abilities in high regard, so he persevered. He knew the words off by heart – everyone did – but he read them again anyway.

When ten hundred years is ten hundred years for the second time, a child will prepare to begin.
When ten years have passed since the union of the last, a new dawn we find within. Rejoice the union 111+

Fabien ran both his hands through the waves of his hair and shut his tired eyes. He was interrupted by the intrusive little buzzer on the wall. He never had visitors and he'd forgotten what it sounded like.

No one but Karen knew he was staying at the offices.

Fabien went to the large windows in the boardroom and looked through one of the lateral blinds. When he could see no one he closed his eyes in an attempt to sense a familiar aura instead. He found it four floors beneath, disjointed and fast paced. It was Rick.

Fabien went to meet him. He found him on the final stairwell panting and sweating, Rick was infecting the air with anxiety. Fabien's heart softened. "Come in my friend," he gestured.

Rick ignored him and slouched in the doorway, exhausted. "Karen's gone," he panted. "To Sublimina, I think. We have to find this prophet or it will never be safe for her to wake."

Fabien glanced around him to see if the commotion had woken Daniel. It hadn't. He could still make out his snores from one of the offices. Strategizing required a peaceful environment, something Daniel was not gifted at creating.

Fabien wanted to send Rick home, but the boy was a mess. "Come in." Rick followed him like a disciplined schoolboy to the cafeteria. Fabien rummaged around the kitchen.

"What are you doing?" Rick asked.

"You need some supper, a wash and some rest. You can help me when all three have been satisfied and not before."

Rick didn't attempt to argue. He found the shower rooms while Fabien prepared them some food. It was eerie in the quiet offices and Rick undressed uneasily. His jeans were wet and stuck to his shins when he tried to pull them off. He pulled his T-shirt off over his head and his muscles ached from the effort.

The water was cold. Rick closed his eyes and tried not to think of Karen. When he stepped out of the powerful shower he felt more awake. Fabien had left him some of Daniel's clothes but they were too big. Daniel was a giant. He buttoned a large blue checked shirt up to the collar and stared at himself in the mirror. He touched the stubble on his face and it prickled the skin of his fingers. He looked older than the last time he'd looked in the mirror. When exactly had life gotten so difficult, he wondered.

Fabien was waiting for him back in the canteen. He handed him a plate of food and they ate in silence at one of the tables.

"How do you live here?" Rick asked eventually.

"You don't like it?"

"It's eerie." Rick shivered. "The silence is deafening."

"It can be peaceful, if you use it."

"So when are you going to let me help find the prophet?"

Fabien shifted uncomfortably in his chair. "Interpreting prophecy is an age-old art, something you have no experience with. I know you want to help but there is nothing you can do."

"Humph." Rick scraped his plate clean with a fork and swallowed the last of his spaghetti. "Sounds a little arrogant coming from someone who once told me we must look before we can find" Rick said, doing an impression of Fabien.

Fabien looked startled for the first time since Rick had known him.

"What was it you said?" One person's conclusions may not be another's. That was right before you told me God must have known of man's tendency to institutionalize everything, to create a hierarchy and pointlessly empower people." Rick shook his head and brought their plates over to the sink. He was straining his eyes sideways, secretly trying to catch Fabien's reaction. Rick was grateful that Fabien wasn't a man. Men were proud and didn't like to admit when they were wrong. Men were blind when they felt undermined. But Fabien was more than a man. Fabien understood the bigger picture; he lived for it.

"You are right." Fabien stood up. "Tomorrow we will examine the passage together."

Rick didn't remember falling asleep. Fabien had given him a hot drink and he woke on the uncomfortable grey sofa in reception. The fabric tickled his chin as he leaned lazily over the side to check his phone. There were no messages. He swung his long legs over the couch to get dressed but paused as a disturbing thought crossed his mind: it was Christmas Day.

The realization disturbed him. Connor and his family would be spending it by Karen's bedside, not knowing if she would ever wake up. He swallowed hard as an enormous sense of guilt seemed to choke him.

Connor was oblivious to the world where his sister resided. He had no idea of the threats she faced. Would he perhaps find solace in the fact that she was safe there or would he despair at the fact that it wasn't safe for her to wake? Rick didn't know. He only knew that he was depriving him of the choice and it bothered him.

He quickly got dressed and dragged himself through the offices in search of Fabien. He found him in the boardroom. A desk lamp was still lit and it looked like he'd been up all night.

"Happy Christmas," Fabien said and slid the manuscript in front of Rick's line of vision. Rick stared at the words.

When ten hundred years is ten hundred years for the second time, a child will prepare to begin.

When ten years have passed since the union of the last, a new dawn we find within.

Rejoice the union 111+

He continued to stare and scratched at the stubble on his chin.

Fabien watched him chew his lips over and over until finally Rick spoke.

"Looks like they like the number ten." He folded his arms at the conclusion.

Fabien overlooked the humour. "Obviously we know that it refers to a period of time following the millennium: "When ten hundred years is ten hundred years for the second time.""

"Obviously." Rick nodded, in a stupor. "What about 'When ten years have passed since the union of the last?'"

"We thought it meant ten years since the union of the two sets of ten hundred years which would indicate the year 2010 but when no one came forward in that year we assumed the arrival was just late, then very late, and now we're just not sure."

"Why not? A child surely wouldn't display anything unusual until it came of age, anyway."

Fabien nodded but he wasn't convinced.

"What about 'Rejoice the union 111+?" Rick sat down.

"The third millennia will be sacred." Fabien rubbed his eyes. "The third millennia will be sacred," he repeated.

Rick examined him and sat back in his chair. "Are you telling me or yourself?"

"I'm not sure."

"So who wrote this?" Rick took up the manuscript.

"She was an angel who resided in Sublimina at the time of St Paul." Fabien spoke in a tone of awe.

"You knew her?" Rick was intrigued by anyone who inspired awe in Fabien.

"As well as anyone could." Fabien smiled at the memory. "Xanthia was ahead of all of us. We barely understood her half the time, she spoke in such riddles."

"And she could see into the future?"

"It was one of the only things she could see. She was blind you see. Her eyes shone so brightly it hurt to open them."

"Cruel twist of fate."

"How so?" Fabien inclined his head.

"Having to suffer such an affliction because you have a gift."

Fabien smiled. "That is a very human way to look at it. We would think of it more as being given a gift to ease the affliction."

"Whatever." Rick wasn't listening. He was still staring at the text. "So she wrote this?" He examined it doubtfully.

"Well, obviously not on this paper. Xanthia wrote on the bark of the trees at Aingeal Forest."

Rick couldn't help himself, "Bit of a vandal, was she?"

"In this world I'm sure she would be. But trees are different in Sublimina." The tone of wonderment returned to Fabien's voice, "In Sublimina the arms of the trees outstretch out over the land extending their branches to all. They supply us with everything we need. I think they're understandably more reluctant in this world."

"Why don't you go and see it?" Rick asked after some time.

"The tree?" Fabien asked.

"Why not? You told me once that the Bible wasn't written until hundreds of years after Jesus left. Some passages, while meaningful, got lost in translation. But you, you have the unique opportunity to interpret the words of a spiritualist written *by* a spiritualist. I think you should visit the tree."

Fabien sat in silence.

Rick lit a cigarette. It was Christmas Day, he consoled himself. He was allowed on such an occasion. He watched the lighter ignite the tobacco and inhaled deeply. He said nothing. Rick was getting good at knowing when not to speak. He may have been in the presence of greatness, but greatness was always learning.

His patience paid off.

"Thank you." Fabien's voice was soft. He left the boardroom and returned with a solitary slim white candle. He took Rick's lighter and lit the wick. Rick watched with wonderment as the flame flickered and failed. The candle wax melted down the middle and separated at the wick. It split down the centre leaving a sheet of bark in its wake.

Your subject is safe and requests your presence, it read.

"You should go." Rick got up to leave.

Fabien sighed with a heavy heart.

Rick was confused. He had gotten the impression Fabien had been missing the world he called home. "Don't you want to return?"

"Returning is not the problem," Fabien said. "Telling Daniel is."

Chapter 51

Karen lay on a bed of soft rushes. It was an unusual sensation. But everything about Sháya's residence was unusual. Sat on the impossibly long branches of a tree she had no name for, it seemed an enchanted place.

Sháya had given her the spare room. The dome of the window filtered the moonlight into rays of blue lines. Karen jumped as a number of knocks echoed from the other side of the timber door.

"Are you awake?" Sháya's voice reverberated in a way that would ensure that she was now.

"I'm awake," Karen called, but the door was already creaking open.

"I brought something to help you sleep." Sháya handed her a hot jug made out of Tuscan pottery.

Karen peered inside and was disappointed to see that it looked a lot like the lake she'd swam in. "Do you think Fabien received our message?" she asked.

"Yes. Angels always light candles to communicate with the waking world."

Sháya nodded to the drink she had prepared. "You should drink that."

Karen made herself take a mouthful so as not to be rude. It didn't feel warm in her mouth but as soon as she swallowed it, it began to heat her insides.

Sháya bade her good night but Karen felt like she'd forgotten how to speak, forgotten how to do anything but close her eyes and give in to unconsciousness.

****

When Karen woke she found Dan by her bedside. He was watching her attentively. Karen immediately pulled a blanket up to her chin.

"Where's Fabien?" she asked.

Dan looked wounded. "He's downstairs with the others."

Sure enough, a chorus of voices carried onto the landing outside the bedroom door.

"It's good to see you." Karen tried to make amends for her insensitivity and reached for his hand. Dan's face grew softer but his eyes still seemed distracted. Karen noticed drooping skin over his eyelids that she hadn't noticed before.

"Happy Christmas," Dan whispered.

"Christmas!" Karen began to panic at the thoughts of her family by her hospital bedside.

"Shush." Dan turned to see if anyone had heard them. "I'm not supposed to remind you, I'm supposed to *acclimatize* you," he said, making imaginary inverted commas with his fingers. "But you deserve the truth; people here don't understand the obligation we have to our families; I do," he told her.

Karen felt helpless, helpless and worried.

"Is there anything you want me to tell them? Anything I can do to comfort them?"

Karen thought about it. "I can't think of a single thing."

Daniel nodded his head slowly. "Me neither."

Dan had grown a field of stubble above his upper lip and down his scar-ridden chin. He scratched at it distractedly before taking his leave. "I'm sorry this has fallen to you." He half hugged, half embraced her before settling for a playful tap on the cheek instead. "I'll check on your family for you." Karen waited for him to go before getting out of bed. The soft light from the window drew her closer; she couldn't help her curiosity. But she didn't find the morning sunshine she'd expected. It was bright, that much was true, but it was the bright blue glow of the moon that lit up the land. The sun was nowhere to be seen.

Some semblance of guilt stirred from the pit of her stomach at the flutter of excitement she felt. Part of her was eager to see this new world. An enthusiasm she hadn't felt the day before. She folded up the nightdress Sháya had loaned her. Karen was sure she had never seen anything so brilliantly white in all her life. She was almost sorry to get dressed.

She followed the voices downstairs to the kitchen.

The little kitchen was crowded. Sháya, Fabien and two others were sat at a little round timber table. Karen recognized the silky red haired Sublim as Sháya's sister.

"I'm Addis," she spoke.

Karen looked to the Sublim next to her but he didn't introduce himself.

Fabien stood then, and Karen couldn't help throwing her arms around him.

It felt like hugging a heated rock, warm and solid.

Fabien seemed surprised but pleased with the display of affection.

"This is Dominic." Fabien gestured to the silent Sublim.

"Dominic will stay with you today."

"Why can't I come with you?"

"I am bound for Aingeal Forest, to examine the prophecy."

"Can't I come?"

"Silence will be of the essence. Addis and Sháya are required at the Senate but Dominic is just as good a host. Karen watched Dominic nod slowly but wasn't filled with hope.

"You must be hungry," Addis interrupted and began cutting bread with a dangerous looking knife

Karen realized she hadn't eaten anything in almost two days now. The bread was hard and course and not what she was used to. There was no tea or coffee but she drank what she was given. It tasted like liquefied old pennies but she did her best not to flinch.

Karen had always been uncomfortable eating among strangers But sitting in a room full of pupil-less eyes made it feel like everyone was watching her.

Chapter 52

Doctor Paul Fahey was the youngest doctor working the intensive care unit where Karen lay. Paul had always been top of the class with a promising career ahead of him. Families generally liked Paul; he was impeccably well groomed, with gelled-back hair and a manner that suggested experience beyond his years. He brushed down the impossibly white coat.

"At this point we're still running tests," he informed Catherine. "Her blood work has revealed nothing unusual." He shrugged. "MRI scans are normal. It could be anything at this point, even a simple case of dehydration."

Catherine looked up from the hospital chart she'd been examining. Paul had not expected the relative to be a doctor.

"Does she look like she just needs a drink to you?"

Paul straightened a little; he wasn't used to being spoken to like this by visitors.

"Where is Dr Vanyak? I want to speak to the consultant."

"Dr Vanyak is in surgery. Being in the medical field yourself, I'm sure you'll appreciate that there are other patients here, too, and everyone gets seen to in order of priority."

****

"What's going on in there?" Esther whispered to Andrew as they sat outside in the corridor. Her long grey hair was falling out of an overworked hair clip; it fell about her face in wiry strands. With wide old eyes she peeped through the glass pane and saw Catherine rounding on a young unsuspecting doctor.

Esther concentrated hard and squinted, but still she couldn't hear a word. It had gone silent. This was when Catherine was at her most dangerous, Esther knew. Lowering her voice usually meant a deadly blow was being delivered.

Esther jumped back with what she thought was speed and saw the young doctor taking his leave with a flushed face. Connor and Esther quickly entered the room. Andrew stayed seated outside. He was holding his head in his hands trying to answer a mind full of questions. How was Karen still alive? What exactly had happened? Had he passed out? Was the key taken?

Please say the key was taken. He rocked his body slowly forward and backwards. Had Karen passed into the other world? Andrew didn't know much about it, or how to get there. The book only mentioned its existence.

"Are you coming in?" a soft voice whispered from behind the door.

It was his mother. It was always his mother. Andrew found it in himself to smile at her. "You know I hate hospitals," he muttered. It was as good an excuse as any. Seeing Karen unconscious was not what he needed right now. He wasn't sure he could bear it.

"How is she?" he asked.

Esther came and sat next to him. "She's stable."

Andrew noticed his mother was trying to sound chirpy. "Go home and be with Katie and Darcy," she suggested. "They need you."

Andrew thought about it. What if Karen woke up? What would she say? *Andrew told the banshee on me*? Unlikely, he decided.

The best place to be right now was with Darcy. If Karen's life failed and the key hadn't been retrieved, it would be Darcy who was in danger.

"You're right." Andrew nodded.

Chapter 53

Dominic had barely helped Karen down from the trees when he found himself drowning in a flood of questions.

"Where are we?" she asked the moment her foot reached the forest floor.

"Pallas," Dominic grunted. "Named after the planet Pallas." He pointed half-heartedly to the sky.

A collection of stone structures in the distance had caught Karen's attention. The flickering of lights inside told her they were inhabited.

Dominic held a branch back so Karen wouldn't walk into it. His eyes were better adjusted to the low light and he knew every inch of this place.

Karen followed him slowly, trying to take in her surroundings.

"Fabien said Sháya was at the Senate today," she thought out loud. "Who runs that?"

Dominic waited until they had reached a clearing before answering.

"One member of each of the higher sentients sits on the Senate."

Karen stopped dramatically to consider what she had learned so far. "Higher sentients are angels, banshee, Gorgons, and converters." She rhymed off like a poem.

"And converters are?" Dominic was interested to learn what she knew.

"Vampires and werewolves."

Dominic raised his black eyebrows, suggesting she should try again.

"Fine, children of Neptune and children of the moon."

Dominic looked impressed and tried to catch her eye but he noticed her flinch when he did. Humans were so easy to read with those black holes in their eyes. He wondered if the unreadable nature of Sublim eyes was making her uncomfortable. Or perhaps it disturbed her to realize her own were mere windows.

"No one else can see through those holes in your eyes you know."

Dominic's voice was monotone and Karen couldn't tell if he was annoyed or hurt.

"The clan of O'Driscoll have no subconscious counterparts here."

Karen felt guilty. She had to get better at hiding her feelings. But Sublim eyes took time to get used to. She would learn in time. She would have to. She fixed her attention on the sky to overcome the awkward moment. Several planets stared back at her.

Dominic noticed her interest. "As above, so below." He stood next to her.

"Where have I heard that?"

"Each of the seven archangels are represented by one of the seven planets visible to the eye." he explained. This was the first time he spoke without apathy Karen noticed.

"They are the seven moving objects in the heavens," he continued. "It's in the Bible. Maybe you heard it there."

"Maybe," Karen lied, embarrassed she had never read the thing.

"Fabien wanted me to show you Hamied's Hub." His bored tone of voice returned.

Karen watched him put his fingers into his mouth and he blew hard. The sound startled her.

"Bracken," he said, as if that explained everything. "You're much too slow for us to walk."

Karen was still deciding whether to be insulted or not when the sound of thundering hooves distracted her. The sight of the muscular horse approaching made her forget the jibe.

Dominic stroked its big black head and jumped astride his powerful back.

"Are you coming?" He stretched a hairy arm down to her.

Karen wasn't sure she could mount a horse as big as Bracken. Not without a boost from the ground upward but she was not going to share this with Dominic. Instead she grabbed his hand. If she fell she would say he had sweaty palms. That always annoyed Rick. She hoped it would have the same effect on Dominic.

Dominic's hands weren't sweaty. They were large and steady. Karen barely had to flex a muscle but he had hoisted her up like she was nothing more than a carrier bag.

He directed her hands around his waist and made sure she was holding tightly before he kicked Bracken into action.

The horse bolted into a speed Karen didn't think possible for an animal.

Karen worried several times that she would fall off, her heart raced with adrenaline. Her fear heightened by the absence of the sun.

She could just about make out the ground beneath them, the passing stone structures and other shapes she didn't recognize, but it wasn't the same without the sunlight.

Everything here was bright enough to see but dark enough to fear.

Finally Dominic pulled on the reigns and the horse slowed to a steady trot. They were approaching a valley and beyond it she could make out the large domed roof of Hamied's Hub.

"Incredible," she whispered.

Bracken trotted onwards into the heart of the valley until they reached the great courtyard that held the Hub. His hooves echoed loudly in the silence.

Karen looked around her. "I thought you said it was a busy place."

"It is." He pointed to a great crystal slab that reflected a lunar dial beneath it. "It's only ten thirty. Everyone will be at the library, documenting observations from their visions."

Karen hadn't considered that these dreams or visions were interpreted before, but they must be if converters were set assignments from them.

Dominic dismounted suddenly and extended a hand to Karen.

This time she took it gratefully. Dominic adjusted his saddle and loosened the straps.

"What then?" Karen asked.

"Then they're taken to Loch Gliese and tossed into its waters."

"What's the point in that?"

Dominic realized he hadn't been explaining himself entirely. "Our observations are documented on bark. When the bark hits the waters of the lake it dissolves and the most important observations are filtered to the angels." Dominic was proud of his short summary. "Documented observations will contain everything from opportunities we observe for good and evil, to what our human counterparts had for breakfast."

Karen's eyes widened with fear. She was grateful no one else had ever seen through her eyes before and had never been more grateful to be a key holder.

They would have seen her take that illegal right turn at the station every day. They would have seen her stuff her bra every time she went out with Sam.

A splash of cold water hit her face and made her jump.

Dominic was holding a container of water under Bracken's enormous chin.

Karen drew her gaze to the building before them. Giant grey slabs were packed so tightly together it gave the stone a polished look Karen had never seen before. Higher they climbed until they reached the stone of the dome that covered them. But there was something unusual at the top. It was as if it existed underwater, slightly blurred with a moving liquid texture. Karen felt dizzy and had to look away. Her eyes rested on two cylindrical slabs either side of the entrance that bore hydrographical inscriptions.

Dominic noticed her star. "It says Hamied's Hub, Hamied is the angel of Miracles."

Chapter 54

Sam's chest felt like it had been stabbed with a wooden stake. She sat bolt upright on her crumpled bed sheets. Her breath came in short rasps, in and out, tight and fast. Her entire Christmas had been wrought with nightmares and here she was on the first Monday morning of the New Year, no different.

She glanced at the little pink face of the alarm clock on her bedside locker. Another twenty minutes. Slowly she lay back down. She shut her eyes gratefully, but images from her dreams still lingered there. She had been in Raptures drinking water from a wine glass, which was enough of a nightmare in itself. But it was the company that made it worse. Sat across from her had been Liam. He looked different and he looked at her with a slyness that told her he knew something she did not. He leaned in to kiss her then and to her disgust she'd kissed him back. It lasted only seconds before she broke away with a jolt. His tongue was thin and forked. It was like kissing a snake. Sam felt like she might throw up.

****

The office was quiet. Sam went straight for Karen's desk to tell her about her dreams. "Where's Karen?" she asked Zara.

"Probably enjoying another late morning," Zara said loud enough for Brenda to hear.

Sam shot her a look.

"Oh, relax," Zara shot back. "Sure, how could anyone hear anything over Cookie Monster over there?" She nodded at Olivia.

"They're crisps, not cookies," Olivia corrected with her mouth full.

"How do you eat those at this hour?" Sam made a face and took her seat.

It was mid-morning when Brenda finally heard news on Karen. It was her mother who called and the conversation had made Brenda's blood run cold. Suddenly being in charge wasn't so appealing any more, and for once she had news she *didn't* want to share with the team.

It was Sam who noticed Brenda approach. It was always Sam because she was always on the lookout for when to shut down her internet browser. Brenda appeared to have lost the springs she wore on her shoes and was missing her habitual look-at-me bounce.

Brenda brought them into one of the meeting rooms. It was cold in there this time of morning, and Brenda could see her breath. She saw everything a little slower since taking that call. "A little bit of disrobing news, I mean disturbing news," she began. "Karen has taken a turn and is commad, I mean in a coma."

Her blunders went unnoticed. Nobody had heard a word she'd said. Will was dipping his hand into Olivia's crisp bag, Zara was criticizing them both and Sam was picking her nails. Brenda slapped the table angrily. "Karen is in a coma," she yelled over them. Brenda loved attention but not of this kind.

Will's brows furrowed and crisps fell from Olivia's mouth.

It was Zara who spoke first. "How long is she going to be in that for?"

Zara was Brenda's favourite. She was easiest to direct, but she was hardest to get through to. "A coma is not a controllable thing," Brenda explained.

"Yes it is," Zara argued. "Doctors induce them all the time. The do it every week on *America's Most Plastic*!"

"I'll put you in a coma if you don't shut it," Sam shot.

This was too much, Brenda decided. "Take the rest of the day off," she intervened. "We'll arrange for some flowers to be delivered." She was talking to herself as much as to the team.

Chapter 55

It had been five days now that Karen had spent in Sublimina. She had been staying at Sháya's. She had risen at dusk and slept at dawn just like the rest of Sublimina.

Adjusting her body clock to rise at night and sleep during the day wasn't hard. In fact it was easy because there was no sunrise or sunset; it was always just dim with a gentle amber light.

Karen spent most of her days at the library. She had read the laws of the land and learned that a feud continuing in Sublimina carried a death sentence at Lake Lilith. She learned that Gorgons had not always been confined to this world. One even featured as a snake in the very first Bible story. They were banished from the waking world by none other than Maewyn Succat. St Patrick, she learned, had been an angel.

Today Karen was on the prowl for a very different book. All this good and evil had her mind working overtime. Her conscience told her repentance was salvation, but what about Marcus? She had been fretting. Would he be forgiven? There was nothing anywhere that she'd read that would explain the gruesome way he'd died. Karen had seen a lot in this world and still nothing disturbed her more than Marcus's departure from it.

"Where is all the doctrine on converters?" Karen asked the Sprite at the desk.

The Sprite stared at her with those unreadable eyes. Karen saw them move beneath her heavily arched eyebrows and couldn't help taking a step back. She looked grumpy. "Children of the moon or children of Neptune?" she snapped.

"Children of Neptune," Karen answered smugly, having brushed up on all her terminology.

"Out of bounds," the Sprite grunted and put her hand on a cylindrical crystal built into the counter.

Karen recognized Addis's face in it.

"Your friend wants to find out about her boyfriend," she said cruelly.

Karen felt her lips curl, almost forming a snarl, but Addis appeared by her side in an instant.

"Don't mind her," Addis said when they were out of earshot. "She's just never known love herself."

"I didn't love him. I mean I don't love him," Karen muttered. "He tried to kill my friend." Karen thought of Dan.

"You don't have to feel bad about caring, you know. You're not betraying anyone by caring." Addis was very matter of fact.

Karen knew she was right, but still she felt guilty as she sat waiting for her book. When the heavy hardback landed on the desk before her Karen jumped.

"I think this is the one you're looking for." Addis gazed at her knowingly.

Karen stared at the gold lettering. "This is a book on Gorgons?" Gorgons were a subject Karen was happy to avoid.

"Chapter thirty-eight." Addis's tone was serious before departing.

Karen lifted the heavy cover and skipped to the heading of chapter thirty-eight, The Blood of a Gorgon.

Karen was still doubtful but something about Addis's tone made her want to read on.

The blood of a Gorgon is a homogeneous mixture of venom and anabolic hormones existing at an exact ratio to lend it the power to both give and take life. Blood taken from the right side of a Gorgon can heal you. Blood taken from the left side is a fatal poison.

Karen took a breath. Days of reading were beginning to take their toll and she rubbed at her eyes. What did any of this have to do with the death of a vampire? She sighed. Karen checked the time. She would be late for the banquet, a ceremony that took place before the onset of dawn, where Sublims and Sprites prepare to awaken in their humans' subconsciousness.

Karen tried to read faster. She did not want to experience the embarrassment of requesting this book again. Vampires were descendants of Gorgons she learned. Vampire blood had similar properties but with one exception – the healing hormones. Unlike their Gorgon masters, vampire blood did not have the power to heal. A Child of Neptune could lose their converter standing and die if the venom in their blood was neutralized. Neutralizing venom is only possible if an emotion pure enough is present. Love would kill a vampire. Symptoms included bruising and lesions on the skin. The blood curdles and cannot flow once the venom dies. Air burns the lungs as they are no longer meant for either world. The subject would suffer loss of appetite as they can no longer digest blood.

Karen's own blood ran cold. The cruelty of it numbed her. How can the world dispel you for love? She thought of Marcus's death and tears welled in her eyes.

****

Fabien sat on the soft grass with his legs crossed. He was examining the Tree of Eagna that held the prophecy.

Dan and Briathos stood a distance away watching him. Briathos stood serious as ever, arms folded. Dan liked Briathos. He was the angel who thwarted demons in the waking world. The Angels expressions were ferocious in nature and he rarely smiled. His blond straight hair formed a fringe over a pair of darker coloured eyebrows, giving him a striking appearance.

Briathos didn't speak much, at least not to Dan. Dan knew he communicated mostly with other angels. Dan was a mere child of the moon to him, but he didn't care. He liked him anyway. Dan liked all warriors. "Is there nothing we can do?" he finally asked Briathos.

"We have no gifts in prophetic interpretations," Briathos answered but kept his gaze on Fabien. "It is Sofia we need," he added in a deep tone.

"Where is she? I can go get her."

"She is meditating."

"After she meditates!"

Briathos stared at him for a moment. "Okay," he agreed. "But I will locate her."

Dan watched him go down the mountain, a bow and arrow strapped to his back. He hoped he was right about Sofia. They were running out of time.

"It's nearly dawn," Dan shouted to Fabien.

Fabien dragged his body down from the summit. "There's something I'm missing, or misinterpreting." He sounded angry.

"You don't say." Dan was being sarcastic. He couldn't help it. He might not have been an angel, but Karen was his daughter at the end of the day.

They met Karen outside the library as planned so they could walk her to the banquet.

"This is your fifth banquet now, right? Do you like them?" Dan asked.

"No!" Karen found them disgusting. The eating and drinking part was fine but the ritual that followed disturbed her. Sublims would kneel before the moon and Sprites would kneel before Neptune. But both groups would cut their own skin. They would collect their own blood with their fingertips and smear it across their eyelids.

"It's not as barbaric as it seems. The blood of Sublims and Sprites is the same blood that flows in the veins of their human counterparts. You will know a person completely by their blood, by how thick it is, how red, even the ratio of plasma platelets and triglycerides holds information about your deepest desires. It helps Sublims and Sprites understand their human counterparts more and deliver more accurate observations."

Karen raised a set of suspecting eyebrows "Are you sure you're not vampire?"

They walked the rest of the way to the banquet in silence. Karen was quiet and Dan was running out of things to say to perk her up.

They reached the gatherings of people around the giant roaring fire that circled the centre of the grassland. They meandered through the crowds. Karen always felt nervous here. The red eyes of the children of Neptune watched her with hunger. Children of the moon were always in packs and they too surveyed her.

"Sofia!" Dan called, startling Karen, who was already on edge.

"Sofia and Dinyl!" Dan nodded in the direction of two beautiful women.

Karen watched him fall on one knee and bow his head before them.

Sofia placed a gentle hand on his head. "Daniel." She smiled.

Daniel? Karen thought.

Sofia made eye contact with Karen then and Karen recognized her instantly. "You were at Rick's tournament!"

Sofia nodded and smiled humbly. "This is Dinyl." She introduced her companion.

Karen was awestruck. There was something about the angel. Dinyl's hair was ivory pale and her eyelashes a silvery white, making it look like snowflakes had landed there and frozen in time. Dinyl, Karen noticed, was examining her with equal intensity and Karen began to feel uncomfortable. "Can we go?" she whispered to Fabien after some time. Her eyes were heavy and it had been a strange night.

Fabien led her back to Sháya's.

Karen stared up at the skies as they walked.

"Would you like to talk about it?"

"Talk about what?"

"You always stare at the planets when your mind brings you discord. Most humans do."

Karen was still silent. They had reached the tree that held Sháya's home in the embrace of its branches, cradling it like a child. But Karen wasn't ready to go inside. She took a seat on one of the large rocks instead and Fabien joined her.

He didn't say anything, he just sat with her.

"You believe in forgiveness, don't you?" Fabien nodded pensively.

"Do you think God would meet someone who left a world they almost destroyed?"

"How did Marcus leave the world?" Fabien asked in a steady tone. "Did you feel the moment he passed?" he asked gently.

Karen tightened her jaw and swallowed hard at the memory.

"Yes." She felt her muscles clenching tighter to form an invisible wall so she wouldn't spill out of herself.

Fabien watched her under the moonlight with pursed lips. "Did he feel you there in that moment, do you think?"

"Yes, I know he did because he inhaled the scent of my hair before he let go."

"And how did you feel about him after everything he did?"

Karen looked at him with fear in her eyes.

"Oh, forget about what you think you should or shouldn't say," Fabien said. "And forgot who you would or wouldn't upset by saying it. Who any of us are or what we did is not important. Just describe the feeling."

"I loved him. I just wanted to rock him in my arms." She slumped onto the rock that suddenly looked very comfortable.

"Well then," Fabien straightened, "I would say that you have your answer."

Karen shook her head in frustration. "I asked how God would receive him, not how I would receive him!"

"It's the same thing," Fabien told her. "You are one and the same. He is inside you, inside us all. He is the love and forgiveness in you. That is how precious you are."

Karen had nothing to say; she didn't feel precious at all.

Fabien watched her uneasily. "I knew he was falling in love with you, you know. The first time I saw you both at the foot of that mountain, and again at the house before he took you. I would never have let him take you otherwise."

Karen's face warmed with the tears that trailed down her cheeks, and Fabien kneeled before her. She was hoping he would put his healing hand on her chest again but he didn't. Instead he lifted a hand like any human could do and wiped the tears with his fingertip.

"How do you do it?" Karen eventually spoke. "How do you keep sight of what's important when the world keeps blinding you to it?"

"Prayer."

Karen forced a laugh. "I don't think a Hail Mary will help."

Fabien chuckled too. "That is because it is a prayer used for a different era, and a different society. It amuses me how it is still used."

Fabien shared his favorite prayer with her. It was only one line long but Karen felt it had greater meaning than any other she'd heard.

"Lord help me to see past what I've been conditioned to see through," he prayed and put his hand on hers.

Chapter 56

Esther was arguing with Catherine. "You haven't slept in days!"

"I'm not leaving," Catherine said. "Do you not smell that alcohol?" Catherine asked angrily. "Someone around here has been drinking before their shift. What sort of care do you think they're giving these patients? " Catherine spread her arm out in an all encompassing motion. "I'm going to find out who it is too!"

"It'll be that Dr Paul!" Esther raised a finger in an accusatory fashion. "Don't worry though, he's not on duty today. She's in the best possible care here, the range is on." She handed her daughter-in-law the key. "There's a casserole in the fridge. You will eat it and you will sleep. You're no good to anyone here!"

"We'll call you if anything changes," Connor promised. He looked worse than Karen did. Black bags hung under his eyes and his lips were an ashen color.

Esther waited until Catherine had left the ward. She could hear the lift being activated.

"Here!" she passed Connor a coffee cup.

"I don't want any coffee, Nan!" he sat forward with irritation.

"Who said anything about coffee?" Esther shoved it into his hand.

Connor looked at her suspiciously and took a mouthful. The unique malt taste of Irish whiskey trickled down his throat. Connor's eyes squinted in amusement as his lips formed a smile and he remembered how to laugh. Esther chuckled along with him, their bodies bobbing up and down on their chairs in unison.

"Don't tell yer mother. It's just, in times like these I need to calm the nerves," she said with a vulnerability that touched Connor's already aching heart.

"You're nearly out." Connor shook the bit of whiskey at the bottom of the cup. "Shall I get us some more?"

Esther didn't need much convincing.

"I'll be back soon." Connor kissed her cheek.

The corridor was empty as he made his way to the lift and a heavy sheet of loneliness descended upon him. He wondered if Karen had been right. It would have been nice to have a girlfriend to share things with. But quickly he dismissed the idea. What would be the point? Just someone else to have to worry about and fail to protect.

His head hung so low that he walked into a woman exiting the lift with some flowers. "Sorry!" Connor caught them before they fell to the ground.

"Connor?" It was Sam.

Connor was relieved to see a friendly face and took Karen's friend in his arms. He squeezed her tightly.

Sam was alarmed. Connor wasn't someone big on affectionate displays and it hurt her heart to realize how low he must be. She hugged him back tightly. His stubble scratched her forehead and he smelled of whiskey. When he stepped back there were tears in his eyes.

"Bloody air con in this place," he said.

"These are from Penbrook." Sam extended the flowers. "Everyone is thinking of her. Do you know what happened?"

Connor rubbed the back of his neck and looked around. "No, but I'm going to find out."

"I can help!"

Connor looked doubtful.

"You don't know everything about her," Sam said. "There are some things only us women share."

"What things?" Connor looked confused and insulted at the same time.

Sam gave a sigh. "Who was the last person she spoke to?"

318

Connor shrugged and Sam shook her head.

"Who called her last?"

Connor shrugged again and Sam slapped his arm "See, you need me."

Connor pressed his lips together and shook his head slowly as if deciding something. "Okay, but not here. Meet me in Raptures later?"

Sam agreed and watched the lift doors close behind him.

****

Raptures was quiet. It was a Wednesday night and not much was going on. Connor and Rick were sitting in a booth waiting for Sam. Rick was staring silently into his pint glass, feeling uncomfortable. His conscience was tearing him up. He was helping his friend try to discover what happened his sister when he already knew. He put his face into his glass and almost emptied it.

"Steady on! I need you sober," Connor said. "There she is." Connor got up from the table so as to get Sam's attention.

Sam was wearing a black blazer jacket and black jeans. All in black she looked as small as Karen. It was unusual to see someone as small as his sister, Connor thought. He suspected her black attire matched her mood. She wore none of her usual sparkling jewellery either.

"Hey." Sam greeted them both.

"I'll get you a drink," Connor told her.

"Not water in a wine glass!" Sam looked terrified.

Connor lowered his eyebrows in confusion. "Wine in a wine glass?"

Sam brightened.

"How are you?" She nudged Rick when Connor had gone.

I'm great … just sat here playing dumb while Karen's guardian angel tries to locate the next prophet and take that blasted key out of her hands, he thought. "I'm okay." he lied.

The evening got more and more uncomfortable for Rick, who answered question after question about the man he'd chased.

"It has to have been Marcus!" Connor argued. "Who else would it be?"

"No, he was too tall to be Marcus," Rick said.

Rick had wondered if it could have been Liam before. But it didn't matter either way. It could have been anyone from the netherworld. The point was that Karen felt in danger and transported herself to Sublimina. Finding who sent her there was not going to change that.

"I feel wrong doing this." Connor produced Karen's phone. "You do it!" He slid it over to Sam.

Sam slid it over to Rick. "No, you!"

"I'm not checking her messages!" Rick was becoming impatient.

"Even if it reveals a phone call just before she went into a coma?" Sam asked.

"Yes," Rick sulked.

Sam took it back and scrolled through the menu.

Rick and Connor were silent for what seemed an eternity.

Sam eventually put the phone down. "Fabien!" she ended the suspense.

Fabien was the last person she spoke with.

"Well, there goes that, then!" Connor threw his hands up. "Fabien's the smallest dude I've ever seen, so definitely not the tall guy you chased."

Raptures was closing and the staff where subtly putting chairs up on the tables around the little group.

"This is hopeless," Rick said. "I'm going to get more drink." He wobbled out of the booth.

"Where are you going?" Connor asked, keen on the idea of more alcohol.

"Some shitty nightclub, I guess!"

"Well, not without me!" Sam followed.

The trio found themselves in a dark and dingy nightclub on Amiens Street.

It was near the train station, which suited Connor, who had the misguided notion of going back to Griffin that night.

All three sat at the bar, which was made of frosted glass, lit up by blue neon lights around the rim. People seemed to appear and disappear in slow motion by a trick of the dance-floor lights that went from off to full beam in a matter of seconds.

"Did you know she wanted to become a vet, when she was younger?" Connor shouted to Sam over the music.

"I did, actually," Sam yelled back. "Why didn't she?"

Connor downed a shot and chuckled to himself. "Because she blew up our goldfish." He threw his head back. Even Rick laughed at this.

"How did she manage that?"

"Well, we were swimming at the lakes, but it was freezing. She said it made her think of Goldie in that freezing water all day long so she filled his bowl with boiling water."

Sam was horrified. "That's not funny."

"It is a little." Rick chuckled.

"No, that's not the best bit," Connor interrupted. "She had the good sense to put a silver spoon in the bowl first, to protect the glass from shattering. But the fish … well, I guess they're just made of much tougher stuff." He shook his head in amusement.

Connor left Sam and Rick chuckling away while he made his way to the toilets. Even in his drunken state he could feel eyes upon him and he searched the club for their owner. He found them gazing at him through the banisters of the stairs to the next level. They belonged to a familiar-looking woman dressed like a temptress.

She had an intense gaze and a longing look in her eyes. Connor stuck to his course. But he must have done so slowly because before he knew it she was standing in front of him. She didn't say anything she just stood there. Connor maneuvered around her and thought he saw surprise in her eyes.

When he came out of the gents' she was waiting for him.

She was wearing a tight black skirt that revealed just enough leg not to be considered a belt. Her heels made her taller than he was. Connor didn't like women who were taller than him. They reminded him he was the only male in his family not over six foot. Connor couldn't help noticing her leather top that was unbuttoned all the way down to the parting of her breasts. She pushed herself against him and leaned in close to his ear. "I don't like being ignored!" she whispered. Connor tilted his head back so he could look her in the eye. There was no arguing that she was a strikingly beautiful woman, her face a sculpture of fine arches and shadows and her lips glowing bright red.

Connor leaned into her ear and whispered back. "I don't like red heads," he said before walking away.

****

Amelia pocketed Connor's wallet before he slinked off. Something was wrong. No one had ever refused her. No one could. There was a change in the boy; she had felt his insides shift as she pressed up against him. He was in the transition. Her eyes widened.

Excitement soared through Amelia's body. If ever his sister were to come for him, now would be the time. She smiled so hard she made her lips bleed.

She was feeling more powerful ever since she had replaced Marcus in the quest to discover what form the key was in. She would find it if she had to tear it from the girl and burst into flames. She would find it and she would give it to Áine.

****

"Where's Rick?" Connor asked when he returned.

"Dancing by himself."

"Yeah, he does that!"

Rick wasn't a bad dancer. But he'd had too much to drink and his coordination left him missing beats, giving the impression he was just punching the air on the dance floor.

Through the bright lights he caught sight of a familiar face.

He hadn't forgotten her red hair, even in his intoxication.

"Diane!" he called. Amelia turned around and gave him an evil smile.

Rick stopped dancing.

Everyone on the dance floor seemed to fall away and all that was left was Diane. She had changed since he'd last seen her, he thought. More confident or more decisive; he couldn't tell.

Rick tried to reintroduce himself and remind her of their meeting in Raptures. But speech failed him. Diane didn't seem to mind. She didn't seem interested in anything but dancing.

Rick watched her hips move ever so slightly, teasingly, to the beat of the music. Steadily she got closer and closer, close enough for him to feel her against him. Her back was arched elegantly and it naturally pushed her chest forward. It created the illusion of space and the void drew him in. Slowly Rick began to move his hips with hers. Unaware of the beat he was happy just to dance to hers.

Amelia put her lips to his ear. "Do you want me?"

Rick swallowed hard, but he said nothing.

Amelia leaned in closer. "You are mine," she told him.

Chapter 57

Karen was having trouble sleeping. Sháya was working at the senate and Addis at the library, and the cabin felt lonely. She stared at Saturn through the arched window from her bed. She wondered how many astronomers were looking at it through telescopes at this very moment. It would be night-time at home, she realized.

The bell chime on the balcony rang and startled her. Karen dragged herself out of the rushes and stared down from the trees.

"May I come in?" Fabien called to her.

Karen was glad to see him. She could use the company. Fabien sat by the rushes and Karen got the feeling he was only there to help her sleep.

"So where are you going today?" she asked him. "Dan said you were meeting Sofia."

"We're going to Aingeal Forest," he handed her a funny-smelling drink. "to the Tree of Eagna."

Karen had thought it a funny name to call the tree until she remembered Eagna meant wisdom. "Why are there so many Irish words here, like Eagna?"

"Because Maewyn spent his years on earth in Ireland," Fabien reminded her.

"Did you ever meet him?"

"Yes."

"What was he like?"

"Quiet, he was quiet. I suspect years in the waking world had made him that way. He had a sacred mission, you see, to rid the Gorgons from the world, or the snakes from Ireland as you tell it. Before that, Gorgons had been making appearances for several hundred years. It was only a matter of time before they were banished."

"Why?"

"Because they had evolved into something more than converters. They were more than just children of Neptune. Their place is here with the rest of the higher sentients."

"Did people ever realize St Patrick was an angel?" Karen wondered out loud.

"I suspect so." Fabien too was pensive. "They called him an apostle, did they not?"

Fabien's words seemed to get farther and farther away as Karen's eyelids drooped.

Fabien stared down at her. He watched her for a moment, her chocolate-brown curls falling over her face.

He could not fail her the way he had Daniel. Daniel had fled the night they heard Áine call through the fields. He tried to cover up his family's identity and then left for Spain. It was there he had made the ultimate sacrifice. He had pledged his life to the angels, knowing the price was his life. They had concocted a fake persona and put Áine off their scent for over twenty years. But now she was back and she wouldn't be fooled again.

****

Sofia was waiting for Fabien in Aingeal Forest. He could make out her delicate shape through the mist. She had already begun mediating in front of the Tree. Fabien sat in silence next to her.

A cool breeze swept the ground and moved the cumulus clouds that clung to the forest floor. They swirled like crowds of spectators being brushed along past a scene of importance.

"You said the human boy told you to come here." Sofia finally spoke. "Why?" she asked, with her eyes still closed.

"He suggested the original text would be more yielding," Fabien told her.

"Why?" Sofia was glowing with concentration.

"I suppose because it was written by Xanthia and not interpreted by others."

"And how does this help us?"

Fabien watched her and wondered where her brilliant mind was taking her. He watched her eyelids flicker and wished he could follow her train of thought.

"We would be taking knowledge from the tree where it was written rather than the pages it was transferred to."

"Precisely." Sofia opened her bright blue eyes to stare at him.

"What makes this tree different than the paper the text was transferred to?"

"I would like to say because it is in the form of nature, but then so is the paper, since it comes from trees."

"What are the properties of paper?" Sofia asked herself as much as to Fabien. "Carbon, polysaccharide chains, cellulose. But what dimension does it exist in?"

"What?"

"The tree is three dimensional." Sofia went to put her hands on the tree. She felt the trunk at the parts that held the text. Her fingertips hovered over the words carefully, reading them like she was blind and interpreting Braille; like Xanthia would have.

She stopped at the words Rejoice the union 111 + and her eyes lit up in pools of light.

"What is it?" Fabien approached the trunk of the tree. He put his hands across the words Sofia had. "I just feel the bumps and grooves of the bark."

"And what shape are they?"

Fabien stroked at the bark over and over again. "The numbers are like an oval shape and the cross is some kind of animal?"

"Could that shape be the base of a ship?" she asked. "Perhaps the numbers 111 are not numbers at all but three ship masts instead?"

Fabien continued across the words and then he felt the shape of the animal in the cross. His own eyes sparkled at the realization. "They are family crests."

"Rejoice the union… Burke and O'Driscoll!" Sofia elaborated.

They both heard a shuffling behind them and turned to find Dinyl approaching them through the mist. She wore a radiant smile and her eyes had been replaced by blinding pools of light that would have caused a human to go blind.

"You knew, didn't you?" Sofia asked. "You sensed it at the banquet."

Dinyl smiled mischievously. "I am Angel of infants, am I not?"

Chapter 58

Rick was on fire with passion for the red-headed stranger. They had found a quiet corner and Amelia was kissing his neck. She pushed her body against him and he could feel her breasts on his broad muscular chest. He felt her nails then dig into his back and she returned her lips to his. They were soft but forceful. He imagined this was what fire tasted like.

"Maybe we should go somewhere else," Amelia suggested.

Rick was on his feet as fast as the alcohol in his blood would allow. When he went to grab his coat, Amelia threw Connor's wallet on the ground.

"Oh," she sang delicately, "your friend left his wallet."

She smiled deviously. Rick looked at her with a lipstick covered face. He glanced at the wallet, then back to Amelia. "It's fine," he told her, "I'll call him later."

"I thought you said his phone was broken."

Rick looked dumbstruck again. "It's fine," he repeated desperately. "Who needs a phone or a wallet?"

Amelia gave him a steady look, giving him time to allow the blood in his body to travel to other places.

"Okay, you're right," he groaned. Rick had never hated Connor more. "You owe me big time," he muttered to the image of Connor's forgetful face in his head.

"If it's not his wallet, it's his keys." he moaned, but Amelia wasn't listening. Her senses were heightened and she could feel that Connor had been close to changing. When he did, Karen would be close by.

They hailed a taxi quicker than any other night Rick had been in the city. He suspected it was down to his companion's legs. People seemed to fall at this woman's feet. The taxi pulled off, leaving the hordes of people behind on the streets. Rick and the woman he thought was called Diane lay back on the leather seats of the taxi.

"You're really something, you know that," he told her.

Amelia could feel the teeth under her gums fight to come down but she controlled them and smiled at him slowly. "I know!" she whispered dangerously. She turned to face out the window and her eyelids began to flicker. A slimy film ran across her eyes like a reptile, making a squashing sound as they did so. She didn't have to wait to go back to Sublimina like other converters. She had a direct line to the banshee now. How pleased Áine would be to receive news of Karen's foolish emergence from Sublimina. Áine herself would arrive once Amelia tortured Karen into revealing what the key was.

"Griffin, did you say, love?" the taxi driver asked. "Coz that's over an hour away, you know."

"Yes, yes, Griffin!" Amelia snapped.

****

Connor had passed out when his head hit the pillow of the family home. Catherine was staying in Dublin. He would take his motorcycle down in the morning. He had managed to undress before pulling a sheet over himself and falling into a fitful sleep.

He had been dreaming of running through the woods with his father. They were looking for something. But Connor kept slowing them down.

He woke with a headache and put his hands to his temples. Breathing a sigh of relief at waking up, he pulled himself up on the bed. Pressing the little button on his wristwatch, he saw that it was two o'clock in the morning. He lay there just staring into the darkness. It was pitch black outside and no cars passed the Bellview Road at this hour. Eventually he fell back asleep.

That was the last his old eyes would ever see of the world. The next time he woke was with a bolt from inside his chest. It felt like his heart had exploded. Connor shot upright on the bed fighting for air, but his lungs wouldn't allow it. They contorted and folded upwards crushing his wind pipe. Blue in the face now he rolled off the bed, his body in spasms. Connor's brow hit the floor first and spilled pools of blood between the floorboards. Oh my God, I'm dying, he thought. I don't want to die. Please help me, God. Help me, Dad! he pleaded, but nothing happened. I have to get up he thought.

Slowly and with great effort Connor bent his knee and raised himself up. He steadied himself with his hands on the bedside locker and stood upright. But it only lasted moments and he heard an unmerciful snap in his leg. Connor looked down in horror to discover his kneecap had burst through his skin. It stared at him, round and oily.

"Jesus!" he tried to scream. But his screams seemed to make things worse. His neck twitched and rocked itself side to side rhythmically like the hand of a ticking clock. It extended of its own accord pushing his head backwards and forwards and Connor fought to maintain balance.

A frightening pain followed as his gums erupted and a sharp vicious set of teeth grew over his own. They crowded his mouth, which was too small to hold so many teeth. But the muscles on his face seemed to have anticipated this and they grew outward, the bones of his jaw protruding like a muzzle.

Suddenly death didn't seem like such a bad thing. Please just make it stop, he prayed as tears rolled down the unfamiliar planes of his face. A further crackling sound ensued and the cartilage in his nostrils erupted, his nose flared, and then nothing. Connor lay motionless; sprawled on the floor in the darkness, passed out.

The rest of the transition was mental and it was a peaceful process. The barriers between consciousness and subconsciousness lifted like a curtain and Connor saw it all.

He was a Child of the Moon and of the Sun now; the only one in existence. He would be the only werewolf in all of history who could live under the sun and the moon. Neither day nor night would present any obstacles for him. He had shared a womb with the key keeper.

Buntie Whelan had been driving taxis for seven years now. He had been hoping to set up his own fleet and work for himself instead of that stingy wanker, O'Neill. But the economic climate was not good. He had even begun taking small wads of money from central office, adjusting his mileage and skimming the fares.

I've been driven to it, he'd think, trying to dampen his conscience when it raised its irritating head. He had planned on skimming some of this hefty fare to Griffin. He'd been wondering what to charge when they'd left the city to take the N11 but he still hadn't decided a figure. His thoughts were hazy; he kept forgetting what he was thinking and where he was going. He wondered if he was falling asleep.

"Drive faster!" Amelia snapped from the back of the car.

Buntie put his foot to the accelerator.

After a number of miles Buntie realized his speed and slowed down. What had he been thinking? He shook his sweaty head. Why had he sped up?

"Wake up!" Amelia shook Rick hard.

"Where are we?" Rick was groggy.

"You tell us!" Amelia stared at him. "Where does Connor live?" she asked hungrily, feeling the tips of her fangs pierce her gums.

"Take the next left!" Rick sat up with a pain in his head. He squinted through the rainy windows. "Pass the train station and take the Bellview Road; there's only a couple of houses. Connor's bike will be outside. You won't miss it." Rick rubbed his temples.

When they pulled up outside an old farmhouse, Buntie released the automatic lock system to let his passengers out. Rick stood in the rain and gave Amelia a wad of money to pay the driver. He was still feeling ill and he put his hands on the wall to steady himself.

Amelia approached the driver's door and opened it dangerously. She didn't give Buntie the fare and he didn't remember to ask for it.

"Where are we?" he squinted.

Amelia put the money down her top. "There is a bridge we passed about a mile out of town." she told him. "Drive into it!" she instructed. "Drive into it as fast as you can and drown in the waters beneath." She smiled.

Buntie nodded and shut the door of his taxi for the last time.

"This is it?" Amelia asked Rick facing the house.

"This is it."

They stared up at the whitewashed two-storey farmhouse. Amelia scanned for movement in windows. There was none.

"Which room is his?" she asked.

Rick pointed to the second story at the front of the house. Rain was trickling down his face and he began to shiver. "He's a heavy sleeper. Bet he doesn't even answer."

Amelia was silent as she took a step closer to the house. Rick followed her. "What now?" Amelia drew her hand across her body to the top of her hip, then in one sharp motion she swept it upwards slamming an elbow into Rick's face.

Rick went down like a sack of peat.

"Now we wait," she whispered.

Chapter 59

Karen's eyelids fluttered as she slept and Rick wasn't there to wake her. She was dreaming of the prophet, the one with the ability to use the key, the one who could choose which converters could enter the waking world by day. Karen was running through fields of red and brown. There was no sky where she ran, just red; everywhere she turned was blood red. The prophet was there somewhere, she could feel it.

A crashing sound coming from the kitchen woke her with a jolt.

"Shit!" She heard Dan's voice from downstairs.

A smile broke across her face. Karen climbed out of bed in search of something to wear. "Ukkk," she groaned at the sight of the clothes that had been left for her. She pulled the off-white knitted robe over her shoulders. She tied it at the waist with the plaited ropes at the sides.

"How long was I asleep?" Karen made Dan jump.

"An hour!" Dan told her disapprovingly. He appeared to be trying to make a drink. "I asked Fabien to leave me more sleeping tonic but he's gone."

"He's at the Tree of Eagna."

"He was at the tree of Eagna," Dan corrected. "No one has seen him since. He and Sofia went to meditate and no one can reach them."

"Maybe that's good! Maybe they found something."

Dan swirled the contents of the cup before deciding the best place for it was in the bin. "Maybe we could go for a swim?" he offered.

"Swimming always helped me sleep."

Karen looked doubtful but Dan was adamant.

"It will clear your head,"

Karen felt like she was the one making Dan feel better when she gave in and they made their way to the lakes.

Dan asked question after question about her family, presumably so she would feel closer to them somehow and less lonely. "Is he happy? Your brother?"

"No one is happy," Karen responded without thinking. She hadn't realized she felt that way. Maybe the last few months were taking their toll on her. Maybe she wasn't the person she used to be.

"He's very masochistic, isn't it?" Dan said.

"How so?" Karen pretended she knew what the word meant.

"Well, he's not very nice to himself, is he? Always thinks everything is his own fault."

"Dad once told him he was the man of the house." Karen sighed. "I don't think he ever took anything as seriously in his life."

Dan looked like someone had twisted a knife in his gut and was quiet the rest of the journey. His silence made everything else louder. Karen could hear crickets and other bugs in the woods. She could hear gulls in the sky and hooves on the land, and then she heard a branch crack and snap under her foot. It set off a commotion inside her. Her body reacted like a bullet released from a gun. The sound reverberated inside her and she saw the bones of her brother twist and brake.

Dan noticed her wince.

"What's the matter?"

Karen stared at him for a moment, her mind racing. What would she say? He would never let her go back. And what could she do even if she did return? She didn't know. All she knew was that she felt an overwhelming urge to go back home. An urge no one but a twin would understand.

Karen had seen his blood. There was so much blood. Who could give him blood? She thought, with panic rising in her throat. Not Dan, and certainly not Fabien.

334

"I have to go," she said.

Dan rounded on her. "What's wrong!"

Karen used her knowledge of his boyish nature against him.

"Woman problems…"

Dan looked like she'd punched him in the face. He even stepped backward from the invisible force of it. "I have to go find Briathos anyway."

Only when he was out of sight did Karen begin to run. She ran all the way back to the tree, to Sháya's spare room. Rummaging through the drawers she found it quickly. Fingers shaking she took the rosary beads in her hands and placed them around her neck. Nothing happened. "Shit!" she muttered. She had overlooked the minor problem of not knowing how to wake up. She rubbed her eyes, squeezed them and pulled them and still nothing. Her entire body was shaking now. She needed to relax. Breathe, she told herself.

Then she remembered Fabien's words. "The heart doesn't lie," he'd once told her, "the mind does."

Karen lay on the bed with the beads around her neck and put her hands on her heart and thought of nothing but home. It didn't work. "Right!" She got stern with herself. "You're thinking again. Thinking of home … Feel home!" she warned herself.

Slowly she began to feel a movement within her, a shift in her state. She inhaled deeply the smell of fresh grass and water. She remembered what it felt like to have rays of sunshine touch her skin. She thought of her life in the city chasing trains and buses. And eventually she knew she could open her eyes.

****

Karen didn't recognize what hospital she was in. She only recognized her mother asleep on a chair in the corner. It was dark and it was raining outside. Clear drips of water were falling against the Georgian window by her bedside. They tapped at the glass gently and rhythmically and she knew she was home. The room smelt fresh and sweet and Karen saw that a large bouquet of flowers was responsible. Carnations – Sam's favourite.

Karen felt a pinch in her arm. She rolled her head over on the hospital pillow to find an IV drip feeding her liquids through a vein of her elbow joint. Carefully she reached for the dressing that held it in place. She ripped it off in one quick motion, taking some hair along with it.

The skin on her arm glared back at her, angry and red. Karen pulled gently on the needle and extracted it carefully from her arm. She looked over at her mother to make sure she was still sleeping, and quietly as she could she got out of the bed.

The hospital floor was cold and chilly. She tried to stand but almost toppled over. She hadn't used her muscles in over a week, she realized. Pounding them with her palms probably wouldn't help but she tried anyway. She flexed and stretched until she was confident enough to move again.

Karen scanned the room for some clothes but there was nothing, only the nightdress she'd been sleeping in. A travel bag lay across Catherine's chair but she dared not check inside. Waking her mother was not an option. She cursed silently.

Then Karen saw that her mother had her legs up on the chair, knees beneath her chin. She was wearing no shoes, Karen realized. She found her trainers under the chair and pulled them on with relief. She spied Connor's leather jacket with its grey hood at the end of the bed and grabbed it enthusiastically. She had never been so thankful for his forgetfulness.

There was no one on the hospital corridors. Karen ran on her tip-toes to avoid the squeaking sound of her trainers on the floor. She didn't risk taking the lift.

Once off the ward she darted down flights of stairs, three steps at a time. She paused between floors to look out the windows and maybe work out where she was. The bright lights of the city stared back at her like old friends. She could make out the high railings of Croke Park in the distance. "The Mater Hospital," she whispered, "I'm in The Mater."

There was no one using the stairs and she made her way to the first floor with ease. Getting past reception in a nightdress and trainers would be trickier. She looked around, searching for ideas. There was the cafeteria and a convenience store.

Karen zipped up Connor's coat and shoved her hands deep into its pockets. There she found a crumpled up twenty-euro note and she kissed it. She knew they didn't sell cigarettes at the hospital but it would give her an excuse to leave unnoticed.

"Twenty Marlboro," she said at the till, imitating Rick.

"This is a hospital, love," a balding man working the night shift informed her. Karen acted disappointed. Adrenaline was pumping through her veins and she used it to improve her acting. "Where is the nearest place I can get some?"

"Daly's across the street," he told her impatiently.

Karen over-thanked the grumpy assistant and left. Once out of the hospital she didn't look back. She made her way down Eccles Street and wondered if she could get a taxi to the station. She would need to get the Nitelink back to Griffin. The rain was getting heavier now and Catherine's runners weren't waterproof.

Karen searched the street for a taxi but found none. It was probably for the best anyway, given her attire. Eccles Street was quiet, with only the streetlights for company. The large redbrick buildings either side seemed to watch her with curiosity.

Karen tried to get her bearings. She could make out the spire of St George's Church through her wet hair and headed in the opposite direction for the station. Finding Gardiner Street, she began to run through the puddles and potholes, splashing her clothes with each step. She could make out the lights of the banks at the IFSC and she headed straight for them.

She was out of breath by the time she cut across Talbot Street but she could make out the big station clock easily now.

It was three o'clock in the morning and she had no idea when the next Nitelink was. Ignoring the stinging in her lungs, she started to run again. What if she was too late? she thought. How did she even know Connor was in Griffin? But every fibre of her being told her he was. She just had to trust her instincts. They had never been wrong before.

As usual, the lifts to the platforms were out of order, so she dragged herself resolutely up step by step to the main hall. Amber and yellow neon lights lit up the digital timetables on the great display wall before her.

Karen wiped the rain from her eyelashes and realized a Nitelink was leaving for Griffin. There was no time to purchase a ticket so she bolted across the slippery floor, almost losing her footing, and jumped the barriers. She caught her shin on the metal bars and her body landed onto the floor with a crash. Her shin pulsated with pain but nothing was broken. She got up to run again. The train was leaving from Platform 7.

Of course it is, she told herself, that's the farthest one away.

Suddenly being back in the city lost its appeal, but she managed to catch the train with only seconds to spare. A young man in his twenties watched her splutter and wheeze before collapsing onto a seat across from him. He looked her up and down. "Rough night?" he asked.

"You can't even begin to imagine."

The young man smiled a college smile. "Oh, I think I can."

"This country's a fuckin' shit!" a voice yelled out to no one in particular.

Karen peeped down the aisles and saw a disheveled looking man, intoxicated and fighting with thin air. He had a bottle of vodka in his hand.

"Shit!" Karen muttered. He'd spotted her.

"Oi!" he shouted. "This country's a fuckin shit!" He waved his bottle menacingly.

"You've gone and done it now," the college student warned.

"It's a shit," he warned.

The young student offered to accompany her to the next carriage and Karen decided there were still some decent people left in the world.

By the time they reached Griffin Karen felt drier. Most of her nightdress was covered by Connor's jacket and the heating on the train had been on full blast. She caught sight of her hair in the window before they reached the platform and suddenly she didn't feel so scared of banshees. She could probably pass as one herself, she thought.

Chapter 60

Amelia waited patiently in the rain. "Tick tock, tick tock," she sang, grinning. It was a grin that contorted her features. She could feel the excitement growing inside herself.

Rick lay concussed next to her in the bushes. She looked down at him and decided she could use a snack. She could make out a vein in the darkness, pulsing in his neck. She was on top of his body before it could beat again, sucking the blood from his core. It wasn't so much the blood itself that fed her, but what it carried within, the unmade decisions, the ingredients of life, the free will and emotion. It flowed into her and filled her body and mind with images. She knew him explicitly in a matter of seconds.

The noise of approaching steps distracted her. It was rare for her kind to hear anything while in a feeding frenzy but she had definitely heard something. She darted her head from Rick's neck and stared intently at the lonely sleeping house. Had she missed something? Had someone gone inside?

Feeding at a time like this had been poor judgment. She would not make that mistake again. She flung Rick's unmoving body onto a bed of leaves and continued her wait for Karen.

Karen climbed the last few steps of the stairs and burst into her brother's bedroom. She found him hunched over. He was getting up from the floor.

"Connor!" she shouted, and a figure so unlike the brother she remembered turned to face her. Karen took in his ferocious form. He looked just like Dan did when she had seen him fight. He was over six foot tall. He stood like a man not like the hound like images most humans attributed with werewolves. Muscles popped from beneath his leathery skin. A pair of red eyes stared at her from beneath a heavy black brow. His lips were pursed to allow for his extra teeth.

None of it frightened his twin sister. She'd seen it all before. Relief flowed through her body. He would know now, she consoled herself. He would be fully in tune with other converters now and he would know everything. It felt like someone had lifted a cement bag from her chest and she ran to embrace him. He held her back with arms stronger than he'd ever had before.

"Missed you," he said in a wonderfully familiar voice.

Karen was about to speak but he silenced her. His new nostrils were wider and sharper; they could smell something in the garden outside. He placed an enormous finger over his sister's mouth and indicated for her to go sit on the bed. He went and stood by the window, his red eyes scanning the darkness, and he growled – a low and ferocious sound.

Karen realized her mistake. Connor nodded to her and she swiftly put her hand to the beads. She needed to return to Sublimina. She slapped at the bare skin they used to cover and looked down in horror. They were gone.

Panic rose inside her and her mind raced to find answers. The hospital, the streets, the train – they could be anywhere.

Connor's eyes may have changed but Karen could still read them. "Oh shit!" he mouthed and everything from there was a blur.

Both Amelia and Connor bolted from their cover, Amelia heading for the house and Connor the garden. Connor burst through the timber of his bedroom door, hoping to meet her on the stairs. The old wooden steps creaked and eventually cracked under his weight as he ran down them.

He met Amelia at the front door. Bursting through the security locks he met her square in the chest with one solid leap and drove her back up the pebbled drive. Waves of stone and grit flew from the ground as she landed.

An evil high-pitched scream of frustration echoed in the quiet night air and Amelia rose in fury. Connor crouched down low, preparing for his second attack. Amelia circled him. Their eyes locked and neither wavered, even when they heard the sound of Karen moving inside, neither one flinched.

Round and round they circled until Amelia's hunger got the better of her. A loud hissing sound came from between her teeth and then she dived at her prey with open jaws. Connor deflected the attack but she anticipated that and caught him on the chin with her heel. Landing expertly behind him, she sank her teeth into his neck. It wasn't a pleasant sensation, not like biting a human. Humans were soft, like butter, succulent and delicious, but werewolf skin was thick and leathery, designed to withstand the sharpest of objects.

Connor howled in pain as she tugged and tore at his skin. Catching her by the hair he threw her over his shoulders, but this turned out worse for him. Her mouth never released his flesh from its grip and he found himself tumbling forward. Connor grabbed and clawed at Amelia, desperate to find a piece of flesh to cling to, to hurt or to tear. He was filled with a violence he never thought himself capable of, but he couldn't release himself from her jaws.

Karen could watch no more. She darted out the front door and into the garden. She had no idea what she was going to do but decided she could figure it out with her fingers in Amelia's eyes.

No sooner had she left the safety of the house than she was tackled to the ground by a stranger. Her head hit the marshy grass with a thud and her eyes shot open to face her attacker. "Rick!"

Dried blood covered her friend's neck and his nose looked broken. "About time you woke up!" he said.

Karen ignored him and peered through his arms at the brawl. "That's Connor!" she called desperately at the two figures rolling across the lawn.

Rick squinted through puffy black eyes and got to his feet. "Then you know he'd want you away from here." He grabbed Karen's arm and ran around the back of the house with her.

"That's your best friend! Where are you going?"

Rick pulled on her wrist as he ran. "Anywhere, through those fields." He pointed to the end of the back garden.

Karen dug her heels into the grass and Rick couldn't overpower her.

He looked at her in shock. Surely he hadn't become that weak, he thought.

They heard a howling and screaming from the front of the house and Rick made a quick decision to throw Karen over his shoulders.

Suddenly Karen felt vulnerable.

Her lower abdomen lay across Rick's broad shoulder and something deep inside her told her not to move.

"Don't hate me!" Rick panted as he ran.

He headed for the ditches at the back of the house and made his way into the fields. But the ground was soft and uneven with the rain and Karen felt heavy on his shoulders. He had to put her down.

"What now?"

"I hadn't thought beyond this," Rick admitted. He looked around him frantically and reached up for one of the branches in the trees. They were slippery and wet, and his hands were blue with the cold and rain, but he managed to break one off. He held it like a baseball bat in his hands.

A hopeless feeling descended in depressing waves down Karen's body and her shoulders fell forward in a hunch. She had ruined everything. She had been safe in Sublimina; the key had been safe.

She had angels bright as the stars to protect her there and yet she'd come here, into a mucky field full of cow dung and no one to protect her but a boy with a branch, a boy she had put in mortal danger all because she thought she knew best.

"I'm so sorry," the words bubbled through the rain hitting her lips.

Rick blinked hard to see her through the downpour.

"Don't go giving up, I swear I'll kill you myself if you give up."

A loud howling sound came from the distance and they stared at each other in silence.

"Looks like Connor won!" Rick eventually broke the silence.

"Looks can be deceiving!" A low and deliberate voice came from behind him. Amelia stared hard at them.

Rick barely recognized her. He stared at her open mouthed and stunned.

Her cranium had doubled in size to allow for a long furrowed brow and a bulbous skull. Her red eyes flared. Her ears were spiked and pointed. She looked like a killing machine.

Karen felt her shoulders almost snap in half as the vampire grabbed hold of her. Amelia's voice was loud and high-pitched, her eyes were bulging wide. "What form is it in?" she demanded. Blood dripped from her mouth. "Where is it?" She squeezed Karen harder.

Rick tried to pry Amelia's arms open. He belted her repeatedly with the branch he'd broken but Amelia flung him to the ground.

Karen said nothing but her face was contorted with pain and Rick made a decision. "It's the rosary beads!" he called from the ground.

Amelia's vice like grip loosened and a disturbing smile crept across her face like a disease.

A liquid film came across her eyes and Karen knew that she was summoning the banshee.

Rick came to stand in front of Karen and stared at Amelia in disgust.

Her eyes were still shut and Rick clenched the branch hard before hitting her full force across the face.

Amelia's fell sideways with the force. Her body began to shake and a high-pitched chuckling sound came from her mouth.

"I suppose it's too much to hope that she's crying," Rick muttered to Karen and took a step back.

Amelia's laughter got louder. Soon it was drowned out by another sound, a sound that came from all around, echoing through the fields. It occupied every molecule of the atmosphere. Rick and Karen shuddered as their skin crawled. They could feel the noise in their guts.

Amelia stared around her with desire in her eyes. She was mesmerized, as though she was seeing things that others could not. The leaves of the trees flew off their branches as a harsh wind swept across the fields, hallow and deep.

Rick held Karen tightly. He knew it wouldn't help; how could it?

He watched the wind take the form of smouldering smoke and mist. Something was taking shape. She was coming.

****

Briathos was angry. It was an emotion he struggled with, one not compatible with being an angel. But that was his cross to bear; it helped him be a better demon slayer he knew. But now was not the right time to feel it. Being angry at Fabien and Sofia was pointless. They were meditating somewhere and they couldn't be reached.

Now the over-ambitious little converter named Dan was jumping up and down like an undisciplined cub scout pleading for help.

"There's something wrong; I know it," Dan pleaded. "If you meditated more you'd feel it too."

Briathos raised a dark eyebrow offended. "I will accompany you, converter. Your heart is pure but be careful how you speak."

Dan nodded dismissively. "Yes, yes, are you ready?" He tried to hurry Briathos.

"No!" came the unexpected response. "As you so kindly pointed out, meditating is not one of my strong points. You know the effect it has if I am not recharged, and it has been six days now I have been in the waking world."

Dan felt his heart sink. He needed Briathos focused or he would be more hindrance than help. He felt his teeth grind and his jaw bulge with anger. This was not the first time Fabien had failed him. "How long do you need?" Dan tried to keep the frustration from his voice.

Briathos didn't know. The truth was that he was having trouble meditating in recent years. It was becoming harder and harder to find peace inside. He knew he needed to work harder. He could not become preoccupied with zealous emotions or they would consume him. He would not become the eighth fallen angel.

"Go to your home and wait for me there. I will come for you."

Dan had no choice. He often had no choice and he wondered if his children would ever be safe. Unlocking the door to his dark stone home he made his way to its only bedroom to prepare. He would not be meditating.

He pulled out a trunk from underneath his bed and unlocked it. A picture of his wife stared back at him. The picture had been taken by the lakes and the wind had swept the hair across her face. She was leaning on a rock, looking at the camera. Two children were by her side. Connor had his feet in the water and Karen was tending to a dead snail.

A fire rose in his chest then and he felt like he could take on the banshee herself and still protect them.

He picked up a handmade choke chain and rolled the beads between his fingers. They were made from his children's fishing nets. He had found them in the back of his truck when he arrived in Spain. There hadn't been time to take mementos; all he had of them was what they'd left in his car. Daniel remembered the night he'd carefully taken the nets apart and used the wooden handles to make beads. Catherine had left a hairbrush in the glove box and he had gently placed some of her hair into a locket.

Daniel put the chain around his neck now and closed the clasp. If his life were to leave his body he hoped it would be the last thing he would feel on his skin.

Carefully, Daniel put the trunk back under his bed. He wondered briefly if it would be his last time to see it, and he didn't care. There were footsteps in the distance. His ears pricked up, and he opened the door to Briathos before he had a chance to knock. "Are you ready?" Daniel asked.

"What do you think?" Briathos drew an arrow from his back.

****

Amelia felt an arrow in her chest. It protruded from her upper body, its spearhead holding parts of her insides, red and fleshy. She broke the tip off with her hands in annoyance, and ripped it from her chest.

As she turned to face her attacker, her red hair blew across her face in time with the wind. "Briathos!" she called in a steady tone. "Taken to slaying converters have we?"

Briathos inclined his head slightly. "Technically demons are converters who have gone astray, so you could qualify."

Daniel ignored them both. He was watching the atmosphere ripple and change and knew something was coming that he could not fight. Calculating his options, he made a dash for Amelia. Taking her out would leave the banshee for Briathos.

Amelia, full of a foresight that made her so dangerous, anticipated his move and she made a rush for Karen. Amelia had the advantage.

Karen could see she was closer to her than Dan was and she ran. The logical part of her brain told her it was pointless, she could never outrun a Child of Neptune, but her heart told her to run and she did. Out into the open fields she ran with a speed she had never reached before. It must have bought Dan some time because she felt the ground shake behind her.

Rick leaped out of the way as Dan and Amelia scuffled.

Briathos was crouched in an assassin's position pointing his arrow at the vortex, a vortex that Karen was heading straight into. Briathos couldn't hope for a clear shot and Rick ran after Karen. But it was pointless – she had travelled too far. Karen saw it too, but she was too late.

This is it for me, she thought. This is where it all ends. Somehow she'd known that she would die here, here in this field. She had been dreaming of it all her life. Her father had died in Spain so why had her dreams always taken her here to witness the cry of the banshee?

Arms collapsing by her sides Karen fell to her knees. Her body felt anaesthetized by an invisible force and she was strangely grateful for it.

Áine had arrived in a shroud of rippling smoky blackness. Ribbons of black cloth and darkness floated in shadows and Karen was reminded of the air around the Hub.

Impossibly long arms extended themselves like tendrils to lift a ghostly veil from her skeletal face. A pair of penetrating wide eyes, swimming with intensity paralyzed her victim. Karen couldn't look away. She had no choice but to stare back into them; they were electric blue and filled with a demonic evil.

Karen saw her wicked smile then. It bore a mouthful of black, diseased teeth.

Áine extended her arms in a mocking maternal manner and Karen was horrified to learn she was drawn into her arms like a magnet. No sooner had her body touched Áine's cold hollow torso than she felt the life drain from her body.

If someone had asked her in the afterlife what her last thoughts had been, Karen wouldn't have known. They had been frozen to a speed inconsistent with life. Her lungs rose and fell for the last time and the blood in her veins slowed to a crawling pace before finally accepting defeat. The life and spirit left her, and the body that had once held her soul fell like a shell to the ground.

****

Rick didn't trust his eyes. He couldn't. He was shaking his head and blinking hard as if somehow that would change things.

Dan made a wailing sound that seemed to last an eternity. It emptied his lungs and when there was nothing left inside he threw up, something he hadn't done since he was human.

Connor crawled through the ditches having caught the last moments of his sister's life, and something died inside him.

He knew she was gone. His mangled body stared at Fabien and Dinyl who had just arrived. "A bit bloody late now aren't you?" His voice came through tears of anger and pain.

When Karen had miscarried, many years before, Esther had tried desperately to comfort her granddaughter.

"This life was too precious for this time," she'd told her. "The world just wasn't ready for someone so special."

Now the world was ready. The child she now carried had been conceived before Áine arrived. It had made contact with the key first and it was the rightful owner. It stirred its developing body and performed its first miracle without realizing. A key-bearing prophet cannot be killed. If it was to live it would have to be born; if it was to be born its mother must live.

****

Amelia searched Karen's body for the key. She ripped her pockets open like they were paper.

She was tearing the seam of her nightdress when she saw them appear around her neck, as though she'd never taken them off. Amelia didn't know whether to rejoice or despair. She dared not touch them but looked to Áine for guidance.

Áine stared down at them now with an unreadable expression on her face. She appeared to have reached some form of conclusion when she pulled a dark hooded veil over her face. There wasn't a word spoken or a glance given but she was gone.

Karen's eyelids opened slowly then; they released tears that rolled steadily down her cheeks. The feeling returned to her limbs then and she placed them protectively over the life she felt inside her.

Amelia appeared to sway as though physical waves of confusion were washing over her. Fabien advanced on her. "The key has already been claimed." he explained. Amelia looked to the ground where Áine had once stood, an expression of confusion still on her face. Fabien decided to put her out of her misery. "Áine has played her part and she has lost. Everything changes now."

Chapter 61

The nurses on G Wing would have to ask the visitors to leave. There were at least seven of them in Room 205. Some of them were sitting and some of them were standing but all of them were around Karen's bed.

"So Dr Paul was right?" Esther nudged Catherine for a reaction.

"How was he?" Catherine took the bait.

"Well, she fainted didn't she? Most likely dehydration in her first trimester. I remember carrying Andrew. I fainted in Heffernan's more times than I care to remember."

"That's ridiculous," Catherine argued. "You can't go into a coma over that. She would have to have hit her head."

"It doesn't matter," Katie interrupted. "All that matters is Darcy will have a cousin to play with." She cradled her baby.

There was a knock on the door and Wayne poked his head into the room. "The nurses are getting grumpy again, we'll come back later."

Catherine and Esther left grudgingly.

"I've got my bump." Karen felt the back of her head from where she'd hit the ground. "We just might pull this off," she told her brother.

"Of course we will, now that I'm not in the dark anymore." Connor was still a little annoyed. "No more secrets." He looked to his father.

Daniel had gotten off easier than he ever could have imagined. All the wasted nights he'd spent rehearsing the disclosure he would someday have to make to his children, and all for nothing; both of them had found the truth in their subconscious, Connor through his transformation and Karen in the face of death.

"This child will be born into nothing but truth," Daniel swore.

"Something tells me we won't have a choice in that." Karen rubbed her stomach. "I still think it was him that showed me who you were," she told her father.

"Him!" Rick repeated. "How do you know it's a him?"

"They'll try to convert him, won't they?" she asked Fabien with fear in her eyes.

Fabien nodded but he didn't seem overly concerned.

"Yes," he agreed, "but that is a fight for another day."